The Piano Man's Daughter

Also by Timothy Findley:

NOVELS
The Last of the Crazy People
The Butterfly Plague
The Wars
Famous Last Words
Not Wanted on the Voyage
The Telling of Lies
Headhunter

SHORT FICTION
Dinner Along the Amazon
Stones

PLAYS
Can You See Me Yet?
John A.—Himself
The Stillborn Lover
The Trials of Ezra Pound

NON-FICTION
Inside Memory: Pages from a Writer's Workbook

TIMOTHY FINDLEY

The Piano Man's Daughter

HarperCollins*PublishersLtd*

Lyrics from "For Me and My Gal", by Ray E. Coetz, Edgar Leslie,
Geo. W. Mayer © 1919 (renewed) EMI Mills Music, Inc.
All Rights Reserved. Made in U.S.A. Used by permission of
Warner Bros. Publications Inc., Miami, FL. 33014. Lyrics from
"Pack Up Your Troubles" © copyright 1915 Warner Bros. Music Inc.
All Rights Reserved. Used by permission. Lyrics from "The Band Played
On" © copyright 1895 Harms Music Inc. excluding the
United States. All Rights Reserved. Used by permission.

Endpaper photography by Jan Becker. Endpaper and part opener
photographs from a collection of photographs courtesy of Timothy Findley,
except *The Intruder* by Charles Macnamara, *The Lane Gate* by Horace
Boultbee, and *'Neath Lordly Oaks* by William Braybrooke Bayley.

First Edition

Canadian Cataloguing in Publication Data

Findley, Timothy, 1930-
The piano man's daughter

ISBN 0-00-224379-2

I. Title.

PS8511.I64P5 1995   C813'.54   C95-930395-2
PR9199.3.F5P5 1995

---

95 96 97 98 99 ❖ HC 10 9 8 7 6 5 4 3 2 1

Acknowledgements

I wish to acknowledge the sources of the factual foundations on which this fiction is built—the people who provided information and images of family history, period costume, piano manufacture and medicine. My special thanks to Beverley Roberts; Isobelle Guthrie; Alan Carlyle; Jonathan Walford; Robert Lowrey; Michael Bennett; Christel Sampson; Nora Hague and Annette McConnell, Notman Archives, McCord Museum, Montreal; The Thomas Bouckley Collection, The Robert McLaughlin Gallery, Oshawa; The Museum of Mental Health Services, Toronto. I must also thank my editor and publisher, Iris Tupholme, for her humour, guidance and wisdom; Mary Adachi, for her all-seeing eyes; and William Whitehead, without whom nothing of this book would exist.

For
Margaret Gibson
and for
my cousin Isobelle Guthrie,
in memory of my Aunt Ruth

*It is their fate to be isolated
and thus original.*

Oliver Sacks

In the summer of 1910, on a still June morning, he took me up the river to the town. Not a sound. No people. Only the splash of a frog or a turtle sliding from the bank. And the reeds all silent on the shore beneath the shade of the willow trees. And yet, when I listened down, I heard a whispering chorus of insects making a seething noise. We drifted there almost an hour and neither of us spoke. In the town, he went away and I never saw him again. And yet . . .

The sun on the hill forgot to die
And the lilies revived, and the dragonfly
Came back to dream on the river.

If only . . .

The Piano Man's Daughter

Prelude

1939

1. I had seen her just the day before—a day of pale blue skies and summer breezes. We had stood on the lawns beneath the chestnut trees and she had said: *the leaves are talking to me, Charlie.*

Yes.

There were wooden chairs and tables painted green. At some of the tables, other patients sat with their relatives. Only relatives were allowed to visit—relatives or deputized lawyers who came with pieces of paper requiring signatures.

"Do you remember Ada? She used to play the piano at The Duke of York when pictures were still silent."

Lily put this question every time I went to see her.

"Yes," I said.

"There she is, sitting thinking Neddy is going to come and take her away. You remember Neddy?"

Yes. He played the violin and wore a bow-tie. He had been in love with Lily.

"I sometimes think he may still turn up," she said, her gaze averted. "After all, we only know he went missing."

No. We knew he was dead. I said nothing.

"It's not as if there was a certificate of death," she went on, "or one of those dreadful cablegrams people were sent . . ." The kind that, in fact, Lily had received herself. But: "he's *missing*, that's all. Missing. Like everyone else . . ."

Her hand went up to shade her eyes when she said this. Not to keep them out of the sun, but to align her focus. I could tell by the expression on her face that she was looking directly into the past, where most of us—she thought—had gone.

"The time will come," she said, "when there will have to be a gathering—everyone brought together in one safe place . . ." She dropped her hand and squinted at the near distance, where a wall defined her confinement. "This is not a safe place, Charlie," she said. "In spite of its being an asylum."

No.

"People like me, I guess we aren't safe anywhere."

No.

"Not in this world."

No.

Then, in that way she had of telling reality to go to hell, she smiled.

"But you and I don't live in this world. Do we."

No. We don't.

"Thank god," I added.

She took my hand and said to me: "you look good today, Charlie."

"Thank you."

"If only we knew who your father was, he could come to the gathering, too."

"The gathering?"

"Yes. The one I just spoke of—all of us brought together . . ."

Yes.

"Do you mind not knowing who he was?" she said.

I lied and said: *no,* because that was what she needed to hear. Lily had never known who my father was. It was not a part of the information she had been handed about her own life. It was one of the reasons she was there in that asylum—her passion for strangers—her belief that we have to put our trust in them—even offer them our lives, if we must. *It doesn't mean they will take them, Charlie,* she would say. *If you give a life, you get one.*

Maybe.

"You know why you look so good today, Charlie?" she asked.

Now, she was being her old mischievous self. She took my arm in both her hands and smiled up into my face. She could break your heart with that riveting gaze and her lips with their crooked, childlike smile. I almost had to look away. But she held me from it with her eyes.

"No," I said. "Tell me."

"You look like a boy I was in love with, once. I don't remember his name, but I know that you are his, and that's enough. What is it people say? *Everything that goes around, comes around*? Is that right?"

"Yes."

"Well, you've come around for me, Charlie. And you've brought him with you—whoever he was."

The smile had begun to fade.

"Shall we sit?" she said. "Or shall we walk?"

"Walk," I said. I wanted to get away from the little green chairs and tables and all the other families who had come to be with their people. And the sight of Lily's friend Ada, sitting alone and looking with expectant eyes at every young man who passed. *Are you my son, Neddy?*

No, ma'am.

Lily, my mother, held to my arm, and we went in further beneath the trees until we were all the way past the tables and walking on the grass.

"That's not the kind of gathering I mean," said Lily, as if she had read my distress at the sight of all the hopeless others. "At the gathering I mean, we will all be brought together into one safe place. And we will dance."

There it was: her catechism. One safe place. The gathering. And dance. Lily dancing—and song.

We went out over the lawns and stood, then, looking back at

where we had been. Her hand on my arm held tighter. Her other hand went up to pull at the brim of her hat. It was odd. I swear I heard her say: *goodbye, Charlie*—but when I looked, her mouth was set—and she was silent.

The next day, I was awakened by a phone call. It was 7:00 A.M., and they wanted me to come and identify her body.

She had died by fire as she had lived, in a circle of strangers. For once, she had made no attempt to escape. Her running—at long last—came to its end in the Asylum for the Insane at Whitby, Ontario, on Monday, the seventeenth of July, 1939. One month after her forty-ninth birthday.

2. Some of what follows I lived and some was told to me. The Lily parts were more in my own life than not because she was my mother. I was there. Her way of saying this was: *you were always there, Charlie—just the way I was always there myself and all of us, long before the visible parts of our lives began . . .*

That was Lily's way of telling everything—all of it sliding sideways, drifting off in little dots—all her sentences unfinished, the way her life was lived—everything always a beginning before there could be an ending to the part that went before. This is the way of any life that is lived on the run.

We were always escaping, you see—escaping, or standing ready to escape; running away from her demons; trying to avoid the outcome of what had been started—making off with the matches just when the fires caught hold.

But first to clarify: the parts about the others—the parts I will tell about Lily's family and the men she loved—all these other parts were written in Lily's notebooks, or told to me by others. Told in the way most family stories are told, some with prejudice, some objectively—always a mixture of myth and reality. The realities are mostly unavoidable: the dates of things, places and circumstances; the irrefutable, undeniable black and white of things that no one can alter—the way a death cannot be altered, or a birth or—as Lily would have it—a flaming. To be born was to be made visible.

As for the myths, take anyone's life and deny that most of it is deliberate self-delusion—an aggrandizement—a mixture of lies and truth, of what was wanted and what was had, producing the necessary justification for having been granted a life in the first place. *I was struck like a match*, Lily wrote. *I had no option but to burn.*

You can put a period after that. Lily did. It was the story of her life.

I see her mostly wearing blue—tall, with a wide-brimmed hat. *My eyes hurt*, she would say, in its shade. *They never shut.*

Lily was beautiful. I say that without apology. Every son thinks his mother is beautiful, I guess—and to every son, every mother is beautiful in ways that have nothing to do with features, nothing to do with graces—everything to do with tones of voice, assurances, the touch of finger ends. But Lily was also physically beautiful. All the way to the very last day, she had men falling at her feet. Me included. When I showed her picture at school, I had to defend her honour. She had that look that says: *beware, I kill*— the look that men will die for gladly. She also had the carriage of a woman who goes her own way without assistance: the carriage that many great dancers and actresses cultivate through discipline, but in Lily it was natural.

She had her father's auburn hair—the colouring I inherited in part. Her eyes were blue with flecks of green—and they seldom, if ever, looked directly into yours. They were nervous, long-lidded eyes, preoccupied with survival—animal eyes—watchful and sad, in the way of all beings living in fear of discovery—of being found. Not that Lily was hiding from everyone—but only from her demons. And these, it seemed from time to time, could be legion. Other times, they went so deep into the dark she was not aware of their presence—but they never completely vanished. A light would flare in a distant corner and Lily would know it was time to run again.

Do not misunderstand me when I speak of *running* and *escaping*. There were places Lily could hide without lifting her feet from the ground. The problem was that when she faded into her illness—the most complete of all her hiding places—it left me out in the open where everyone else could see me. Being a child, I had no defence against this scrutiny. It was hard to bear—and sometimes I hated her for it.

I will tell you honestly there were moments when being Lily's son was on a par with almost any persecution you can name. On the other hand, I look back now from beyond her death, and I know that my life, without Lily's presence in it, would have been no life at all. Not a life, at any rate, I would want to claim.

3· You already know that my father had disappeared without leaving his calling card. He was gone before I was born—an echo of Lily's own birth. We took on her mother's name and this way I became Charlie Kilworth.

Now, at twenty-nine, I am *Charlie Kilworth, Piano Tuner*. This is apt. You may well have heard of the Wyatt Piano Company. Perhaps you own a Wyatt yourself. At the height of their success they were the largest piano manufacturing company in the British Empire. Today, in 1939, all that is gone. Nevertheless, it was from the Wyatt Piano that we got, in part, our money—and, in part, our family history. But that comes later. For now, it is enough to say that pianos have always been an intimate part of my life and therefore there is some poetic justice in what I do. I cannot sing. I cannot play worth a damn—but I can recognize a piano in distress from a mile away.

Every piano has its own voice—unique in its sound as the voice of a human being. And when that voice begins to waver—when it strays, the way human voices do under stress—my job is to restore its resonance—tighten its enunciation—clarify its tone. I have an unerring ear for these voices. That is my gift. In the music business, we call it *perfect pitch*.

Sometimes, especially since the radio and the gramophone have taken up permanent residence in just about every house in North America, I feel as though I am trying to save an endangered species. Pianos were once the universal adornments of living-rooms and parlours. Now, they are lucky if someone makes room for them out in the garage. Discarded. Discordant. Passé. Silent—unless the thunder of a passing storm should happen to shake their wires.

I am almost thirty years old. Married. No children. My wife has left me. I don't like to talk about that. I live in Toronto, at 32 Dunbar Road. I tune, on the average, one piano every two weeks. There was a time when I tuned one every day. But now, the times are bad. The great Depression has done us all in—so, at least I am not alone in this situation. I am fortunate, too, that when Lily died there was still some money in the bank. She left it there for the children I've never had. And won't.

My mother believed in continuance—in what she called *the songs in the blood*; but my definition of those songs is far from benign. No child of mine will ever sing Lily's song. Once—for all its marvels—was once too often.

4. On the day I went to identify her body, the smell of smoke was so overwhelming I felt as if I had gone into the fire itself to find her. I removed the rings from her fingers and took a lock of her hair. She was not so badly burned that she was disfigured. The smoke had killed her—that, and her own determination to stay with the others when she might have gone on running.

All that was left of her possessions, besides some clothing and her collection of hats, was a wicker suitcase I instantly recognized. It was of a kind no longer manufactured and had been a part of my life since the day I was born. It was made of laminated straw, with bindings of leather studded with brass.

In the years before she was institutionalized, Lily had always kept this suitcase packed and ready for escape. In the Asylum, the nature of its contents had been altered. There were no more changes of underwear—no more combs and brushes—no more ropes and screwdrivers. These were all gone and in their place she had collected what she called her *songs*.

The suitcase had survived the fire intact, though its surface was stained and somewhat darkened. It smelled, when I had it first, of smoke—the scent being the same as a richly cured tobacco.

The items she had placed inside had a perfume on them, too. It was so evocative of Lily, I found it distressing—as though I need only turn and she would be standing there behind me. This perfume had no name that I was ever able to find, but she used it always. Sometimes it was in her hair, or it clung to the back of her neck or the undersides of her wrists, but mostly it was in her clothes. Rosemary, ferns and roses. I cannot describe it any other way. I know that she hung such things to dry in her closets—or layered them in sachet bags amongst her underclothes and hand-kerchiefs. And now the ghost of their scent was on everything in the wicker suitcase.

The *songs* that Lily referred to had little, if anything, to do with music. They were artifacts, mementos, notebooks. There were also photographs in an album and others tucked into envelopes. In some of these my own face stared out with Lily's—but most of them were of her mother's family. Also, the men she had known, one of whom might have been my father. In her notebooks, the writing was small and squared—almost hieroglyphic. She used black ink exclusively and fine-nibbed pens with which she also drew.

In a box that had once contained some expensive item from Ryrie-Birks, there was a wreath of long-stemmed grasses interwoven with flowers whose faded colours could not be read. I looked, but dared not touch it. A jar of pure white stones meant nothing to me—but a box of All-Weather Matches was like an old friend—or enemy, all too reminiscent of my mother. A brown paper parcel revealed, when opened, a small boy's sun-suit—my own from childhood. Above its heart my mother had embroidered *Charlie*, using a crimson thread.

Much else was there—most of it known to me, some of it not. These were Lily's *familiars*—her totems, her reassurances that what her mind could not retain of her life could be collected in a suitcase. They were, as she had written, her songs. Each of them had its own voice.

"You might want to disown me," she had said to me when I was still quite young.

I had no idea what she meant. To *disown* was a word I recognized as having negative connotations, but I did not understand what those connotations might be. When she explained that it meant I might one day want to deny her—in the way that Peter had denied Jesus—I was horrified.

"Oh, no," I said. I was seven. "I will never disown you."

How little we know.

I did, of course, disown her in time and—to my shame—in the next communication I had from her, she reminded me of my seven-year-old's indignation by addressing me as *Peter*.

There were other, happier meetings after that—but the cloud of that memory was never to leave me. I suppose I could be excused for having denied her on the basis of her own willingness to be denied. She urged me, after all, to call her Lily and to treat her as any relative other than the one she was. It was not as if the denial came out of nowhere. But I have not forgiven myself.

It happened in a public place—the quad at King's College, where I had been sent when still a boy. The occasion, I guess, was some sort of parents' day or prize day—I don't remember. The memory of what I did overwhelms it.

Lily had one of her episodes and fell to the ground. There were a lot of people there and I was mortified.

"She's fainted," someone cried. "We must get a doctor!"

But I knew she hadn't fainted. I knew too well precisely what was happening and what was going to happen next and I could not bear to be present with her when it happened in that particular place.

"Does anyone know who this woman is?" someone asked.

No.

I was silent. I turned away. And ran. And left her to the mercy of her demons, anonymous and alone. I remember looking back and thinking: *if she dies, I will have to claim her.* So I prayed that she would not die. Not for her sake—but for mine.

Now, she is dead and I claim her.

I will not disown her.

I will give her back her life.

One

1889—1890

Shine on, shine on, harvest moon
Up in the sky.
I ain't had no lovin' since
January, February, June or July.

Shine On, Harvest Moon
Jack and Nora Bayes

1. All that is left of the others now—or most of them—is Lily's album of photographs. Its pages can be dismantled, mingled and rearranged at will, forcing them outwards into a circle of exploded time. Though each of these photographs is titled and dated—*Lily with Charlie, August, 1915—Ede with Lily, June, 1891*—the dates, the faces are of less importance than the circle of light that closes round them—the aureole whose radiance they share.

Nothing within the circle fades. Time, it seems, is powerless here—loses its authority and casts no shadows. Each of these lives is equal in its moment with each of the lives that surrounds it—all of them reaching out together through the camera's lens to meet the common gaze that greets them.

This is me. This is us. This is now. Forever.

The tall grass field in which Ede is standing holding Lily, one year old in 1891, is the self-same field where the hay has already been cut in the summer of 1915. In this latter image, because of the War, there are very few men and many women. They are spreading the hay with wide wooden rakes so it will dry when a summer storm has passed. The sun is shining. The women wear aprons over their skirts and their hair is bound in scarves or pulled up under pale straw hats with brims like overturned plates. Lily is now twenty-five and she pauses to squint at the camera, one arm raised to shield her eyes from the sun. I am standing beside her, wearing a hat and the sun-suit embroidered with my name. Ede is not with us here. Perhaps it is Ede who takes the picture—calling out: *Lily! Charlie! Look at me! Look!*

The summer Lily was twenty, she is shown with others sitting on blankets that have been spread beneath the trees by the side of an English country road. This would be somewhere near Cambridge. A tablecloth has also been spread. A picnic is in progress. Someone has hung his jacket from the headlamp of a motor car. A low stone wall cuts through the frame beyond the picnickers. Lily by now is fully possessed of her disturbing beauty. She is holding out her hand—her right hand—towards the camera. Something is meant by this—something the eye cannot decipher. The hand, palm up, is empty—and yet it seems to offer something—what?—to the picture-taker.

All the others, but one, in the photograph are staring straight at the viewer. The expressions on their faces are a mix of suspense and amusement. Something has been said, perhaps, which demands a response that is yet to come.

The gaze not fixed on the viewer is fixed on Lily. It is intense and vulnerable. This watcher is wearing what must be a uniform, though he wears no cap. His hair is trimmed in a military cut. He is hoping, this young man, that Lily will turn to look at him. Clearly he is beguiled. Is he my father?

If you turn this picture over, you will find that none of the figures shown is named. There is also an unseen presence—my own. I am there in Lily's womb. The date is August, 1910. I will be born the following October. Beneath this photograph—displaced and out of sequence—is a photograph of Lily's mother.

Edith Mary Kilworth.

A formal portrait.

She is posed in a studio, leaning back against a pasteboard tree. In her hand, which rests at arm's length against her skirts, there is a bunch of field flowers: daisies, clover, vetch. Some grasses.

Behind her, a painted field of hay stretches upwards over a painted hill to a painted skyline of distant trees.

Lift your chin, Miss Kilworth. Try to ignore the camera . . .

That's right. Think of your favourite song.

It is 1890. The songs are various, crowding Ede's mind, but the one she chooses has not yet been named.

2 . Ede had been pregnant now not quite the full term: eight months, two weeks, four days. She had lapsed into an extended silence—partly because she was still in mourning—still enraged and afraid of speech. And partly, too, because the child itself had taken up dreaming in her belly—dreaming and, Ede was certain, singing. Not singing songs a person knew, of course. Nothing Ede could recognize. But songs for certain. Music—with a tune to it. Evocative. A song about self. A song about place. As if a bird had sung it, sitting in a tree at the edge of a field. Or high in the air above the field. A hovering song. Of recognition.

3 . Ede knew the field was partly in her mind—a version of it hanging there in a kind of mist, without the confining edges of the skyline and the split-rail fences that defined it in fact. It had become the landscape of half her recent dreams and almost all her conspiracies. This was Ede's word for fictions—the fictions by which she extrapolated hope from hopeless situations and surprise from certainties: *conspiracies*. Against reality.

The field was beautiful—enchanted in all its forms and seasons, whether conjured from the past or conjured from the present as one approached it. Ede's first encounter with it had been when its grasses had loomed up over her as a child—and when she had watched it, the way one watches a sleeping animal, safely from the upper branches of a tree—or the roof of her father's house—or a window. It had always seemed to be the hiding place of all the mysteries of life—to be the life itself of other living things. Its nearest edge ran parallel to the road that cut through the middle of her father's property—called *Munsterfield*—and Ede had been born within sight of it in a north-facing room at the front of the house. It was by the windows of that room that her mother had held Ede up to see the world—and the world was the field. *And the field was the world* . . . That had been the first of Ede's conspiracies.

Once you had crossed the dirt road, you were confronted with a wide but shallow ditch—a haven for weeds, mice and creeping ground cover that rabbits were partial to.

The ditch rose onto a scrub-infested, rock-strewn median that had been created out of the chaos resulting from the ditch being dug in the 1850s, almost forty years ago. And that was twenty years after the road had been drawn—first on the survey map, then on the earth. Every boulder, blade of grass and tree that had stood in the way of that narrow straight line had been removed. The boulders had become the foundations of fences and the trees had become the stuff of potash fertilizer and the fodder of kitchen fires. The grass had gone in clods against the walls of early barns and houses to keep out the cold. But none of these labours was in the memory of the living. They were the gifts of ancestors: great-grandparents, grandparents.

Beyond the median, a split-rail fence had been raised along the ridge of a gently falling slope that formed the whole south end of the field. The slope, in its turn, rolled down to a watercourse that could be crossed in a single step. To the west, where the slope cut deepest, there was a warm expanse of pond water, glistening with frogs and reed reflections.

If the field was breached beyond the stream, you entered the world of grass that had once been so intimidating to Ede. The slope that had fallen gently from the fence line now rose steeply to a greater height from which, once gained, a person could turn and see the wind-blown giant that was Munsterfield, with its angled porches, its shuttered windows and its gabled roofs. Its clapboard walls were painted white and its trim was the green of Ireland—all of it shaded by trees. Farther west, the wide, dark shape of the river came from the marshlands off to the south. It twisted—seen, unseen—northwards into the woods beyond which the town opened up around the millpond. Three church spires and the fire-hall tower gave evidence of the town itself. Always, the church bells could be heard on Sundays and, if the wind was right, three congregations trying to shout each other down with the clamour of the hymns.

Like the singing town, the field itself was invisible in the pitch of night, though the songs of its creatures came clear enough through the open windows at Munsterfield. Ede would conjure the field in the dark and walk in it barefoot through her dreams. She did this every night through most of April and all of May that year. 1890.

When the heatwave began in the first humid days of June, Ede would lie on her bed in the afternoons and imagine the field on the ceiling above her, tracing its boundaries with her finger. All she had to do to see it was rise and cross to the windows. But she avoided this. The field in her mind was safer than the field beneath the sun. That field was menacing. The sound of its cicadas drowned out the humming in Ede's womb—and drifting hawks and buzzards left their shadows on the hill. This way, the field presented itself until the third week in June. Then, on the 17th—a Tuesday—Ede was awakened in the night by a shout so loud that its vibrations shook the bed.

Now!

Though turning up the lamp made it clear she was quite alone, she knew she had been told to go about the business that would set this day apart for the rest of her life.

4. The house had the burden of seven sleepers besides Ede Kilworth, and this did not include the cats asleep on windowsills and the dogs asleep in the hall. Nor did it count the two hired men who shared a truckle-bed in the loft above the buggy in the drive shed. Nor the third hired man who slept in the tack-room. It did include Ede's family. Also the simple-minded girl whose job it was to feed the chickens—and her mother, the German woman, whose bed was in the summer kitchen. But none of these awoke in time to be aware of Ede's morning journey through the house. None of them heard the straining floorboards nor the creaking doors as Ede, barefooted, retrieved the cotton robe from its hook in the armoire and went to her bureau to lift some handkerchiefs from a squealing drawer and to take the silver scissors on their chain from the sewing box she had dumped last night on the table—the table whose lamps would need refilling before the night to come. Automatically, she turned over the book in whose favour she had set aside her mending and noted she had reached page 645 of *David Copperfield: I was a boyish husband as to years,* she read, and marked the place and closed the book. And all this while the music continued inside her—almost the music of a dance.

By the door, before leaving the house, Ede took up a pair of rubber boots discarded there by her brother Liam. If he found they were gone, he would be angry—but Ede would be back before he woke, or so she presumed. She would be back before anyone awoke, with the possible exception of the German woman and whichever of the three hired men whose job it was to fire the stove.

The sky was yellow—almost green where the fading moon still shone. Ede went over the lawn and through the gate. The sun had not yet risen—but its light was everywhere. She crossed the road barefooted. She did not attempt to struggle into the boots until she had reached the stile and was able to use its wide board steps as support. This whole operation made her laugh and she thought what a pity it was that women were forced to make a dignified withdrawal during pregnancy. For all its discomfort, there was still a wonderful entertainment to be had from the war with balance.

At last, the boots drawn on, Ede clambered over the stile with handfuls of nightgown and robe held up against her thighs. *Pray God, my rear end doesn't show*, she thought as she felt a draft of morning air reach up the backs of her legs.

In the field, she paused, letting down her skirts and closing her eyes. She held out her arms and breathed in the thick scent of clover and alfalfa. A bird sang somewhere off to her left, but when she opened her eyes she could not find it. Not that it mattered. In moments the air would fill with so many songs and birds in flight that watching them would make her dizzy. She wanted, from sheer exhilaration, to run deep into the field and fall on her back where the sea of grass was deepest and where she could drown in green. But there would be no running. It was quite impossible. She would surely topple sideways—backwards—or, worst of all, face down.

To her right, the sun at last made its appearance. At once, there was a shout from the rooster back in the barnyard. *Tattletale*. Ede still wanted to be alone.

The stream was thick with billowing grasses laid out flat in the current. Stepping across to the other side, Ede began to climb on an angle—shaping her journey so it would carry her westward. There she knew she would find a thick, rich spread of wildflowers and, if she was lucky, a few early branches of honeysuckle in the corner where the fence and the tree line met. It was in her mind that she would create a wreath of those flowers and the grasses from the field—because it was here in this field that the child who was soon to be born had been conceived. And one day, after the child was old enough to be told the truth of its parentage, she would offer the wreath as a token of . . .

What?

Her rage?

No.

That could not be told. But something could be told. Must be. Of course, it would depend on the lies that had preceded it—the conspiracies that remained to be invented.

Ede undid the belt of the robe that had only been loosely tied and withdrew the scissors on their chain from her pocket. The first thing she cut for her wreath was a strand of bindweed set with pale blue flowers, so pale they were almost white. And then, the first of that summer's ox-eye daisies. And a dozen spikes of purple clover and a . . .

What?

Something was wrong.

Very wrong. Or right.

The humming had stopped. The singer was silent.

Ede sat down on the ground.

Not here, she thought. Not here.

And then she thought: but why not here—and be done with it. To finish where it began.

5. The harvest moon of 1889 rose on the evening of Saturday, September 28th. It rose above the field and over the town of McCaskill's Mills and over the road and the river that joined them. By night, it would be of a pumpkin colour, but all that afternoon it haunted the horizon, pale as milk glass, silent as snow.

Saturday. Not, in its usual connotation, the most relaxing day of the week. Shopping took up most of the morning. Boring visitations took up most of the afternoon. But this week was different. For over a month, it had been known that on Saturday, the 28th of September, *The Piano Man* would arrive to give a demonstration of the newest instruments being offered by the Williams Piano Company of Oshawa.

The Piano Man himself was more than the usual salesman. He was an artist. Or, as his flyers would have it: *an artiste.*

"An artiste of the keyboard!"

There were three pianos, each of a different size and each in a different price range, which The Piano Man would *play upon one-by-one* throughout the afternoon in the showroom of the Queen's

Hotel. That evening, he would give a concert and accept requests. According to the flyers, he had no name aside from *The Piano Man*. Ede had read every word and found no mention of it, though his credentials were given. He had played in public concerts in Boston, Toronto and Atlantic City. He had, so the reader was informed, a *degree in music*, though which degree was not specified. All of this was discreetly offered between brackets, in italic letters. Each of the handbills—and there were larger versions for posting in public places—gave the names of a dozen towns laid out along the Toronto–Nipissing Railway Line. To each of these towns The Piano Man would bring his *demonstration of the newest dance tunes and the greatest classics of the keyboard*.

Ede went into the Queen's Hotel that afternoon with her brothers Liam and Malahide and her sister Willa. Ede was the eldest of the Kilworth children. James, who was known as Jamie so as not to be confused with his father, had been the eldest son, but had died in his twentieth year of a burst appendix. That had been last October. 1888. October, as a consequence, was not as much anticipated as the rest of the year had been. On the anniversary of Jamie's death—which came on the 25th, the Kilworths would all go into mourning for a week at their father's request. The first-born male—the namesake child—*the darling one*, as he had been known to both his parents, would never be forgotten.

Ede was now resplendent in her twenty-third year—and the search for a husband had already begun, although Ede would have none of it. *You can look*, she had said to her mother, *but I'm not ready yet.*

The local prospects were without a hint of promise. She wanted more than a butcher's son—and less than a *prominent citizen's boy*, as one or two had been classified. Her father was prominent enough, when it came to that, and wealthy enough with his huge successes as a dairy farmer and landowner. Ede would take her own time and go her own way into marriage. The thought of it made her laugh—that a person should hand herself over to another person and say *I'm yours forever*. Ede's edict was: *I'm* mine *forever*.

Joining—being joined to another person's life—was a bookish

concept with no reality in it. That her parents, who were innately at odds with one another, had stayed together was a quirk. A trick. They were beguiled, somehow. Ede had never felt the mysterious pull of another person the way it was described in novels. No one had *stopped her dead in her tracks.* No one had *immobilized her with his smile.* To love without reason was to condemn yourself to misery, all for the sake of mindless custom.

Oddly enough, the fact that Ede had distanced herself from marriage satisfied Eliza Kilworth, though it left James somewhat disgruntled. He was all for getting the next generation started on its way. Eliza rebuked him. *Ede is not one of your cows,* she said. *She has intelligence and wit—which means she has an independent mind. She can have any life she wants—and the longer she has to dream up a future, the better off she'll be.*

This was the Ede—still *dreaming of her future*—who walked into the Queen's Hotel with her brothers and her sister that Saturday afternoon in September, 1889. Liam was to buy them all tickets to The Piano Man's evening concert. While he did this, and while Malahide went off to stand in the poolroom door, Willa dragged Ede away to see the pianos.

The air was filled with the satisfying smell of furniture wax— of lemon oil and dust. All the gilt chairs on which they would sit that evening had been pushed against the walls to make room for the Williams display, with its placards and tabletops of pamphlets and its three pianos gleaming with polish. Ede would have preferred to leave the viewing of the instruments until the concert. She wanted an atmosphere of music, not of commerce. "He'll just try to sell us one," she said to Willa. "And you know Papa won't allow a piano in the house."

"I don't want to see them," said Willa. "I want to see *him.* Everyone says he's beautiful."

"Don't be silly. You're only a child. What would you want with a beautiful man? Besides which, men aren't beautiful. They're handsome."

"Not The Piano Man," said Willa. "The Piano Man is *pretty as a picture*—he is *every woman's dream and every man's rival!*

The Piano Man is *lovely as a rose* and *perfect as a piece of pie!* He is . . ."

"Stop that, Willa," said Ede. "Wherever do you hear such things?"

"Standing on the corner, waiting for you outside the Queen's. Mrs Donaldson, Mrs Fairhurst, Mrs Hunt and Miss Bransby, the nurse."

"You're not to listen to gossip. You know that."

"But . . ."

"Just be quiet."

As they entered the showroom, a group of women was clustered around the Williams Grand, whose lid had been raised and whose wires were ringing with a boisterous tune that Ede did not recognize. The Piano Man could not be seen because of the cluster of women (which included Mesdames Donaldson, Fairhurst and Hunt) but he could be heard:

> *A wandering minstrel, I,*
> *A thing of shreds and patches,*
> *Of ballads, songs and snatches,*
> *And dreamy lullaby!*
> *And dreamy lull-a-by!*

There was enthusiastic gloved applause and there were muted cries of *oh! Oh! Oh!* and murmurs of *isn't he wonderful!* and *have you ever!*

Still, he could not be seen.

"Let's leave," said Ede.

"But I want to see him," said Willa.

"Tonight," said Ede. "We'll see him tonight." She turned to leave, but just as she turned, there was a break in the cluster of backs. Two of the women were moving away to inspect the upright pianos.

In seconds, the gap had been filled by the crowding in of others, but in those seconds, Ede caught a glimpse of The Piano Man. Only a glimpse—but it stopped her cold. In the pit of her stomach it seemed that a hand reached out and held her in place.

"I thought we were leaving," said Willa.

"We are," said Ede. But she was rooted.

"Are you all right?"

"Yes. Fine."

"You look funny."

"Do I?"

"Yes."

"Maybe we should go and have a glass of lemonade," Ede said. "All the windows must be closed—it's so hot in here."

At last, they moved off. But as they went, Willa noted that all the windows were open.

6. It had long been Eliza Kilworth's ambition to own a piano and to install it in the front parlour where it could be heard by all—*even by those passing by on the road*. A piano, she argued, was *a sign and signal of civilization*. And *a gift of gentility to all the generations to come*. But James would have none of it. A piano, in his lights, was *a pagan instrument*. As if he were God-fearing. As if he believed the Devil lived in the cellar and only waited to hear a single chord in order to come up through the trap to claim his victims. As if the world would end if a musical soirée were held in the Kilworth parlour and the neighbours invited in to hear the piano being played. As if . . .

James was adamant. Money would not be provided for it and that was that. The truth was, James Kilworth feared the piano in much the same fashion and for much the same reason that later generations of fathers would fear the radio and the gramophone. He was afraid of its distractive powers—its ability to seduce the otherwise industrious child into a world of dreamy inactivity. He was afraid he would lose his children's attention, and thus their devotion to labour. He was not a mean-spirited man, but—as his wife would have it—an ignorant man. But: *ignorance can be cured*—a motto Eliza had copied from *The Farmer's Advocate and Home Magazine.* Time would tell.

Ede's association with music was that of most others in the community. A person sang on Sundays and in the choir at school. There were concerts in the Queen's Hotel, and there were all the local marching bands—the *Boys' Brigade*—the *Battalion*—the *True Blue Orange.* Groups of visiting musicians came and played in the auditorium upstairs at the Town Hall, where a stage with a sylvan backdrop awaited them. There was gay music, too—waltzes and polkas, gallops and reels at public cotillions and private dances. In three of the local houses—*mansions,* according to their owners—there were ballrooms. Most of the homes Ede visited had pianos. But not her own.

She had touched one only once. With mysterious results. It happened at the Allertons' in town. Martha Allerton had been Ede's best friend in school, but was married now and gone to London, Ontario. Most days, when Ede was in the Allerton house, the piano was closed. Not because it should not be played, but only because the dust got down between the keys and *clogged the workings.* One afternoon, however, when Ede was waiting for Martha Allerton to change into a cooler dress than the one she had worn all day, she saw that the doors to the parlour were pushed aside and the grand piano stood there open and inviting.

Ede went in slowly, hearing—she thought—the echo of some music sounding along the strings. As if some player had just arisen and walked away. Perhaps the breeze from the open windows had created it. There the piano sat with its lid raised and propped in a tipped position. There was a round, cushioned stool in front of the keyboard. Ede put her knee down into the plush and leaned forward.

Mason and Risch, she read: *the piano with a soul.*

This made her smile.

All right, she thought. *How does one do this?*

She had seen it often enough.

One splayed one's fingers.

One used both hands.

One placed them so—having drawn back the sleeves of one's dress—and waited.

Her hands were birds, all at once, poised there above the keys—capable, as birds are, of song—of singing. But how?

She knew that one did not use all of one's fingers—only some, as if to make a pattern. She knew, as a singer in the Orpheum Choir, what music notation was and how to read it. But not how to read it through her fingers, down to the keys in chords. If only she had been allowed . . .

The image she had was of placing a sound—of laying it out—of displaying it. But when her hands descended and her fingers touched the keys and the first intimations of sound began to gather, a stronger sensation than sound reached out along the wires to touch her. Enter her. Connect.

The shudder of it passed all the way to her shoulders, up into her skull and down her back.

It was thrilling. Mystifying. Dangerous.

Whether the chords she had made—left hand, right hand—were coherent musically, they were certainly coherent in ways Ede felt but could not articulate. All she knew was, she wanted it to happen again.

What—oh, what was it—this rush of heat through her nerves all the way to her groin? What—oh, what was it?

Ede bowed her head.

She lifted her left hand up and pressed it hard against her mouth. Hard. Harder. Fisted.

She waited, wanting—why?—to weep. Tears came—but none fell. A current passed through her. It was difficult to breathe, as though her throat were being clutched. But she was not alarmed. She was not afraid. She was waiting.

Slowly—very slowly—she lowered the casing over the keyboard. *Click.* And then she lifted the extended hand to join the other—turning both of them to cover her face.

She stood up straight. Then straighter. Her shin and her thigh had almost gone to sleep. Both of them tingled as she put her weight on the leg that had knelt on the pillow.

Oh, she said.
Oh.
No one heard her.
Oh.
She stepped back.
The tears now escaped and rolled down her cheeks.
Ede blinked and stared at the piano.
Oh.

She was twelve years old when this happened. Not quite twelve, but on the verge of it. The cusp, as it turned out, of womanhood. That night, while preparing for bed, she commenced her first period and the next day, she wore a red bow in her hair. Martha Allerton, on seeing it, smiled. She had worn the red bow herself six weeks earlier. It had been their prearranged signal that life had begun.

7 • *Sunday, 29th September, 1889:*
I have never done this before—write to myself—speak privately, alone—whisper into my own ear. There has been no necessity till now. I have never felt the desire. Not to write. Not to put things down on paper. But this . . . I must explain what I have done. I must explain it so that I will understand it. Why it happened. And how.

The words look funny—odd—set out like this. Words written down have always been for other people. So others would know and understand some event—some aspect of my life. But this is not a letter. No one else will ever see this. No one. Ever. When I have written it, I will burn it.

I went in—only yesterday—to see The Piano Man. To hear him play. Willa went. And Liam. Mama. Papa. Malahide. We all went in to hear him. This was in the evening. Seven-thirty. I wore my yellow dress. The one with buttons down the front. There must have been forty or fifty people there—all sitting down, or most of them. Sitting in those lovely little chairs I've always wanted to steal and bring home. The gilded ones—gilt?—gilded? The ones they use for the New Year's Ball and the times when the politicians come and there's not enough room in the Town Hall. Everyone sat in a golden chair.

I had seen him in the afternoon. One glimpse only. But it made me feel . . . I don't know. The sight of him was like a match being struck. And it burned me.

The Piano Man is small. He is a little man. Small, with perfect proportions. His hands, for instance, being the hands of a man who "must play the piano or die," are extremely small—small if you think about what they must do. Accomplish. *Achieve.* But they do achieve it—music. They accomplish it in spite of their inappropriate size. Beautiful music. I could not believe my ears, any more than I could believe my eyes. In the afternoon, he was sitting down and I thought he was a giant. Almost.

Tonight, he sang for me. To me. Right there in front of everyone. It did not embarrass me. Even as it was happening—even as he sang—I wondered why it did not embarrass me—the way it used to embarrass me when Mister Callaghan made us sing to each other when the Orpheum was rehearsing. "You are singing for other people," he would tell us. "To other people!" Angry. Shouting—as if he was angry with us. "The song is not for you. The song is for the world!" And we would sing it—he would make us sing it, whichever song it was, into each other's faces. So embarrassing. Then, I *was* embarrassed. But not yesterday.

Right there in front of everyone, he sang looking right into my eyes, and I couldn't look away. Right into my eyes, while he sat on his special chair—the chair that raises him up. I had been invited out of the audience to stand beside the piano with my hand on the lid of it because he said: "the song I am going to sing must be sung to a pretty girl." I am not a girl, of course, I'm a woman. Still, that is what he said.

I admit I was afraid. Nervous. Everyone knew me. I knew everyone out there—sitting, watching.

But that didn't matter. I didn't care. I was not embarrassed. Afraid, but not embarrassed. And I stood there—in front of everyone—facing everyone, the way I would have stood if I had been the singer and The Piano Man my accompanist, the way the soloists stand beside Mister Callaghan. And when The Piano Man played, my hand was on the lid and I could feel the vibrations.

This is what he sang. To me.

> *Once, in the dear dead days*
> *beyond recall,*
> *When on the world the mists*
> *began to fall . . .*

It was mesmerizing. It was wonderful. His voice was so rich and sweet and reassuring.

> *Out of the dreams that rose*
> *in happy throng*
> *Lo, to our hearts*
> *Love sang an old sweet song . . .*

I could see Little Eva Willard watching me. Jealous. She was sitting up front, in the closest seat to the piano. I suppose this made sense, since her father owns the Queen's Hotel. He, of course, was not there—off in his office, no doubt, making sure the Queen's will reap another fortune this year. But Mrs Willard attended—acting as her daughter's agent—showing her off for all the world to see. *She's going to be a great concert artist—you wait!* Ho-hum. I saw her reach out to take Little Eva's hand, but Little Eva snatched it away. The child—I think this year she is eight or nine—was wearing white as always—long white gloves and white kid boots. Eight years old. Or nine—and already *a shining star!* Ha! One thing was perfectly clear. Little Eva was in love. *Everyone* was in love with The Piano Man. But he was singing to me.

And in the dusk, where fell
*   the firelight's gleam,*
Softly it wove itself into our dream . . .

Just a song at twilight
When the lights are low,
And the flickering shadows
Softly come and go. . . .

He sang the whole song through to the end, with me standing up there, listening. I felt like an actress in a play—as if all the lights were shining on me. And I could not back away.

When the song was over, The Piano Man stood up and faced the audience. And just as he turned towards them, he spoke to me through the applause. "Do not go away," he said. "When it is over, stay."

I said nothing. Not a word. But I nodded.

Why?

Now, my whole life is changed. My whole life. Changed forever. Because I nodded. Because I stayed.

8. "No one ever calls me Edith," she said. "Except my father when he's angry. And Mister Callaghan, who's always formal and wouldn't give his dog a nickname."

"Who is Mister Callaghan, then?"

"You don't know Mister Callaghan? You must know Mister Callaghan. Mister Callaghan knows everyone in music."

"No. We've never met."

"He's the Master of the Orpheum Choir."

"The choirmaster."

"No. He won't let us call him that. Choirmasters are church people, he says. Mister Callaghan is Master of the Choir. He calls us all *young gentlemen and ladies*. Even the boy sopranos are *young gentlemen*. And we all get our full names off him. It's unfailing. Mister Callaghan fires them at you like pistols and cannons! *Edith Mary Kilworth! BAM!*"

They both laughed. And both fell silent, standing still by the piano—the upright—the same one from which The Piano Man had sung to Ede.

"Tell me your name," she said. "It isn't posted on the bills."

"I never tell my name," he said.

"But we haven't been formally introduced. That's a rule with me. I have to be introduced."

The Piano Man looked around at the ebbing crowd as it filed away past the golden chairs. "I suppose I could make an exception . . ." he said, with a hint of a smile. A signal.

Before he spoke again, he stepped in closer to Ede, turning very slightly to one side. She could smell him now. He laid his fingers on top of her brown gloved wrist. Ede closed her eyes. She did not dare see him so near to her for fear she would reach out and touch him with her free hand. She also held her breath—drinking in and holding the smell of his hair. Men had the most wondrous smelling hair . . .

Say your name.

O, say it . . .

"Thomas Wyatt," he said at last, almost whispering. Wet. His eyes turned away from her—then slid back again, cloaked in the longest lashes Ede had ever seen—using the lashes as a hiding place from which to watch her—a place of ambush.

His hand was still on her wrist. Ede could not move. All the pale down on her arm was raised as she waited, ignorant of what might be going to happen next but certain that, no matter what it was, she was in danger.

Thomas Wyatt. Tom.

9. A dozen people must have seen them walk out through the lobby—and, on Collins Street, a dozen more.

Just in front of the hotel, Liam Kilworth sat in the democrat, waiting for the rest of the family to emerge. Ede broke away from The Piano Man long enough to tell her brother she was going to walk home with *this gentleman*. Liam seemed unimpressed. He nodded and, looking at Thomas Wyatt, he said to Ede: "so, you're not going over to Gallaghers with the rest of us?" Ede said no. Edna Gallagher was Eliza's oldest friend. The visit there would be intolerably long. She was glad to have an excuse to avoid it.

She did and did not want to introduce The Piano Man to Liam. Protocol demanded it—but Liam was Liam. So critical of everyone but himself, it would be difficult—possibly embarrassing. Besides which, Thomas Wyatt had already turned away. Clearly, he did not want any introductions. That decided it.

Sitting on a bench near the corner, Billy Barns—the town drunk—was enjoying his jar of whisky. Tom said: "good-night, old man," and Ede thought that was kind of him. Thoughtful. Tom said: "there's one in every town I play. They all seem the same lost soul. They have the saddest eyes in all the world."

Ede took Tom's arm and led him to the carbon street lamp that lit the corner. "This is the way," she said. And then, before moving on, she looked back and did what she had never done before. "Good-night, Billy," she said. And they went on.

Moonlight showed them one tall, angular house after another—each house showing lamplit windows in a brick façade—all its doors and windows closed—all its people hidden. A covered phaeton went by on whirling, almost silent wheels, but Ede could not identify the driver. Nor the horse, in spite of the richness of the moonlight. Too many leaves remained on the trees and, this way, too many shadows plagued the roadway.

All that could be heard was the sound of their footsteps on the boardwalk as they made their way to the outskirts, passing the last of the houses, passing the last of the drive sheds, passing the last of the high board fences. Then, all at once, stepping down to the dust of the road, their feet were silenced. Later, Ede would remember this as floating—being floated up the hill and down the other side—swum with—carried weightless. And the moon rose higher, brighter, larger—until it seemed to engulf the whole sky. Ede would never again inhale the smell of wet, fallen leaves without closing her eyes to find the moon in her mind.

10. There was a hollow in a corner of the field to which Ede had always retreated when she wanted to be alone.

"Here," she said.

It was the only word spoken.

Afterwards, in memory, she forgot that she had been afraid. She forgot that she had not known what to do. She could not remember having said *yes* or *no* or *do* or *don't*. Or anything. The words for everything meant nothing.

In time, the silence was broken by crickets and frogs and the cry of a fleeing killdeer—all of which Ede fed back into memory. Not where the moment had found them but where her sense of the moment put them—a wash of sound like a sea of whispers.

These, too, became the instant occupants of memory: the warmth of Tom's breath at her throat—the smell of his hair—the feel of his fingers turning her yellow buttons under and open one by one and the slide of his hand as it found her shoulders and breasts—the nodding descent of his head and the weight of it, pressing inward until his fingers and then his mouth were on her nipples—a sucking so gentle a child might have been there.

She remembered, too, his kneeling between her legs, his hands making wings as he lifted his suspenders wide of his shoulders and his shirt all undone with the moonlight beyond it shining through the cotton. She remembered him leaning forward, the moonlight now in his hair and the dew on his fingers when he pressed for entry and the shudder of pain that sent her knuckles flying to her lips and the cry she had heard that was her own. And the sudden presence of him inside her and the gradual overwhelming yearning that this would never end—that he would never leave her. She remembered all this, but not a single memory of words.

They had lain in the field for an hour. For longer. Surely it had been longer. The clock tower belled eleven. Maybe midnight. Ede had lost count.

Tom had smoked a cigarette and Ede had watched him, both of them seated now—Tom with his knees drawn up and his elbows digging into the earth and the field giving up the smell of clover, alfalfa and sweetgrass while the firefly of the cigarette danced over it.

Far, far away to the south, where the river wound through a forest, a pack of wolves began to yip and sing. Something had been cornered—killed—and now there was the news of it to be spread and celebrated. This was not a sound Tom knew but one that Ede had lived with all her life—the ritual of song as a life is ended. More than once, the men had returned from the woods with the carcass of a calf, or the trophy head of a deer that had been killed by wolves.

When the singing was over, Tom said: "I should deliver you to your door."

Ede wondered: *will I be able to walk?* And then: *do I want to?* But she rose and stood beside him as he placed his arm around her waist.

All the way back through the field, across the stream and up the slope to the stile, they paced each other step by step. And Tom sang—whispering—leaning in to kiss her hair and away again to see the moon.

> *Roses love sunshine,*
> *Violets love dew,*
> *Angels in heaven,*
> *Know I love you . . .*

And Ede believed him.

And then he was gone.

11. In May, a month short of the birth of her child, Ede went back to the field one night to the very place where the child had been conceived. She had watched a cow, once, giving birth in the hollow of this corner. It had been the first such event that Ede had witnessed. She was six years old and had strayed from the kitchen yard, passing along the side yard beneath her grandmother Portia's lilac trees, into the front yard over the lawn.

The gate was an irresistible beacon, like all gates to a child of six. Ten thousand times Ede had been told not to open this gate—never to pass beyond this gate, any gate, all gates. But she had just discovered she could master the gate from the kitchen yard—and why not this gate, too?

This was in the days before the German woman and long before her simple-minded daughter. Also in the days before the present young hired hands—but not before Ephraim Allward, who was the eldest hand—older by five years (or more) than James Kilworth. Ephraim, as he aged, can be seen in photographs dating back to the 1860s. He does not appear too often, but over the years, for a man of his reticence, he turns up often enough. His expression never alters—his essential appearance barely changes, always and ever an upright figure hiding his hands behind his back or deep in his pockets. Ephraim never smiles, but children adore him.

On the day of Ede's escape from the kitchen yard, Ephraim was in the drive shed sawing new sides for the wagon. The sound of his sawing gave a rhythm to the steps Ede took—and as Ephraim paused to select a new board, Ede stood looking at the tall wrought-iron gate that had come all the way from Ireland. Through its ornate metal lacework, she could see the road and, beyond the road, the fence with its stile.

Come over, come over, whoever you are, the stile seemed to say. To sing.

Ephraim gave his newly selected board a slap and began to saw again.

Ede stepped forward. She did not look back.

Gates were easy. Heavy, but easy if the hinges had been oiled—and these had been. There was not a sound as she pushed at the latch with her chubby fingers. For a moment, Ede stood hard up against the cool iron coils, somehow excited by their shape against her dress. She would remember that always—of pressing and of yearning through that gate as if an act of magic had allowed her to pass.

The road was wide and dusty—a high-summer road much stirred and flustered by a season's worth of wheels. The clapboard front of the house and the screens on the windows had taken on a patina from its billows of grit. In the driest times, the house took on the colour of golden brown sugar.

Ede did not look either way. A magnet was at work—the road, the stile, the field. Ede was wearing a blue cotton dress with an apron over it and the ties of the apron blew out like skimpy wings as she climbed one step at a time to the top of the stile. Strands of yellow hair blew over her face and in reaching to pull them aside, Ede almost lost her balance. She was, from her new perspective, a mile—two miles—above the ground.

The grass was blowing, too—blowing in lime-green waves that sounded like a thousand children whispering: *scissors—scissors—*sibilant and mesmerizing—*scissors—scissors—scissors—*throwing up clouds of scent and winged insects—unidentified—unidentifiable—everything with wings going up at once into the air around her—*scissors—scissors . . .*

Ede climbed down. She went out into the sea of grass and began to swim towards the gully—down into the deep green heart of it, flurries of hair in her eyes—her honey-hair rising, lifted, being floated beyond her reach.

She went to the shallow valley, down to its river and through the river, wetting her slippers and ankles and, pushing the grass aside, angling sideways, upwards over the hill and down again towards the corner—down to the corner as if a track had been laid and the map of it was in her veins.

For a child, this journey was immense and yet, as Ede approached the end of it, she was running, vaguely aware of the squelching sound in her slippers and overwhelmed with the sound of the tall grass jungle through which she moved.

Someone was there.

A creature lying on its side.

What? What was happening?

As Ede approached, she heard the creature groan—not in pain, but in behalf of some effort it was making. She stopped in her tracks and removed a strand of hair from her mouth and said out loud: *Lena?* As if the creature would answer her.

What are you doing here, Lena?

Ede squatted down to wait.

Lena was a small Jersey cow. She gave another groan and lifted her head to look at the child. She knew this child. This child was harmless. Lena looked away again.

Something instinctive made Ede fall silent. She knew—and did not know—what was happening. This was either death or birth. When you die, you lie down like this. And when you sleep. And when you're born.

The cow gave a heave and her legs made pawing motions, as if she wanted to rise. Ede did nothing. She waited.

Lena groaned once more. And then again. And then again. The final groan was almost a cry. And then, with what Ede thought was a *jellified* sound—like a pudding tipped from a mould—a calf emerged. A folded calf in a bag of wetness.

Ede! Edie! Ede!

Someone was calling.

Ede! Edie! Ede!

Eliza. Ephraim. Jamie, who was still alive that day, and seven. All of them calling: *Ede! Edie! Ede!* But none of them calling: *Lena!*

The calf, on its side, was wet all over. Lena got up and moved in its direction—speaking to it softly—ignoring Ede altogether.

Ede was still squatting—and had pulled some strands of grass with which she now made knots to chew and suck on.

Ede! Edie! Ede . . . !

Lena was licking her calf and nudging it—pushing at it gently with her nose. Clearly, she wanted the calf to stand.

"He can't," said Ede—the first words spoken since the calf had appeared. "He's tired."

Nonetheless, Lena kept nudging him until—at last—he staggered to his feet and stood there wavering.

Ede! Edie! Ede!

Where, oh, where can she be?

Ede was still silent.

She knew something now she had not known before. To give birth, you must go into the field as far away from everyone as possible. To give birth, you must find the tallest grass in the furthest corner—and when they call for you, lie down there and be silent. You must refuse to answer. Giving birth is a secret between two people only: the one being born—and the one who . . . what? The one who was giving up the life of the other. Birth is a parting, a separation forever. Lena and her calf had been one. Now, they were two.

That had been—when?

It didn't matter. It had been long before Ede would give up her child—long before the moment when it would be parted from her. *Now, my life is my own,* it would say to her. *Now, I am me. Entirely.* But not yet.

All of spring, the year of Lily's birth—all of that season had been a wonder, one day after another of perfect weather—no floods, no droughts but only a balance that comes perhaps once in a decade. It was the time of blossoms and the first sweet flowers in the fields and along the ditches. And Ede went into the field that night in May and lay down as best she could and stared up through the dark all the way to the stars.

Her hair was unbound, as she preferred it now, and she could smell it where it lay along her cheek. It had the smell of rainwater in it and of the inevitable grass that seemed to be a part of this expected child's every nuance, even as it burgeoned—the field where it was dreamed—the field where it was imagined—the field where it was got.

We lay here and sang, Ede thought. *We lay here and sang* Down in the Valley. *Beneath the moon. That mischievous harvest moon. No moon now, just stars—only stars. But all of them. All. Every one.*

Ede stared up and raised her arm and moved her fingers, drawing lines between them, all the stars with her fingers—joining the great constellations—naming them: *Orion—Cassiopeia—Ursa Major—Ursa Minor . . .*

She drew lines, too, in her mind—as her finger moved amongst the stars—from the field to the town—to the rest of the township—the county—the province—the country—the continent—the world; lines, lines. Lines like train tracks—sending out the connecting trains of thought—joining, joining, joining . . .

And The Piano Man—young Tom Wyatt, dead already. Gone to the earth—lying down to die and dying. And his child—his blood—his love of music—all his songs inside her, reaching through the dark to touch her, searching up and out in order to join—to be joined with Ede, in order to sing their child into life.

Killed, he was.

Gone now—like Jamie. Gone like all the dead brothers and sisters—Elizabeth, Joseph, Jane and Patrick—her mother's rosary of grief. Gone, as they were gone, utterly.

And yet—not utterly. Surely not every last vestige of him. Jamie and the Rosary Children had died *without issue.* Isn't that what it says in scripture? Books? Certainly Ede had seen the phrase *died without issue* somewhere. But not Tom. Not entirely—utterly.

It was not just the fact of the child—of there being some issue; it was more than that, more than a mere statistic. And more, too, than the music—the singing, the song. Ede had a sense of his actual presence in that moment. It happened when she lay back into the grass, feeling it the way she had felt it on that September night—a bending aside of all resistance—making of both the grass and of her will a pillow on which to spread herself. She had wanted to take him so deep inside that he would never leave her. Could not.

He might as well have been there, kneeling above her now, saying *I am here*, his presence was so absolute. Ede thought for certain she could smell him and feel the pliant angle of him bending into her as she lay back under the stars—the Pleiades watching over her.

A bell in the town began to toll the hour, but Ede was asleep before she could finish counting—one hand clutching a palmful of grass. She had drifted off on the song of the field itself—and of its endless life, and the endless lives of the stars spread out above her.

12. Tom was buried on a hillside in Toronto and all his brothers came and stood beside his coffin. It seemed there were no women in his family—only men. His father stood alone at the foot of the grave and his brothers appeared to have no wives. Certainly no wives were present.

The brothers were dressed in what Ede came to think of as *Wyatt suits*—of a blue so dark it was almost black. They were taller than Tom had been. Taller and more angular. Their faces were all clean-shaven and would have been handsome if they had not been so determined to grieve. Their father—who gave the impression of being at war with them—had a double-pointed beard that reached his breastbone. He wore old-fashioned 1870s' attire and it was only on seeing him that Ede realized how poor he must be—and all his sons. It wasn't just that his mourning clothes were cut in the old-fashioned way. They were also ill-fitting and somewhat threadbare.

Ede stood back beneath some trees. The propriety of her presence had been difficult to manage. Only one of the brothers—Frederick, the eldest—had met with Ede before the Toronto visit.

He had been kind enough to bring the news of Tom's death in person. The scene in the Kilworth parlour had been muted, almost silent, and all the clocks, Ede swore, had stopped mid-stroke.

Frederick Wyatt at first seemed more like a distant acquaintance of Tom's than a brother. He spoke with the kind of authority you expect when grief has no blood in it—a self-controlled kind of grief—an objective grief. Reasoned, utterly without emotion and yet with deep concern.

There had been an accident in the streets. Some horses had run away—a trolley car had been involved—a wagon had been overturned. Tom and another man had been killed. Some children had been injured. That was all. It was both horrific and ridiculous. *A matter of minutes . . . seconds . . .*

How had Mister Wyatt known about Ede?

"You surprise me, Miss Kilworth. It was common knowledge in our family that you were Tom's young woman."

"I can't believe he told you that," said Ede. "I don't even know who you are. Tom never spoke of you once."

Clearly, Frederick Wyatt did not know what to make of this news—that his brother had never mentioned his name. "Tom certainly spoke about *you* to us," he said. "And of his feelings for you."

Ede looked away, unable to breathe. Not that she did not believe Tom had loved her—but that he should have been so confident that he announced it to this stranger here, who called himself Tom's brother; that was not credible.

"After all, he was going to marry you, Miss Kilworth. He told our father so. And all our brothers—of whom there are three, besides myself and Tom."

"Marry me . . ."

"Yes. You must have known this."

Ede said nothing.

Frederick Wyatt continued. "There were plans to bring you to us so that you could be met beneath our roof. Train tickets were bought so that you would not have to go to any expense. Tickets for you and your father. And for your mother, of course. Tickets for all three of you. Two-way fares from McCaskill's Mills to Toronto."

"Toronto."

"Where you were to live, of course, once married."

"Yes. Yes. Of course."

Married. To Tom.

Ede, having so far succeeded in masking her grief with decorum, all at once broke free of her restraint and made a sound in her throat that had no meaning. It was just the violent sound of air being taken in—as it would have been by a diver breaking to the surface.

"Dead."

"Yes, Miss Kilworth. I'm sorry."

Ede regained control of her breathing and said: "how did you know about this journey I was to make, Mister Wyatt?"

"We had to be prepared for your coming. Reservations were required. I made them myself. At the Sherbourne Hotel."

Even at a distance of seventy miles north-east of Toronto, Ede had heard of the Sherbourne Hotel. It was considered to be among the finest—*an hotel for the élite . . .*

"The train tickets were in Tom's pockets when we emptied them. And we . . ." Frederick Wyatt got no further.

Ede stood up and turned towards the windows. *Emptied pockets.* Winter beyond the windows, held at bay by the glass, had done its worst that year. Blizzards and cold spells had lasted for uncommon periods of time—days—weeks. Now, years. Or so it seemed. *Emptied pockets. Tickets. Reservations. For a journey she would now not make.*

Dead.

Ede looked down at her folded hands. Also emptied.

She could not turn around. It was impossible.

"What . . . else did Tom tell you, Mister Wyatt, about our relationship?"

Frederick Wyatt looked at the woman who, if some horses had not broken free of their traces, would have become his sister-in-law. If some liveryman had not neglected his harnesses. If Tom had not been running to catch the trolley. If.

Her back was still to him. The grey light of March made an aura around the whole of her body.

"Why, nothing," he said. "Only that he loved you. And would marry you. Only that. Nothing more."

Ede's shoulders fell from their rigid tension before she turned again to look at her visitor.

"Thank you," she said, "for all your trouble, Mister Wyatt."

"I'm only sorry that our meeting should be the cause of sorrow, and not the meeting we had expected."

"Expected?"

"Yes. We were, after all, intended to be kin."

Ede stood back. "Oh," she said. "Yes."

Kin.

It had not occurred to her that, in loving one, you gain a multitude of strangers who were intended to be kin.

Now, Ede stood beneath the barren trees beside Eliza. Liam stood behind her. James had declined the invitation. Refused it. No dead young man he'd barely met could make him leave Munsterfield. He was needed there—he was *indispensable.* Indispensable was his favoured word when it came to describing his own importance. *The cows!* he had said. *The horses! The hands! The German woman! Her half-wit daughter! The barns! The fields! The house!* They could not survive without him. Ede had once listened to him spin out his list until it contained twenty-five items—of which his wife and children were the last.

If only it had not been Liam whom James had deputized, with all his overwrought dignity and silent disdain. Ede could feel the emanation of her brother's discomfort and disapproval even though she could not see him. He had been silent all the way down on the train and had spoken only the minimum of courtesies when introduced to Tom's brothers. Liam's sense of formality led him to bow very slightly over any hand extended to him and this curious habit—so entirely out of keeping with the Irish manners common to the rest of his family—made him seem, somehow, Prussian.

All Tom's brothers wore their Wyatt-blue suits and laced boots. Their overcoats were of plain, grey wool and their hats, now held in ungloved hands, were shiny black bowlers worn without rakishness of any kind. Not at all like Tom, whose hats and caps had always been worn with a tip in one or another direction. They nonetheless had a brotherly look about them, in spite of their greater height and heavier figures. The boy among them would clearly be tall one day. Still, they had a sameness to Tom in the eyes and the shell-like shapes of their ears. And their hair was the same as Tom's, with a deep auburn sheen that a woman might have dyed for. Strange, almost furtive eyes—the lot of them. What was it? A hint of something withheld, and a blue that had green in it, another Wyatt trademark.

The service was Anglican—known to the Kilworths, though it was not their native faith. There was, however, a psalm that took Ede by surprise. She had forgotten it and found it a curious, almost cruel choice. It began: *I said I will take heed to my ways* . . . and it was read on this occasion not by the clergyman but by Frederick Wyatt.

Ede had begun to drift away from the service into a kind of frightened lonesomeness in which she felt she had been abandoned not only by Tom but by all his kin and her own. She could not, in this moment, make any connection between herself and them. Her feet were cold and a wind had risen, driving a clutch of birds from the branches above her and as she looked up to watch them depart, her loneliness embraced their absence, too. Then, all at once, she heard Frederick Wyatt's voice.

"My heart was not within me," he read, "and while I was thus musing, the fire kindled . . ."

Ede turned to watch him, his hat in one bare hand, the prayer-book in the other and she thought: *they played together as children, my Tom and this man. They sat together at table, laughed together, argued as brothers—fought and forgave one another, pumped one another's hands in the formal way of boys, sang together, cajoled one another, slept together, woke together—all these brothers here in ways together only brothers know—and sisters—which I will never know of Tom and his childhood.* But none of that was in Frederick's voice as he spoke to God in Tom's behalf.

"When Thou with rebukes dost chasten man for sin, Thou makest his beauty to consume away, like as it were a moth fretting a garment: every man therefore is but vanity . . ."

They had gathered behind the chapel in the graveyard, the whole of which was poised at the lip of a wooded hill. This hill, with many graves cut into it and markers all the way down, had a gentle roll to it and over the years the plots had been set out in terraces. Paths led the eye in a maze that could not be deciphered. Watching now, Ede saw the snow-laden trees below her, sitting like islands in a grey winter sea and all the tombstones like the hulls of sinking ships. She wondered if Tom had time to cry for help as he went down under the storm of horses hooves and wagon wheels—down like a man who was drowning—drowning in snow and mud and slush.

The service went on without her. She could not stay put at its centre, but kept returning to the drift of her thoughts about Tom. The horses, waiting with such ironic stillness to take her away and all these others with her, were breathing visibly at the curb some yards to Ede's left. The carriages were uniformly black. Five of them. Broughams. The hearse that had brought Tom's body had been driven off to be of service elsewhere.

The collect was read by the clergyman, who wore a wide grey scarf with his overcoat. He had seemed from the very beginning to be quite divorced from the whole proceedings—decent enough, but unavailable for personal contact. *Out*, Ede decided. *Not at home today!*

O, Merciful God, she heard—as from a hollow building. *We meekly beseech thee, O Father, to raise us from the death of sin unto the life of righteousness* . . .

Ede would be more than glad when it was over. She hated—and always had—those moments in the service of Christian burial when the clergy held out their collective hands and reached for the souls of the living, using the death of loved ones as a trick—as a trap—to gather more converts. It was despicable.

I do not, she wanted to shout at this endlessly talkative man, *need to rise from the death of any damn sin unto any damn life of righteousness!*

She blushed.

Had she spoken aloud?

Wouldn't it be wonderful if she had. Tom would have approved of that. He would have laughed, if only she could bring her defiance into the open.

Then, just as she was thinking *will no one sing? Will none of us sing for Tom and all his music?* a voice began to sound away to her right. A child's pure voice, at first alone and tentative, and then, as it continued, with more and more strength and even with a kind of affirmative joy as one and then another of the brothers joined in the song.

It was Lizzie—the only brother Tom had ever mentioned—cap in hand and the vapour of his breath in the air around him like an aureole—almost a halo. His eyes were closed and he sang with unwavering authority, all the words as clearly sung as written words that were visible. The song itself was unknown to Ede. It was called *The Beautiful Isle of Somewhere,* and it went in through to her heart that morning beside Tom's grave and took up residence there for as long as she lived.

> *Somewhere the sun is shining,*
> *Somewhere the songbirds sing.*
> *Somewhere, there's no more pining—*
> *There's joy in everything.*

The tune was full of dreams and longing and Lizzie's voice was rich as the voice of any boy she had ever heard in the Orpheum Choir, a clear, strong contralto. *Somewhere, Somewhere,* he sang.

> *Beautiful Isle of Somewhere,*
> *Land of the true,*
> *Where we'll live anew,*
> *Beautiful Isle of Somewhere.*

There was silence then, the first real moment of sorrow that held them all together. And then the clergyman said: "the grace of our Lord Jesus Christ, and the love of God, and the fellowship of the Holy Ghost, be with us all evermore."

Amen.

They were free to go.

No, Ede thought. *Not free to go—but able.*

13. Snow began to fall. Mister Wyatt, having said: *good-bye to all*, stepped into his rented carriage and departed, taking the boy Lizzie with him. Snowflakes, blown on the wind, made a series of screens beyond which the cab's black shape dissolved as if being melted down to nothingness.

Frederick, Franklin and Harry Wyatt clustered on the curb to the left of the grey brick chapel, where the cabs were waiting. Each in his turn bade a formal farewell to Eliza, who was then lifted up by the driver into the brougham.

Liam, still hatless, nodded over each extended Wyatt hand, gripping them with an iron tenacity.

Turning to Ede, Franklin all at once embraced her with emotion and begged her to remember all of Tom's brothers as loyal and friendly servants if she should ever be in Toronto and need assistance. "Even in the least of matters, we hope you will call on us to help you."

"I will," said Ede, "but I must remind you, Mister Wyatt, I haven't the slightest notion where you might live. My letters to Tom were always addressed to his boarding-house on Crawford Street."

Franklin, puzzled, looked at Frederick. "Boarding-house? Crawford Street?" he said.

"Yes. Number 106."

Frederick put his hands behind his back and looked at his shoes. Then he said: "it's more than likely I will be taking on Tom's rooms as my own, Miss Kilworth. Why not continue your correspondence to that address. After all, you have it by heart."

"Thank you."

Frederick then took Ede's elbow and led her forward. Liam

stood at attention by the cab door, being snowed upon as statues are snowed upon, without apparent notice and without complaint. He gave a brief nod as Frederick and his sister approached.

Ede lingered long enough to thank the grey-scarfed clergyman for his words, after which Frederick helped her in beside Eliza. Liam followed her and shut the door with a bang, perhaps intending to punctuate the ending of the funeral. Ede watched him dust the snow from his hat with a handkerchief as they drove away, and saw by his expressionless face that he continued to be unmoved by what had taken place around him that morning. He was, it seemed, barely present.

They drove down Parliament Street, crossing on Wellesley to Sherbourne and that way up to their hotel. While Liam organized the bags and got them to the cab with a bellboy and the driver doing the carrying, Ede and Eliza made one last visit to the Ladies' Salon.

Ede took note in the mirror of how pensive her mother had become. Funerals were stimulants for too many griefs and the Celtic side of Eliza had a tendency to fall into mourning at the least provocation. When the leaves fell, she mourned, and news of the death of any neighbour's most distant relative could bring disaster to her spirit. On the other hand, Ede was grateful for the rise and fall of her mother's emotions. Joy had an equal effect on happy occasions—driving Eliza's spirits skyward—just as they were plummeted to earth in the throes of sorrow.

Ede adjusted the veiling on her hat and pulled on one black glove.

"Mother?"

"Yes, my dear?"

"Thank you for coming. It was good of you to make the effort."

Eliza turned and put out her hands so that Ede could hold them.

"Pray God, the next time you fall in love," she said, "there will be a happier ending than this."

"Yes." Looking down, Ede wondered if now was the time to speak. To tell. "Mother . . ."

"Yes, my dear one?"

"I wish . . ."

"Yes?"

"I wish you had known him better. I wish there had been longer. I wish . . ."

"Yes? You wish?"

"I wish . . ."

Eliza waited, smiling, expectant.

Ede looked away and back again and then looked down at her mother's hands in her own. Gloveless, for the moment—ringless because in mourning Eliza wore no jewellery and kept her wedding ring on a chain round her neck—they were the hands of a woman whose strengths were hidden and whose graces predominated on the surface. How could they be so square and soft and lovely, given the labours she had performed?

"What is it, my darling?" Eliza said, her head on one side, peering to see into Ede's averted eyes. "Tell me."

"Nothing," said Ede—and withdrew her hands into her lap, where she busied them drawing on the second glove. "It was childish." She would have to conspire. She would have to lie. The truth was too violent to tell in this moment. Instead, she said: "I wish that Tom and I had never met. I wish—I only wish we had never met so we might never have to have parted—be parted this way."

"My dear, my dear, my dear one," Eliza said—almost crooning the words as she rose and leaned in over her daughter, holding her as close to her breast as hats and clothing and propriety would allow in this public place where strangers might open the door at any minute. "Oh, my dear one . . ."

Ede had prepared for the moment when she must expose her predicament by linking it to the imagined moment when Tom said: *marry me.* Even then, if the proposal had come soon enough, she might not have had to tell at all. There were ways of hiding the birth of a child, even from one's family, if only a person could be at a distance from home when the birth took place.

This, of course, was madness and well Ede knew it. *A pregnancy cannot be hidden forever . . .* She got out her powder box—lifted her veil and dabbed the tip of her nose. Then she stood up.

"We must go," she said. "We have that train to catch."

"Yes," Eliza said, briskness overtaking her wish that, for a minute, they could just be still. "A train to catch—and before the train, one other visit we must make."

Ede said: "oh? To whom?"

Eliza was already walking to the door and her back was to Ede.

"Saint Michael," she said—and was gone, leaving only the hint of some rosewater perfume in her wake.

Ede looked out beyond her veiling at herself in the mirror. She stood as straight as she was able and, satisfied with what she saw, turned to her left until she was reflected sideways.

Nothing showing.

Yet.

14. Liam would not go in. When Eliza had asked that they be driven down Church Street to Shuter, he had guessed what his mother was up to and told her he would stay in the cab. His excuse was that, in a city—any city, presumably—one could not trust one's luggage to strangers. The truth was, Liam had recently become a Methodist and he knew that his mother's destination was St Michael's Cathedral.

Now, Ede got down from the carriage and walked behind Eliza through the snow towards the porch of the cathedral. Liam remained by the window, drawing the lap rug Eliza had left behind her over his knees. The driver, having gauged how long it would take two Catholic ladies *to fall on their knees and grovel for Christ,* decided there was time enough to victual his horse and he commenced to fill the animal's feed bag.

Ede had to struggle to drag the doors of the cathedral open, they were so heavy. Eliza passed through and as Ede was following, the wind gave a push that almost slammed the doors behind her. All the lighted candles wavered. A multitude of shadows—a congregation of ghosts—fled along the walls. The air was thick with the residue of incense and the smell of it mingled with the smells of musty prayer-books, melted snow, damp wool and hand-rubbed wood. Eliza raised her face to the vaulted caverns of the ceiling above her, closed her eyes and filled her lungs. The whole of this forbidden atmosphere, as she breathed it in, held the essence for her of every morning and every evening of her childhood when, hand in hand with her grandmother Fagan, the child that Eliza had been was escorted into the presence of Jesus Christ Himself and made to lie face down at the foot of his Cross.

There had been joyous, less fearful moments, too, of shouting choirs and thundering organs before she was taken—still a child—away from that church in the City of Dublin, and away from Dublin itself and all of Ireland—carried off aged six to become a child of the wilderness in a place called Upper Canada. This history, encapsulated in a glance through the incense-laden air past the wavering streams of dusty candlelight, was Eliza's instant response to where she was. For a moment she wanted to fall, as the child Eliza had fallen, on her face in the presence of Jesus Christ. For surely He was here, if He was anywhere.

Ede made a modest genuflexion and waited for her mother to rise. Eliza had gone to her knees—but no further in her desire to prostrate herself. There was no time for more. There was a train to catch—and before the train, a duty to be fulfilled in this place.

"Come," Eliza said to Ede, as she rose. "We have candles to light."

Ede bowed her head. As she watched her mother begin to walk away from her, using the ends of the pews as a series of touchstones—brushing the top of each with the tips of her fingers almost in the manner of a playful child—it was clear that Eliza was engaged in a ceremony of her own that Ede could witness but not take part in—except as an acolyte.

This way, they went down the centre aisle and veered to one side where the Mary Chapel offered its banks of votive candles.

"Give me the taper."

Ede took the taper from its ledge, lighted it from one of the candles already burning and handed it to her mother.

"Pray for your brother Jamie," Eliza said, reaching with the taper to light one of the candles in its red glass jar.

"I do," said Ede—and crossed herself.

"On your knees," Eliza said.

Ede got down on the stones and Eliza, using her daughter's shoulder as support, got down beside her—the taper still in her hand.

"A prayer for Thomas Wyatt," she said.

Eliza lighted a second candle and Ede again crossed herself.

Then Eliza said: "you have another to light, have you not?"

Ede looked sideways—alarmed.

"This is a candle you must light yourself, my dear. And I will pray with you."

Eliza handed the taper to Ede and Ede, without a word, reached out with it and touched the wick of the candle next to Tom's. As she did this, she could hear that Eliza was praying—though she could not hear the words.

Nothing more than that was said.

Ede's child had been proclaimed in silence.

15. The wreath in Ede's hand was not yet completed. Daisies and clover had been joined together with strands of bindweed, whose flowers had closed the moment she had picked them. There were branches of budding honeysuckle still to be cut and dog roses caught in the fence row and day lilies not yet in bloom, whose stems were pliable but strong. These latter, Ede was thinking as she moved towards them, would serve very well to make the braided hoop on which the rest of the wreath could be shaped.

This was the corner—the very place where she and Tom had made this child who was straining now to be free of its prison; a nurturing prison to be sure, but nonetheless a prison in which there was no more room to grow. *Out—out—out*—down through a well of rich red light and the first rude shock of gravity—no more floating now, but only falling.

Ede felt a strange ballooning of pressure—of pressure only, not in any way painful but nonetheless alarming. The process had begun; the initial signal had been given. What had Eliza told her? *First, the water will break . . .*

Ede had expected a tidal wave, but there was nothing like that. Not like a flood and not as if a dam had burst. It was more as if a basin she was carrying had been filled to overflowing and the contents—warm as Sunday wash water—were streaming down her thighs.

She lifted up the skirts of her robe and nightdress and held them above her waist. The wreath and the sewing scissors were still in one hand and with the other she locked her garments in place by pressing her fist against her diaphragm. She knew that she was not going to leave this corner until she had shed the child and the certainty of this provided some relief. She did not even have to consider trying to reach the house, nor the top of the hill before the child was born. Too late for all of that, the process of birth had begun and the sequential consequences could not now be interrupted.

She removed her robe and tore it apart at the seams. Half of it, she folded into a pad onto which the child could emerge. A second part was set aside in which to wrap the child against the morning air. With the sewing scissors, she cut a length from the twisted cotton belt with which she could tie off the umbilical cord. *Praise God,* she thought, *for the scissors themselves.* All this was done as she squatted waiting for the next event in the sequence.

Warnings were given. Cramps made knots in parts of her body where pain had never before occurred in the whole of her life. Spasms uncoiled like springs in all the muscles of her back and thighs and stomach. Someone, too—so it seemed—was playing with matches inside her body—lighting and fanning fires that were clearly intent on burning her alive.

The words *get down—get down*—kept coming to her—flooding her brain with the noise of voices she had never heard before. At one point, between the bouts of girdling pain, she rose all the way to a standing position and, carrying the birthing pad and the remnants of her robe and the scissors on their chain and the wreath in all its flowering parts, she made her way to a place near the fence where the grass gave way to beds of moss and where, by reaching out, she would be able to grasp the rails for support in her final struggle to deliver the child.

The spasms were now more regular and were being repeated with shorter intervals between them. Ede could not kneel, which was too confining, but she hunkered—squatting with her knees as far apart as possible. She raised her nightdress until it rested like a shawl around her shoulders.

Perspiration poured down her face—stinging her eyes and salting her lips.

She thought of Tom and wanted to shout his name. There seemed to be a great deal of noise all around her—insect noise and birdsong—her own pounding heart—and the rush of a wagon whose horses had broken into a canter out on the road—and the memory of Eliza's voice, *Ede! Edie! Ede* . . . that day long ago when a cow—which cow?—oh, what was her name?—when a cow gave birth in this very corner—*Lena, Lena.* That was her name. And I was six. I was six and I had never seen a cow giving birth—a calf being born—a life beginning—*Ede! Edie! Ede!* The whole world was calling—is calling my name—*Ede! Edie! Ede!*

Tom went under beneath the horses—trampled—rolled in the slush—everyone shouting his name, everyone crying out: *STOP! NO, DON'T KILL TOM!*

Tom's final song—oh, God, the roaring of it—had been that flurry of hooves—and someone shouting his name.

And now, again, someone shouting—the air filling up with his name to greet his child.

This way, Lily Kilworth was born. In the corner of a field, in the shadow of her mother's body, and all the birds leapt up from the grass at the sound of Lily's first song.

16.

"Don't go away," Tom had said. "When it's over, stay."
This is what my grandmother Ede had written—his words and the fact that she had not replied. That she had merely nodded—saying nothing—standing away from the others, proving she had a mind of her own and did not depend on someone else's permission to be seen with this notorious man who used a theatrical pseudonym. I found the scribbled notes that told of this in Lily's suitcase. Having sworn she would burn her words, Ede had relented. The pages were rolled—not unlike a diploma—in one of the flyers announcing Tom's arrival. *The Piano Man will give a demonstration of the newest dance tunes . . .*

Ede always smiled when The Piano Man was mentioned. *Charlie,* she would say, *we were both so young—but only I got old. You would have adored him.*

It was a perfect night, that Saturday when the harvest moon arrived in 1889. A perfect night for a concert of music, the sound of it spilling into the street; and a perfect night to linger on the porches and to listen on the sidewalks. When the concert was over, the whole town was left adrift with indecision. There was a general move towards the bars of the two hotels, the Queen's and the National across from the station. Many folks, especially those with children in tow, made a languid beeline for Islay Lambert's Emerald Café, where angel food cakes and phosphates served in tall green glasses awaited them.

But Ede, over time, began to look back on it all as upon an event more in Lily's life than her own. And with this, my mother concurred. It seemed that Lily herself was already there and that it was she who led them out of the town, along the dusty road and over the fence and into the field. The child and the harvest moon were conspirators, so it seemed. As though the moon had placed the child in her parents' path.

Here, it had said, *is where Lily Kilworth's song begins.*
Nine months later, my mother told me, *I was made visible.*

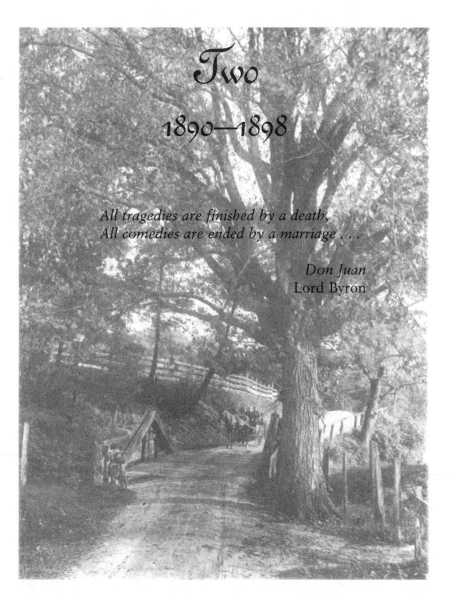

Two

1890—1898

All tragedies are finished by a death,
All comedies are ended by a marriage . . .

Don Juan
Lord Byron

1. When Ede came out of the field with Lily in the crook of one arm, she was wearing only her nightdress and Liam's rubber boots. Her torn and ruined robe provided Lily with swaddling clothes and the wreath, newly finished, provided Ede with a crown. She looked like a female Lear returning from the heath.

It was Liam who saw her first and who went to the wrought-iron gate and let her through.

"So, you're back," he said. And then: "you're wearing my boots." As if she had intended to abscond with them.

The child was not mentioned.

Liam's greeting became a part of Lily's legend as it was recounted to me by my grandmother. The field, the harvest moon and Lena, the Jersey cow, were also woven into it. I must have been told about Lena at least a dozen times. *When I was a little girl,* Ede would say—and off she would go, back to *scissors-scissors* and the stream she had splashed through and the waving blades of grass *above my head.*

I once asked Ede what her father's reaction had been when he discovered she was pregnant—and she froze in her place as if I had struck her. *I never talk about that,* she said. But she gave no explanation. I was ten. Perhaps that was why. Something to do with the impertinence of a child who seemed to be suggesting there could be a conversation between a ten-year-old boy and a fifty-four-year-old woman on the subject of having an illegitimate baby. *And what did your father say?*

It was none of my business.

There are so many fathers in this story—my own, Lily's, Ede's—others. Aside from parenthood, they have only one thing in common: their habit of disappearing when you least expect them to. James, in his way, was not unlike The Piano Man in this. He disappears from Ede's story—and from Lily's—when you most suppose he will be there.

As for my own father, it could be said he disappeared twice: once, when Lily lost him in the fog of her illness, and again, when he disappeared with her death. After that, all memory of him passed into time, including his name. But I have not given up the search at least for his identity. Someone's finger descending to his face in a photograph and saying: *him*.

Lily's memories of James, who died in 1912, were mostly pleasant. It was, after all, in his house that she spent the first eight years of her life. *He loved inventions,* Lily told me. *All new-fangled things intrigued him—telephones and automobiles and flying machines. When he did his accounts, he used an abacus! Hardly new-fangled— but it was, to him.* She stole it from his office once, because she thought it was a toy, and when it was found underneath her bed, she was made to return it to him with a formal apology . . .

"What's this?" said James. "Another of your playthings? Like my watch?"

She had also taken his pocket watch, just to listen to it, and a paperweight with snow in it, and a pair of his shoes to walk in— and other things, over time. Lily did not consider these acquisitions as thefts. She knew what thieving was. The fox came and did that in the hen house. But watches, paperweights and shoes to walk in were different than stolen chickens; they were the focus of her attention, sometimes the whole of her attention. They were like magnets to her, utterly irresistible and fascinating.

And now, the abacus.

"Who does it belong to?" said James.

"No one," said Lily. She was four. *Ownership* was foreign to her.

"Seems to me it belongs in here, on my desk," said James.

"Yes, sir."

"Are you going to put it back where you found it?"

Lily said nothing. *Where had it been?* She did not remember.

"No," she said.

"I see. Well, what are we going to do about it?"

"Mam found it under my bed," said Lily. And waited.

"Yes, so I'm told."

Did he want her to put it back under the bed?

James was looking at her sternly. And some other way as well. As though there were something wrong besides the question of the abacus. As though there were something he could not decipher in her.

Lily looked away.

Finally, James said: "didn't I tell you it belongs on my desk?"

Lily did not answer.

"Show me where that is," said James. "Point to it."

Even though James was sitting right behind it, the word *desk* had flown out the door. *It* was all that remained. The word *it*, and the word *point*.

Lily bit her lip—and played an ace. "Mam told me *not* to point," she said.

She was still looking away at the wall, with its books in glass cases and its clock with a pendulum. She did not see James smile.

"Quite right," he said. "I should not have asked you to do that."

Then he told her to cross the room and hand him the abacus. If she did that, all would be forgiven.

Abacus.

Lily stepped forward.

She went around the corner of *it* and stood before her grandfather, looking at the floor.

"What do we say when we've done something wrong?"

She hadn't done anything wrong.

"Tell me."

"I don't know."

"All right. Then I'll tell you. We say: *I'm sorry.*"

Lily was silent.

"Lily?"

Nothing. She was staring at his shoes.

"I'm waiting."

They were not the ones she had walked in. Those had been brown. These were black. With laces. That looked like worms. And there were . . .

"Lily."

. . . spots where the rain had wet them.

"Tell me you're sorry."

Finally: "I'm sorry." Still looking down at the shoes.

"Thank you for your apology," said James. "You may go now."

"Yes, sir."

Lily turned and walked around *it* again, making for the door. The carpet had a tree on it—a tall, thin tree whose branches had tiny little . . .

. . . *somethings* . . .

. . . hanging down.

Green.

And the carpet was . . .

Brown.

And the tree was . . .

Black.

She had reached the door.

The door was open.

Lily went through.

She was gone.

The abacus was still in her hand.

2. On her fifth birthday, Lily went missing. This happened in the afternoon, when the only people about were the German woman and her crazy daughter. *Crazy*, so-called. She was in fact nothing of the sort. But everyone, including her mother, thought of her as a simple-minded girl and, in the parlance of the town, this was called *being crazy*.

The German woman had come to Canada in the employ of a couple whose children required a nursemaid. They had been living in Heidelberg, where the husband had taught in the university. On their return to Canada, he had joined the Faculty of Medicine at the University of Toronto. It so happened that one of his students there was from McCaskill's Mills—a man called Robert Melbourne. A few years later, when Melbourne had become the town doctor, he was instrumental in bringing the German woman to Munsterfield after the birth of Willa Kilworth. There were six children then in the household, and Eliza had thrown up her hands, demanding that James procure her some help. This way, Freda Hoffstaeder and her daughter, Minna, joined the family. That had been fourteen years ago.

Now, mid-afternoon on the day of Lily's fifth birthday, Freda was in the kitchen making the cake for that evening's celebration. Minna had gone to the hen-house to collect the required eggs. Lily was supposed to have gone with her, but did not. Instead, she crouched in the kitchen garden while Minna went on marching to the barns. Seconds later, Lily had gone round to the front door. Ephraim, returning in the wagon from the mill, had seen her there. After that, she disappeared.

When Ede came downstairs to take Lily up for her nap, no one could tell her where the child was.

James had been working in his office. Eliza had been resting in the parlour. Malahide and Willa were at school—and Liam was at work in town.

"Lily?"

There was no reply.

"Father?"

"Yes?"

"Have you seen Lily?"

"No."

Ede went back along the hall.

"Mother?"

"What is it, dear?" Eliza was half asleep, lying on one of the figured maple sofas. Both hands rested on her forehead. "Is something wrong?"

"I can't find Lily."

"She went upstairs."

"I've just come from upstairs."

Eliza lifted her hands and opened her eyes. "And you didn't see her?"

"No," Ede said.

Eliza sat up, swinging her legs to the side. "But I could have sworn I heard her . . ."

Ede, still in the hallway, called one more time.

"Lily?"

Not a sound.

Turning, she noted the front door was standing very slightly ajar. The air was so still, there had been no draught to blow it open or pull it shut after Lily went through. The day was now monstrously hot, almost suffocating. Ede went over and pulled the door aside so that she could look out.

"Lily?"

Nothing.

Vanished.

Because of the open door, Ede could only assume Lily had gone through onto the porch and into the front yard.

Closing the door behind her, she went across to the screens and peered out beyond the road.

There was the field.

Was Lily in it?

Ede went through the screen door and across the lawn. At the gate, she was thinking: *when I was a little girl . . .*

Then she crossed over.

Back in the front hall, Eliza stood listening.

"Is it serious?" James asked. He, too, had come into the hall from his office.

"I don't know," said Eliza. "Lily has disappeared."

"Well," said James, "children do that."

"Yes," said Eliza, "but this is Lily . . ." And then: "I'm going out to look in the barn."

Lily was standing transfixed on the middle step of a mysterious stairway. Behind her, there was a closed door. Above her, a pale light shone beyond what seemed to be the underside of a dusty lake.

Tall, shrouded figures loomed to one side at the top of the stairs, and to the other side, a bannister cut through the light, reminding Lily of the branch from which the swing was hung in the garden.

Slowly, she began to climb again.

She did not know where she was going—or what she might expect to find when she got there. The word *attic* was not a word she knew. No one had ever spoken of this place in her presence. When you went *upstairs*, you went up one floor only. No one had said there was anything above the ceiling but the roof. When she had heard the mice in the night, she had assumed she was hearing birds. Now, at her approach, the mice went scurrying, seeking shelter in the shadows. Lily was not alarmed by the sound of them. She had been listening to them all her life.

When she reached the end of her climb, she was standing on a wide-planked floor of incalculable size. It rolled off into unseen corners, populated with clusters of wooden boxes and the curled-up, animal shapes of canvas bags and paper packages.

To her right, the looming figures she had seen from below turned out to be the Kilworth family luggage. Steamer trunks, suitcases, hat boxes, carpet bags and Liam's prized pair of pigskin Gladstones—all of these were neatly collected on a wooden rack, covered with dust sheets and smelling of distance. If Lily had been able to read their travel scars and labels, she would have been informed of journeys to Philadelphia and Cambridge, Massachusetts—to Montreal and

Winnipeg—and from Cobh to Halifax—and Dublin to Boston. This way, the routes of Kilworth and Fagan arrival could be traced and the lifelines to members of the clan who had chosen to settle elsewhere.

Furniture which Eliza refused to abandon was also stored in the attic—pieces from her Fagan ancestry, for which there was no room downstairs. One day—so she dreamed—her children would want it to furnish the houses in which they would live resplendent lives with wives and husbands as yet unknown. *You must have some of it, Charlie,* she told me on the day I discovered the wonders of the Munsterfield attic. *Take it and be proud of who we were . . .*

Lily, my mother, found all this that June afternoon of 1895. Crates of dishes, shrouded paintings, cedar chests filled with children's clothing—Ede's, Jamie's, Liam's—all of it outgrown, all of it outmoded, all of it layered in tissue paper and cedar boughs to ward off the moths. In another box, there were velvet drapes for seven windows, smelling of camphor, smelling of menthol—and all the Christmas decorations, carefully labelled—and a mourning wreath in a rounded box that had once contained cheese.

Because the roofs at Munsterfield were so variously angled, the attic windows looked out in six directions. They were not very tall, these windows as I remember them. But they were wide and gave a breadth of filtered light through several yards of square-paned glass. I remember squatting down to count the chimneys rising beyond those frames, and the distance smudged with dust and blurred with cobwebs. Lily, I think, did not look out, but inward, at the surrounding minacity of that silent assembly in the midst of which she continued to stand immobilized.

Mam?

There had been a noise.

She was not alone.

Mam?

A curious figure stood before her, seemingly advanced from the shadows.

Mammy?

Not a word.

Yet it had a human shape.

Human dimensions.

Human menace.

Who are you?

What?

The thing did not respond.

Lily stared.

She was not so much afraid as baffled. Alarmed.

It had no head, this person.

It had no head and no arms.

Lily could not move. She wanted to—but could not.

What? Who are you?

Speak.

At last, Lily took a step backward.

Then another step sideways.

And another.

And another.

Her gaze never left the creature—but the creature still did not move.

From the top of the stairs, Lily took her last look. No head. No arms. But otherwise, utterly human—Mam-shaped and Mam-sized—but decapitated.

Lily ran down and began to pound on the door, forgetting she could open it.

No one came. No one. They were all off looking for Lily elsewhere.

She stayed there, crouching for half an hour before she remembered what the door knob was for—and, turning it, she was released.

The next day, Ede went up and brought down the dressmaker's dummy and hid it where she was certain Lily would never again encounter it. In the root cellar, standing in the sawdust with the last winter apples. Even so, Ede did not yet understand what Lily had seen.

3. In November of 1895, James Kilworth had a stroke. This happened in the bathroom while he was shaving. The razor fell from his hand and clattered to the floor. Leaning forward, he tipped the basin. All its hot water splashed over his knees and down to his feet. James could see himself in the mirror, but did not know who it was he was looking at.

Someone . . .

His eyes rolling upwards, he fell—and when Eliza found him, he was lying on the floor bent over backwards with both arms flung out. There was foam at the corners of his mouth and he could not speak.

Doctor Melbourne was summoned and the stroke was diagnosed as having been severe but not life-threatening. James could survive. He could also—given the right care and treatment—recover his faculties.

A nurse was brought from Toronto, where she had worked in the neurological ward of St Michael's Hospital. Her name was Isobelle McClintock and her special skills lay in the world of physical therapy. She would live at Munsterfield for the next five months. This was acceptable. She was Irish. James adored her.

Household routines were altered. Eliza now spent more than half the day with James and took her dinner with him every evening, sitting where he could see her at a small table facing him up in their bedroom. Or rather, the bedroom they shared under normal circumstances. So long as James lay stricken, Eliza slept in the room next door, which meant that Willa had to be moved down the hall. This was not popular. Willa had entered that phase of her life when men become central to every waking thought. *Men*—not boys. Willa had decided *boys* were beneath her. Only men held her attention. She was sixteen.

In order to accommodate her, a curtain was hung between one half of Malahide's room and the other. The men brought an ancient Fagan bed from the attic and set it up on the windowed side, so that Willa would have access to the view. Mal had to give up half the drawers in his tallboy and half the space in his armoire to Willa's belongings—and half the night to her endless chatter. In the long run, he moved across the hall into Liam's room where, at least, the residing presence was male. And silent.

Down came the curtain—back went the bed and Mal found every stitch of his clothing piled on the carpet on Liam's floor. He had thought the victory of the move had been his—but it was Willa who had the last gloat. *I always wondered what it was like to live on this side of the house*, she said. *And now, I much prefer it*. Mal had lost his room forever. In April, when Eliza reoccupied her old accommodation, Malahide was deported to Willa's room *in the interest*—so Willa put it—*of fairness*.

In the meantime, rest and Isobelle McClintock's therapeutic massages had begun to work their magic. By Christmas, James was sitting up in bed and by mid-January, he was being dressed and encouraged to spend his mornings seated in a chair. On February 1st, two and a half months after the stroke had felled him, he said his first word. It was: *Lizzie*.

Eliza burst into tears.

James had not called her *Lizzie* since he had courted her, thirty years before. The best of times came flooding back to engulf her, riding on the crest of that single—and singular—endearment.

All this while, Lily had been in pursuit of some way to populate the world in which she lived. The door to the attic was now kept locked. There was no way of getting back up there.

She wondered how, if the door was locked, the person who lived among the shrouded others could be kept alive. Perhaps the birds—she did not yet call them *mice*—would feed and care for her.

Or was it a him?

She could not tell. True, the figure had looked like Mam. But Liam, in his bathrobe, looked like Mam—if you caught him in the shadows between his bedroom and the bathroom.

The figure had been so still. How could that be?

Perhaps, like her grandfather, it had been stricken in some way. A *stroke*, she had learned to call this. Lily had often gone to the door of her grandparents' room and stared in—still and silent—at the still, silent figure lying on the bed. In the night, it might very well be that Miss McClintock went up into the attic and performed her miracles for the mysterious stranger. And if the birds fed it and the miracles were successful, the figure might be revived. Morning after morning, Lily waited by the attic door, convinced the mysterious stranger would knock and request admission to life on the second floor. *Are you there?* Lily would say, with her ear pushed hard against the wood. *Do you want me to let you out . . . ?* But there was never any answer.

It was then, in the days before Christmas, that Lily took up her life with Willa's dolls.

Willa Kilworth had once collected dolls the way her mother collected handkerchiefs and Malahide collected postcards. She had been given the first of them around the time she was Lily's age—five, going on six. By the time she was twelve, she had dozens of them—cloth dolls, china dolls, wooden dolls, papier mâché dolls—every kind of doll that can be imagined.

Her relationship with them was odd. Peculiar. Unique. Though avidly collected, they were just as avidly abandoned. It was not simply a question of tiring of them. Loving them excessively at first, she grew to dislike them excessively. To despise them. Which brought her to scorn them—even to ridicule them. One by one, as hugs and kisses gave way to spankings, arm-pullings and head-twistings—the dolls would be thrown to the floor and kicked into the farthest corner.

Over time, as she retrieved them at Eliza's insistence, Willa's dolls were piled face down in the chairs between the windows in her bedroom. These mounds of doll cadavers had grown until they looked like the victims of some universal doll catastrophe— their legs and arms spilling down from the edges of the chairs towards the floor where they had first been thrown. This way, Willa's playmates became her prey.

Photographs reveal why this might have been. Between the ages of six and twelve, Willa passed through a fat phase, of which there is little evidence now. But then, it was more than evident— verging on the grotesque. Framed by round, wide hats, her round, wide face seems older, in the photographs, than its years. She is always standing apart, stubbornly refusing to join the human race—perhaps afraid of the negative comparison between herself and its taller, thinner, happier members. She never smiles. Her chubby hands are always fisted and her body has the appearance of having been wrapped in a gingham parcel of which the strings have been too tightly tied. Clearly, Willa's violent relationship with her dolls was nothing more than a reflection of her violent relationship with food. And her violent refusal to be loved.

At twelve, Willa put all the dolls together in a common grave—set them on fire—relented, doused them with water and buried them. The next week, she dug them all up and threw them into an apple basket. Not that she mourned them—or wanted to re-establish her authority over them. It was just that she could not bear to think of them being underground. The thought of being buried alive in the earth gave rise, as she stared in the mirror, to the thought that she had buried herself alive in fat. From that moment on, she began to lose weight.

One day, Lily found Willa's apple basket in the corner of the bedroom then being occupied by Eliza. When she withdrew the lid, she saw a mass of doll arms—all reaching up, imploring her to save them.

Help, she heard. Whispering. *Help us.*

Lily stared.

Arms. Legs. Faces.

Burnt hair.

Burnt dresses.

Burnt eyes.

Shoes.

She knelt in closer. Nearer.

Fire—but no flames. Smoke—but only the smell of it.

She reached in over the top and grasped a doll hand between her fingers.

Please don't leave us here.

No.

One out.

Two.

Three.

Four.

Then more, without number, there being no numbers in Lily's mind beyond *four*.

When the final doll was retrieved, Lily sat in their midst and wondered if these could be the children of the woman in the attic. Or the man. Someone's children—lost.

Perhaps her own.

It did not occur to her to put them back in the basket in order to transport them to the room where she slept with Mam. Instead, she placed them all on a blanket, taken from the foot of Eliza's bed, and drew them through the hall as she would draw her sled through snow. Clearly, she would have to hide them until she discovered who had put them in the basket. If Mam had put them there, she would only put them back. If Grandmam had done it, she would be angry. But if anyone else had done it, Lily might bring them into the open where their real mother could find them. Or their father.

That night, while Lily lay in the bed pretending to be asleep, she heard Ede opening and closing doors as if she was in search of something lost.

The children?

No. It was something else.

Ede went into her parents' room where Eliza still sat up with James. Lily could hear them talking—after which, Eliza and Ede returned to the open doorway and Ede said: *there—do you smell it?*

"No."

"I don't understand. It's faint enough, but I swear it's there . . ."

"Smoke?"

"Yes. As if someone had been burning something."

Eliza took three steps into the room and gave a series of violent sniffs. "No," she said. "I don't smell a thing but your lamp. Maybe it's been smoking . . ."

"No. It's not like coal oil, what I smell."

"Maybe it's just the residue from one of the fireplaces, dear. If there's a sudden down-draught, it can set quite a bit of smoke adrift."

"Perhaps. I suppose it could be that—but . . ."

"Ask Miss McClintock. She has a younger nose than I have."

"Did you want me?" Lily heard.

Isobelle McClintock came and stood in the doorway. "I was coming up the stairs," she said, "and I heard my name."

"See if you smell smoke in here," said Ede. "Mother can't—but I can."

The nurse stepped forward, took a deep breath through her nostrils and said: "no—not a thing but the coal oil lamp. Perhaps it's been . . ."

"No," Ede cut her off. "It's not the lamp." And then: "well . . ." laugh, ". . . I guess I'm crazy. Thank you, ladies, for your olfactory opinion."

Eliza and Isobelle McClintock withdrew.

Lily heard Ede humming as she moved around the room. *I don't want to play in your yard—I don't like you any more . . .*

And then the lamp was blown out and her Mam crawled into the bed beside her. *Good-night, my darling,* she heard—and felt Ede kiss her on the cheek and roll away. Lily gave a sigh and, smiling, fell asleep.

Under the bed, the dolls leaned closer together—safe, at last, and loved. Their painted smiles were a match for Lily's.

A few days later, as Doctor Melbourne reached the top of the stairs for his weekly examination of James's progress, he was greeted by a curious sound.

Off to the right, he heard a rhythmic but gentle shuffling noise, almost like someone doing a two-step in their stocking feet. Turning, he peered off down the murky hallway towards the rear of the house. Only the furthest doorway was open—the doorway to Liam's room, and through it, a fall of afternoon light illuminated the floor.

What on earth was he seeing?

A toy train?

A chain of miniature wagons?

Whatever it was, it was slowly disappearing, being drawn by

an unseen hand around the corner that led to the bathrooms, the back stairs and Miss McClintock's room.

Surely it had not been what it most seemed to be—a string of dead cats and rats and mice, some of them wearing tiny dresses . . .

As the last small figure turned the corner, it had raised what appeared to be a paw—or was it a hand?—in a gesture of farewell.

Doctor Melbourne thought it best not to mention the incident to Eliza and Miss McClintock as they greeted him at James's bedside. No telling what they might make of it. Or of his explanation.

Dead cats, rats and mice in tiny dresses . . .

No. He would leave it alone.

Doctor Melbourne might have been surprised at how close he had come to the truth. Surprised—and relieved. For it was not the string of dead animals he had feared, but a string of smoke-stained dolls. And when he thought he had seen a *gesture of farewell*, it *had* been a gesture of farewell. Not from the cat-paw he had suspected, but from the hand of a doll whose name was Attica—child of the attic woman. Or man.

This was Lily's way of keeping the survivors of the doll basket entertained. She would take them for walks through the hallways of the house, endlessly searching for their parent and their past. But it was all to no avail. Neither Willa nor the attic woman stepped forward to claim them. They had been abandoned for certain, and were now in Lily's care. Forever.

Or, at least, until she was seven.

4. In time, James returned to a relatively normal life. He reestablished his weekly tours of the barns with Ephraim, went out with Richard and Davey to inspect the herds in their various summer pastures—supervised the accounts and placed all orders that had to do with the running of the farm. What he could

not take on was delegated to Liam. This included supervision of the land holdings and management of the household.

Liam was, by this time, twenty-six. His job, as junior partner in the town's only law firm, was undemanding, even stultifying. He wanted, above all, to make his name and, to do that, he should have been in Toronto. But the combination of his father's health and *something else* kept him at McCaskill's Mills.

The *something else* was never mentioned. Liam, outside of his profession, was basically a silent man. He was reticent and private—guarded—even secretive. Lily was intrigued by him, wondering if perhaps the disappearance of the headless figure might have been caused by Liam. Or could be explained by him.

He knows something he won't tell, she decided. *Something no one else knows.*

One night, Lily discovered what this was.

She was six. Liam had been in charge of the household not quite a year. He had started coming home rather late. Sometimes he missed dinner altogether and, once or twice, he did not come home at all. Nothing was said about this. James was largely unaware of it and Eliza felt it was not her place *to interfere in the life of a grown-up man.* Privately, she hoped that her son might have fallen in love. *It would do him so much good.* But a woman was never mentioned.

Because she had wakeful moments through the night, Lily often heard the sound of Liam's returning. The buggy in the yard—the door being opened—the stairs being trod upon—his negotiation of the darkened hall—water in the bathroom—once or twice, a light cursing, something falling, something being struck. Sighs.

Other times, she was certain he was not alone. Whispers could be heard. Voices. Yet, there were no other footsteps but his—and these always guarded, careful, sock-muffled. *He must come up from the hall without his shoes, carrying them perhaps, or leaving them behind.*

On the night of Lily's discovery, the arrival noises began at 2:00 A.M. She knew it was 2:00 A.M. because the clocks in the parlour and the dining-room had struck.

Ede was sound asleep. Utterly.

Lily was in the truckle-bed and got up without a sound. The door—as always—was partially open. Ede had put a shoe on either side of it to keep it in place. The windows—this being the height of a summer heatwave—were also open, and the consequent draft was welcome.

Lily could see the bathroom lamp, far, far away at the end of the corridor. It was kept alight all night as a safeguard. The spill of its beams reached out along the floor, almost completely dissipated by the time it got to Ede and Lily's room.

Liam was partway up the stairs when Lily, who was standing at the top, heard him sigh and sag.

"Uncle Li . . .?" A whisper.

"Go to bed . . ." A hiss.

"I can't sleep."

Lily moved down one step at a time.

She could see him, slumped on the stair below her, with his back against the wall. The hall light, though turned down low, was enough to guide her.

"You should not be out of bed," he said. "Go away."

He sounded funny. Almost as if he might have been crying. And she could smell him . . .

"Why are you sitting here?"

"I'm sad."

She said nothing.

"Well," he said, "if you're here—you're here. Sit down."

Lily sat below him, using the bannister as a backrest. She made a tent for her legs with her nightgown and wrapped her arms around her knees.

"You smell," she said. It was not a bad smell—just distinctive. Different.

"I've been drinking Memory Potion."

"What's that?"

"Memory Potion? Helps you remember . . . helps you forget."

Remember what? Forget what?

Liam's tie was pulled aside, his vest buttons loosened. Lily had never seen him so undone. He pressed himself further into the wall, with his head lying back and his hands hanging down between his knees.

"Memory Potion is not for you," he said. "You have to have a special permit to buy it. A secret permit—got from a secret agent in a secret place . . . You understand?"

Lily was silent.

Liam said: "no one knows I have this permit. No one but me and you. Me and you—and one other person. You see? You and me and one other person . . ."

Who?

"I don't tell—I never tell anyone who she is. Never. You . . . you mustn't. Tell. You have to promise . . ."

Lily waited.

"Do you? Promise?"

"Yes."

"Only me—and you. That's all that knows. And her."

Who?

"She's the princess . . . the duchess . . . the *Queen of Memory* . . . the one who gives out the potion. *One for you, and one for you— and one for you, and one for you* . . ."

"Me?"

"No. Not you. Never." He gave an elaborate sigh. "But others . . . others . . . others . . . damn them . . ." His voice began to drift away—to fade—to die. Lily wondered if he was falling asleep.

Then he said: "did I say she was a princess?"

"A queen."

"Oh, yes. The Queen of Memory . . . all in white. And I . . ."

Yes?

The sentence was never finished.

Lily could see there were tears in his eyes—spilling over—sliding down. And his nose was running. Wet.

"Uncle Li?"

"Go to bed."

"But . . ."

"Go. To. Bed."

He raised his hand towards her.

"Never, never, never," he said. "Never, never tell . . . *anyone*. No one. Promise."

"Yes."

"'Night, then. Go."

Lily stood.

Liam sat there, his head descending.

Lily went around him and up the stairs. At the top, she turned, looking back.

"Good-night," she said.

Liam raised his hand—but not his head. He gave a backhanded wave, his head still lowered—bowing into sleep.

From her truckle-bed, Lily heard him half an hour later, crawling up the stairs and down the corridor.

Whatever the *Memory Potion* was, it worked. Liam forgot which door was his and turned the wrong way, into Malahide's room.

In the morning, nothing was said.

Liam never mentioned it again.

But Lily, having no access to the *Memory Potion*, did not forget—and never would.

Liam managed the household as he might have run a military outpost. Or rather, Liam's version of a military outpost—disciplined as if survival depended on sitting down to breakfast at precisely 7:00 A.M., and not one second later. In Kilworth parlance, *the year 1896 was the year we joined the army!*

By the autumn of '97, they had been *in the army* for just over one year. This was hardest on the young. Willa became more rebellious—more demanding—and Malahide began the long withdrawal that would end with his failure to go on to university. He spent more time in the fields with the men and in the barn with the animals than he did with his family.

Lily was becoming increasingly difficult to entertain and to educate. Her attention was almost entirely given to worlds that Ede could not enter—the doll-child world—the under-bed world and the world of silences which no one could penetrate.

On the other hand, Ede had discovered there were worlds to be shared with Lily—into which they could both retreat. In these, they took up residence as happily as castaways on a sunlit island. One of their shared retreats was the world of cards.

Ede had always been devoted to cribbage, double solitaire and casino. But Lily's interest was in card architecture—card houses—card farms and card towns. Sometimes, she and Ede would use as many as ten decks at once. Their creations included card cathedrals, card palaces—even *card heaven*, replete with pearly gates and card angels.

One November afternoon—this was in '97—Ede and Lily were standing side by side at the round oak table in the back parlour, carefully putting the crowning cards in place on *Windsor Castle*.

"We must set the Queen at the top of the tower," said Ede.

"Which queen?"

"Queen Victoria, of course."

"Yes, but which queen is she in the pack?"

"Ah—" said Ede. "There you have me. Let's see . . ."

Before the decision could be made, Freda Hoffstaeder opened the door and said: "there was a gentleman to see you."

Ede affected amused confusion. She was leafing through the royal houses, selecting all the queens.

"A gentleman to see Miss Lily?" she asked.

"*Nein*. A gentleman for yourself."

"For me?"

"*Ja*. He was here now," said Freda.

"Oh?"

"Yes. And was in the front parlour."

Ede handed the cards to Lily. It was late afternoon and the snow beyond the windows was bright with slanted reflections from the sun. November had shut down nearly all the roads. There had been two blizzards already and a freezing wind had blown for days. Any visitor would have to have an extraordinary reason to venture all the way to Munsterfield.

"Who is this gentleman?" said Ede—already searching for her

image in the clouded mirror. Her hair—her sleeves—the buttons at her neck . . .

"Mister . . ." Freda hesitated. The man's name was troubling because she was always being corrected regarding such words.

". . . Vyatt," she said at last.

"Mister Wyatt?"

"Yes. Friedrich."

"Is he German?"

"I think no. Perhaps I have him wrong."

Friedrich Wyatt.

But, of course.

Ede said that Lily was to stay in the back parlour and Freda must stay there with her. "You wait here for Mam," she said—giving Lily a kiss on the top of her head. "When I come back, we can decide about the Queen."

Lily said nothing.

Ede, on leaving, closed the door behind her. No sense taking chances. Always best to be safe.

The hallway was dark along beside the stairs. "We can't light the lamps for *mere gloom*," Liam had decided. They were lit for darkness only.

Frederick Wyatt had come all the way from Toronto—seventy miles by train—to call on her. Ede was astonished. She had not maintained communication with the Wyatt family after the first anniversary of Tom's death. Then, she had gone down into the city to see the marker over his grave. Before her arrival she had written to Frederick Wyatt to say she was to be expected. She had hoped *we might meet at the Crawford Street boarding-house where Tom had once lived.* It had been in her mind that she might at last be able to stand where Tom had once stood and look from the very same windows out on the very same view. She had longed for some aspect—any aspect—of everyday life to share with the Tom who was living still in her mind. This way, he had an ongoing life, and for the longest time, Ede woke up with him beside her, walked with him in the field and spoke with him in a private continuum that only she was aware of. Now, that had passed. Tom had faded back into memory, where his death was absolute.

But Frederick Wyatt had not agreed to meet with Ede at Crawford Street. Instead, they had met again at the Sherbourne Hotel. Harry and Franklin Wyatt had joined them there for lunch in the dining-room and it was after that meal that all of them had gone together to view Tom's marker.

In the graveyard—the street—the cab—Ede had lost a glove that day but had no way of judging where it might have fallen. It was black, as suited her mourning for Tom, but otherwise there was nothing to set it aside as hers. Each of the Wyatt brothers had promised to locate it and return it to her. But it was gone—the way of all gloves—and Ede forgot it.

Polite enquiries made by Ede at that time—now six, almost seven years before—had produced no more than polite replies about old Mister Wyatt's health and young Lizzie's whereabouts. Lisgard, Senior, was *in decline* and, although the impression was given of some disease or condition *which might be going to kill him,* neither the disease nor the condition was given a name. As for Lizzie—he was enigmatically *at school.* But the school remained unidentified and the boy's well-being was discussed no further than a muttered acknowledgement that *Lizzie is well. Quite well.*

Now, Frederick Wyatt was waiting for Ede in the Kilworths' front parlour beyond the door that stood ajar to her left—and her only thought as to why he might have come to call was that he had found her glove and was about to return it to her. This, of course, was madness, and she almost laughed out loud.

At the foot of the stairs, she paused to compose herself. A caller. A gentleman caller. All the way from Toronto through the snow. No callers had been accepted since Tom had died—been killed. Not that she hadn't been courted—not that no one had tried to break down the barrier of her self-imposed exile at Munsterfield. *Little Elba,* she had called it, her home for life in its sea of fields. But none of her suitors had been accepted. They had been banished.

Now, there stood Frederick Wyatt. Not a suitor, but a man all the same and, because of the distance he had come and because of his name, Ede had consented to see him. See him—and be seen.

She was wearing carriage slippers, normally worn only on journeys. Today, she wore them because they were warm, but also because she enjoyed the feel of them—quilted blue satin with soft leather soles, low heels. Because of these—and because she had put on two heavy petticoats that morning whose weight prevented her skirts from rustling, she knew she had not been heard as she came along the hall. This silent arrival gave her an advantage in the moment before she entered the parlour to pause and look at Frederick Wyatt through the space between the partly opened door and its frame.

He was not entirely as she remembered him, having seen him last nearly seven years before. The difference between the man she remembered and the man she now watched from her secret station had mostly to do with the way in which he presented himself. He stood—if it was possible—even straighter than he had in memory; straighter and yet with greater ease. His shoulders no longer looked as if they had been cast in iron, preventing him—as they had—from any but the most formal, almost mechanically performed gesture.

And there were other differences, too. He no longer wore his Wyatt-blue suit—nor anything even remotely like it. Not that he had become, as Liam had, a cold-blooded fashion plate. But he was dressed with some elegance in what had all the appearances—given her narrow view of him beyond the door—of being a suit of some quality, beautifully cut from dark blue Melton. His profile was to her—slightly angled on a bias that denied her the fullest sense of his expression—but his demeanour was one of patience. He had come to call on Edith Kilworth—and if she took an hour to arrive in his presence, so be it. His hands told her this—folded behind his back entirely relaxed in the warmth of the fire—the fingers of his left hand at rest and barely clasped in the palm of his right.

Ede retrieved a small lace handkerchief from the underside of her sleeve and held it to her lips. She was fearful of betraying her presence by means of a sudden, inadvertent cough and she held her handkerchief firmly against her mouth. It smelled of Taylor's Valley Violet Perfume, Eliza's favourite—of which Ede took advantage from time to time. Her eyes were fixed so intensely on Frederick Wyatt that she failed to notice she was holding her breath—still as an animal watching its prey. Or its predator.

Then, in that very moment, the fire in the grate gave a sudden *crack!* And Ede, as though the crack had been her cue to enter, pushed the door wide and went in.

"Good-afternoon, Mister Wyatt."

Frederick turned.

"Good-afternoon, Miss Kilworth."

"You have come such a very long way through all this snow. Will you stay to dinner? Surely, I can persuade you."

"No. Though I thank you. It would be quite impossible."

"You cannot mean you will return to the city tonight."

"In the morning. But I am engaged this evening elsewhere."

"Then you must let me offer you some tea."

Ede turned, already leaving for the kitchen.

"No. No. I beg of you, do not go to the trouble."

His formality was excessive. Ede thought this must be due to nervousness, rising from the need to come to grips with the purpose of his visit. He was performing and saying all the necessary proprieties—but briskly. Efficiently.

"I suspect you might accept a glass of whiskey, Mister Wyatt," she said. "That, we have right here. Do be seated."

"Thank you."

Frederick sat down. Ede went over to the Empire sideboard— her grandmother Portia Kilworth's pride and joy—where square glass decanters and Waterford tumblers were always set out for James and his Friday-night cronies. The decanters held whisky that was got from the local distillery—inferior, but quite acceptable. There was also a single decanter—there being four in all—which contained *the very glory of the world* from the home county of Munster. Irish whiskey—whiskey with an "e". It was the whiskey either of Buttevant or of Ballyporeen or of Kilworth itself. All three were kept in the cellar. James would not have a drop of Scotch whisky in the house—*not even if it arrives inside a guest.*

"There you are." Ede handed Frederick Wyatt a tumbler of Ballyporeen. She had also provided a lesser quantity for herself and, sitting down on the edge of a chair, she breathed in its ether as protection against what might now be said.

"Your health."

"And yours."

They drank.

Frederick indicated the Empire sideboard.

"Bird's-eye maple," he said.

"Indeed," said Ede. "My grandmother Portia left it with us when she returned to America. Boston." She smiled "My grandfather Jonah Kilworth, in spite of being an Irishman, was a Loyalist. Portia was not. She had Republican tendencies—so when my grandfather died, she went back."

"I see. And left this wonderful piece behind."

"You are fond of woods, Mister Wyatt? Of furniture?"

He nodded—and drank again before he said: "I'm in the furniture trade, so to speak."

"You are?" This was the first indication Ede had received of what it was the Wyatt brothers did.

"Oh, yes," said Frederick. He was smiling—and watching the whiskey in his tumbler, turning it this way and that in the lamplight. "I make pianos, Miss Kilworth."

Pianos.

There it was. A signal. Just as if Tom himself had walked into the room and said: *I'm back.*

"For whom do you make pianos, Mister Wyatt?"

"For anyone who will buy them, Miss Kilworth." Frederick was smiling.

Ede laughed. "I meant, of course, for which firm. Don't tell me you work for Mister Williams, too."

Frederick shook his head.

"For myself, Miss Kilworth."

Ede was genuinely confused. Could pianos be manufactured in

someone's backyard? In a shed? In a barn? Did it not require a factory to provide all the shaping and tuning?

"Tom never told me his brother was in the piano business, Mister Wyatt. I thought music was in his blood only. And Lizzie's."

"No. All the Wyatt brothers have music in their veins, Miss Kilworth. But before Tom's death, there was no piano factory, only an agency."

"An agency?"

"Yes. We represented the firm of Bolt & Bryden—piano manufacturers in England. My father established the business, but . . ." Frederick made a deprecating gesture. "There were years of endless . . . *misfortune*, I suppose, is the best word. A long, long history of losses—one and then another, over time."

"Losses, Mister Wyatt? You mean of people?"

"A combination of personal losses—yes—and of—let us say, financial *setbacks*."

"I must say, your father struck me as being a man of exemplary unhappiness. Was this the reason why—all these losses you speak of?"

"To some degree, yes."

"Why are you smiling, Mister Wyatt?"

"My father, Miss Kilworth. I see he has succeeded in catching you, along with all the rest of us. If sorrow were a hammer, he would have the entire population nailed to the wall."

"You're telling me he exaggerates his unhappiness?"

"Not the causes of it, no. But the prolongation of it. The Queen herself has not been more successful than my father in using grief as an excuse to retire from the world of other people. This has been a burden to his sons, as you can imagine."

"I am more than sorry to hear it."

"You mustn't be. It is not a proper subject for discussion—certainly not in the light of my business with you, Miss Kilworth."

"Your business with me, Mister Wyatt?" Ede was more and more convinced they were playing a scene from a novel by Mrs Henry Wood. Would he tell her next that he had somehow discovered the existence of Tom's daughter and had come to take Lily away?

Frederick stood up and, turning his back to Ede, faced the fire and finished his whiskey.

"Miss Kilworth . . ." His back was still to her.

"Yes?"

Frederick set the emptied tumbler on the mantelpiece—straightened his shoulders and turned once again in Ede's direction.

"I . . ."

Ede was watching him as one might watch a villain—waiting with apparent calm for the axe to fall. She set her unfinished whiskey aside and folded her hands.

"You will—I think—have been unaware, Miss Kilworth, that my father had three wives and that each of them died before their time . . ."

Frederick raised his left hand in order to prevent any expression of sympathy. He wanted no interruptions.

"The last of these women was Lizzie's mother. The first of them was mine and Franklin's and Harry's. The middle wife gave birth to Tom. My own mother died when I was young. Quite young. Tom's mother barely had a life at all, and Lizzie's mother died at his birth. You can tell by this, Miss Kilworth, there has been a dearth of women in the lives of my brothers and me. We had no sisters—none was born. Only boys—the ones who lived, and the ones who died . . ."

Ede looked away. She felt as if she must stand, but could not. Clearly—all too clearly—Frederick Wyatt had come to claim Lily. However it had been managed, he had been told of The Piano Man's daughter. Now, she would be taken. "Mister Wyatt . . ." she said. But he would not listen.

"I have been thinking of you, Miss Kilworth," he said. "I have been thinking of you and the irresistible image of your having so very nearly become a member of our family."

Ede could not believe her ears. Or her eyes. He was smiling.

"How very close you came to joining us then," he said. "And how very close I felt to you at that time. Close, because your grief at Tom's death was equal to my own." Now, he looked at his shoes and placed his hands behind his back.

Ede saw the top of his head—with its waves of auburn hair and the width of his brow—leaning forward into the light. How white his skin was, she thought as he looked back up and away from his shoes and the carpet. White as Tom's had been.

"I am thirty-six years old today, Miss Kilworth. This is my birthday, and—*no*: say nothing. Please. I am nearly done." He stood to his full height, now. "I have come here because I have not been able to forget you since all that long while ago—seven years and more—when I saw you first. Even then, I wanted to say to you . . ."

Here he stopped. His gaze wavered.

Ede, no longer able to bear the distance between them, stood up. Later, she would not understand this feeling, but in the moment it was strong as any feeling she had experienced since Tom died.

She took a step forward. "Tell me, Mister Wyatt, what it is you want."

She could barely raise her voice. All at once, she was keenly aware of the heat from the fireplace.

Frederick was looking at her the way a drowning man might look at the last departing lifeboat.

"You," he said. And then his hand went out towards her and he spoke a single word that Ede would never forget. "Please," he said. *Please.*

He might as well have said: *help!*

5 • Ede had given no answer, though the answer was already in her mouth. Before she could speak it, however, she was interrupted by a sound that immobilized her.

Far off at the rear of the house something—or somebody—fell with a terrible crash. Instantly, Ede knew what it was.

Frederick Wyatt—hanging on Ede's unspoken reply—nonetheless stepped away from her.

"Miss Kilworth?"

Ede's right hand had risen to her lips, as if to silence herself. And then: "please forgive me, Mister Wyatt," she said. "I shall come back directly. I know what has caused this commotion and it will require my presence—but only briefly." She turned towards the hallway, leaving him helplessly lost behind her. "Do feel free to help yourself to more whiskey," she said from the doorway. "And would you be good enough to add another log to the fire?"

She was gone.

Frederick sighed—his proposal in ruins. There was more he had wanted to say, but the chance for that had withered. He must pacify himself by doing her bidding as he waited for her return. Moving towards the wood box, he calculated that once he had fulfilled her request, he would take another drink of whiskey from the square-cut decanter on the Empire sideboard. At least he could find some pleasure in the moment, running his fingers over the sideboard's layered surfaces, waxed and rubbed, no doubt, by the palms of ancestral hands.

Ede went hurrying down the hallway, cursing Liam's lamp-oil stinginess. Light was essential now—it being almost completely dark—four or four-thirty in the afternoon.

Passing her father's study, she heard the clicking of the abacus. James was sitting at his desk in a quilted robe, his hair brushed up in distracted tufts where his fingers had massaged his scalp while he laboured over his accounts. Seeing her, he attempted to rise.

"No," said Ede. "I'm going. You stay where you are."

"I only wondered . . ." said James—but Ede was already gone.

As she neared the back parlour, she could hear the sounds of the struggle within and see the turmoil of tumbling shadows in the play of light beneath the door. She paused for precisely seven seconds—time enough to close her eyes and pray. And then . . .

"It's all right. It's all right . . ." Into the blinding light. "Mam is here. She's here. I'm here."

The figure on the floor gave a heave and, thrashing still from side to side, attempted to put its arms out—upward. But no discernible direction could be achieved—sideways only—only sideways—this way, that way—banging against the floor while reaching up for the ceiling.

"Don't. Oh, don't," said Ede. But only to herself—only to placate herself as she began to fall towards the carpet—already raising her skirts in order to ease her descent. "Don't. Oh, don't. No, don't, my darling . . ."

Lily.

6. Freda had been gone five minutes, no longer. She had wanted to bring the child some *selbstgebackenen Kuchen mit Marmelade und ein Glas Milch*. But once she had reached the kitchen she became distracted by the fact that a cast-iron kettle set too near the centre of the stove had almost boiled dry and then she was required to go to the sink for more water and, once at the sink, she had found that the pump required priming and the water for that must be fetched from the shed where seven pails of it were kept beneath some sacking, hard up against the wall behind the stove to prevent them from freezing. All this—and in the meantime, *Die Krankheit*—"the sickness," which had no other name, since no other name had been permitted.

Freda Hoffstaeder, too, had suffered the indignities bestowed on the parents of children who are beguiled. Her daughter, Minna, had been considered dim-witted until last year, when it was discovered that, in fact, she was almost completely deaf. The results of this discovery had been miraculous. All at once, there was a means of communication that could be learned. A language of the fingers—and, once that language had been mastered, there was the language of letters—the whole world in print on the pages of books.

This way, Freda had been able to acknowledge the depths of Ede's suffering when it was finally clear that Lily's illness would not go away. It would be a part of her forever like Minna's deafness. *One can live with deafness, yes—but still one will never hear.* This was why one suffered as the parent of such a child—that one could not go out into the world of medicine, or wherever it was that one might look for such things, and come back home with a new pair of ears—or a new, untroubled mind—or a . . . what? What could one bring to Lily Kilworth that would give her back the life she had lost at birth? The life of an ordinary child.

Freda went now to Ede and to Lily without the biscuits, the jam and the glass of milk, and she stood at the door as a guardian might to prevent the rest of the world from coming in.

"Get up now, Miss Edith," she said. "You should."

Ede said: "I can't."

She could, of course, but she did not want to. She wanted to stay where she was—on the floor beneath the table with Lily wrapped in her arms—lying on the carpet singing *all is well, my darling* so that only Lily could hear it.

Lily's eyes were open wide and staring. Her lips were parted. Blood stained her chin and the front of her dress. Ede held her close, but not so close that Lily would not be able to turn if she needed to. The image they made beneath the table—shadowed, fragmented—was the image of people under bombardment—seeking shelter where the falling sky cannot touch them. Freda had seen many such images before she had come to Canada. She had seen them when the French had taken her city. Saarbrüken, where both her parents and all her sisters had died.

"Be remembering you have a guest," she said to Ede. "I will be taking Lily now and sit me with her until she sleeps. You come away, Miss Edith, and let me take her."

"Yes. Yes," said Ede. She was exhausted. The burden of the last fifteen minutes had almost been equal to the burden of giving birth, since every ounce of her will and every grain of her energy had been focused on Lily's survival.

"Let me help you," said Freda. "*Ja.*"

Ede came out from under the table, crawling on her knees. She pulled Lily's dead-weight as far as she could and lifted her into

Freda's arms. Freda sang: *soo, soo, soo* into Lily's ears and closed the child's eyes. *Soo, soo, soo.*

When Ede looked down at the tabletop, she saw the card ruins of Windsor Castle. This was the turning of the screw. *Ruins.* If she had finally guessed correctly at Frederick Wyatt's purpose, her answer to him was now secured. Kissing the top of Lily's head, she laid her hand on Freda's cheek in thanks and moved towards the darkened hallway.

All at once, beside the staircase, she came to a stop in the pool of dim light that Liam had allotted. She closed her eyes. Frederick was waiting for her—and she must somehow compose herself. Her eyes opened. *Frederick.* She had called him Frederick for the very first time, even though it was only in her mind. *How strangely people gain their names,* she thought, as she smoothed her hair and stepped towards the parlour door.

7. "Mister Wyatt."

"Miss Kilworth."

He was standing on the hearth with his back to the room. The fire burned brightly, but gave less heat than it had. Ede went straight to the nearest lamps and turned them up in order to offer a decent light. To hell with Liam.

"I trust," Frederick said, "that whatever was amiss has been rectified."

"Yes, yes. It has—as best it can be."

Ede picked up her tumbler and finished the modicum of whiskey that had waited for her there. She then decanted a further two fingers—a drink of some strength, given the small amounts she was used to.

"Have you sufficient, Mister Wyatt?"

"Yes. Yes, I have." He was distracted, now, wondering how to return to the subject of his proposal. He noted, too, that Ede was distracted in another fashion. Her hands kept exchanging the tumbler of whiskey—first to one and then the other and back again. She meanwhile fussed and fidgeted with elements of her dress, the folds in her skirts, the buttons at her neck. The silver bracelet on her wrist.

She stepped inexplicably away from him just as he was about to speak. She went past the hearth and past the dark-stained mantel, making for the deep-set alcove whose twin flanked the fireplace. The windows there were curtainless—drapeless. Wide wooden shutters with small brass handles stood open, waiting to be closed in the worst of weather and at night.

An occasional chair—one of four in the room—had been placed in the centre of this alcove and Ede now made her way towards it, not to sit, but to use its seat as a resting place for her knee. Kneeling, she steadied herself with one hand on the chair's frail lacquered back and raised her whiskey tumbler with the other. Beyond the window, the sun was setting.

"You had something you wanted to say to me, Mister Wyatt," she said—but not before she had swallowed a mouthful of Ballyporeen and raised her handkerchief to dab her lips. She did this, turning at last to be seated. Behind her, the window filled with orange-red light.

"I must ask you," he said. "I am asking you . . ."

"Mister Wyatt, I cannot marry you."

Frederick was so stunned by this reply that he was virtually silenced—incapable of speech. His mind, on the other hand, was spinning off like a Catherine wheel, sputtering gibberish.

Ede stood up. She turned in profile to the dying light beyond the window. "It is not," she said, "that I would not. Not that I do not wish it, Mister Wyatt. Vehemently," she added. "But, when I say I cannot marry you, that is precisely what I mean. I mean that I can not. My refusal has nothing to do with a lack of desire." She faced him. "I had not thought to ever marry. Not after Tom. As far as I was concerned . . ." Here she was careful: ". . . he and I were married. And when he died—was killed—I felt like a widow. I was a widow."

She looked at Frederick—all his destroyed hopes cutting his gaze free of her. His drowning, she surmised, had commenced. Certainly, this part of him—in which he had invested so much— was dying right before her eyes.

"I cannot bear your answer," he said at last. "And I will not accept it, Miss Kilworth."

Ede began to speak, but he prevented her. He raised his voice and cut her off. "There is nothing," he said, "*nothing* that I will allow to prevent this. Nothing. If you told me you were going to die tomorrow, I would marry you today."

"Mister Wyatt . . ."

"No. I refuse to hear you. I am deaf—and will remain so to every answer but *yes*."

He was already walking towards the door. Ede could not think how to stop him.

"I have some business to deal with in town, Miss Kilworth, and will now return to the Queen's Hotel. If I may prevail upon one of your men . . ."

Ede relented. "Of course," she said. "I will ask Freda to bring your coat."

She moved without pausing to set down her whiskey tumbler. She carried it with her past Frederick Wyatt into the hallway where Malahide at last was turning up the lamps. Liam would return at any moment with the sleigh and Davey Burns, the youngest of the hired hands, could take it back into town with Mister Wyatt as his passenger. She said as much to Malahide and kept right on walking down the hallway until she had reached the kitchen. Not once in this parade did she stop to look back at Frederick, not even to acknowledge his presence by introducing him to Malahide. Neither did she say: *goodbye*. She simply left him standing where he was.

Coming to the back parlour, she opened the door and told Freda to fetch Mister Wyatt's things. Lily was now asleep on the recamier, under a blanket. Ede went on to the kitchen.

Eliza was busy at the stove with Minna. They were cooking something that otherwise would have given Ede the greatest pleasure—a chicken stew that would soon be garnished with German dumplings.

"Where are you going?" Eliza asked.

"To the privy."

Ede went on walking.

"You'll freeze to death," said Eliza. "Put something around you shoulders . . ."

Ede kept on walking.

A door banged open and slammed shut, sending an icy draught past the dogs on the kitchen floor. All the steam from the chicken stew was blown up into Eliza's face. Minna went running into the shed to make sure the door stayed shut. It had a habit of slipping its latch.

All Eliza could think was: *Ede's gone out to the privy with no coat and no lantern. And with . . . had it been a tumbler of whiskey? Surely not.*

8. Liam did not return that evening as usual, but stayed in town where he worked until long past the supper hour. This meant that Davey Burns had to hitch old Kate to the sledge and drive Frederick Wyatt back to the Queen's Hotel, both men side by side on the box seat up front. It was not the elegant transport Ede had thought to supply, but it was all there was on hand. Eliza, making excuses that gave the impression Ede was suffering from headache, went to the door with Frederick and wished him well and said *goodbye* in her daughter's absence.

"Shall we see you soon again?" she asked.

"I cannot tell," said Frederick. "I have a very great deal to contend with at the moment. But I trust this will not be the last of our meetings, Mrs Kilworth. Let us see what transpires in the next few weeks."

Eliza had drawn the correct conclusion in supposing Frederick

Wyatt had come to speak to Ede about marriage—but nothing formal having been said, she was in no position to put the question she wanted most to ask: *would Mister Wyatt repeat his proposal?* Or had Ede, as Eliza feared, been so vehement in turning him down that his hopes had been entirely dashed?

As she stood on the porch and watched the sledge pull away down the drive, Eliza saw that beyond the rise of land over which the lights of McCaskill's Mills lit up the sky, a storm of some magnitude was brewing. A wall of solid black cloud was looming and a low distant moaning gave warning of a rising wind. This winter, only just begun in the calendar, had already proved to be uniquely forceful. The men had had to trek three times to bring back stranded cattle into the yard beside the barn and two young heifers had perished of cold out there in the fields. Now this, that looked to be the storm of storms.

Closing the door against this distressing news, Eliza could only think that the weather outside was conspiring with other dark forces at work in her household. Liam increasingly aloof—Malahide refusing to continue his education, seemingly without ambition—Willa being courted by half a dozen young men, not one of whom was acceptable but all of whom she *adored*—and Ede in this binding contract with a child whose crippling illness had driven them all into a corner from which there seemed to be no escape.

Eliza veered to the right and entered the parlour her daughter's would-be suitor had just vacated. The fire still burned beyond the screen and the lamps, which Ede had raised, were beacons of welcome Eliza knew she must decline.

There was so much to do. *When was the last time all of us sat together in this lovely room,* she wondered. On the furthest wall, the portraits of Malahide and Cathleen Fagan begged to hold court with the children of their children's children. But it had been a month—*two months—a year ago?* when the whole family had gathered here.

Eliza crossed the Turkey carpet making for the Empire sideboard. The tumblers and decanters gleamed and beckoned in the lamplight.

She was not aware of whether the decanter of Ballyporeen had been filled to the brim as the day began—but its level seemed inordinately disproportionate, now, in comparison with the others.

Well.

A good shot of whiskey was a blessing, time to time. And a shot of Ballyporeen would be a double blessing . . .

Eliza poured at least three inches into a tumbler and returned with it to the centre of the carpet, where—closing her eyes—she swallowed half the contents without a moment's pause.

She waited. It was not her daily habit to drink more than wine—and even that she watered, except on formal occasions. The whiskey burned its way into her system, causing her to raise her other hand to her diaphragm. *Lord protect me, what have I done?* It crossed her mind that she might have killed herself, the liquor was so potent.

When at last she was able to open her eyes—which had been inflamed along with the rest of her—she was confronted with her grandparents, watching her from the wall. Each stared out directly from a smoke-darkened canvas framed in gilt, each in the dress of another time and place—Dublin, Ireland, 1812. How formal they had been. Their portraits showed them just as they were—all their anguish hidden—all their woes denied in their proud carriage. All the disasters of Ireland had been their inheritance, but they had borne them one by one, as if disaster were God's greatest gift—the surest sign of His attention and approval. When Cathleen had forced the child Eliza to lie face down on the stones beneath Christ's figure on the cross, she had said to her: *there is nothing in this life that cannot be borne with grace.*

Eliza raised her glass in the portraits' direction. It was only she who knew that in a dark room high in the attic, her own father's brother had been hidden from the world in her grandparents' house. Lovingly cared for—but publicly unacknowledged—he, too, had suffered from Lily's illness. Her condition. Well . . . *there is nothing in this life that cannot be borne with grace*, she repeated in her mind. And then she said: "amen," out loud and raised the tumbler of whiskey to her lips and emptied it.

Behind her, the fire that had burned all afternoon collapsed with a sigh in its grate and Eliza, tumbler in hand, returned to the kitchen.

9. A bed was kept for Lily in Ede's room—the room at the front of the house whose windows looked out onto the road and then the field. In the wintertime, the leafless trees afforded a wider scope to this view and all the snowy hills rolled off towards the town, whose Fire Hall tower and spires gave some appearance of holding up the sky.

Some nights, Lily slept with Ede in the largest bed and Ede would sing to her and stroke her hair. The bed had a wondrous smell to it—warm and washed and scented with straw from its mattress. They would lie there safe as burrowed animals or birds in nests and the moon would light the window-panes whose bubbled glass made underwater stars. This way, Lily drifted into her dreams and Ede would lie awake beside her telling Tom that all was well.

Weeks would go by and there would be no convulsions. Ede's heart would lift and she woke to her days without fear. Then, all at once, the convulsions would return and multiply—as though they had been in hiding in order to breed.

As always with such maladies, it was hoped the convulsions would pass in time, that age and growth would cure them. Doctor Melbourne told Ede there was every possibility that Lily's body would shed them *just as it sheds its scabs and baby teeth*. But whatever inducements were offered—bromides and diets and, when Miss McClintock was there, her miracle massages—nothing done would draw the seizures off. Eliza, knowing the source, was silent. She had watched each child of her own curve past the danger point and achieve maturity without a sign or signal of the condition. Common knowledge informed the most ignorant that all

such curses are rooted in the blood—but no one said so. No one
ever put the question: *who has this come from?* No one. Not even
Doctor Melbourne. The burden was Lily's and Lily's only. *Not
one Fagan—not one Kilworth before her—had suffered from such
a thing . . .* So it was said.

The night of Frederick Wyatt's visit, as soon as she had eaten, Ede
went up to be with Lily. In the bedroom, she set a lamp on the
bureau next to Lily's truckle-bed and watched the child for twenty
minutes before she realized how long she had stood there immobilized, counting over the features of Frederick Wyatt's face and
listening again and again to his proposal. And her answer, rolling
on a wheel inside her mind: *I cannot marry you, Mister Wyatt. I
cannot marry you. Will not. Must not. Cannot.*

And yet—she wanted to. Wanted to. Not for love. *Of course
not for love! But . . .* His proposal had opened a door that Ede
had imagined was shut forever. The door to freedom.

Being at the front of the house, Ede's bedroom bore the brunt
of the wind. The storm that Eliza had seen in the sky before dinner was now upon them. Beyond the glass, the world was awash
with blown white streamers of snow being driven through the air
as if some great machine were grinding it up and spewing it out
from the top of the hill.

God bless all beasts and men who must survive out there. Ede
made the sign of the cross as she whispered this prayer. She had
seen the cattle huddled in the lane on her return from the privy
earlier. She was grateful for their sake that Richard and Ephraim
would now have herded them into the barns. Inside and out of the
wind, the body heat of their numbers would save them from the
cold. *It's the wind that kills,* so Ephraim said. *An animal can
stand more cold on a windless day than a person can. But when
the wind is up, pray God they're near the barn.*

She wondered if Davey and the sledge had returned from deliv-
ering Frederick Wyatt to the Queen's Hotel. She had not heard
them do so, but then, the dining-room was not on the driveway
side of the house and, if all had gone well with his journey, Davey

must have returned while the family was still at table. This left only Liam at the mercy of the storm—and given his stingy nature, he would certainly try to get home. The sensible thing to do, of course, would be to take a room at the Queen's and wait for the storm to pass. But Liam would call that wasteful.

Ede wondered, too, what Frederick's mysterious business engagement might be. Surely he would not have stayed overnight to negotiate the sale of a single piano. Such transactions could be dealt with in an hour.

This left the possibility there might be other women in Frederick's life, in spite of his claim that none had intruded there since the death of Lizzie's mother. And that had been ... when? Ede did a short calculation. Fourteen—fifteen years ago, at the most. The boy could not be older than that. When she first encountered Lizzie, he must have been seven or eight. She could not remember.

What she could remember was Lizzie's auburn hair and his pale wax complexion cut across with scarlet lips. Almost scarlet. *No one's lips are really scarlet.* But Lizzie—Lizzie had a face that someone might have painted. A portrait's face—or an actor's face, perhaps. Lizzie was like a boy written in a book—an illustrated boy. Drawn in black ink. Incised. Hand-tinted. That was Lizzie Wyatt, who opened his mouth and sang like an angel.

> *Just a song at twilight*
> *When the lights are low*
> *And the flickering shadows*
> *Softly come and go ...*

That was Tom's song. Tom's, not Lizzie's. But in her mind, she heard Lizzie's voice.

Ede, looking out through the storm towards the town, began to conjure Frederick's room at the Queen's Hotel. White, white curtains blew at an open window—not a winter room, but a summer room. She could see the washstand—basin and pitcher—towels all white—and a bureau with Frederick's brushes laid out side by side—his pocket watch with its brand new chain—a book, perhaps—a folded handkerchief. And there, reflected in the mirror, Frederick himself seated on a wide brass bed, its pillows thrown aside, its covers in disarray—and lying beside him . . .

Who?

A woman.

Which?

I am engaged this evening, elsewhere, he had said.

". . . engaged this evening, elsewhere," Ede said aloud.

She turned. Had Lily wakened?

No.

Lily. *The cause of all my joy. And all my grief.*

Don't say that. It isn't true.

Ede dropped the curtain, shutting out her vision of Frederick.

It wasn't true. It wasn't.

And it was.

She turned back into the room and began to undress.

If only Lily . . .

No. She must not think that. She must never think that again. She had thought it once in the throes of some despairing moment. She had thought it and said it—cursing the child to her face. For some denial of access to a moment's freedom—for being the impediment between a life Ede wanted and the life she had: *damn you!* Meaning: *damn you for having been born!*

But oh—if I should ever say that again. Or think it.

Sitting before the mirror, undoing her hair, Ede looked up and saw Lily's birth-wreath hanging on the wall. *She is mine,* she thought, *and dear God, I love her. Dear God, I love her. Dear God, I love her . . .*

Ede closed her eyes and began to plait her hair. *Just to watch her. Just to see that extraordinary concentration. Just to hear her talking to the string-dolls. And to see her dance . . .*

And Lily was all there was of Tom. All of him that could be touched, all of him that could be held. All of him that breathed.

The wind blew. A shutter banged.

Ede, in her nightdress, crossed the room and looked at the child asleep in the lamplight. The storm beyond the windows was not unlike the storm in Lily's mind. It would pass, as all storms pass, leaving whatever havoc in its wake that wind and weather decreed—and fortune.

We get what we are given, Ede thought. *What we are given is all we have. There is no way back for Lily into non-existence. There she is—and she is mine. And I am hers. She was given to me—and I was given to her—no other. I cannot marry you, Mister Wyatt.*

No.

10. In the morning, Ede was awakened by the sound of sleigh bells.

Surely not Liam returning at such an early hour. The sun had barely risen. And yet—a horse was neighing in the yard and there were voices.

Ede, who had slept in a chair beside Lily's bed, got up and, at once, fell down. Her legs were asleep. It almost made her laugh out loud to find herself on the floor in her nightdress, having to crawl like a baby to the window. But she was silent, fearful of waking Lily.

At the window she knelt and pulled the curtains aside, revealing a clear bright sky and utter stillness everywhere. The field across the way had been redesigned—resculpted in snow, with drifts as high in places as the fences. Ede could not see the yard—but she could see where a sleigh had passed beneath the trees that lined the drive. And all the trees were black on one side, white on the other, the wind having blown the snow against them all night long.

Now, there were voices down in the lower hall—men's voices and a woman's voice. Freda? Eliza? It was impossible to tell. There was so much muted chatter—urgent whispering and admonitions *not to wake the dead* that Ede could not tell who was there.

Someone was now on the stair. In slippered feet—and skirts.

The door behind her opened. She turned where she was, on the floor, her legs still coming awake and tingling beneath her.

"Edith Mary." It was Eliza. "Put on your robe and come downstairs at once."

"But, Mother . . ."

"At once. You have a visitor."

Five minutes later, Ede was descending into an otherwise silent house, brushing her hand along the wall to steady herself—her other hand on the bannister. Each step she took made a cracking sound that was either in her bones or in the stairs.

The door to the parlour was open and it was only when she could see inside that she realized what she was hearing. It was the cedar kindling of a fire newly lit, exploding like Christmas crackers in the grate.

No one was present there—or, at least, no one could be seen.

A visitor? At dawn?

Ede took a breath at the bottom of the stair. She could smell the fire. She could smell the kitchen: coffee brewing—toast being made on the grill.

The robe she wore had been her father's gift when he and Eliza returned from their annual trip to visit his mother in Cambridge, Massachusetts. Silk brocade with velvet facings. It was the grandest thing she owned and she was grateful for its elegance now, when she must face some stranger at this ungodly hour. Her plait of hair, pulled back, had been hastily tied with a blue satin ribbon.

"Miss Kilworth."

Frederick.

He was smiling—beaming—flushed with good health. Ede could only blink with surprise.

"I hired a sleigh with a driver from the livery," he said. "We were first on the road out there. We broke the way for other traffic. It was the finest—the most exhilarating ride I've had since I was a boy."

"But, Mister Wyatt—why have you come? Surely you must understand that I have given you my answer."

"Yes," still beaming. "I understand. But you must understand that I do not accept your answer, Miss Kilworth."

"Mister Wyatt . . ."

"No, Miss Kilworth. There will be no argument. I have not come here this morning merely to reiterate my proposal of marriage. I have come here in the hopes that I might meet my brother's daughter."

Ede was speechless. She stared at Frederick Wyatt for such a long moment in silence that he came at last, across the floor and led her to a chair.

Seated, Ede looked down at her hands. Frederick had stepped away again and could not see her face. She wanted desperately not to weep. It would be so demeaning. She made a knot of her fingers in her lap—one hand locked in the other. And when she spoke her words were barely audible.

"Tom never knew there was a child," she said. "I had hoped to be his wife before she was born. And then . . ."

"And then he was killed."

"Yes." Ede looked up and then away again. "Mister Wyatt—I have been such a long time in hiding. It is difficult to tell you what I had thought would never be told."

He said nothing.

"I thought," Ede went on, "I kept thinking, someone will come and I will be able to trust them. Someone—a stranger—will come and I will be able to trust them and then I will be able to tell. But that person never came. Until you. And then . . ."

"Then you did not trust me."

"No. Not that. I did trust you. But—I couldn't trust myself any more. When you spoke—when you asked me to marry you, I realized then that I had no right to accept—to say yes, because I was not alone—not just me alone—but me with Lily. And you had not asked for her. You had no notion I was attached to another life."

"And so you sent me away."

"I had no option."

"But you had been inclined to say yes?"

Ede did not answer this. Instead, she said: "how was it you found out about Lily? Who told you?"

"I cannot answer that, Miss Kilworth. I'm afraid I'm sworn to secrecy, and I'm sure you would not expect me to break a trust."

Ede nodded. Nonetheless, she said: "I suppose it was your dinner guest of last evening. Your *engagement*."

"That is a fair assumption. But I can say no more."

"In that case, Mister Wyatt, we shall set the question aside."

They were silent for a moment. And then: "Well, Miss Kilworth? What is your answer, now?"

Ede looked away. She smiled. And then she laughed.

"Mister Wyatt," she said, "if I do say yes, you must promise never to call me *Miss Kilworth* again."

"Then you must give up calling me Mister Wyatt. Have we a bargain?"

Ede put her hands out towards him.

"Yes," she said. "We have a bargain."

11. Half an hour before his departure, Frederick stood again in the front parlour where Ede was beginning to think they had taken up permanent residence. Aside from the dining-room, where they had eaten their breakfast—this was the only room at Munsterfield in which she had met with him.

Though each had wanted to settle more details about the immediate future, it was imperative that Frederick return to McCaskill's Mills in order to be on the spot if the train should have ploughed its way through the storm. He would be wanted in Toronto at the piano factory.

It was Eliza who urged them to introduce Lily to the situation without an immediate announcement that Frederick was to be her *father*. "Such things are so difficult for children to understand. Let her see Frederick first as a family friend. As her uncle."

Both Ede and Frederick approved of this, Ede being nervous of the moment, as it was. Eliza brought Lily downstairs, having dressed her first in blue. Pink was forbidden. It turned Ede's stomach.

"Come along, my dear," Eliza said, "and meet your Uncle Frederick . . ."

In her grey morning dress with its tiny pearl buttons and its hint of a bustle, Eliza entered with the child beside her. Silent.

Frederick had never seen such a sight. Lily's hair was a paler shade of red than Tom's had been—but she had his blue-green eyes and his long, thick lashes. Her flat, oval face with its tilted lips and thin nose was a Kilworth inheritance—Ede in miniature.

"There you are, my darling," Ede said—reaching out to take Lily's hand and draw her forward.

But Lily would not go.

She told me this herself. "I would not go. I hated him on sight, Charlie. He terrified me . . ."

"Why?"

"His eyes," she said. "They contradicted everything else in his expression. Smiling, Charlie—smiling lips, his whole face beaming. But not his eyes. To me, they were cold. Frigid. Chilling. I'd seen them already—dreaming. There was a man in my dreams— a stranger—who stared in at me through a window. Now, there he was—inside the house. And Mam—my mother—was standing there beside him, unaware. And all my defences went up against him—so, when Grandmam let go my hand and gave me a push, I would not move. I could not . . ."

I watched Lily conjuring the moment. Her voice faltered. I might have been seven or eight years old when she told me this story. I remember we were seated in the very room where the scene she was describing had taken place. At Munsterfield. Winter was on us then, just as it was in my mother's narrative.

"Frederick himself stepped into the space between us," she went on. "He put his hands out in my direction. *Come,* he said, *let us be the best of friends in the world . . .*" She laughed. "I'll give him this much, Charlie—he tried. But he made a dreadful liar. For all the warmth in his smile, his eyes had caught hold of me and wouldn't let go. I still couldn't move. Mam came past him, then, and picked me up. I can feel it even now—oh, Lord—being lifted up so that Frederick and I were face to face. And Mam's fingers on my elbow—bending my arm until it was extended in his direction . . ."

Here, Lily placed her own fingers on the underside of her elbow—forcing her right arm outward to Frederick's phantom self, who might as well have been standing there before her.

"He took my hand," she whispered—raising it even then in Frederick's direction. "He took my hand and kissed it. The palm of it. *There*, he said. *Our friendship is sealed.*"

Her hand descended.

I waited.

"All I know now," she said, "is the scene, word for word, was straight out of *David Copperfield*. Mister Murdstone had risen from its pages and forced himself into my life."

12. Lily would escape from time to time. This was Ede's word for it: *escape*. It had started long before Frederick's arrival on that November day in 1897 when he came to propose. It was during the time when Ede still imagined the rest of her life would be entirely devoted to Lily and Lily's needs—to Lily's protection. It was not a life Ede rejected, but she regretted that so much vigilance was required. *If only the child was content—even from time to time—to be still.*

But this was not Lily's way. To her, at even the earliest age—when she began to walk—something waited for her beyond every door in every room. She became enamoured of the stairs—of height and depth, of climbing and descent. The attic, in time, was forbidden. The cellars could be reached only through a trap in the kitchen, over which Freda stood like a policeman. Still, this left the barns, and when Lily came to them, she found they were the havens of every mystery a person could imagine: *animals who spoke in languages I understood—chickens under whose brooding bodies I could thrust my hands for warmth—swallows whose flight was laughter personified. And, oh Charlie—oh!—beyond the barns, there was all that distance!*

But distance came later into her life. At the start, there was Munsterfield itself—the house to be challenged, each individual room within its walls a foreign country. The first time Lily escaped, she was gone no more than a minute before it occurred to her that, going into hiding, she had found a way to rid the world of others—and to claim it for herself.

One day, she stood in a long grey-lit corridor that had no windows and no lamps. It was, in fact, the walkway between the wash-house and the summer kitchen. Its walls were heavily screened, and in the draft created between the open rooms at either end, this screening gave off a humming sound that was not unlike the sound inside a beehive. Closed out with board-and-batten drop-leaf shutters, the only light that reached this corridor found its way through knot-holes and spaces where part of a batten had been broken. Lily's first encounter with this place was mid-afternoon on a winter's day. She was two years old—plus.

When her hands reached out for support and found the screening, an electric thrill ran up her arms from her fingertips to the nape of her neck. This was such an extraordinary sensation she tried at once to repeat it. Turning to face the screening, she stood on tiptoe and applied her fingers to it as a harpist might have done. The corridor began to thrum with song.

Found by Freda five minutes later, Lily was standing at the centre of a storm of sound—having managed to spring the screening into life from end to end—the noise of it sustained by the draught. Lily was immobilized—overwhelmed by resonance. Freda, hearing all this droning, came out running and was terrified by the expression on Lily's face. Snatching her up, she carried her back into the lighted kitchen.

"Liebchen, Liebchen," Freda cried. "*Wo bist Du hingegangen?*" Where have you gone . . . ?

Lily, in Freda's arms, was staring past the woman's shoulder—staring, but not at anything visible to Freda, who turned in order to see what held the child's attention.

"*Liebchen*. What is it?"

But Lily went on staring and was staring still when Ede came into the kitchen to retrieve her.

"She will not close her eyes," Freda said—her voice still shaking.

Lily's hair stood out from her head—an aureole of red. There was saliva running down from the corner of her mouth and her hands were working the air convulsively—as though the screen were still beneath her fingers. And the sound in her throat was a *click-click-clicking* sound—a sound that Ede described as the sound of *keys being turned in broken locks—keys that won't catch.*

"Take her,"said Freda. "Make her eyes to close."

Ede took Lily in her arms and tried to turn her attention from the unseen wonders in the air. But Lily twisted away in order to go on staring. Ede was astonished at the child's strength. She had the crazy impression that Lily was trying to fly—writhing back and upwards, beating her arms against the pull of gravity.

"Stop this! *Stop!*" Ede shouted, still trying to turn Lily round to her face. "Stop it! *Stop!*"

Even the fact that her mam was shouting had no effect on the child. A motor—whatever it was—had been started inside her and nothing could be done to shut it off. It roared and spun through her system with a growing intensity until it seemed its shaking was going to part her from her wits.

"Help!" Ede called, not knowing who could help or how. Freda stood frozen. Ede began to run with Lily down the hallway towards the front of the house. She did this instinctively, the way she would have fled if a maddened animal had suddenly entered the house. And all this while, the clicking sound was beating like a heart in Lily's throat.

By the time Ede had reached the bottom of the stairs, Eliza had come out into the hallway. "Let me—let me have her," she said, knowing—with a sinking heart—but refusing to say what was happening.

"Bring her in here. *Now.*"

Eliza spoke with sharp authority, having seen that Ede was in the throes of panic.

They went into the parlour where a fire had been laid but not yet lit. The room was cold, like a cellar—and its shutters were closed against the wind. Only one lamp burned.

"Put her on that sofa," Eliza said. And then: "let go!" She had to force Ede's hands to open and give up their burden. "*Let go.*"

Ede subsided.

Eliza took the child, whose head was now tilted backwards as though she had found new demons on the ceiling. "Give me your bracelet," she said to Ede.

Ede removed a thin, double twist of braided silver from her arm. It had been her gift from Jamie the year before he died. Asking no questions—speechless—she handed it over to her mother.

Eliza forced the silver coil into Lily's mouth, using it to hold the child's tongue in place. She knew that Lily could do no harm with her baby teeth, but she also believed the old wives' tale that people can choke on their tongues.

Dumbly, Ede watched her mother's actions as though some part of her already knew that she herself would have to do these things from now on. The word *convulsion* floated to the surface in her tumbling mind. Other words also tried to rise up beside it— *epilepsy—seizure*—but Ede refused to see them—hear them— even to recall their existence. *There are no words for this*, she insisted. *There is only babble.*

She was watching, now, with the appearance of absolute calm. Her shoulders were squared, but not rigid. She leaned very slightly forward, her hand at rest on the back of one of the rose-wood chairs. Lily lay rigid as a corpse on the nearest sofa—her arms locked stiffly at her sides, her head still yearning backwards. Eliza knelt beside her, smoothing the child's hair, crooning words that Ede could not decipher—singing what seemed to be a lullaby into her ears.

Then she said: "bring me that shawl from the chair," her hand reaching back towards it. When Ede had given it to her, Eliza drew the shawl up along Lily's body like a shroud, and *there, there, there*, she said—*there, there, there* . . .

It was over.

Eliza sat on her heels, lifting strands of hair away from Lily's forehead—almost smiling in her relief that Lily's eyes, at last, had closed. Then, sinking sideways onto her hip, she drew the silver bracelet from Lily's mouth and dropped it into her lap.

After a moment, having seen the child's breathing had taken on a normal rhythm, Eliza said: "she will sleep, now. An hour, perhaps. Or more." And then she said: "we should light that fire."

Ede went across the room and lifted the screen in its metal frame away from the hearth. She struck a match against the stones and touched it to the shavings she had put beneath the kindling only an hour before, or less. When had that been? She was laying this fire when Freda gave her cry in the kitchen and Ede went running.

Now, as she watched the flame go crawling through the shavings, curling up towards the grate and its cargo of cedar logs, Ede thought of Tom, and wondered if this—whatever it was—had been his legacy. It was not an angry thought—not accusatory. Merely a pondering. *There's something in everyone's blood,* she thought. *A gift or a curse—or both* . . .

"Mother?"

"Yes?"

Eliza was seated still on the floor, her weight on one hand, her gaze still fixed on the sleeping child.

"Can it kill her—this?"

Eliza said nothing. She looked at the coil of silver in her lap and touched it with her finger. Lily's teeth, however few and small, had marked it nonetheless.

Ede said: "is this to be her life? Mother? Yes?"

Eliza still said nothing. Better that Ede should decide how to answer these questions herself, since Eliza knew the answer to each of them was *yes.*

Ede said: "tell me. Is it in us all? Or was it Tom?"

Eliza stood.

She looked at the portraits, inwardly cursing her love of them. Cathleen and Malahide looked back at her. Their expressions, locked in paint, did not reflect the scene before them—only their aloofness from it—their noble but foolish certainty that all was for the best. The future they had dreamed did not, of course, embrace Lily Kilworth, now lying comatose.

Eliza—nodding at the paintings—said, without turning: "there is your answer."

Ede sat down and stared at her child. *Oh,* she thought. *Oh.*

Later, as Lily slept, Eliza sat in the shadows and told Ede The Story of Uncle John Fagan . . . This was the way Ede would describe it forever after—as if the story was a legend with a title. Or a fairy tale by the Brothers Grimm. *Once upon a time, in Dublin town, there lived . . .*

"He was my father's brother," Eliza said. "Dead before I had been told he was alive—though he lived into my time. This was, of course, in Dublin—back as long ago as that. My parents were married in 1840. I was born in 1843 . . ."

"I know all that, Mother."

"No, no. I'm telling the dates for my own sake. I need to calculate."

"Sorry."

Eliza gazed at the fire. "1843," she said. "Which means my Uncle John and my grandparents died in 1849."

"Why?"

"Because I was six."

"You came here when you were six. To Canada."

"That's right. And the story of Uncle John Fagan will tell you why."

Eliza drifted for a moment, somewhere inaccessible in the past. Finally, Ede spoke.

"Mother? What happened?"

Eliza leaned forward into the light.

"There was a fire," she said. "The house burned down. You know that, of course, but . . ."

Ede waited.

"What you don't know is . . . I've always lied about this. Lied. Deliberately. Even your father doesn't know the true story. Now—" she looked at Lily "—it has been forced into the open. I'm sorry, Ede. I'm sorry, my darling. I wish I didn't have to tell you."

Ede sat back.

"Tell me."

"Yes."

There was another pause while Eliza collected herself. And then: "Uncle John Fagan had the falling sickness. That's what they called it then. *Epilepsy.* But not. Not just epilepsy—but worse. It was . . ."

"Oh, God," Ede said, barely audible—and put her head down, covering her face with her hands.

Eliza continued as if she had not heard or seen this.

"He was . . . mad," she said. "He had visions. My father told me this. Uncle John lived in another world. Not—not this one. Not ours—where there is reason. He spoke to God. God spoke to him. Not in voices, but in writing. God wrote . . ." Eliza paused, with her eyes closed, as though to see the next words in her mind. "God wrote on the walls," she said.

"What?" Ede said. "God wrote? What did he write?"

Eliza stood up, forcing herself out of the chair, using her hands against her knees to push herself upright. Ede heard the heavy folds of her mother's skirts rearranging themselves as she stepped towards the Empire sideboard.

"Death," Eliza said. "It was all about death."

She lifted the stopper away from one of the decanters and Ede heard her pouring whiskey into one tumbler—and then another.

"Death by fire." Eliza brought the tumblers to Ede and handed her one. Nothing was said about the drink. Eliza did not even pause. Having sipped, she went to the mantelpiece and collected a tin box of matches. Then she set her tumbler in its place and turned back into the room.

"*Life is a flame,*" she said, "*but if we flame, we die.* My father saw that written on the walls . . ." Eliza removed the chimney from one of the lamps and struck a match. "Attic walls. Under a sloping ceiling, I suppose. I never saw it. This was the Dublin attic where Uncle John Fagan spent the whole of his adult life. Hidden—but not in hiding. He was kept there by his parents—*for his safety's sake*. And because they were ashamed . . . which in itself is shaming. But . . ." She shrugged.

Ede watched as the corner where Eliza stood began to fill with light.

Now, Eliza passed methodically from lamp to lamp, lighting them one by one as the story unfolded.

"Another thing written," she said, "was: *blessed be the name of God forever and ever—for wisdom and might are His. He revealeth the deep and secret things—He knoweth what is in the darkness, and the light dwelleth with Him.*"

Ede was watching Lily. Eliza was now at the centre of the room. Two of the six lamps had been lit. Moving on, she said: "the writing itself was painted onto the plaster with paintbrushes. Quite elaborate. Uncle John had some artistic talent, apparently—but he was childlike . . . childlike and simple. Not a simpleton, but simple—the way that children are simple. He used pure colour—water-colours—all the letters in red and orange. Green and blue. This, too, my father told me, saying: *God's writing on the wall was like an illuminated manuscript. All the capital letters were decorated with leaves and bees and singing birds . . .*"

Ede drank. Her throat burned. Her throat and the underside of her tongue.

Eliza said: "*every man that shall hear the sound of the cornet, flute, harp, sackbut, psaltery and dulcimer—and all kinds of music, shall fall down and worship the golden image.*" She struck another match. "I remember having to learn the names of those musical instruments when I was five years old," she said. "Not only all their names, but the order in which they were given. I didn't know why, of course. My grandmother forced them on me, the way that geese are force-fed in France, so their livers will be enriched. And swollen. *The cornet, flute, harp, sackbut, psaltery and dulcimer . . . and all kinds of music.* Yes?"

Four lamps had been lit. Two with red shades, two with green. Eliza now moved to the rear of the room, where the lamps had golden shades—glass shades with blue pendants on tall chimneyed lamps—the tallest in the parlour.

"All who did not fall down," she said, "were to be *cast into the midst of a fiery furnace.* Uncle John's chosen colour for this was red. Of course. Of course it was red . . . My father said there were drawings, too. Paintings of the fiery furnace. One whole wall was a depiction of flames. Drawn—painted—illuminated by God's hand. Shadrach, Meshach and Abed-nego . . . *bound in their coats, their hose and their hats, cast into the midst of the burning fiery furnace.*"

Eliza paused before she lifted the last chimney. She removed one of her prized linen handkerchiefs from its hiding place in her shirt-waist and wiped her eyes. Irish linen. Cream-coloured. Laced at the edges. Her eyes had been smoked with sulphur fumes from the matches. They were watering profusely and her nose was running. She dabbed at its end before she returned the handkerchief to its burrow. Then she struck the final match and flamed the last lamp. "There you have it," she said. "Uncle John Fagan—and fire."

Ede sat, staring. She held her tumbler of whiskey in both hands, cupping it between her knees. Eliza seemed a long way off, lambent in a yellow nimbus, almost floating in the lamplight.

Ede said, almost whispering: "the Dublin house was burned to the ground . . ."

"Yes."

"And Uncle John Fagan in it?"

"Yes. Uncle John Fagan in it—and Malahide—and Cathleen Fagan with him."

Someone sighed.

It was Lily.

But not awake—merely stirring, turning her back on the room, reaching with one hand up to the top of the sofa.

Eliza returned to the mantelpiece, where she set the tin box back in its place and drank from her tumbler. Looking down, she saw that she had closed her other hand around a bouquet of dead matches.

Well. It was fitting.

She threw them into the fire.

Beside her, Ede was transfixed. Still seated, she could not remove her gaze from the portraits on the farthest wall—lit now with wavering light.

And Malahide—and Cathleen Fagan with him.

She had never known this. None of it.

Reaching out blindly, she took Eliza's hand and squeezed it.

"Thank you," she said, "for telling me."

Then she stood up and went to the sofa. Lily was fast asleep. Ede pulled the shawl-blanket higher.

"I may be late, Mother, coming in to dinner," she said. "I'm going to sit here with Lily."

13. In Toronto, they looked at houses on Huntley, Colby and Linden streets. Ede had a predetermined image of where in this city she could abide. If there could not be fields, there had to be trees—if there could not be hills, there had to be ravines— somewhere to walk—somewhere to breathe.

The long, wide residential streets of choice were Jarvis and Sherbourne—laid down side by side beneath a canopy of elm and chestnut trees set out from end to end in matched straight lines on snowy boulevards.

Ede had seen the houses along these avenues drawn in magazines. The families who lived in them had names evocative of wealth and fame: Massey, Gooderham, Mulock, Trent—and others, not so well known. It was Frederick's hope one day to join his name to theirs, to take his provisions from Michies and his suits from Lowndes. But these were conventional ambitions. They in no way set him apart from the majority of determined young men with their eyes on the twentieth century about to blossom in their path. Anything would be possible in this coming time. But the realist firmly rooted in Frederick's character told him to play the present within his means.

This way, they turned their eyes to the streets in the shadow of Jarvis and Sherbourne, where the houses bore a more modest relationship to the pocketbook.

On Huntley Street, there was a house Frederick favoured which Ede found dreadful and forbidding. It had all the necessary attributes for a house that was intended to accommodate a family with children and servants, but not a single attribute for a person who wanted to see the sun shine. It was cloistered in the extreme, with doorways and windows so deeply recessed that not a hint of light could penetrate beyond them. Its hallways were narrow and dark and its stairways were steep and enclosed. The reception rooms were thin and cold and only one of them had a fireplace—and this so tiny, the grate would not hold more than a single shovelful of coal at a time. The dining-room was inhospitable and the kitchen had all the warmth of an institution.

"No," Ede said emphatically. "I could not live here."

"But the price, Edith. The price."

"Do you want me to marry you?"

"Of course I do."

"Then we will not buy this house."

Having said this, Ede stepped out through the door onto the verandah, where the agent was waiting for their decision. "I hope you will forgive me for saying so," she said, "but men do not know how to buy houses. They see them only as real estate, whereas women are looking for somewhere to live."

Frederick, donning his hat, came out to join them.

"I have a house just north of Bloor Street you might want to see, Mister Wyatt," the agent said. "It has . . ."

"I thank you, no," said Frederick. His mind was set on the proximity of the *barons*—the leaders of industry who lived east and west of where they stood. "We will continue our search in this neighbourhood."

The agent nodded and pulled the door to behind him. Having heard the tone of the argument that preceded Ede's exit from the

Huntley Street house, he decided he must now conspire with her if he was to sell anything to the Wyatts. He would have been greatly—though pleasantly—surprised if they had purchased the house just viewed. Now he better understood Ede's taste, he was confident that, with her help, he could turn the situation to his own advantage. There was a house on Selby Street that was unlisted, expensive—but irresistible.

Knowing that Mister Wyatt was not available to look at other houses that day, the agent turned to him and said: "perhaps your wife would care to inspect something else."

"We are not yet married," Frederick told him. "And, no—she will inspect nothing else."

"I beg your pardon," said the agent. "I assumed . . ."

"We will not be married till April," said Frederick. "You have until then."

14. The Wyatt Piano Factory had its gates on the south side of King Street, east of the Massey-Harris Manufacturing Company. Together, their red-brick buildings covered more than twenty acres of land. To the south, the Canadian Pacific and Grand Trunk Railway lines gave access *to the whole of Canada—and beyond.*

These were the brave words of brother Harry Wyatt as he greeted Ede, Eliza and Lily Kilworth on the morning of January 10th, 1898—a Monday. He was standing in the corridor waiting for them with Lizzie, the youngest Wyatt of all. Like the Kilworths, Lizzie had come to the factory at Frederick's invitation to see *its wonders as it prepared to enter the twentieth century.* Frederick himself was not present. Public relations were Harry's purview. And his pleasure.

Going to sleep the night before in the room she shared with Lily at the Sherbourne Hotel, Ede had been restless and ill at ease. All the way down in the train she had been fearful of Lily's reaction to the journey. The child—now seven—had never travelled before; never been in the presence of so many strangers; never been forced to sit still for such a long time. And tomorrow . . .

They would take a cab to the factory. The trolley would be unbearable, lurching along on its bumpy tracks through the snow. God knew what might happen. The thought of Tom's death was unavoidable—all those wagons and carriages—all those horses and people in the streets. And the slush and the mud in which Tom had died.

These thoughts were bad enough, but the thought of the factory itself was worse.

In Ede's imagining of them, all factories were fiery furnaces into which the poor and the despairing were driven, only to emerge with tormented spirits and broken bodies. She subscribed to Blake's image of *dark, satanic mills*, where human beings were bonded to diabolical machines—machines that were capable of killing them. The accounts Ede had read in the papers of industrial accidents had left her terrified and nauseated. *GIRL'S ARMS TORN OFF BY GIN-WHEEL! WORKER DECAPITATED IN PIANO FACTORY! MAN CRUSHED BY STEEL PRESS!* Why would one go willingly to such a place to be shown its *wonders*?

Beside her, Lily was already sleeping. Leaning down, Ede pulled some strands of hair from the child's mouth and kissed her on the cheek.

There had been no seizures now for a fortnight. Two weeks of freedom—two weeks of peace. And tomorrow . . .

Ede rolled away and watched the snow falling through the light of the street lamps beyond the windows.

The best thing about tomorrow—the most reassuring thing—was the prospect of Lizzie's presence. Ede had asked that he be there for Lily's sake. *Children give other children confidence*, she had told Frederick. *And Lizzie is such a gentle child.*

He's not a child any more, Edith.

How old is he, then?

Fifteen.

So—he's a boy. But still close enough to childhood.
He's twice Lily's age.

Ede had smiled at this. And said: *I seem to recall that you are somewhat older than me. And, if we were children . . .*

All right. All right. Lizzie will be there.

Another victory.

Ede, in her bed, smiled again—and on that smile, she had drifted into sleep.

The buildings of the Wyatt Piano Factory had once been the property of S. and A. Nordheimer. More recently, they had been in the hands of the Nordheimers' one-time partner—now their rival—Gerhard Heintzman. When Heintzman had moved his piano factory to the industrial wasteland known as The Junction, Frederick Wyatt had made his move and acquired the King Street property. He had waited ten years to do so. This was the terse, abbreviated version of the Wyatt story—the version that came to be *the Wyatt legend*—another of Harry's achievements.

The twists and turns of fortune that accounted for this legend were not discussed. The piano business was like any other in its time. Attempting to seize the new century as his own private territory, each man whose name appeared on the instruments of the new age was determined to dominate the field. Not, by outward appearances, a cutthroat business, it was nonetheless competitive to the last degree. There were millions to be made in the surge to put *a piano in every parlour*—as the Wyatt slogan proclaimed. And every manufacturer wanted those millions in his own pocket. There was no polite way of saying you wanted to bury your rivals—but the Victorian Age, then drawing to a close, had found a dozen ways to put a good face on it. The word *finesse* was the current substitute for *bury*. If you could *finesse* your rival, he went under—and you were the king of spades.

Harry Wyatt had seemed the least impressive of the Wyatt brothers when Ede first encountered him in 1890. Then in his mid-twenties, he was now thirty-four—two years younger than Frederick, one year older than Tom. Of the three wives of Lisgard Wyatt, the first had been Harry's mother—and Frederick's and Franklin's. Clearly, she must have died very soon after Harry's birth, since Tom was born barely one year later to the second Mrs Wyatt.

Ede could not help receiving an impression of the second Mrs Wyatt waiting in the wings, already wearing her wedding dress. *Who can these women have been?* she wondered, each of whom had followed so closely on the departing heels of the other. Each of whom was doomed to die in childbirth or its aftermath. Each of whom was nameless. Every time Ede contemplated these women, the image of a dark, unhappy house rose up before her— filled with motherless sons and its Ahab of a patriarch. Now, she would join them there—the current *Mrs Wyatt*. One more victim—or the lone survivor. *At least*, she thought, *I can be identified. I have a name—I'm not just someone's mother . . .*

Harry wore elegant, custom-made shoes. It was more than clear that he loved his feet. He went to great lengths to show them off. His trousers were cut unfashionably short though, in every other sense, they were stylish: tight around the buttocks and thighs; tighter still at the calf. But it was Harry's shoes that told the tale. Ede had never seen their like. They must have cost a fortune— beautiful shoes, with fine, soft toes and high inset arches—laced, not buttoned. Black. The heels were of layered leather and they made the slightest clicking sound as Harry walked. With every step he took, Ede fancied he might be going to dance.

Lily had no interest in *Uncle Harry*. She had been watching *Uncle Lizzie*—looking at him guardedly, sideways. She saw very few other children at Munsterfield and those she saw were seen at a distance—schoolgirls and farm boys in aprons and overalls. Lizzie was not like them. His eyes were unsettling—mysterious— mischievous—and his skin was white—pale as the paper she drew on with her pencils. Why had her mam not told her about him— Uncle Lizzie, with his girlish name and his storybook eyes. And his wide, white smile.

When he caught Lily staring at him, Lizzie grinned at her and gave a waist-high wave with his hand—like a secret signal. He also winked.

Very slowly, Lily smiled. And immediately looked away—alarmed. Lizzie had seen her, and she felt as though she had never been seen that way before.

"This is what we call the rubbing deck," Harry told them, pulling open a massive wooden door, covered with battered, shiny tin.

"Oh, my goodness," said Eliza. "Smell the oil and wax! It's wonderful!"

Harry pulled the door closed behind them.

"That's lemon oil," he said. "We use it to protect the wood and enhance the sheen."

"Any woman knows that," said Eliza—smiling as she said it.

Two dozen men in heavy cardigans and cotton aprons were disposed about a large, airy room whose beams were twenty feet above the floor. Long frosted windows faced north, each window topped with an angled transom.

"The transoms have to be open in every weather," Harry informed them, "because of the fumes from the oil and the wax. That's why so many of these men are wearing sweaters." Some men, Ede noted, were also wearing scarves.

The air, though cool, was not icy. Still, it was cold enough to see your breath. Lizzie turned his collar up and wrapped his arms around his chest.

"Why aren't they wearing gloves?" Eliza wanted to know.

Harry laughed.

"They couldn't work in gloves, Mrs Kilworth," he told her. "It's their hands they use as buffers."

"I don't understand," said Ede.

Harry introduced them to a quartet of men, all of whom were working on the same dark piece of wood. Clearly, by its shape, it was to be the top of a grand piano and the men who were clustered around it were polishing it with paste wax, using only the palms of their hands and the tips of their fingers to do so.

Two of the men looked to be in their twenties or early thirties. One of them could not have been more than sixteen. The fourth was much older and had, himself, the look of someone cut from wood and carved with a knife. His skin was like the finest leather, stretched so tight on his bones it gave the impression of being mummified.

This man's name was Robinson, *master of oils and polishes*. The boy was one of six apprentices on the rubbing deck.

Robinson showed off his hands for the tourists—and prodded the other fellows, urging them to do the same. Ede was reminded of schoolchildren forced into a display of cleanliness. But the men did not seem to mind. On the contrary, they held out their hands with pride. The skin on the backs was the colour of rosewood—and the palms were a deep, shining red.

Eliza asked Mister Robinson if she might touch him.

"Of course," he said. "Everyone wants to touch me. Being *touched* is almost my second profession." Still holding out his hands, he displayed them, top and palm. "It takes many years to get such a patina."

Eliza removed her gloves and reached for the pads of the old man's fingers. They were like velvet.

"There are oils in the palm," he told her. "Human oils that are beneficial to the wood. This is why my crew and I polish barehanded. No rags, no chamois at this stage. Before this top is finished, other polishes, other waxes, various tinctures will be added—and these will be applied with cloths and brushes, but not at this stage."

"Don't you ever get splinters?" Ede asked.

Before Mister Robinson could answer, Harry said: "Mister Robinson wouldn't work in a factory where he was allowed to get splinters. By the time the pieces get to him, there has been so much sanding and smoothing there isn't any possibility of splinters."

"What do you do when you wash, Mister Robinson?" Eliza wondered. "What on earth would ever get rid of all that wax and oil?"

"Turpentine," said Lizzie.

"No, no, no!" Mister Robinson shouted while the other men laughed. "No, no, no!" Then, he held up his hands like prizes.

"The finish on these fingers is my fortune. Without it, I am dead."

"But . . ."

"How do you take care of the rest of your body?" This was Lizzie.

"Yes," said Ede. "A person, after all, must bathe, Mister Robinson." She was smiling.

The old man beamed. "In the bath house," he said, "I am famous!"

"Why is that?" Ede wanted to know.

Lizzie laughed—and Harry glared at him.

Mister Robinson was not perturbed. "I am the only man who goes to his bath in gloves," he said.

Ede smiled. "That must be quite a sight," she said. Now it was Eliza who was not amused. Ladies should not be discussing gentlemen's bathing habits. It was unbecoming. She coughed and gave Ede a tug at the elbow. "Ahem," she muttered.

"Thank you, Mister Robinson," said Ede, still smiling. "I hope we meet again."

Mister Robinson gave a nod and touched his forehead.

Standing back to let the tourists pass, the whole of his crew followed suit—touching their foreheads and bobbing. Ede was distressed. The apprentice actually went so far as to pull at his forelock.

"My goodness," she whispered as she walked away. "I don't think I care for that."

"You'd best get used to it," said Eliza. "You'll be living in a world where place has a different meaning than it does at home."

"So what am I supposed to do in return when they start pulling forelocks? Curtsey?" Ede was angry.

"Don't be ridiculous. Accept it as your due."

"But it's not my due, Mother. I haven't done anything to deserve it."

"Who has?" said Eliza. And when Ede looked, she saw that her mother was grinning. "Nonetheless, it's part of your station now. Nod a little—and breeze on by."

Ede stopped dead in her tracks.

"Yes? What?" said Eliza, still retaining the ghost of her grin.

"*Nod a little and breeze on by?* Where on earth did you learn to talk like that? *Breeze on by!* Good heavens, Mother." Ede began to walk again.

"I've been reading," said Eliza, following her. "Magazines. We're in a new age now—almost a new century—and that requires a new language."

"Unquote—no doubt. Was that in your magazine, too?"

"I suppose. I don't remember. But it does make sense—what with motor cars and talking machines and so forth . . . *Everything* is new . . ."

"Yes . . . well," said Ede. "Don't renew your character, Mother. We like you just the way you are."

All this while, they had been following Harry down a long, cool corridor with windows on both sides. Looking out, Ede could see a lumber yard on the one hand and a bay of loading docks on the other, with horses and wagons standing by.

Harry already stood at the far end of this covered walkway, with his hand on the lever of another massive door. "Next stop—the assembly department," he said. "This way, ladies." Then, seeing Lizzie, he added: "and gentleman."

Harry gave the lever a pull and the door slid away behind him.

A deafening roar of men and mallets greeted them.

Thirty workers stood on platforms set on either side of what appeared to be a rippling canvas river.

"What on earth . . . ?" Eliza exclaimed.

Metal rollers beneath the canvas allowed a series of upright pianos to be moved with relative ease from one pair of workers to the next. Each man had only one job to do and for each of these jobs a wooden mallet was employed.

"The rolling river is brother Franklin's innovation," said Harry. "You may not know that he loves the theatre—all things theatrical and tricky. He saw this contraption in a production of *Ben Hur* at the Hippodrome in New York and thought it was just what we needed here." Harry gave a wave at the canvas. "Sometimes I think he's a genius."

Lizzie at this moment suddenly leapt up onto brother Franklin's invention and, after a running start, took a long, rolling glide to the end of the assembly line—waving his cap at the workmen, as he sang:

> *I've been working on pianos*
> *All the livelong day!*
> *I've been working on pianos,*
> *Just to pass the time away!*

Everyone but Lily cheered and applauded. Lily stood thunderstruck.

At the far end, Lizzie jumped down and ran back, laughing, to the others.

"Yessiree," he grinned. "Brother Frank is a regular genius, all right!"

Then he turned to Lily and said: "you want to go for a ride?"

Lily looked at Ede. *May I?*

Ede nodded, smiling.

Eliza said: "no—don't let her. She'll fall."

"No she won't, Mrs Kilworth," said Lizzie. "I won't let her."

All the workmen set their mallets aside to watch, standing on their platforms with folded arms. Between them, the gleaming pianos formed a train.

"All aboard!" cried Lizzie, stepping up to the canvas track. He put out his hands for Lily.

Eliza heaved a sigh, and said to Ede: "be it on your head."

Lily stepped forward.

Lizzie offered her his arm.

Lily was smiling. Ede was enchanted. Most often, Lily's round, sad face was expressionless.

"Are you ready?" Lizzie asked.

Lily nodded, still not having uttered a word.

"Here we go, then."

Taking Lily's hand, Lizzie placed his arm around her waist—just as he would on a ballroom floor. Lily felt giddy. She had never danced with a boy before—only ever alone, or with her mam.

"One! Two! Three!" Lizzie cried. And they began their run.

Eliza held her breath and closed her eyes.

Smooth as skaters on ice, Lizzie and Lily rolled along the assembly line—two perfect dancers, gliding through a waltz.

The workmen applauded and cheered. Some of them whistled. Harry went to the other end of the canvas, where four or five pianos awaited transport—finished except for their top lids and face boards.

Standing in front of one of these, he began to play and—to Ede's astonishment—to sing.

Harry was not a professional, like Tom, but he had determination and energy—and a sudden burst of joy, almost theatrical, rose up around them all, as if they had been transported onto the stage of the Hippodrome itself.

> *Casey would waltz with a strawberry blonde*
> *And the band played on!*

Still holding Lily, Lizzie jumped down from the ride and danced her round and round and round—waltzing her all the way back to where they had begun.

> *Da-da-dee-da-da-dee —*
> *da-da-dee-da-dah!*
> *And the band played on!*

The child in Lizzie's arms had been transformed. Ede almost wept. She had never seen Lily so alive.

As Harry closed the rolling door behind them, Ede took Eliza by the waist and did a waltz turn. "Oh!" she said, "Oh, Mother! Mother! I've never been so happy. Never."

In Lily's wicker suitcase, I found a souvenir of this occasion. I don't know why, but she had never shown it to me. It was a drawing—pencilled and painted—of *Lizzie dancing*. Clearly, my mother had put him on paper within hours of her return from that initial foray into the piano factory.

It is, of course, an image created by a child—but a child who could infuse her drawing with character and energy. Lizzie looks like George M. Cohan, standing there with one leg bent, its knee turned out to the side and one arm placed akimbo, hand on hip and the elbow making a perfect balance for the jutting knee. He also points his toes—and with his free hand reaches out—as though he were asking you to come down onto the page and dance with him.

Lily was seven years old, nearly eight, when she made this drawing—and the arms and legs, and Lizzie's clothes are crudely achieved. She has coloured him with brighter colours than he could have worn and the paint doesn't always stay within the lines. But the feeling of it is all too clearly an expression of love— of a childish passion for her subject.

My mother often broke her reveries—those mystifying, over-extended silences into which she fell from time to time—with a fragment of song. *Casey would waltz with a strawberry blonde, and the band played on* . . . And I would wait for it to end. But it never did. Instead, it would degenerate into a barely audible humming of the tune—and I would hear the unmistakable tapping of her toes. Seated—always seated—in whatever twilight she was in, she would waltz with Lizzie until it got dark.

In the drawing, she has overlaid his face with white—and the only features shown are two smudged eyes and a pair of scarlet lips, whose smiling redness has still not faded—even now, though more than thirty years have passed since Lily sat above the page and placed it there.

15. The house they ended up buying was indeed the one on Selby Street—the unlisted delight the agent had hoped would catch Ede's attention. This put them squarely in Frederick's neighbourhood of *barons*. It was also the district Ede knew best in the whole of Toronto.

There were trees in front of all the houses on Selby Street and the Rosedale ravine was quite nearby with its cart track and its bridle path. The graveyard where Tom was buried lay within walking distance and you could catch the electric street railway right around the corner on Sherbourne.

The house itself might have been the house of Ede's dreams.

Sitting well back on the north side, its lot also contained a stable and a vegetable plot. There were fences and gardens, porches and a vine, rooms filled with light and a staircase with landings wide enough to dance on. Ede was particularly pleased it was not hemmed in on either side by houses built so close that a person could not walk in between them. Closeness was a feature of city life that Ede could not get used to.

"Some people live in houses where the people next door can hear them breathe!" she told Eliza. "Strangers can look right into your dining-room and tell the rest of the world what you had for dinner! I don't know how they live like that—I know I couldn't."

Eliza blinked and wondered what Ede would do when she discovered the noise a city makes, and the fact that a city never sleeps. And the sorry news that she'd seen her last cow and would never hear a rooster crow or step out the door into a world of fields. Well—there was always the train to McCaskill's Mills and a person could always come home.

"I'll be at home," said Ede.

"No," said Eliza. "Home is where you were born, not where you bide."

There was only one aspect of the Selby Street house that Ede found alarming. It had an attic.

She had thought it was just a cupboard when she first saw the door—a door that should have opened on a linen closet. Instead, it opened onto a staircase.

There was a key in the lock and once Ede had turned it and seen what lay beyond, she felt like Bluebeard's wife. Her first impulse was to turn away. All she could think was—*Uncle John*

Fagan . . . A staircase had been the last thing she wanted to find. A shiver passed through her.

Down on the first floor, some workmen had begun to install additional electric lighting in places that Frederick had decreed. Perhaps they would lend her a lamp or a lantern. She would not go up without one.

Descending, she was able to persuade a young Dubliner to give up his kerosene lamp. Perhaps he could find some work to do in a less dingy corner than the one she had found him in. Because he was Irish, she almost asked him to escort her—but she resisted this. Her fear of the attic would not be solved by someone else's presence. It would only be solved if she faced it alone.

At the bottom of the narrow stairs, she removed her hat, not knowing why. *People do things all the time they can't explain,* she told the air. *The doing has a reason of its own.* Perhaps she removed the hat in order to leave it as a signal: *she's gone up,* the hat would inform them when they found it by the open door. It was her version of fairy tale breadcrumbs: *this way into the woods . . .*

And so—*go up.*

Yes.

The stairs were narrow—ladderlike, with open sides.

The lamp preceded her, held at arm's length, the fumes from its kerosene magnified by the lack of air into which it was being lifted.

When she got to the top, there had been fifteen steps in all. It was only then she discovered the trapdoor blocking her access to whatever lay beyond.

If you resist me, so be it. I refuse to use force.

But the trap was unbolted and light enough to be pushed with one hand. Some quantity of dust was disturbed in doing this and it roiled about in the lamplight while Ede tried to keep it from her eyes. Two steps more and she was onto the floor, the trapdoor lying flat beside her.

Some atavistic instinct made her speak.

"Is there anybody here?"

Yes.

The soft reassuring patter of mouse feet fled from the light. On the farm, if you heard no mice, you knew there was something wrong. A house in the country whose walls and ceilings did not announce the comings and goings of mice has been visited by creatures far less welcome: a ferret, perhaps. Or an owl.

This attic, so far as Ede could see, was large enough for storage and tall enough to stand in. It did, however, have steeply sloping ceilings and its rafters ran east to west. The house faced south.

Known dark was not alarming to Ede. Moving through familiar rooms, walking along the road or through the fields at home on a moonless night did nothing more than make you sensibly cautious. After all, a person didn't want to trip and fall. But the unknown dark of unfamiliar spaces—this was troublesome. It made her cringe, in spite of being able to lift the lamp against any part of the dark that was ominous.

Windows.

There was not a sign of them. Nor of any kind of ventilation. This was extraordinary. The first thing you learn on a farm is that barns and houses require ventilation. Otherwise—*what was it called?*—*spontaneous combustion*—a place could explode into flames.

Ede crouched down and felt her way along the walls. There must be some way light and air could be introduced to this dreadful space. But there was nothing—not the slightest hint that windows had once been present—boarded over or removed.

Don't tell Frederick . . .

Or what?

Something.

Attic.

Attic.

She did not like it.

Instinct—sudden as a banging door—spun her all the way back to the legendary attic in faraway Dublin. Fire . . . And the whole house razed.

Ede held the lamp out further into the dark. The mice, who might well never have seen such a light, raced from corner to corner—panic-stricken. All Ede could think was: *don't be afraid.*

And she said it: "don't be afraid." The mice fell silent, watching her. Waiting.

As Ede departed, the thought came back to her: *don't tell Frederick.* As if it could be kept from him. As if he did not already know.

By the time she had descended and closed the door, the cold dark feeling had begun to leave her and all her fearful thoughts were crowded, like the mice, into corners out of sight. Blowing out the lamp and retrieving her hat, she turned towards the room that would be Lily's. Already, it was papered in her mind with a pattern of field flowers—curtained with muslin. And on the wall, the birth-wreath tied with ribbon, waiting to welcome her daughter.

16. On a Friday morning in February, Ede took the streetcar down from in front of the Sherbourne Hotel to the piano factory. She wanted to have a few words with Frederick about one or two last-minute details regarding the house. She might have telephoned, but there were samples of curtain material she wanted him to see. On the 1st of March she would be returning to Munsterfield, where she would complete her trousseau with Eliza's help. Work on the Selby Street house had gone quite smoothly. Most days, Ede had spent time there making lists of its future needs; working with the seamstress hired to make the curtains; supervising the blending of paints and enamels so that every colour would be just right.

The streetcar ride was pleasant enough. Best of all, you could get off near enough to the factory gates that you had to walk only eight blocks—and that was nothing. From Sherbourne Street, the car turned west along King, making a loop up Spadina to Bloor, and back to Sherbourne.

Ede sat mid-car, right across from the pot-bellied stove. Outside, it snowed. She was glad to be alone. It gave her room to focus on the vital questions that needed answering in the few remaining weeks before the wedding. Lily was with Eliza. Loved and safe. Yes, Ede missed her, but during the days of separation, she knew—by its absence—the weight of the burden she had been carrying.

Burden. No. That's not the right word, she thought. *It's not a burden, but . . . what? Attention. Focus. The ordeal of endless watching—endless waiting. That was all. The constant vigilance, watching for the next sign—waiting for the next cry.*

At the factory, she went straight into the offices, where Harry and Frederick were discussing an advertisement soon to be placed in all the newspapers and magazines. It showed a pretty young woman seated at a Wyatt piano while she sang to a handsome young man. Off to one side, an older woman sat a little too primly, overseeing their courtship.

Frederick thought the ad was tasteful, elegant and reserved. Harry thought it should have more *zest.*

"*Zest,* Harry?"

"Yes. To begin with, take out the chaperone. That way we introduce an element of romantic tension. Also, it should be the young man playing the piano—while the woman dances for him."

"You must be mad," said Frederick. "Men only play pianos in saloons. As for a dancing woman—thank you very much—we have not descended to blatant displays—and we never will. No. I like it just the way it is."

Ede said: "why not let her dance, but keep the chaperone?"

Frederick was adamant. "Absolutely not. No dancing. Not with a Wyatt in the picture. These are *parlour* pianos, not . . . not . . ."

"Honky-tonk pianos?" Ede said. She was smiling.

Harry laughed.

Then Ede said: "why not let her stand by the piano, listening to him play? With a rose in her hand—and a faraway look in her eyes. Every woman in the world associates love with music."

Frederick said: "women don't buy pianos. Men do."

"Yes," Ede conceded. "But it's women who persuade them it's a necessity."

Delighted, Frederick sat back in his chair. "You hear that, Harry? You should hire this woman. All right," he said. "Let the man play the piano while the woman listens. But no rose. And leave in the chaperone."

Satisfied, Harry left them.

When Ede had discussed her few suggestions for the house, she showed Frederick the swatches of curtain material. Having received his approval, she returned them to her bag and, snapping it shut, she prepared to leave.

Frederick said: "tomorrow, I'm afraid I won't be able to take you to the station. I want you to promise me you'll take a cab."

"Yes, I will."

"Have you ample money?"

"Thank you." Ede nodded. "You're very generous."

"Will you be all right on the train? I'm nervous of your being alone."

"I'll be perfectly fine, Frederick." Ede was smiling, amused by his almost pompous concern for her safety. As if she did not know how to fend for herself. Still, it was equally charming. In his way, he was telling her he loved her—words he had not yet used.

"Will you promise to send a telegram the moment you step off the train in McCaskill's Mills?"

"I will."

They fell silent.

Ede made a pass with one hand over the pins at the back of her hair. She had started sweeping it up in a tight, rather married look which gave her a matronly appearance her years did not deserve. She was wearing a Prussian blue overcoat cut in the military fashion currently popular. The hat she had chosen that morning was a circlet of auburn sable—also military in style and the most expensive hat she had ever owned.

Frederick, she thought, looked truly splendid seated at his desk, with all his *presidential* insignia around him—the marble inkstand, the shiny telephone, the electric brass lamps. Behind him on the wall there were photographs of various Wyatt pianos. Also of Wyatt employees, gathered together in groups: the stringers, the carpenters, the felt-cutters, the polishers. And the office staff. It was all extremely impressive.

"Well, then," she said.

"Yes," said Frederick. "Indeed."

He stood up and came around the desk. Much to Ede's surprise, he all at once leaned forward and kissed her on the forehead.

"Goodbye, my dear," he said.

"Goodbye." She rose.

"Shall I walk you to the door?"

"No, no. Please don't bother." She did not want Frederick to know she had come on the streetcar and intended to return the same way. So long as she was alone, she wanted to learn as much about the city as she could. Its buildings—and its people. Streetcars, that way, were a gift. For a nickel, you could meet the whole world.

17. Outside, it was still snowing. Turning east on King Street, Ede began to walk towards the nearest crossing.

She had decided to *complete the loop* by taking the streetcar north on Spadina. This way, she would see parts of Toronto she had not yet encountered. Heading for the car stop, she glanced at the street signs she was passing. *Lockhart . . . Reynolds . . . Crawford . . .*

Crawford.

Crawford Street.

Ede felt as if she was going to drop. Eight years fell away and Tom's own voice spoke into her ear: *I live on Crawford Street . . .* he said.

Crawford Street.

Number 106.

Now. She would do it now. Alone.

Oh, dear heaven—at last, I'm going to see where he lived. I'm going to stand where he stood.

Turning north, she suddenly realized she had no idea of what to say when she knocked on the door of number 106. What if the woman who ran the boarding-house in Tom's time had died? Ede would have no way of knowing which room he had occupied. She thought it must be towards the front, because he so often described the sights and the sounds of the street in his letters.

The houses were not so large as she'd thought they might be. Semi-detached for the most part—tall, thin dead-looking houses with sickly trees—or none—in the yard.

10, 12, 14.

Little picket fences that might have been children's toys had been set down unpainted to show the shapes of tiny gardens. Newspapers blown up out of the gutters seemed to be all the hope of flowers that might bloom in the spring. Grey, icy snow was on everything.

64, 66, 68.

She had crossed over Adelaide Street where two wagons were blocking the traffic while their drivers argued and their horses stood numbly in the falling snow.

Ede began counting again.

82, 84, 86.

Finally, she walked into the shadow of a large, grey brick factory. Queen Street with its mass of cabs, carriages and pedestrians lay before her.

Queen Street.

Ede knew—as anyone did who lived in Toronto—that the dreaded Lunatic Asylum was just beyond that factory on her left. Even the thought of it made her shudder.

And there, just shy of the corner, was Number 106 Crawford Street.

Dear God.

Poor Tom.

Ede was stunned.

Had he gone home, all that time, to this? And not complained.

Though he'd always said it was simple enough, he had never said it was mean and broken down.

Thank heaven, there was a park on the far side of Queen where he could sit in the sun. But the house . . . so dreary and dead-looking.

On the other hand, Tom had lived here eight years ago and a lot can change in eight years. Change for the better—change for the worse.

All the windows had shades, most of them pulled over halfway down—some of them torn. None of the windows had curtains.

Ede went along the shovelled bricks that led to the front stoop. The walk was six feet in length, no more, the street was that close to the house. The door—solid wood—had no handle, only a keyhole.

Ede wondered why there was no sign that told of *Rooms To Let*. And not a sound from inside that made you think people lived here.

She knocked three times.

There was no response to this. She knocked again—louder.

At last, she heard an energetic step approaching. Her spirits lifted. Someone young, perhaps—someone smiling would greet her.

The door opened—halfway.

"Yes?"

A tousle-headed figure stood there in shirtsleeves and slippers. Ede was speechless.

It was Lizzie.

18. Ede had to play against her surprise—Lizzie was so obviously pleased to see her.

"Have you come to see my father?" he asked.

"Why, yes." *His father?*

"Don't stand out in the cold," said Lizzie. "Come right in."

The vestibule was small and dark, square and boxlike, leading to a hallway. What light there was came at an angle through open doorways. At what seemed a great distance—narrow and tunnelled—Ede could see the kitchen. To her right, there was a dingy room that passed for a parlour—rarely, if ever, used. The windows needed cleaning and one of them was cracked. Dust was layered evenly on tabletops and chair-backs. To her left, where a door was held ajar against a brick, a bedroom had been fashioned. A washstand and an iron cot could be seen—and a wooden chair painted red. On a table there were pots of daffodils and paperwhites, whose leaves had just begun to show. Ede knew at once this was Lizzie's room—a clearing in the woods.

In the far-off kitchen, a chair had been set in the middle of the floor so that anyone sitting there could watch along the passageway and see whoever came and went.

Lizzie said that his father was going blind. He was also bedridden.

"Have you brought him here because of Tom?" Ede asked.

"Tom?"

"Yes. This is where Tom lived when I knew him first," she said. "It was a boarding house then . . ."

Lizzie laughed. "That's crazy!" he told her. "We've always lived here—the lot of us."

"You have?"

Lizzie said: "sure. Never been a boarding house that I was told. I been here all my life and my brothers mostly. Well . . ." he smiled. "Maybe not mostly. They were gone from here ten years ago, when I was still a kid."

Tom had lied. And no wonder. Looking around her, Ede could not imagine there ever being room for all the Wyatt men.

Still, she could not understand why Lizzie and Mister Wyatt had stayed when there was so much Wyatt piano money. She did not, however, say this.

"Where might we find your father?" Ede was anxious to get away from the dark of the hall.

Lizzie said: "in the kitchen—where he always is."

"Should you tell him I'm here before I go through, do you think?"

Lizzie nodded and went along the passageway to the kitchen, where Ede could hear him talking to Lisgard, Senior—shouting almost, because the old man must be deaf as well as blind. She wondered how on earth a fifteen-year-old boy could cope with such a burden. And why did he have to? It seemed unconscionable.

She wished now she hadn't come. Better not to know how Tom had lived—in this squalor—in this darkness. Every word of description in his letters had been a lie. A necessary lie, she had to suppose—a lie required in order to survive this place. It might even be that Tom succeeded in transforming what he saw into an acceptable reality by filling it with his own light—the way that Lizzie survived, by means of a red painted chair and paperwhites. Light—that's what mattered.

When Lizzie came back, he said: "my father's not too good with visitors. He won't know who you are, I reckon."

"If visitors upset him, maybe I shouldn't go in."

"Oh, no. You've got to go in now I've said you're here. He'd be mad if he felt the draught from the door and thought you'd left without letting him look at you."

"You said he was blind."

"Near blind. Not total."

Lizzie turned around and started back to the kitchen. "There's a dog out here," he said. "I hope you don't mind."

"I love dogs," said Ede. "We always have dogs at home on the farm."

They came to the kitchen.

Lizzie went on through and turned towards the left-hand side of the room.

At a glance, Ede took in a sink, a stove and some chairs—a table off to the right and a door that led to the yard or perhaps a shed. Windows gave a view of the leaden sky. Nothing more.

Lisgard Wyatt lay on a bed whose side was pressed in hard against the wall. The dog was lying at his feet—a yellow dog, perhaps a Labrador—Ede wasn't sure. Its tail was working a slow, hard thump against the blankets, the only sign of greeting from the bed. The old man lay, propped up against some pillows whose cotton casings were grey with age, not grime. His hands lay flat against a turned-down sheet of the same description.

The wood stove gave a cracking sound, as if to prove it was alive. Its heat was welcome. Ede took off her gloves and went to stand where Lisgard could see her.

"Hello," she said.

He did not reply.

"Can he hear me?"

Lizzie nodded.

Ede drew a chair from the table and placed it beside the bed. She petted the dog, whose tail went on thumping.

"The dog's name is Buster," Lizzie said.

"Hello, Buster," said Ede. And then, to Lizzie's father: "I've come especially to see you."

She sat down and laid one hand on top of his.

"Get out," he said. His voice was just a whisper.

Ede sat back, unsure of what she had heard.

"It's all right," Lizzie told her quietly. "He doesn't mean it for you—only for who he thinks you are."

"And who might that be?"

"My mother, perhaps. Or one of his other wives."

"Get out," the old man repeated, but the words were flat and without inflection. Anger wasn't in them, nor demand. He was simply making noise. "Get out."

Ede said: "do you know who I am? I'm Edith Kilworth, Mister Wyatt, and I'm going to be married to your son Frederick."

"Alice," he said.

"No, not Alice. *Edith*."

Lizzie said: "Alice Williams was Frederick's mother."

"I see."

"Get out."

"But I've come especially," said Ede. "Do you remember meeting me all those years ago? In 1890? I came to Tom's funeral."

"Jane," said the old man.

"That's Jane Williams. Alice's sister. She was Tom's mother," said Lizzie.

"Horses," said Lisgard. "Get out."

"Tom was killed by horses," said Ede. "He remembers that."

"Yes."

Ede leaned forward. "Is Lizzie taking good care of you, Mister Wyatt?" she asked.

"Margaret," he said.

"Margaret Beeton," said Lizzie. "She was my mother."

"Get out."

"That's always his reaction when my brothers are mentioned. And me," Lizzie explained. And then: "*Harry*," he said. And his father said: "Alice."

"You see?" said Lizzie. "It's just as if you pressed a button. He only remembers us by our mothers."

Ede was thinking: *Alice. Jane. Margaret.* Named at last.

"Perhaps I should let him be," she said. "Whoever he thinks I am, he obviously wants me to leave."

"It's only because they died on him," Lizzie said. "He blames them, you see—for dying."

Ede stood up. She had no desire to stay, but she wanted to find some decent way to say goodbye. She moved her chair away from the bed and knelt in its place.

"I'm going to go now, Mister Wyatt," she said. "I'm so very glad I've seen you."

She gathered both his hands in hers. Buster lifted his head and watched with interest.

Lisgard said nothing. His gaze remained fixed.

Just as she began to rise, Ede felt the old man's fingers tighten against her own. Once she was on her feet it was clear that he wanted to draw her down in order to speak without Lizzie hearing.

Leaning in close to his lips, Ede said: "I'm listening."

Then he said, quite clearly: "Tom was a good boy. Remember that."

"Yes," said Ede. "I do remember. Thank you."

"Goodbye, then."

"Yes," said Ede. "Goodbye."

She straightened.

He let her fingers withdraw from his and closed his eyes. Ede stood and watched him for a moment, thinking how extraordinary it was that he did know who she was. *Tom's girl—everybody says so.*

She looked away. "I'll go along, now. We'll meet again, I'm sure."

The door that would release her seemed a great way off.

Lizzie said: "I'll come and let you out."

When Ede was at last on the walk, she heard the door close behind her. But when she heard its key being turned and the bolt applied, she stopped dead in her tracks.

No, she thought. *No. This is wrong.*

She turned around and went back onto the stoop and knocked.

When Lizzie answered, she opened her arms and took him into an embrace. Nothing was said. Lizzie's arms slowly rose to hold Ede against him. She was crying.

All she could think was that she and Lizzie were in the same boat—adrift on the same sea—he with his father and she with Lily.

"It's going to be all right," she said. "It's going to be all right, I promise."

It was then that she knew what he needed to hear—knew it because she wanted so desperately to hear it herself.

"You aren't alone," she said. "You are not alone."

19. My grandmother told me that story long after Lisgard Wyatt had died. By then, her parting words to Lizzie had become one of Lily's songs. The first time I was aware of them, however, the words themselves were unvoiced.

Lily had taken me into a restaurant during one of our escapes. I was seven years old—maybe eight. The War was not yet over, that's a certainty. Maybe I was only six. It doesn't matter. The thing is, I was still very much a child.

Sometimes I would lose her. She would disappear. I constantly had to be on the alert—especially during our escapes, when Lily was already in a travelling mode. She could say to me: *sit here, Charlie. Wait for me. I'm only going to the washroom . . .*

Then she would not come back.

On this particular escape, we ended up in a restaurant. Dead of night—mid-winter. I don't remember why we had to escape—it was probably the usual: a demon in her dreams. *Get up,* she would say in the dark, *we're leaving now.* After we were dressed—we ran. It was always the same. She carried the wicker suitcase in one hand—and with the other, she pulled me after her. In the suitcase, she kept our *escape kits* . . . ropes, screwdrivers, wrenches—a change of clothes. Chocolate bars. We ran until she felt safe. Safety was distance—the distance she could put between herself and the demon.

In the restaurant that night, we chose a table near the door—in case the escape should have to be continued. Lily ordered coffee and toast. I had cocoa. That was all I wanted—besides my bed.

Lily sat and smoked while her toast and her coffee got cold. Her eyes had the look I later came to recognize as her *mirror gaze.* I might just as well not be there during these episodes, when she went back into herself the way a person will enter a haunted house. *Is there anybody here . . . ?* She never came back out until she knew the demon was gone.

As always, I sat waiting for her return. There was no point speaking. Sometimes I dozed. Sometimes I even fell asleep. But not this night. I was physically tired from the running but I was wide awake.

"Charlie?"

She was back. Whispering.

"There's a man over there. Do you see him?"

He was behind me. My job had been to watch the door. No one had entered, so I guess the man must have been there when we arrived. Now that I saw him, I turned away so quickly, I knocked my cup aside.

The man had alarmed me. Frightened me. He seemed to have no face. His nose was gone and there was just a hole where his mouth should have been.

What could have happened to him?

"He must have been in the War, Charlie," Lily said. She was looking at him frankly—not staring, merely gazing almost languidly in his direction.

"More than likely fire did that to him."

I wanted desperately to leave. But Lily stayed. So I stayed, too. We sat there another five minutes before she spoke again.

"Stand up," she said. "Bring the suitcase."

At last, we were leaving.

But no.

We didn't leave.

Lily started to walk towards the back of the café.

Now, I knew what was happening.

Lily had found a stranger—who needed her.

"It's so cold up there at the front by the door," she said to the man. "Do you mind if we come and sit back here?"

The man—whose eyes were lidless—shook his head and ducked back into the collar of his overcoat. He stared down into his coffee cup—perhaps alarmed, perhaps relieved. I couldn't tell. I was so afraid of looking at him that I barely saw him there. Only the shape of him, with his lowered head and his shoulders hunched.

Lily sat down across from him at his table and gestured for me to do the same. I did—but I still wasn't looking.

The waiter came and Lily ordered another cup of coffee and another cup of cocoa. When the waiter had gone, Lily took off her heavy scarf and laid it down beside her. Then she undid the buttons of her overcoat and gave a sigh.

"I was so relieved to see someone sitting here," she said. "The city offers so few people at night . . ."

The man nodded.

I was now peeking out from my own lowered head. I had pretended to read a menu up until that moment.

"Can you speak?" Lily asked.

The man shook his head.

"That's all right," said Lily. "Everyone doesn't have to speak."

The man looked up at this—directly into Lily's face.

She smiled.

Then, quite slowly so as not to alarm him, she reached across the table and took his hand in hers.

The man—I think unbelieving—looked down at the knot of their fingers—entwined. It was just as though someone had handed him a thousand-dollar bill—or a diamond big as a fist.

In his throat, he made a noise—the breath, but not the shape of words.

The waiter came.

And retired.

No one spoke.

We sat that way for half an hour.

At first, I didn't understand why they went on holding hands for so long.

And then I did.

Lily was telling him that he was not alone.

Three
1898—1903

Love, oh love, oh careless love,
Love, oh love, oh careless love,
Oh it's love, oh love,
Oh careless love,
You see what careless love has done.

Traditional

1. All of this happened before I was born, but all of it is known to me as though I had been there. Granted, there are places where I lose my way in the connective tissue joining events that are known. Questions remain: *how did Lily get from here to there—from this episode to that?* The days and months in between are clouded. On the other hand, these clouded moments exist in the lives we know most intimately—our own.

Of the years in the Selby Street house, I know the following: that Lily suffered there; that Ede, my grandmother, suffered also because of the torment of what was done to Lily—and for other reasons, too. But good things also occurred—decent things—amusing things—happiness.

Ede and Frederick were married in the spring of 1898, away from the world at large. In spite of the fact that his own mother's sister had married his father, Frederick did not want to publish the news that he was going to marry his brother's "wife." For so he thought of Ede—and so her status had been described. Otherwise Lily would have to be acknowledged as Ede's illegitimate child and Frederick was not about to put up with that. So far as the world at large was concerned, he was marrying a widow—a mystery woman. Anonymous. She was beautiful. She was charming. She was discreet. Her soon-to-be-eight-year-old daughter would not appear until the honeymoon was over.

The wedding, not unlike Tom's funeral, was conducted in a chapel by a minister who gave the impression he would rather be elsewhere. Certainly, his mind was elsewhere, burying the dead. At the very instant the ring had been placed on Ede's finger, the reverend minister intoned: *man that is born of woman hath but a short time to live, and is full of misery* . . . Not exactly what Ede and Frederick had hoped to hear in that moment.

A lounge on the second floor of the Queen's Hotel on Front Street in Toronto had been rented by James and Eliza for a small reception that afternoon. *It seems every town and every city in the country has a Queen's Hotel,* Eliza had said. And James had added: *more than likely every town and city in the whole British Empire . . . Yes,* the manager had said, *but this is* the Queen's Hotel. Which, indeed, it was—the grandest and most sumptuous Toronto had to offer—with the railway station just across the street and, beyond that, a view of the islands sitting in their bay.

Eliza had spent their money lavishly—little round tables with cloths—fresh flowers on every one—and an elegant meal—and a cake, all served by waiters in dark blue jackets and starched white aprons. James had ordered a bar with Irish whiskey—and three cases of champagne. It was splendid.

Partway through the meal, Ede had a sudden fit of giggles about the minister's grim mistake and could not contain herself. The guests—to say nothing of Frederick—were astonished when she ran all at once from the room and gave way to peals of laughter in the corridor. Brother Liam went to retrieve her, furious because she was disgracing herself in a public place.

"How?" she asked, still laughing, "am I disgracing myself?"

"By making a spectacle here in the hall."

Ede looked around and said: "but there's no one here, Li. No one but thee and me . . . !" And off she sailed again, head back, her hands on the wall and her feet doing a dance on the parquet floor.

"Will you be quiet!" Liam hissed. "They'll be sending the manager to see what's wrong."

"Tell him we've just returned from a funeral," said Ede. "He wouldn't dare interfere with grief."

"You're incorrigible."

"Damn right I am."

"I beg your pardon."

"I said: *damn right* I'm incorrigible. Damn right I am! And what a pity you're not."

"You s-s-swore," said Liam, stuttering, his cheeks going red. "You *swore*," he said again. "You *swore!*"

"Oh, for heaven's sake!" said Ede, turning on him angrily, all her laughter gone. She splayed her feet, set her arms akimbo and shouted both ways down the corridor. "Damn, I said. Hot damn and God damn! Did you hear me? *Damn!*"

"Edith . . ." Liam paled with alarm.

Ede went past him along the hall to the door that opened into the reception lounge. Stepping across the threshold, she looked back out at her brother and said to him: "go to hell!" And slammed the door.

Liam stood there immobilized.

He did not know what to do. He could not go back to the party—everyone would know what she had said to him. A man with wit would have gone straight in and said: *Ede just told me to go to hell—but I've decided to stay right here . . .*

Instead, he retreated to the bar beside the dining-room, where he calmed himself with a glass of whiskey. One—and then another . . . and then one more.

Family—and family only—had been invited to the reception. None but family had been in the chapel. Franklin and Willa had made up the rest of the wedding party. Even so, not everyone invited could attend. Lisgard did not attend—and, therefore, neither could Lizzie. Malahide did not attend, being too devoted to his pregnant cows, refusing to leave them now, as the birthing season had begun. And Lily did not attend because . . .

Ede had to pause before she could bring herself to think of the words.

Lily could not attend, because . . .

Out it came. But only in her mind.

Frederick would not acknowledge her until after the honeymoon.

Ede's lovely moment in the chapel would not be shared by her daughter. The Piano Man's daughter.

Frederick had forbidden it.

His *no* had been an iron fist. He slammed it down and nothing more was said.

2. The wedding had been mid-April—*after Easter and before the first of May*. That had been Ede's decree, because she had wanted to avoid her period. The honeymoon was taken at Niagara Falls in the Duke of Wellington Hotel. That had been Frederick's decree. In Niagara Falls, the whole world had just been married. This way, he hoped to escape attention. *Anywhere else*, he had said, *our brand new luggage and your new clothes would have screamed the word NEWLYWEDS for every ear to hear. At least, at Niagara Falls, we'll be lost in the crowd.*

On the train, Frederick was silent. Ede took his arm where they sat and watched the passing fields through the window. April was such a promising month. The first wet hint of green was in the grass and the trees had visible buds. A few of the dogwoods standing along the fence rows even had a branch or two of blossoms. *Look,* said Ede, *there are deer over there at the foot of that hill.* Three of them, each of them pregnant and near her time.

Ede thought of Lily, far away at Munsterfield with Malahide. Lily, born in a field, watching now the same late afternoon light as the sun began its long descent. Lily, born in a field, who would sleep that night in a truckle-bed at Freda's feet. Lily, born in a field, who had never known her father.

One day, Ede knew, she would have to reveal Lily's condition to Frederick. *Tell him—yes—but not yet.* Not yet. She would have to find some way to explain it so that he would not be fearful about the children she knew he wanted them to have together. Sons and daughters. *Sons and daughters. Children. Children. Oh . . .* How could she tell him—what could she say—why must she break his heart?

And her own.

She knew that Frederick's ignorance of Lily's seizures had been abetted by his determination to hold the child at a distance. And because—in the moment—she was glad of this ignorance, she forgave him. Besides, so much was going on in his own life, what with the weight of the factory and his impending marriage and the buying of the house, he clearly had no inclination to be in the company of children. That would come later, when they all lived together under one roof. For now, he extended a cordial greeting, a friendly hand and a kindly smile. And the express wish—never voiced in Lily's hearing—that she remain for as long as possible with her grandparents at Munsterfield.

As long as possible, Frederick? Ede had asked. *What does that mean?*

Until we've returned from the honeymoon and have settled into our house. And the servants are in place. I want you to have every bit of help you require.

Don't be ridiculous, Frederick. I've brought Lily up and taken care of her for eight years all by myself.

Oh?

Yes!

You mean without the support of your parents and your brothers and your sister—three hired hands—the German woman and her daughter? My, my! However did you manage?

He was smiling when he said this—smiling amiably—indulgently—the way a father might have smiled at a child's exaggeration of her adventures. *All by yourself? You are extraordinary!*

Ede had been forced to laugh.

Charming. He could be so damned charming, she thought, sitting there beside him on the train. *Charming. But still arrogant.*

And right.
Dammit.

On the other hand, the fact remained that Ede had carried the terror of Lily's illness—the dread of its consequences—the fear for Lily's safety—her survival—her rights. All of these, she had carried alone.

And the fear of telling Frederick. That, too, was borne alone. Emphatically.

Frederick watched their reflections in the window, static against the moving sky as it began to redden beyond the glass. His wife was seated there beside him, leaning down towards the handbag in her lap. He wondered when, if ever, she would fall in love with him. Truly, truly fall in love, as he had fallen in love with her. That had been eight years ago, when he'd gone to Munsterfield to tell Ede of Tom's death. Eight years, one month, fourteen days and sixteen hours. The minutes were beyond Frederick's powers to calculate. They passed before he could give them numbers. *Tonight*, he was thinking. *Tonight. Tonight.* And then, all at once, he stopped. Ede was pressing a handkerchief against her cheek. Had she wept? He dared not look. Instead, he kept his gaze on her reflection. From the lowered angle of her profile as she replaced the handkerchief in her bag, he knew Ede's thoughts were not of *tonight*, but of something else. The child, no doubt. No doubt, the child. Not of *tonight*, but of *Lily*.

Neither word was spoken.

3. As the wedding reception was coming to an end at the Queen's Hotel in Toronto, Eliza turned to James and said: "where is Liam?"

"Perhaps he went across the road to the station, so he could wave goodbye to them."

"You think so? Oh, no, James—I doubt it." That would have been too congenial.

It was not as if Liam and Ede had ever been the best of friends. They tolerated one another, but that had been the extent of their relations. Ede had loved Jamie—*adored him*—and Liam had known this. Besides which, there was his own coolness—his own aloofness. Even as a little child, Liam had never wanted to play with the others—talk to them—chat or chatter. He had seemed, at the best of times, a distant relation—a cousin who came to visit and stayed against his will. The impression given was: *when will someone come and take me away from all this?*

Of all her surviving children—who then included Jamie—Eliza had been most concerned about Liam. The Rosary Children were dead. She would never know if one of them had been cursed with Uncle John Fagan's illness. *But Liam . . .* what had it been that made her so cautious—so watchful? *His silences. His loneliness. His wilful, stubborn apartness.* These could be signs—though, in time Eliza came to see them as signs of something else. *Not Uncle John Fagan's condition. Not Lily's. Something else, unreadable.* She loved him, sometimes, with desperation, because she could not reach him.

Liam hated the farm. He hated the animals. As a child, he had been afraid of them. He treated his parents with respect—but little more. If Eliza attempted to cuddle him, he drew away. Even when ill, and therefore more dependent on her care, he had accepted it with a strange formality that had always baffled her. As for his siblings—Jamie had been too glamorous for Liam's liking, with his huge laugh, his curly hair and his athletic enthusiasm for the playing field. Other children and a multitude of adults had always flocked to be in Jamie's company, while Liam stood on the sidelines. But whether his position there was maintained because he was jealous, or simply because he was hypercritical, Eliza had never known.

Ede had always tried to take command of Liam—to control him. She had treated him, early on, as a possession. But Liam would have none of this—any more than he would accept Ede's love, which was genuine. She might have thought he was *odd and quirky—stuck up and affected—*but she treated all these negatives with affectionate good humour. He was a *silly goose—a character.* It was only later, when Liam had opted to study Law and gone off to Toronto, that she began her serious war with him. It was Ede's perception—right or wrong—that as Liam prospered, he treated his family with increasing condescension. *He thinks we're beneath him!* she had once yelled at Eliza in a state of fury. *He thinks, because we live on a farm, we're potato Irish! Damn him!*

Unlike Liam, Eliza had not reacted to Ede's cursing. She liked a good cursing herself—though never in mixed company. Only with other women. *Men think so well of us,* she said, *they don't understand that we know such words . . .*

As for Willa and Malahide—they were eternal children in Liam's eyes. Willa had bratted her way through his life like a noisy dog. She was *ill-mannered, common* and *vulgar.* Her mouth was always open, ready to take the next bit of food.

Only Malahide received his brother's serious attention—which, later, Mal would come to know as a tentative kind of love. Liam understood Mal's focus—his single-mindedness—his devotion to the wilderness of life apart from other people. His fear of proximity. His need for the eternal privacy of separation. *We do not choose our lives,* Liam believed, *our lives choose us, and we must hold the choices of others at bay, lest our lives lose sight of us.* That was his definition of single-mindedness—*not of choosing, but of being chosen.*

The train bearing Ede and Frederick had departed at two-thirty. Now, at four-thirty, the last of the wedding guests were at the doors of the lounge, in their overcoats—the men with hats in hand, the women in a storm of millinery splendour.

Franklin and Harry had attended with female cousins—relatives from Paris, Ontario. Neither man had yet married and there was doubt that Harry ever would. But Franklin was a notorious *womanizer*—this was Eliza's word—and he was often seen with *actresses and stars of the concert stage and of vaudeville! Honestly,*

James, one has to wonder what sort of family we've married into!

James's cousin, Muriel Kilworth, was the last to leave. She was his youngest brother's widow and had spent the entire afternoon in tears. When she finally left, James turned back into the lounge and walked straight to the bar, where he requested a very large whiskey.

"Remember your condition, James."

"I've had nothing but champagne since noon. Leave me alone."

Eliza took a slow tour of the whole room, smiling at the waiters, whose wages James would pay, and mourning just for a moment the loss of her daughter. *Married. And gone. Gone—and married. Someone else's, now.*

And where was Liam . . . There was his overcoat. There was his hat. But not the man. *Oh, well. He's an adult now. He can take care of himself* . . .

She turned to the two large urns set where the receiving line had been. They were filled to overflowing with hothouse flowers—with irises and roses—with tulips and with lilies . . .

Lily.

"Oh, my god—James! Lily!"

"What about her?"

"She's still up there in our rooms, with that woman!"

Unknown to Ede—and contrary to Frederick's wishes—James and Eliza had brought Lily with them to Toronto. She was now ensconced with a nursemaid, hired for the occasion, in the suite of rooms the Kilworths had rented in the Queen's Hotel for the duration of the wedding. It had been in Eliza's mind that Frederick might relent and that Lily might be allowed to come to the reception, if not the ceremony. Of course, it was a pointless hope. Eliza had begun her reading of Frederick with the words: *be careful*—and she was already beginning to understand her initial reaction had been correct.

"I will come back," she told James. "Don't you dare have more than you know you should. We can't afford another stroke . . ."

With that, she was through the door and down the corridor. The stairs seemed two miles high, but that was all right. *I've climbed enough miles in my life to handle a few more.*

Oh, my dear Lily. My dear, dear Lily—I'm so sorry I left you alone for so long with a stranger . . .

This was Eliza's thought as she hurried towards the doors of the rented suite. Just as she entered, she heard the familiar voice— and, turning, she saw him sitting in the splendour of the sunset, and the child and her nursemaid sitting opposite, enraptured. It was Liam—telling Lily the story of *The Hidden Child.*

4. "What he told us that afternoon," Lily said, "was a fairy tale."

When I laughed, she said: "no, I mean it, Charlie. Uncle Liam sat there and told us a fairy tale."

Oh.

This was her version of the scene, as she remembered it in the years after the asylums claimed her, long after Liam had disappeared from all our lives and gone his own way.

Lily and the Nursemaid—whose name was now forgotten—had been playing cards when Liam came in. At first, the Nursemaid did not know who he was, but Lily reassured her.

"He's my uncle."

Liam gave his military nod, heels together, hands at his sides, and it was then that Lily realized what was wrong. *The little bow didn't quite come off, and he almost fell . . .* It was just like the night when he'd sat on the stairs at Munsterfield and told her that other story—the one about *The Memory Potion* he was forced to drink, from time to time.

Coming over to the table where the card game was in progress, he gazed down at Lily's hand and said: "you should play that nine. You can pick up her seven and her two . . . and her four and her five with it."

"I was just going to do that when you came in."

The Nursemaid smiled.

"Miss Lily's good at cards," she said. "She's kept that nine in her hand to trap me."

"Yes," said Liam—somewhere off behind Lily where she couldn't see him. "She's good at laying traps . . ."

The Nursemaid must have recognized the menace in these words, but she said nothing. Nor did Lily. She played her nine and took in the others, adding them to her winnings.

Liam said: "not that she means to lay traps. It's more that she *is* one."

He was standing now where she could see him. "Aren't you, Lily. A trap."

"I don't know," she said, "what you mean."

She began to fiddle with the cards. The Nursemaid was watching her, concerned but silent. Lily concentrated on the woman's uniform. It was sky-blue and over it she wore a plain white apron. In her breast pocket there was a puff of white handkerchief and, on her head, a high, white, ruffled cap . . . there were so many details to be counted . . . the stitching . . . the buttons . . . the woman's dark hair tied up in a knot beneath the cap and . . .

Liam had started to hum a tune. And then he gave it words.

"A wand'ring minstrel, I, a thing of shred . . . and patches . . ."

He stopped singing and looked around the room.

"This wedding," Liam said—as if to the world at large—"almost did not take place. You realize that. In fact, it would not have taken place at all, if it hadn't been for me."

The Nursemaid said: "Mister Kilworth . . ." Her voice was harsh and firm.

She stood up.

She was formidable.

Liam blinked at her—amazed. He was being challenged. Without charm. Without pleading. Without anger. Simply challenged. *Stop*, he was being told. *Don't.*

He sighed.

"Ah, me," he said—but smiling. "A dragon."

The Nursemaid said: "perhaps you would like to return to the party, Mister Kilworth. To the reception."

"Perhaps," Liam shrugged. "Perhaps not."

He moved in the same way Lily remembered from the time before, on the stairs—clumsily, almost—without dignity. His shoulders had fallen, rounding down and forward. His backbone had loosened. His hands were like rags at the ends of his arms and he shook them out, the way Freda shook out her dusters at home. He went over first to the bureau, then to the closet—into which he disappeared.

At this point, the Nursemaid said to Lily: "I think we won't play cards any more, dear. Let us go and sit over there . . ."

She gathered her charge and took her across the room to a sofa, angled outwards towards the window. Liam could be heard rummaging behind then—and then: "eureka!"

Neither of them watched.

Still, they could hear him. A glass was found in the bathroom. A bottle was opened. Liquid was poured. "Thank you," Liam muttered. "You're welcome."

Then he drank.

Down went the glass.

More was poured. Not much—a little—and then, he reappeared.

He came around the sofa, carrying both glass and bottle. It was James's *emergency whiskey.* Liam held the bottle up to the light, and squinted at its amber contents—*The Memory Potion.*

Lily watched him, sideways.

The Nursemaid sat up very straight and folded her hands.

Liam sat down in a chair about eight feet away from them. His back was to the window. He set the bottle on the floor beside him—and he sipped, like a child afraid of burning his tongue, one sip—two—and three . . .

"All right," he said. "What I'll do is tell you a story. The story of *The Hidden Child and Her Mother* . . ." This made him laugh. But silently. And then: "once upon a time . . ."

He told about the wandering minstrel, *I*, who met the girl with the flaxen hair—and of how they were joined by the light of the moon and of how, when he'd wandered away again, the minstrel, I, was drowned in a sea full of horses—who thundered over him in waves—who swept him far, far away—and under—*down and down and down* . . .

He told how the Hidden Child had been born *in a field of hay—in a field of hay* . . . and of how the girl with the flaxen hair had sequestered her child *in a tall white house—in a wide white house—in a tall, wide house that was white* . . . *and all its roofs— its several roofs—its many roofs were green* . . .

And for countless years, Flaxen Hair had pined for her poor, lost Minstrel, I—and many suitors came—ten thousand suitors came—*but all were turned away* . . .

And why—tell me why—were they turned away—shunned for their loving and driven from the door? Why—tell me why?

Because of Flaxen Hair's secret child—her silent child—her Hidden Child. That was why—and how sad it was. How sad.

But Flaxen Hair was not alone in the tall white house—in the wide white house—she was not alone with her Hidden Child. There were others there—her family—and . . . chief among her family, her eldest brother. *Me.* His name was *Me.*

And?

One day, during a blizzard, a man appeared—another suitor, writhing through the snow. When he knocked on the door and the door was opened, the whole world came in after him—carried on the wind—*the whole, wide world* . . .

Flaxen Hair was shaken. This man who had come from the snow to ask for her hand in marriage was not like any of the others who had come. An aura shone around him.

Flaxen Hair had become so tired of living her little life alone with the Hidden Child and her family that, with all her heart, she wanted to say *yes. Yes,* to this Suitor. *Yes.*

But . . .

But . . .

But, there was still the fact of the Hidden Child—and of her silence—of her silence—her long, long quietness . . .

No.

No.

No.

Flaxen Hair said *no.*

And this is when her brother, Me, stepped into the story and saved the day.

Suitor, rebuffed, went back into the blizzard where, in time, he found a town with a grand hotel—a town that was drifting in the snow—a town that, by morning, would have disappeared.

That night in the grand hotel, all at sea in the wind and snow, Suitor went in to the dining-hall, where Brother Me was sitting. Having met Brother Me on another occasion, Suitor wondered if he might join him for the evening meal.

Of course, said Brother Me. *I beg you. Sit down.*

Here, Liam refilled his glass. The Nursemaid had subsided into the corner of the sofa, watching him, spellbound—one hand tapping the verses with its fingers on the velvet and the other reaching out for Lily, as if to share the story with her. As for Lily . . .

I knew—and I did not know—what he was saying. I knew— and I did not know it was us . . .

Brother Me was not alone when Suitor sat down. A lady was seated there with him. I will call her *Lady Snow and Ice,* because she was soft as the one and cold as the other—and also white. Every stitch of her clothing was white. Even her shoes were white. And her hair was almost white—pale yellow beneath a white, white hat. She was seated there because it was her father who owned the grand hotel, and Lady Snow and Ice was more grand, grander than anything or anyone in the whole town.

Brother Me had once shown an interest in Lady Snow and Ice, but that was over. That was done with. She had accepted him— and rejected him—just as she accepted and rejected many men. In fact, it was perfectly clear—the moment that Suitor appeared— she was prepared to accept him, too. He, however, though plainly attracted to Lady Snow and Ice, was in love with Flaxen Hair, and nothing could be done about it. She had refused him.

Lady Snow and Ice offered her sympathies. Her condolences. Her tears. *What a sad, sad story . . .*

Now . . .

Liam leaned forward.

"Now, Brother Me stepped in to save the day . . ."

"How?" This was Lily. She couldn't help it.

"Yes," said the Nursemaid. "How?"

Brother Me wondered aloud if Suitor had ever heard of the Hidden Child.

No.

Brother Me was careful. *Very* careful. He did not want to spoil his sister Flaxen Hair's last chance at happiness—and so he decided he would say nothing—nothing about the Hidden Child's silence, her everlasting quietness. He knew, you see, that silence was a quality that Suitor would find . . . disturbing. He knew, you see, that silence frightened Suitor . . .

And so, he told of the Hidden Child and of Flaxen Hair's fear that Suitor would not accept a child that was not his own.

Oh! said Suitor, with a great loud thump on the table. *Oh!* he said. *Oh—how wonderful! If that is the only reason she has turned me down, I will go off at once, before the town disappears in the blizzard, and I will tell her I know of the Hidden Child and that a child—whether hidden or not—can make no difference to my love—and again I will ask her to marry me!*

And this he did, and Flaxen Hair said *yes!—yes* to the Suitor who would accept her Hidden Daughter—and they were married. Wedded. Wed. All because of Me.

There.

Lily sat staring. Silent. She was waiting for Liam to say *they all lived happily ever after.*

"But that," she told me, "is when Eliza walked in. And so, he never said it."

She looked at me and smiled.

"I never told you that one before, did I, Charlie?"

"No," I said.

"I thought so. Yes. I mean—if I'd told you, I'm sure you would have remembered."

I watched her. It was growing late. My visit would soon have to end.

And then, not looking at me, staring instead—as usual—into that distance I could never find, she said: "Charlie—in that story, do you think the child was hidden—or do you think she was in hiding?"

I shook my head.

"I don't really know," I said. "I guess it depends who's telling it."

She looked at me.

I smiled.

So did Lily.

5. Frederick told Ede the Duke of Wellington Hotel had been recommended by a business acquaintance. *You won't find a better hotel in the whole of Niagara Falls—costly, not fancy— rich, not gaudy!* On sight, it actually seemed to pander to good taste. The lobby was not too brightly lit, its furnishing almost staid. Having heard that Niagara Falls was a *perpetual circus* and made *an entertainment* of marriages, he had not been prepared for propriety, in spite of his friend's recommendation. No one shouted, the bellboys all wore red, but without gold braid and the clerks all spoke with cultured respect. There was not a trace of ribaldry in anything anyone said. This was not what Frederick had imagined and he was greatly relieved.

He had asked for and been given one of the larger suites on the topmost floor, which would afford them a view of the falls *unmatched from any other hotel. Wait until you see it!*

While Frederick dealt with the formalities, Ede chose to sit away to one side of the lobby in a straight-backed chair with a velvet cushion. Her hands were folded in her lap and her feet pressed close together so that her ankles met beneath her skirts. She wore the Prussian blue overcoat and the sable hat, having been assured by Eliza they made her look like a queen.

"Not *the* Queen, I hope," Ede had said. Victoria was then eighty-two years old.

"No, dear, of course not. I mean like the queens in fairy tales."

The problem with wearing gloves was that you didn't get to show off your rings. And with overcoats, that your pearls weren't visible. Two strands of pearls with an opal clasp and an evening ring with three round diamonds in a silver filigree setting. And, of course, her wedding ring and the ring of engagement—sapphires. She might have worn the sapphire brooch her parents had given her, but what was the use of wearing it beneath the coat? If they took their evening meal in the hotel dining-room, she would wear it then, with the pale mauve evening dress not yet worn, but saved for this occasion. Her trousseau was not extensive, but had been assembled with the greatest care. Nothing white, of course. Her wedding gown had been the colour of dark red plums. She wore no veil, but flowers in her hair and Frederick's gift of long kid gloves with pearls as buttons—twelve on each arm. The gloves, like her shoes, had been peach.

Waiting for Frederick to finish his business at the desk, Ede counted over every item of clothing in her steamer trunk and every article of toiletry in the green leather case at her side. In another part of her mind, she was observing Frederick and the registration clerk. Frederick's back, displayed to advantage in his tailored overcoat, was straight as the back of an athlete. She had always liked the way he stood—erect, with his feet apart. Not in any sense military—more relaxed than a soldier, but definitely *there*. In all of them—in all the Wyatt men, including Tom in her memory of him—there was a gentle sense of aloofness—something to do with the way they held themselves and the way they pulled their chins in close, which gave the appearance of someone looking down from a height. Whereas, if their chins had jutted out in the manner of some actors she had seen in magazines—

Richard Mansfield—John Drew—the Wyatt men would have looked nothing less than arrogant. Liam-like. *Chin stuck out a mile! And his eagle eyes half-hooded in their Kilworth lids—the eyelids of marble heroes, wide and smooth and white as milk.* Ede had those eyelids herself. Pray God they did not portray the arrogance her brother's did . . .

Poor old Li. Poor young Li. A young old man. The youngest old man she knew. Sad—if he hadn't been such a . . .

Ede gave a laugh at the advent of *bastard* rising into her inner mind, as if it had been a word she used every day.

It had always been there, of course. In her mind. But in another context. The context of Lily. Perhaps, because she feared the word, she had pushed it under the surface in Lily's behalf—hidden, but riding closer to the top than she had known. *I'm rid of it, now,* she thought as she watched the lobby filling up with people. *I'm married—married—and Lily has a name.* The very name she would have had if Tom had lived. Lily Wyatt.

What a reassuring name it was. Secure.

All at once, a voice came sailing across the lobby—a woman's voice sweeping in Ede's direction.

"Edith Mary Kilworth! I'd know you anywhere!" it said.

Little Eva Willard—little no longer, but still dressed up in white and with her mother still in tow and at least six men in dark blue overcoats in a swirl around her.

"Is that you, Eva?" said Ede. As if it needed saying. The beautiful angel child with the curls of pale blonde hair was now an angel young lady of eighteen or nineteen and a great raging beauty with powder in her hair, which gave it a kind of ethereal look—a halo spun from gossamer.

Eva waved her attendants towards the desk—her mother with them—and stood before Ede, the very picture of something—what?—*commercial.* Ede, however, could not imagine what the product was. The white fur trim on her pure white evening coat? The pallor of her perfect skin? The white kid boots? The ostrich plumes on her wide, white hat? Something surely was being advertised. Sold.

"May a person ask why Edith Mary Kilworth is sitting here alone in a hotel lobby in Niagara Falls? Would it be too rude for words to ask such a thing straight out? What *are* you doing here? Tell me. Tell me."

Eva's words were spoken as one might expect to hear them in an elocution class. Each vowel perfectly rounded—each of the consonants crisply fired as salvos from a gun.

Ede declined to say she was on her honeymoon. That might lead to the kind of gushing, little-girl enthusiasm she dreaded. What she offered instead was the news that she was here with her husband on business.

There was the slightest pause before Eva spoke.

"Married, Edith Mary? Married? Oh." She sat down in the chair next to Ede. "So . . ." She managed a smile. "What I heard was true."

"I'm not sure I know what you mean," said Ede.

"Oh, nothing. Just a rumour. You know the sort of thing!"

"No, I don't. Tell me."

"Only that—*some*one was thinking of proposing." Eva gave another smile. A sweet one. Small. "Do I know him?" she said. "Is he here in the lobby?"

"I don't think you do know him," said Ede. "His name is Frederick Wyatt."

A cloud appeared on Eva's horizon. A squint took hold of her eyes.

"Frederick Wyatt? Of the piano Wyatts?"

"That's right." Ede did not know whether to be flattered for Frederick's sake or wary for her own.

She had no chance to speculate further, however. Frederick himself stepped into the breach.

"My dear," he said, putting out his hand in Ede's direction.

Picking up her green leather case, she rose to her feet and took his arm. Their steamer trunks were already being wheeled towards the elevators on elaborate carts by dwarfish men in short red jackets. Frederick turned to Eva and lifted the ever-present Homburg. "Miss Willard," he said.

"Mister Wyatt." She extended her hand.

Frederick took it and bowed. Ede let go of his arm.

"You've met," she said. But without inflection.

"Oh, yes," said Eva, brightly. "Some time ago."

Frederick said: "may one enquire if you have prospered, Miss Willard?"

"Yes, indeed. I have. My purpose here is a professional engagement."

"Ah, yes. I see."

Ede remained silent—watching.

"Shall we hear you?"

"If you're inclined."

Ede thought: *butter would not melt . . .*

"I'm appearing in the Wintergarden. Up on the roof . . ." She lifted her hand towards the ceiling. "Twice nightly."

"We should be delighted."

"I thank you." Eva rearranged the skirts of her overcoat. "You may or may not be aware, Mister Wyatt, that my father has been expanding his empire—and is now the owner of this hotel."

"The Duke of Wellington?"

Eva nodded. "Yes. And three others. One in Montreal. One in Toronto. And one in Buffalo, New York."

"He must be congratulated."

"I will tell him you said so, Mister Wyatt."

"And you?"

"I give my *Night of Song* in each of them. And I must say, I have enjoyed some success. That is my entourage over there at the desk with my mother. My manager—my stage-manager—my director—my vocal coach—and my pianist."

"I trust he plays a *Wyatt*." Frederick smiled.

"Well—no, as a matter of fact. I'm afraid not. We use a *Mason and Risch . . .*"

Ede thought: *yes—the piano with a soul!*

Eva said: "of course, these things *can* change."

"I would like to think so, Miss Willard. It would be a great honour for my company."

Eva nodded. "Perhaps we shall talk about it."

"Any time," said Frederick. "At your convenience."

Ede said: "it was good to see you, Eva." Civil—but nothing more. They retired—and followed their luggage.

From the elevator, Ede glanced back and saw Eva turn and move towards her mother, still at the desk. The look on her face was quite unreadable. For a change, however, there was nothing angelic about it. A hardness had caught at the corners of her mouth and the expression in her eyes was frozen—caught between anger and frustration.

Well. And so.

The elevator operator closed the doors. Looking out at the passing floors, Ede said: "I didn't realize you'd met Miss Willard."

Frederick said: "everyone knows Eva Willard. She's famous. Isn't that right, lads?" He said this last to the child-sized men who were riding with their luggage.

"Yessir," said one, whose voice was pinched and piping.

The other said nothing.

"I guess I didn't realize she'd gone so far," Ede said, "for a girl from McCaskill's Mills."

"She's not *world famous*, of course," said Frederick. "She's just beginning. But—it seems she's off to a good start."

"Yes," said Ede. "It seems so." *In more ways than one!*

The elevator had begun to slow.

"I had the impression she knew you quite well," she said, half smiling—wondering what Frederick would say.

He waved it aside. "Not really," he said. "But then . . ." smiling back at her, "don't forget—I'm famous, too."

They had arrived. The elevator operator held aside the gate.

"This way, please," said the little man with the piping voice.

Ede took Frederick's arm and they stepped out into a corridor of muted, golden light. *Well,* she thought. *The honeymoon has begun.*

6. The bed had a canopy—six pillows—one blue blanket and a yellow spread. The sheets were white, with blue stitching. All very elegant—all very reassuring. The yellow of the bedspread was anything but insipid. It was almost orange—shot silk and lined. The same material had been used to cover the chairs—faux-French, but very well done.

Having prepared herself according to Eliza's instructions, Ede waited in the semi-dark, in a kind of gloaming spread from glass-shaded lamps that had been turned down low as Frederick retired to the bathroom. He had been gone now fifteen minutes. What might be keeping him, Ede could not imagine—but equally, she knew that men were as mysterious as women when it came to bodily functions. Liam, at home, had always taken what seemed like hours in the bathroom, holding everyone at ransom with his fastidious hygienics. Running taps and gargling noises—toothbrush and nailbrush noises—razor-stropping noises—more running water . . . It could be endless.

On the other hand, Ede always loved the chance to be next in line for the morning bathroom after Liam had gone down the hall in his long blue robe. The scent of his soaps and lathers was intriguing, smelling of dark green forests and lemon groves.

This would be her first encounter with the private side of Frederick—that closed-door part of life she had been privy to only through her parents. What did they laugh about so often in the dark, or when—as they often did—they went into the bathroom together on the excuse of washing one another's back? Always there would be sudden outbursts of laughter and giggling and Eliza saying: *oh-James-stop-that! Stop!* and sailing off into more delight. Baby-talk, sometimes. Quite embarrassing. Quite outrageous. Also wonderful. Joyous *shushing—dear-not-so-loud* and *no-we-shouldn't* breaking through the gaiety. What had it all been about?

With Tom, there had never been a door to close, only the grass to lie on, never a bed; no walls, no ceiling to shut them in—or others out. Only the moon to see them, only the moon, some stars and whatever it was that had flown up out of the field when Ede had cried *don't* in the final seconds of their embrace. *Don't*—meaning don't withdraw. But he had, as he must, and she had never borne his weight again. And from that bearing, Lily.

Lily. Now elsewhere.

Ede lay back against the pillows. From the bathroom came the sounds of taps being turned and of water being run. A sink full of water . . . Just like Liam.

Married.

Lily would have a home, now. A house and a name. *We will all be together. Safe.*

The bathroom door opened.

Ede had thought he would speak, but nothing was said. He came across the room, turning off lamps, refusing to look at her. He was wearing a dressing gown, beneath the hem of which she could see his bare legs and slippered feet. When the last of the lamps had been extinguished, Frederick came and sat on the edge of the bed. Ede wanted desperately to hear him speak—his voice could be so reassuring—but when he said nothing, she too was silent.

She felt him rise in order to remove his robe and then she heard him kick the slippers aside and throw the robe on a nearby chair. The next thing she knew, he was pulling the covers down to the foot of the bed and clambering on top of her the way a man would hoist himself from the water onto a raft—stiff-armed and taut. Ede almost laughed, it was all so perfunctory.

Frederick?

Had she really spoken? Certainly she'd tried, but her voice had failed to materialize and all she heard was the sound of her nightgown ripping as Frederick pulled it over her head and threw it aside.

He was kneeling, now between her ankles, pushing at her, forcing her knees apart and then her arms until she was entirely splayed on the bed beneath him.

Nothing was said. Not a word.

Ede felt his hand between her legs, forcing the way for the rest of him. *Stop,* she wanted to tell him. *Stop. I don't understand what you're doing.* But nothing—still nothing was said.

He seemed to be raging inside her, moving his hips in a circular fashion, all the weight of his upper body held above her, resting on his arms, his hands pushing down into the mattress.

Stop! But he didn't.

Don't! But he did.

Nothing. Not one word.

The only sound he made was a choking noise in his throat at the end, as though he might be going to strangle. But when he rolled away from her onto his back, she felt the shudder of his first free breath and she heard him sigh. It was over. *Tonight.* It was done.

Ede could not bear the thought of seeing him, or of being seen. Still without speaking, she rose from the bed and, through the dark, found her way to the bathroom. She had brought the torn nightgown with her, but when she turned on the light and saw it, she threw it down in the corner. Ruined. Spoiled. Everything.

When, at last, she returned to the bed, Frederick was sound asleep beneath the covers—and nothing—nothing—nothing was said.

7. The household then was made up of Ede and Frederick and Lily, plus a man who groomed and drove the horses, waited sometimes at table and kept the garden; a maid whose name was Agnes and a small round cook whose name was Charlotte. The man had no first name—certainly none that anyone was told. He was known universally—even to his dog—as Bateson. "Come to Bateson," he would say, when his dog was with him. "Walk with Bateson." Sometimes he was granted *Mister Bateson*, but his other names—if such existed—remained a mystery.

As the men on the farm had been, Bateson was squinny-eyed and taciturn—measuring the world around him by standards he would not discuss. Why it was that men who worked in flowerbeds and barns should have so little to say was a mystery to Lily, but one she had learned to accept. She had no concept of class and, of course, the brief exchanges between those who laboured and their employers had much to do with the distance such relationships required. The variety of silences that could be had from Bateson regarding his intimacy with nature enchanted Lily—but they were not of interest to Frederick and Ede. Or so they must imply. This was called *propriety*, and was *understood by Master and servant alike*. Unquote.

On Frederick's instruction, Ede had commenced a thorough reading of *Our Deportment* by a man called John H. Young whom Ede complained was *an American!* Mister Young had collated a mass of instruction on the MANNERS, CONDUCT AND DRESS of what he called THE MOST REFINED SOCIETY—all set out in capital letters. Ede just laughed, but Frederick's insistence could not be brooked. He quizzed her on the book's contents day by day, until she finally consented to take it seriously. He also provided her with a copy of *Beeton's Book of Household Management* in order to acquaint her with a proper relationship with servants.

"I've worked with servants all my life," said Ede.

"No you haven't," Frederick told her. "You have submitted to the ministrations of an ignorant German woman, her idiot daughter and a passel of hired hands."

Ede took a deep breath and closed her eyes. "You shouldn't speak of them like that. To begin with, she's not an *idiot*. She's deaf. And they are all—they are *all* my beloved friends."

"*Were*," said Frederick.

"*Are*," said Ede, and bit her lip.

"Servants cannot be friends," Frederick insisted. "To speak of them as friends is to undermine the whole system."

"What system?"

"The social system."

Ede saw the words set out in her mind much as Mister Young had set THE MOST REFINED SOCIETY on the title page of his book. She kept her silence, fearful that she would weep with frustration or burst out laughing at such a ridiculous situation. Surely Frederick would come to his senses and allow them both to be the people they were. Ede had no pretensions about this. Or, at least, she thought she had no pretensions. She took great pride in her Kilworth past, and her Fagan ancestry. "We lived," she told Frederick, "in a great tall house in Dublin. *Brick*. With dozens of rooms—and maids galore and a cook and a housekeeper. We even had a butler at the door!"

"Why are you shouting?"

"I'm not shouting. What makes you say things like that? *I'm not shouting!* I'm explaining."

"No," said Frederick, who was seated in the Selby Street parlour. "You are not explaining, Edith. You are lying. Through your teeth."

"We lived in a great tall house . . ."

"You did no such thing."

"My people did. My mother did when she was a little girl. My people did." She faltered.

Frederick watched her with seeming diffidence. In a moment, she would be calm, his demeanour told her. In a moment, she would tell the truth.

"I'm not lying," she said.

He was silent.

"You've seen the furniture," she reminded him. "The Empire sideboard. The rosewood chairs. My grandmother's settee. The portraits on the wall. You've seen them. You loved them."

Nothing.

"I am not lying. We lived in a tall . . . brick house."

Ede, who was standing, laid a finger on the nearest table, which—it so happened—had also been rescued from the ruins of the Dublin house and had crossed the ocean with Eliza's parents. It seemed that all her weight was poised on that finger-end—all her weight and all the weight of every Fagan who'd ever been born.

"That table needs dusting," said Frederick.

Ede blinked in amazement. What on earth was he saying? Dust? She looked—and there it was.

"I'll see . . . I'll see to it in the morning," she said.

"No."

"Why not? I want to."

"Agnes will do it."

"Agnes cannot do everything, Frederick."

"Agnes will do it, and if there is ever dust on that table again, you will let her go."

"Frederick, don't be ridiculous."

"The duties of the housemaid are set out for all the world to see in *Beeton's*," he said. "I know, because I read them. You will never learn how to run a household unless you read them, too."

Ede removed her finger from the table and put her hand behind her back.

"What you have to understand, Edith, is where we are going. And what it takes to get there. *Money. Know-how.* And *acceptability.*"

Ede blinked. She did not know where to look. She had not been lectured since James had dressed her down for being pregnant. And even that lecture had ended with an embrace. Not that she could expect an embrace at the end of this one.

Frederick continued. "The money and the know-how are my affair. The acceptability is yours. In a year—no—less: in half a year, I want that empty silver tray in the front hall *filled* with cards. I want your name on the lips of every hostess in this city—and mine on the lips of all their husbands. Do you understand that?"

Ede did not answer.

"Do you understand that?"

"Yes." And then: "I thought you loved me."

Frederick sat back and banged his fists on the arms of his chair in exasperation. He shook his head, as if in disbelief. He sighed.

He stood up.

"No man," he said, "would have said that. Only a woman."

"I am a woman."

"Yes. Alas."

"I beg your pardon."

Frederick had started to turn away from her. Now he turned back.

"Edith," he said, his voice on the verge of cracking, "I do love you." Each word was given the same careful weight. "I do," he said. "But . . ."

Ede waited, her eyes refusing to waver.

". . . this is not about love. This is about survival. This is about our future. And about our work—the thing we have to do—the *job*," he said. "The accomplishment of place."

"Why did you say *alas*?"

"When did I say *alas*?"

"I said I was a woman and you said: *yes—alas*. Why?"

"Did I?"

"Yes."

"Then I apologize."

Ede stared at him. He hadn't the slightest idea how dismissive he was. Not the slightest idea.

"What's for dinner?" he said.

Damn him.

And in bed that night, the same performance and the same dead sleep.

And yet, to her amazement, Ede was entirely at his mercy. This amazement was confirmed by the fact that she now began to try to hear and to play with the word *love*. Love in the neighbourhood—love in the possibility—love in the preserve of Frederick Wyatt.

Love, oh love, oh careless love . . . That was now a thing of the past. This was different—utterly. *Yes.*

It was true—there was pity in her love for him. She knew it was a patronizing kind of love—or at least there was a patronizing element. She felt—what?—sorry for him. Sorry—recognizing that, for whatever reason, the loss of his mother, his fear of women—he did not know how to connect. He was afraid of losing control. And she—*yes*—she pitied him for this. And—*yes, too*—Tom was beginning to fade from memory. Days on end would pass without his name in her mind. *Going—going—gone* . . .

It did not occur to Ede to challenge what she was feeling. Any more than she challenged—against the odds—her feeling for Lily. *Love is not about* why, she wrote to Eliza. Why *is a madman's question when it comes to love.* It was the sort of question Liam might ask.

Ede began to sink into the depths of her marriage, thinking

only *I must learn how to swim*—swim with graceful, accomplished strokes, and smiling all the while. She was not—and would never be—aware that in *learning to swim,* she was exercising her instinct for survival at all costs. All. Including the cost of her integrity.

8. Towards the end of May, Lily would be introduced into the household. The lilacs were in bloom. The word had gone up to Munsterfield to bring Lily down and *all her comforts with her.* These would be her jars of feathers and butterfly wings—her photographs of James and Eliza—her vast collection of stones—and her playing cards. Her bedroom, with its field-flower paper and its muslin curtains, awaited her. On the wall above her bed, the birth-wreath was hung with ribbons.

Ede knew the moment had come when she must tell Frederick the truth about Lily's condition. Her *illness*—her *inheritance*—her *problem*—her *seizures*. Her dependence—her absolute dependence on Ede. On Ede's watchfulness. On Ede's ears and eyes and heartbeat. On everyone's understanding. Everyone's awareness. Everyone's . . .

None of this would do. It was all too stark. It sounded as if the child would have to be leashed—belled and monitored—as if a dangerous beast were being brought in out of the wild. As if she might not know how to live in houses—eat at tables—lie in beds—sit in chairs.

Between the main course and the sweet the night before Lily's arrival, Ede sat forward in her place and looked at Frederick, far away beyond the candles and the flowers. She had seen to it that everything offered that evening was a special favourite—a jellied consommé, a loin of beef with Béarnaise sauce, potato croquettes and hothouse spinach, rolled in butter and spiced with nutmeg. Also, the promise of chocolate almond ice cream and ladyfingers. Coffee and brandy. One cigar.

"What's the occasion?"

"This is our last night alone."

"Yes, of course. Tomorrow, our daughter arrives."

"My daughter."

"Yes. And mine."

"Tom's."

"Mine." He smiled. "Ours."

"Yes. Ours. I will concede that. So long as . . ."

Frederick was sitting back. Relaxed. With one hand, he turned the wineglass before him, watching its facets catch and lose and catch again the candlelight and the mirrored light from the silverware and the twin decanters set within his reach and Ede's—one at either end of the table. Perfect.

"So long as?" he asked.

"So long as your acceptance of Lily is more than a mere formality. It's not a duty, you know. I mean—you aren't obliged . . ." Ede laid her hands on the table—one with its rings, the other with its napkin. She was letting her fingernails grow to lady-length. Beautifully shaped and buffed, and all her *moons* as white as . . . ladyfingers. Edible sweets. Dessert.

"Fred."

"Yes."

"I have to tell you something. I have to tell you something—and I'm nervous about it—sorry."

She could not quite bring herself to look at him—but if she had, she would have seen that his lips were pursed, that his eyes had narrowed and the goblet stem between his fingers had been stilled.

"Something?"

"Yes. About Lily."

Frederick moved in his chair, resting his right elbow on the arm, shifting his weight so that he could achieve an unobstructed view of his wife.

He said nothing. He waited.

Now it was Ede's turn to sit back, holding the edge of the table with her fingertips.

"When she was two years old . . ."

"Lily . . ."

"When she was two years old—not quite, but almost . . . Something happened."

Frederick's chair creaked.

Ede did not look up.

"She had . . . She was taken by a seizure."

"A seizure."

"Yes."

"That's not uncommon."

"No. But . . ."

There was then such a silence in the room, Ede could hear the candles burning.

Speak.

Say this: it was not the last . . .

"It was not the last."

It was the first of . . .

"It was the first of . . ."

Many.

Many others. Say it.

". . . There were others, Fred."

Nothing. And then:

"Still?"

"Yes."

Ede heard Frederick straighten.

That damned chair . . .

"Are you saying she is—epi . . . leptic?"

"No. Not epileptic. Something else."

"What, then?"

"We don't know. I don't know. They don't."

"They?"

"Doctors."

"Specialists?"

"Yes. And others."

Frederick lifted his head. His lips were parted. He took a deep breath and exhaled.

Now, Ede looked at him.

He was tired. Another nail was being driven into him—she could not tell where. His wounds were in secret places—never spoken of. Never revealed.

He rubbed his lips with the back of one knuckle—his index finger crooked.

Ede could see his tongue attempting to form a word.

"Do say something," she whispered. "Do say *some*thing."

He sighed. Barely audible.

"Is this . . ." he said. "Are we . . ." he said. "Are we . . . going to live with this forever?"

Their eyes locked.

"Yes. For as long as she lives."

Lily.

At last, Frederick lifted his wineglass and drank. And, while he refilled it, he said: "I often wondered what it was—over these last six months—that kept you from me. What it was that stood between us."

"It doesn't have to be a barrier."

"No."

"I've dealt with it all her life. It is possible to live with. It can be lived with."

"How often do they occur? These . . ."

"Seizures."

"Yes. How often?"

"It's unpredictable. But—in all the time you've known her, there's never been one—she has never had one in your presence."

"No."

"Well." Ede sat up. "There you are. I've said it. It's been said."

The door to the pantry opened.

It was Agnes. Tiny as a plump mouse.

"Madam . . . ?"

"Yes, Agnes."

"It's just—I thought—there was such a long wait. And I wondered if I hadn't heard the bell."

"There was no bell. I didn't ring."

"Thank you, madam. I'm sorry."

She began to retreat.

"Agnes . . ."

"Yessir?"

"You may clear."

"Yessir. I'll just get my tray."

She was gone—the door swinging to and fro behind her.

"What's for dessert?" said Frederick.

And that was all. It was over. Done.

The next day, Lily arrived.

9. In time, my mother was to write about that moment in her life. Her notebooks were not journals in the formal sense, but dislocated paragraphs, sentences—chapters, even—in which she made attempts at articulating her response to being alive. And to being Lily. Not Lily Wyatt. She forbade that name to be spoken. Or written. She was *Lily Kilworth*: none other.

This, for instance, written in 1910—addressed to me in the year of my birth: *Those first years at Selby Street were stilted and confusing. I was not, it seemed, to be sent to school with the other children who lived in the area. Because of this, the only education I received of the world around me was what I got in gossip from Agnes, the maid, and Charlotte, the cook, and Mister Bateson, the man. The education I had from mam was mostly got from books—gossip of another kind: that the world was round—that it spun amongst the stars—that the stars had names and made their way through the heavens. I could only verify this gossip— these rumours—by stealing into our garden in the dark, where— staring upward—I was dizzied by the shifting sky . . .*

It had not been Ede's original intention to keep my mother from school. In the back of her mind, where Lily was given the eternal promise of a normal life, Ede saw the years advancing as they had for herself. Grade school would one day offer Lily a formal education—and friends.

But not yet. Not now.

Ede knew the moment must come when Lily would rise from her desk in the classroom, spin out her chittering words and fall to the floor in a clatter of books and pencils, only to lie there helpless under the stare of her fellows—never to recover their esteem. Always thereafter, she would be their fool and their cretin—the butt of all their jokes and the object of their pity.

No.

Lily would not go to school.

Instead, there would be lessons at home, books to be read, letters to be formed, pictures of the world to be drawn at the dining-room table. The dining-room was bright and spacious. Huge! Lily, eight years old, could be seated on double cushions in a high-backed chair. She could spread her pencils, paints and crayons over a wider surface than any measly school desk could offer. All the room lacked was companions. Friends. That was the worst of it.

Frederick's return from the King Street factory was the same every day. The front door would open and Lily, seated halfway up the stairs, would hear him call out: *where's my girl?* And there she would be—mam, coming from the kitchen to greet him with: *Fred! Fred! I've waited all day to see you!* These private affections were broadcast for all the household to hear—since all the household depended on the state of the marriage that held it together. If a voice was raised in anything other than tenderness and rapture, the house would shudder and fall.

That *my girl* should be Ede and not Lily did not fail to raise Lily's interest. It gave an edge to Frederick's relations with Ede that seemed to be parental. Lily had witnessed enough of a father's behaviour in James Kilworth to be aware that grown men had girls for children—not for wives. Her Aunt Willa had been the *girl* on the farm.

It was in this moment of ritual greeting that Lily first sensed she had lost her place in the order of Ede's affections. Sitting on the stairs, she felt her mother's arms letting go of her as she watched them being offered up to this man whom Ede claimed to have waited all day to see.

But she'd spent the whole day with me, Lily wrote.

Once their greetings had been exchanged and their embrace had ended, mam took away Frederick's hat and coat and hid them in the cloakroom. This was where the telephone was also hidden. I could follow mother's voice as it babbled on non-stop about the day's events and the meal that would soon be eaten.

The hallway below was wide and square, with doors on every side but one—where the stairs rose up towards me on the landing.

The cloakroom was small and secretive, lying between the kitchen door and the dining-room. It was like a cave, with a green velvet curtain at its mouth. In there, all our overshoes and rubbers sat on sisal mats and all the household overcoats hung from hooks, like savage robes at the end of the hunt. They smelled of everywhere we'd been.

The telephone was boxed and hung from the wall beyond my reach. I had not yet heard its voice, but I knew it was alive and I never failed to be relieved by its ringing. Living things should not be speechless.

Mam's voice inside the cloakroom was muffled, so it seemed, by all the fur and wool that was hanging there. Sometimes it would dip and swoop as she leaned towards the floor to straighten the rows of boots and galoshes. After a moment, she would return like Eurydice from the Underworld, and follow her Orpheus into the drawing-room where Frederick would be lifting the decanters from their table, pouring out whiskey and sherry.

I had been told that in a moment, mam will come and bring you to say hello to Papa *and sometimes those* moments *lasted hours until she came to the bottom of the stairs and called me down.*

Hand in hand, we would then return to the drawing-room, where mam would lead me forward and release me into Frederick's arms. He never failed to lift me onto his knee—and seated there, in the aura of his whiskeyed breath, I would close my eyes and feel him kiss my cheek. He rarely kept me there and put me down as soon as the ritual kiss had been delivered. I was

not required to kiss him back. I had smeared saliva on him once,
and ever since, reciprocal kisses had been repulsed. I never told
mam I had done it to him on purpose . . .

The thing is, he put me down from his knee because he was
afraid. Afraid that I would be there when the whirlwind began to
throw me across the room and hurl me up to the ceiling. He didn't
understand the whirlwind can't get out of me. It can't hurt anyone
else. It's mine.

10.

Agnes, Charlotte and Bateson also had to be instructed in the matter of Lily's *whirlwind*. This was left, in the natural order of things, to Ede. *The natural order of things* was an invention of John H. Young's—or so it seemed. In it, everyone had their place and thus their functions. Duties. Responsibilities. Obligations. Mister Young's compendium, *Our Decorum*, became the family's bible. *Beeton's Household Management*, the Apocrypha.

On the day of Lily's arrival, Ede called Bateson into the kitchen and, with Agnes and Charlotte standing beside him in the middle of the floor, she informed them of her daughter's illness.

"Have any of you encountered seizures before?"

"You mean in the street?" said Agnes. She thought that a seizure might be something that reached out and grabbed you from the bushes.

"No, Agnes." Ede was patient. Charlotte, however, had a nephew who, it was explained, "is *ecopleptic*. I know all about it," Charlotte said. "Poor, dear child. Is Miss Lily violent?"

Ede said *no*.

"Does she require restraining, then? My nephew sometimes has to be held down at all corners."

"In the street, you mean?" said Agnes. This appeared to be her question of the day.

"No, dear. Hand and foot—spread-angled on the floor. I seen it take four of us to hold him. Poor, dear child."

Ede explained that Lily herself was not violent. Nor Charlotte's nephew. "It's the seizure that makes them seem so. Do you know, besides holding, what needs doing?"

Charlotte said: "rest is what they give him, afterwards. The boy, I mean. And a warm blanket."

Ede confirmed this.

"Are they frequent, madam?" Charlotte wanted to know. "I mean, Miss Lily's apprehensions . . ."

"No. Thank heaven. Lately, so I'm told, they seem to have abated. I only wanted you to be comfortable about them, so they would not alarm you unduly. The thing to remember is to go to her at once, not to go running for help. That just wastes time."

Agnes, who was small and delicate, suddenly begged permission to be seated. Ede allowed this.

"If you're going to swoon on us, Agnes, put your head down 'tween your knees," said Charlotte.

"I couldn't do that," said Agnes. "Not with Mister Bateson here."

"Better your head between your knees," said Charlotte, "than your body on the floor."

Ede was satisfied that Charlotte would make an able attendant if anything should happen. Thank God for that, if nothing else.

"I need hardly add," she said, "that Miss Lily's sickness is not to be discussed beyond the walls of this house."

"No, madam."

"Bateson? You've been entirely silent," said Ede. "Have you any questions about this?"

"No, ma'am."

"Very well, then. If questions should occur to you, please feel free to ask."

"Thank you, madam."

"Agnes?"

"Yes'm?"

"Are you recovered?"

"Yes, madam."

"Stand up, then. There's work to be done."

Agnes stood up, wavering only slightly.

After informing them Lily would be arriving at three o'clock that afternoon, Ede walked out of the kitchen—through the front hall and into the drawing-room, where she poured herself a glass of sherry and sat with it on the sofa. Having delivered her news, she was suddenly shaken by it—almost as if it was the first time she had heard it herself.

In the kitchen, Agnes spoke hoarsely: "I think I can't work where people's crazy."

"Miss Lily's not crazy," said Bateson. "She's obviously blessed."

"Blessed, is it?" said Charlotte. "I think not. Maybe not *crazy*, but not for certain blessed. My nephew . . ."

Bateson was already heading for the side door, where he'd left his rakes and brooms. "Blessed of God," he said. "Saints, some of them. It's a sign. You mark my words."

The screen door banged and he was gone.

Agnes sat back down in her chair. "Oh," she said. "No. I know I can't work in a house where there's going to be saints. The minute there's saints, the devil sends messengers."

"Fiddlesticks," said Charlotte.

"No," said Agnes. "Swear to God! It's true! I know it for a fact."

"You're barmy," said Charlotte. "*Barmy*." And laughed.

"No," said Agnes. "Not barmy. Catholic."

11. Lily was on the landing, reading *Beeton's Book of Household Management*. Morning sunshine poured in all around her, some of it streaked with red and blue from the stained-glass window. Down below her in the entrance hall there was a duster lying on the carpet. Agnes must have dropped it from her apron, unaware.

"*CLEANLINESS IS NEXT TO GODLINESS,*" Lily read, "*. . . the housemaid then may be said to be the handmaiden of two of the most prominent virtues.*"

Lily did not know the meanings of *prominent* or *virtues*—but, having the meanings of CLEANLINESS and GODLINESS by heart, she could grasp the burden of what was being said. *Agnes was in trouble.* Having lost her duster, the housemaid had failed the handmaid.

Lily hugged her knees and bent in closer over the book. There were pictures there in the margins of *Housemaid's brushes.* That is what it said. There were twelve of them—disciples: the handmaid's apostles. *Three scrubbing brushes. Two carpet brooms. Two stove and grate brushes. One staircase broom. One crumb brush. Three hearth and fireplace brushes . . .* Twelve.

And one of them Judas.

Which?

The crumb brush, Lily supposed—tracing its sickle-curved back with her finger. The Judas brush, used at the Last Supper. The sunlight shifted. Lily turned pages. Behind her, the stained-glass window glowed. Beyond it, the branches of the elm trees waved their brave new leaves in the wind. A flock of starlings flew up—shouting—wheeling—spooking the sunlight so that it stuttered and flickered—flickered and stuttered—red—red—green—red—orange—on the pages of *Beeton's Book of Household Management.*

Fire-lighting, Lily read, *however simple, is an operation requiring some skill . . .*

A shiver ran down her back. A breeze, all at once, walked up the stairs and lifted her hair in its fingers.

Who let you in?

The back door.

Lily read on.

. . . a fire is readily made by laying a few cinders at the bottom in open order . . .

Cinders.

Open order.

. . . over this a few pieces of paper, and over that again eight or ten pieces of dry wood; over the wood, a course of moderate-sized pieces of coal . . .

Coal.

. . . taking care to leave hollow spaces between for air at the centre, and taking care to lay the whole well back in the grate, so that the smoke may go up the chimney and not into the room . . .

Lily raised her gaze from the page and bumped herself down three steps so that she could see all the way into the drawing-room, where an empty fireplace waited for the day's instructions.

Fire-lighting, however simple, is an operation requiring some skill . . .

Lily closed her eyes. In her mind, the flickering—prompted by the window beams—continued: red—red—green—red—orange . . .

Is that you?

Fire.

Waiting.

Where?

That's for me to know and you to find out.

Lily smiled.

Fire had never spoken to her before in such a direct way. Not with a human voice. The language had always been in flames, augmented by the wind-words high in the chimney. Sometimes there was so much roaring it was more like song than speech. Music. Singing. Song. But not words.

This was words.

Fire?

Yes?

Still there?

Yes.

Let me see you.

Later.

When?

Later.

Lily's eyes were still closed.

She waited.

No. The voice did not return.

This was tantalizing. Lily knew that fire was both her friend and her enemy. It contained her secret people—gave her glimpses of them far away down the flames, where they huddled in rooms she had never seen in life. Tall, high-ceilinged rooms with tall bright windows. It also brought the sparkling sickness—dousing her in light before the whirlwind rose to lift her, wrapped in its wings of noise.

Lily opened her eyes and looked back down at the book on her knees.

. . . fire the paper with a match from below, and if properly laid, it will soon burn up, the stream of flame from the wood and paper soon communicating to the coals and cinders . . .

Matches. Paper. Communicating.

. . . provided there is plenty of air at the centre.

Someone was coming. But Lily could not give up her reading.

The several fires lighted, the housemaid proceeds with her dusting, polishing and sweeping.

Agnes walked into the hall and stood on the carpet with her back to Lily.

"There you are," she said, as if speaking to a disobedient child. "I've been looking everywhere for you. Naughty!"

Then she stooped over and picked up the Voice of CLEANLINESS.

Lily put her hand to her lips.

The Voice of CLEANLINESS said nothing. It allowed itself to be carried off in Agnes's left hand—one end hanging down towards the floor.

Agnes, the handmaid of CLEANLINESS and GODLINESS, was also the handmaid of fire. Lily had watched her—Agnes—with her box of matches and her paper—communicating.

Lily closed the book and stood up.

She went down into the drawing-room and stood in front of the fireplace.

I know where you're hiding, she said.

High in the chimney, the wind blew.

Birds—those starlings, perhaps—must have been sitting up there as Lily had seen them do before in order to catch the warmth of the house when the fire was not lit. Now, they flew off all at once, with a great clap of wings. And a shout.

The wind—the whirlwind?—increased and grew louder.

No, Lily said. *Not here. Not now.*

She felt herself falter. Her mind, in its place, leaned backward, as if it were about to launch itself into the air with the birds. She waited.

And waited.

Nothing happened.

The wind abated.

Silence.

Silence.

Someone, somewhere, must have heard her.

12. On a bright spring morning scented by a warm south wind, Lily went to the garden to watch Bateson dig. She was wearing a dark cloth coat, long black itchy stockings and a wide straw hat that was tied beneath her chin. The coat was pulled in tight at the waist and the hat had been dyed to match its particular blue. Bateson was humming a tune.

Don't sing that.

He stopped.

Lily made a show of interest in some ants crawling up a tree. She counted them, watching them pass as on a highway. She did this glancing sideways. She wondered where their city was. They kept going up, but none came down.

Bateson, silent, went on digging. Lily's gaze flicked in his direction from time to time, but nothing was said.

She walked along the edge of the flowerbed that ran between the lawn and the fence at the front of the house. Bateson was off to her right. The ant tree was behind her.

She had been looking up words in the dictionary, and she now rehearsed their meanings.

Handmaiden: *one who serves, often in a religious context, as in: handmaiden of the Lord.*

That was Agnes for you.

Agnes: *chaste—Lamb of God*—followed by something unpronounceable in a language Lily could not decipher. But there was God again: *Lord. God.*

And also:

Cinders: *res-i-due of coal and wood that has ceased to flame, but which still has com-bus-ti-ble matter in it.*

Com-bus-ti-ble: matter capable of burning.

Bateson had made a pile of dry dead leaves in one corner of the yard. Lily turned in its direction.

Ede came and stood on the side porch, pulling a cashmere shawl around her shoulders.

"You warm enough, Lily?"

Lily nodded.

"Bateson?"

"Yes'm?"

"Is the gate . . . ?"

Shut.

"Yes'm."

I knew that. It's always shut when I come out.

"Tomato soup for lunch, Lily. Won't that be nice? Charlotte made it herself, with those tomatoes we brought back in jars from Munsterfield." Ede and Lily were now on parallel paths, about ten feet apart, Ede on the porch, Lily on the grass. "This afternoon, don't forget your Uncle Lizzie will be here. He's going to bring his dog. Won't that be fun?"

Lizzie. Dog. Buster.

"Bateson?"

"Yes, ma'am?"

"You don't mind if the dog comes into your garden, do you? He's a dear, sweet dog. I don't think he'll hurt things."

"Not to worry, Mrs Wyatt. I like dogs."

"You have one, don't you, Bateson?"

"Yes, ma'am. Name of Toby. I keep him in the stable."

Ede nodded. She turned again in Lily's direction.

"Lily?"

Where was she?

"Bateson?"

"Yes, ma'am?"

"Where is Miss Lily?"

"She's gone round the house, Mrs Wyatt. Been doing that all morning—round and round. I expect she's on some kind of mission."

"Mission?"

"Yes. Not to worry. I seen Miss Lily on missions here before. She saves things."

"Saves things? You mean a collection?"

"No, ma'am. Saves things in peril. Toads and the like. Worms. Moves them off the lawn into the flowerbeds."

"I see. Well—keep an eye on her." Ede started back towards the door, but stopped just short of it. "Something's burning," she said. "What is it, Bateson?" She turned around. "Those leaves are on fire," she said. "Was that your intention?"

Bateson looked across the lawns at his pile of leaves. A long grey curl of smoke was lifting itself from the centre. Deep at the core, he could see a few orange flames. Mystified as to how the fire might have been started, he nonetheless took credit for it. "Yes'm," he said. "That's my intention."

Satisfied, Ede went into the house and the door clicked shut behind her. Bateson walked across the grass and inspected the pile of leaves. It was now quite thoroughly on fire. He reached out and touched it with his garden fork.

Lily came around the far corner of the front porch. She stopped and looked at Bateson's back.

Good.

The only problem that remained was returning the matches to Agnes's work-box without being caught. But that was for later—after lunch, before Uncle Lizzie came. For now, she had to solve the problem of the ants.

She went and stood at the foot of their tree, looking skyward. No city up there—so what were they all doing marching in single file to the top of the tree without returning?

Ant heaven—that must be it.

All these ants were dead and climbing up to heaven.

Lily looked down at her feet.

No ant hell that she could see. Maybe no such place existed.

She looked across at Bateson. The leaves were all on fire. Leaf hell, yes—ant hell, no.

Lily smiled and went across to sit on the steps. She would watch the daffodils until the tomato soup was served. The world at large was wonderful, she decided. Things pushing up to heaven. Others burning down to hell. And in between, the living walking sideways on the earth.

13. Lizzie arrived at three that afternoon. The yellow dog was with him. Lily watched their arrival from an upstairs window. She could hear her mother singing out her greeting.

"Hallo, Lizzie!"

"I hope you don't mind my bringing Buster," he said, opening the gate and coming through to the walk.

"Not one bit. It's lovely to see you both."

Buster's tail was wagging. His whole rear end was swaying side to side with pleasure. His eyes, though merry, were old, and his muzzle had white on it.

Lily thought she had never seen anyone as beautiful as Lizzie Wyatt. He was seventeen years old, now, and always seemed to be smiling, even when he wasn't. Something indefinable shone in his face. *His broad clear brow in sunlight glowed* . . . And his eyes were the eyes of the knights in her picture books—drawn on his face with a smudge of charcoal. Even his hair was poetic—like the hair of Lancelot, only red—not black. Dark, dark red and curling at his neck. He wore no armour—only a brown linen jacket and a wide cravat. His trousers were tan and his shoes were grey and his *helmet* was a plain straw boater—but still, her view of him was always the same—of *someone riding down to Camelot*. In his hands today, there were yellow tulips for Ede.

Lily left her room and went to the top of the stairs. She had put on her white cotton dress, the one with the pale blue sash and the cloth-covered buttons. Its collar rose to her chin. She still wore the hated black stockings. She had been, it seemed, condemned to them for life.

When Ede called her down, Lily took a deep breath and walked all the way to the landing with her eyes closed. Then she opened them and there he was.

Lizzie looked up and gave his famous smile *out loud*, as Lily thought.

"Hello," he said.

On the bottom step, as Ede had taught her, she bobbed in a silent curtsey.

Buster came across the carpet and put his snout in the palm of her hand. His nose was cold and wet and friendly.

Hello.

Lizzie had something hidden behind his back. "I saved this tulip for you," he said—and gave it to her. Yellow. Maybe he was going to ask her to marry him. She wanted that. She was so in love with him, it hurt her insides. She decided that if Lizzie did not ask her, she would have to ask him. *Not now. But later . . .*

Then, they all went into the parlour.

At 3:35 that afternoon, Lily tried to excuse herself, but got no further than rising from her chair. Ede looked up and could see what was happening.

"Don't be frightened," she said to Lizzie. "Take the dog away and come back to help me."

This was the first in a series of three seizures that were so severe Ede had to call in Doctor Cooper. Sadly, they had returned just as everyone's hopes had been raised because there had been no sign of Lily's illness for weeks.

When Agnes had let Doctor Cooper out of the house, she stood in the parlour, staring down at Lily on the floor. "Will she live, madam?" she said.

"Of course she will, Agnes. You must learn not to be so afraid."

Lizzie said: "let me carry her upstairs."

Lily heard him, seemingly from far away. Then she felt him lifting her.

Later—much later—she would write of this: *he carried me up to Camelot—with Agnes going before and Buster walking behind. And all the doors flung open by the Lamb of God . . .*

Lily's world was peopled, then, with illustrated heroes, Mrs Beeton's handmaid, a father killed by horses, some figures seen in flames, ants on their way to heaven—and a headless ancestor. She sat long hours in the sunlight, staring from beneath her wide-brimmed hat.

Is she out there with you? Ede would say to Bateson.

Yes, ma'am.

With him—and not. Not with anyone visible.

14. When Lyon Wyatt was born in August of 1901, Lily had only just turned eleven. Her swollen mother had disappeared for a week and when she returned, she carried the swelling wrapped in a blanket.

"This is Lyon," said Ede. "Your brother."

Lily looked at him in silence. He was sleeping. Why had they called him a lion? She thought he was the smallest living creature she had ever seen. He was nothing like the playmate she had been promised—besides which, he was not a girl. She disliked him at once and turned around and left the room.

Later, she said to Ede: "why did you have to leave home to get him? Couldn't you have found him here?"

Ede said: "I didn't have to find him, darling. He was already here inside me. You know that. It was all explained."

Lily wasn't satisfied.

"How do I know he's really my brother?"

"Because I say so. Don't be tiresome, Lily."

"He could be somebody else's brother. You might have found him anywhere."

"I did not *find* him. I gave birth to him."

"How?"

"He was inside me. I let him out."

"How did he get inside you?"

"Your father put him there."

"My father is dead."

"I mean Frederick."

"Frederick is not my father."

"No. But he is your stepfather, Lily. You must learn to call him *Father*."

"I don't want to."

Neither of them spoke. Ede was preparing Lily for bed and had just finished brushing her hair. Lily pulled away and went and stood by the window. In the garden, the robins were still singing. It was half past eight and the sky was an incandescent blue.

"Where did you find me?" Lily asked.

Ede gave a sigh and set the brush aside.

"In a field," she said, giving in to Lily's fantasy of birth. To be born was to be found—nothing would convince the child otherwise and Ede thought maybe it was best to let her think so for the time being. Perhaps the image was a comfort to her.

"Why in a field? Was I lost?"

"No, dear. That was where I went to find you. I've told you this a hundred times. Surely you know it by heart." Ede looked over at the birth-wreath, hanging above the bed. "I made that the day you were born, so you'd always have a part of the field you could touch."

"You *were* looking for me, then?" Lily persisted.

"Yes."

"Where else did you look?"

"Nowhere else. I knew you would be in the field."

"Did you know where Lyon would be?"

"Yes. In the hospital."

"Why? Was he sick?"

"No. Not sick at all. He was just fine."

Ede hoped this would be the end of it.

"Maybe he'll die," said Lily.

Ede sat down on the bed and closed her eyes. She had no idea where such a thought had come from and it saddened her. And frightened her.

"Will Lyon have spells like me?" Lily asked, just as if she hadn't mentioned death.

"I don't know." Ede was exhausted. The burden of Lily's persistence was unbearable, but she had no way of stopping it short of crying out or striking her. Reason played no part in dialogue with Lily. A person had to weather it, surrender to it—or leave. Ede knew better than to thwart the question by walking out and closing the door. That led to tantrums and the tantrums led to rage—and the possibility of seizures.

"How will I know he's my brother if he doesn't have spells?"

"Everyone doesn't have spells, Lily. You know that."

"Why not?"

"I don't know."

An extended silence followed this, in which Ede sat inwardly praying for the session to end and for Lily to lie down at peace. The torment in the child was not entirely mysterious. Simple jealousy was part of it. That much was understandable. Lyon's arrival had undercut Lily's supremacy—or so she imagined. Telling her that nothing could displace Ede's affection for her would only lead to more accusations: *you're lying—I don't believe you—prove it.* Some of these feelings, though never articulated, had taken root in Ede herself when Liam had been born—and Willa. Especially Willa—another girl. *As if another girl was needed!* she had cried to Eliza.

The thought of this memory made Ede smile.

This was unfortunate. Lily turned and saw her.

Ede tried to pass it off, but the expression on Lily's face was one of hurt and anger. Did her mother not take her feelings seriously?

Say something. Please.

Ede looked down at her hands. How sad it was, this unnecessary hurt and anger that could not be soothed away.

"It's time for bed," she said.

"How can I go to bed when you're sitting on it?"

Ede swallowed her exasperation and stood up. She did, however, say something.

"I don't speak to you in that tone of voice," she said. "And I expect more courtesy than that from you."

Lily kicked off her slippers and drew back the covers.

"In this family," Ede said, "we pray at bedtime."

"Yes, ma'am." Lily's back was to her. She got to her knees and gazed through the window, pretending her eyes were closed.

"Out loud," said Ede.

Lily sighed. Then was silent.

"Gentle Jesus . . ." Ede said.

"Gentle Jesus, meek and mild, bless the wishes of this child . . ." The voice faltered.

"Yes?"

"If I should die before I wake, I pray the Lord my soul to take . . ."

Ede waited.

"And?" she said.

Lily did not respond.

"Aren't you going to thank God for Lyon?"

No.

Lily's folded hands were turning white.

"What do we say at the end of prayers?" Ede asked.

"*Amen.*"

"Thank you."

"You're welcome," said Lily, rising.

Ede almost laughed out loud. She went to the door.

"Good-night, Lily," she said.

There was no answer.

Ede could see that Lily's back was to her. Rigid.

Nothing more was said.

Ede stood waiting. Mourning.

Something between them—something vital—was over. Had ended. When Lyon's cord had been cut, so—it seemed—had Lily's. Irrevocably.

Ede closed the door and went downstairs to Frederick.

15. On a Friday night in December of 1902, Ede and Frederick gave a dinner party. It was notable for several reasons. The first of these was the grand success of the guest list. All of those to whom invitations had been sent responded with eager anticipation of the event.

The Wyatts were now moving in towards the centre of a coterie whose cachet was the glamour of their wealth. Not that mere money gave them this glamour—but the glittering accoutrement of what could be had through its auspices: clothing and jewellery, motor cars and servants, houses that were grander by far than the Selby Street house, for all its acknowledged charm and warmth. These were insignia of achievement in the market-place—of domination in the world of finance—of power that reached all the way to London, New York and Paris.

A secondary glamour—the glamour of *charm* was got from the interest this circle had in the arts and culture. Its boxes at the Massey Music Hall, the plaques that named its members as the donors of paintings and the sponsors of literary events; stationery that acknowledged them as the Honourary Patrons of music festivals and members of the senates of universities—these were the emblems of their concern for their community and their place in its history. And, of course, from Frederick's point of view— because he was lodged at the heart of a cultural industry, namely the manufacture of pianos—it did him no harm as a businessman to be one of this circle.

Ede had a natural ability and, indeed, a proclivity for creating an atmosphere of gaiety and charm that bathed her guests in a warm light of welcome. People did not merely like or admire her—they *adored* her. Stepping into Edith Wyatt's drawing-room, her parlour and her dining-room, one never failed to be reassured by the presence of a few acquaintances and the intriguing possibilities of one or two strangers. None would be stranded on the shore—all would find welcome at the centre. And the centre was Ede.

Flowers abounded—hothouse roses and lilies, bulbs that had been forced by Bateson to an exquisite burst of scent. And, on this particular occasion—given the Christmas season—wreaths of spruce and holly hung with velvet bows had been added to the décor.

Ede's table, too, was becoming well known—much appreciated and even more talked about than the tables of hostesses with twice her money. The secret of this was in Charlotte's blossoming as a cook who would dare all to please the palates of strangers. She fell upon the joy of food as entertainment with all the relish of a Paris chef.

There were two more servants now, besides Charlotte, Bateson and Agnes. These were a governess, who went, like Bateson, by her last name only—Browning—and a second housemaid whose name was Emily.

Browning was severe and testy, but she was wonderful with Lyon and after the births of Annie in 1905 and Alice in 1907, she became a household institution whose presence was so valued, Ede kept her on until Browning's death in the flu epidemic of 1918. But in 1902, she had not yet deciphered the secret of mastering Lily. Lily remained aloof from the nursery, claiming she was *not a child* and therefore not in Browning's charge. This was later to be refuted with a vengeance—but not just yet. Lily—too briefly—was managing to define her own existence.

On the night of the dinner party in December of 1902, when Lily was halfway through her thirteenth year, she was given permission to sit on the stairs and watch the guests arrive. She pretended, as she did increasingly in public situations, that no one could see her where she sat. She was invisible, and thus unaccountable. The wraith on the step below the landing was nameless, silent and perfectly still. If smiled at or spoken to, it closed its eyes—as rabbits do when the fox is about to pounce. She wore a blue wool bathrobe and a long white nightgown and—abjuring slippers—she had pulled on a pair of white lisle stockings that gave her feet the look of birds at rest.

The fires had been lit in all the grates, which was always a mix of wonder and fear to Lily. The smell of burning applewood and birch was more than pleasant—almost an opiate—but the flames had fingers that seemed to beckon her and she turned increasingly away from them.

There were twenty guests in all that night. Ede had arranged to seat them at two round tables, instead of the usual oblong of mahogany with all its additional leaves in place. Beyond the three sets of uncurtained French doors, a snowfall could be seen, as if by command performance. The flakes were large as bits of lace, cut into shapes that echoed the shapes of apple blossoms. These fell into the beams of houselight gleaming through the windows, lingering—so it seemed—to show themselves to all the guests.

Lily watched from a crouch, her arms around her knees, as men in white ties and tails walked in to be greeted by Frederick near the central fire—and as women in gowns of plum and blue velvet, coffee-coloured lace and cream-coloured silks moved towards one another with sibilant sighs as their skirts met the carpets. The smells of powdered shoulders and of perfumed handkerchiefs mingled with the dark green scent of the wreaths and the tall oriental vases filled with flowers and the applewood fires. To these was added a transfusion of aromas emanating from Charlotte's kitchen. Lily closed her eyes and drank it all in.

To be precise, what Charlotte had concocted was nothing less than a banquet. To call it a mere meal would be to insult its integrity. Words such as *dinner, supper* and *repast* were equally unworthy. After all, this food would be set before Masseys and Baldwins and Gooderhams—palates whose memory of this feast would carry it far beyond the Wyatts' table into the upper-upper echelons of society, where Mister and Mrs Frederick Wyatt had but a finger-hold.

Perusing the guest list, Charlotte had dreamt that her culinary genius would push her master and mistress all the way to the centre. Given the month of planning already invested and the well-rehearsed timing of each of the courses—besides the imagination with which the menu had been charted—it seemed that Charlotte had a triumph within her grasp.

Emily and Agnes had been schooled in the ways of handling the various serving dishes so as not to disturb their contents before each one had been uncovered and displayed. Part of the pleasure of food was in its appearance and Charlotte would hang that night by the door of the butler's pantry, pinching herself with pleasure as each of her concoctions was presented.

A consommé came first. Besides its rich aroma, larded with sherry, the broth was afloat with razor-thin slices of lime and lemon and scarlet crab-apples. Only Charlotte knew the secret of these coins of fruit. Prior to being submitted to the knife, each of the lemons, limes and apples had been partially frozen in a snow-bank out in the garden. Fearing this technique would reach the kitchens of the mighty, Charlotte had laid down the law. "Tell no one," she had said to Bateson, Agnes and Emily, "or I'll have a word with madam!" *Having a word with madam* was the penultimate threat of the household. The ultimate threat, of course, was *having a word with Himself.* Frederick could intimidate the moon.

Once the consommé had been cleared, and the *coquilles Florentine* dispatched—scallops in a light cheese sauce, nestled on beds of Charlotte's bottled spinach—the sideboard was graced not with one but with two roast suckling pigs, the carving of which had been taught to Frederick by Charlotte herself. Lily, on hearing that baby pigs were to be eaten, had attempted to spirit them away from their place in the cold room—but on discovering they were already slaughtered, she demurred and gave up animal prayers to the Ant God in the garden, instead.

These crisp and succulent meats were served with a course of vegetables whose gleaming Christmas colours drew cries of pleasure from the tables.

Charlotte retreated to her kitchen and drank a whole glass of sherry straight down. When Emily and Agnes returned from their latest flurry of serving, they were laughing and giggling with excitement. Emily, who was a perfect match for Agnes in height, but not in girth, might have been her anorexic sister—if that word had been used in those days. As it was, she was painfully thin and brittle, having been given up as an orphan to an agency that sent young girls and boys to be servants in institutions. These institutions—reform schools and the like—were so poor in themselves that only the sparest meals were offered.

Tonight, the Wyatt staff had been promised *leftovers. Roast suckling pig!* Agnes would whisper in Emily's ear—and they would close their eyes and pinch each other and laugh behind their hands. *Soup with sherry in it!* Simpering. Dancing. *Wait till you see the dessert!* Almost shouting its name aloud. *Gâteau Saint-Honoré! Gâteau Saint-Honoré!* That afternoon, in her hiding place in the dumb waiter, Lily had heard their cries, but could not quite make out the words. *Stron-array!* She wondered what it might be. It was not a sweet she had yet encountered.

But there was more yet to come before the final course. After the suckling pig and vegetables, Bateson was given a silver tray to *carry forth*, as Charlotte would have it—an array of sorbets *for cleaning* the palate, she said. Agnes was to accompany Bateson and lift each serving from the tray, setting them one by one before the guests. Emily's job had been to run to the garden, wearing her overcoat and gloves, and there to recover the frozen sorbets from their hiding place in the snowbank.

Agnes had asked if the snowbank was given its name because it was a place for hidden riches. Charlotte, having gained much practice in reading Agnes's intelligence, was certain the girl was not making a pun.

The ices were taken from moulds in the shape of Saint Nicholas, whose suit was of raspberry sherbet. His face, gloved hands and fur-trimmed hood were of frozen grapefruit juice and cream.

Once these figures had been dispensed with and after the tomato aspic and celery salad had been received, consumed and praised, and after all the emptied plates had been removed, Charlotte's great moment had arrived.

In the kitchen she kissed her hands and smoothed her hair before putting on a clean white cap and apron. She herself was to bring her *chef d'oeuvre* from its hiding place in the cold room— to which the key had been turned and pocketed—and march in its presence to the dining-room. Perhaps, given the business of the household, there should have been music for this. On the other hand, given the majesty of the confection which preceded Charlotte into the presence of the guests, music was not required. It would, at any rate, have been drowned by the round of applause that greeted the appearance both of the wonder itself on its silver tray and its creator.

"What marvellous thing is this?" someone asked.

"Madam," said Charlotte, sweeping a chubby hand in its direction, "this is a *Gâteau Saint-Honoré* . . ."

More applause. And sighs of delight.

Charlotte was requested by Ede to describe the dessert, which was quite unknown to all the guests, before she made the first cut.

"Yes, madam," said the cook—very like a schoolgirl all at once, who has won an unexpected prize. Before her on Bateson's serving tray was a glorious Christmas tree almost two feet high. It was made of dozens and dozens of puff pastries, each one filled with pastry cream and dipped in the sugar syrup that would bind them together. These had been assembled by Charlotte in circles that grew increasingly narrower as the hollow tower had risen up beneath her hands. A myriad of candied cherries, some red, others green, had been sliced and fixed to the surface of this monument to Charlotte's kitchen skills.

"Then, madam," she went on, "the whole creation is filled with whipped cream, glazed with spun sugar and dribb'ed with chocolate sauce . . ."

"It is a masterpiece," said Ede, "and we thank you for it, Charlotte."

"Madam." Charlotte blushed and wrung her hands in her apron before she picked up the knife with which she would cut her way into the tower. Emily had been instructed to bring a silver jug of boiling water to dip the knife into, but she had forgotten.

Agnes was dispatched to bring it.

In the pantry, she encountered Lily, dressed in robe and night-gown.

"Aren't you supposed to be in bed, Miss Lil?"

"I don't feel well," said Lily. "Get my mam."

Agnes was thrown by this. The entire company of diners was waiting for her to bring the hot water so their sweet might be served. Charlotte was already fuming. There might be *words with Madam* over this—or even *a word with Himself* if Agnes tarried.

"Can't you go up to Browning, Miss Lily?" she asked—already pushing through the far pantry door into the kitchen. "Emily can go and fetch her if . . ."

"I want my mam," said Lily, her voice a dead weight in her throat. She was pale and cold and her hair was wet with perspiration—signs that a seizure was on its way. Still, Agnes hesitated. The *Gâteau Saint-Honoré* awaited dispensation. The success of the whole evening now depended on a single jug of boiling water, without which the cake-knife would refuse to cut.

Emily was carting dirty dishes, trayload by trayload, into the scullery—and was otherwise sorting the flatware into piles of knives, forks and spoons. Her mind was entirely engaged in the thought of leftovers. Now that at last she was living in a house-hold where she was allowed to eat, she could think of little else.

"Emily?" This was Agnes.

"Yes, Aggie."

"Go fetch Browning. She's up in the nursery. Tell her *be quick, Miss Lily's going to have a spell . . .*"

Emily ran to the back stairs.

Agnes, at the stove, nearly scalded herself as she tried to pour the boiling water into the silver jug with its ebony handle.

"You hang on," she said to Lily. "Browning's coming and I'm going to whisper to your ma. I just have to get this water in . . ."

But Lily wasn't listening. Wasn't listening—or could not hear.

She started for the pantry door at the very same moment as the Lamb of God.

Lamb of God.

Lamb of God.

There were lights.

Flickers.

Flashes.

The wind was rising. Whirlwind.

Lily stumbled forward, to and through the first swinging door. Agnes was barely a single step in front of her, balancing the jug with its scalding contents.

Lamb of God.

Lamb of God.

Lily flailed.

She thought she was singing a hymn, but all that Agnes heard was the dreaded chittering, announcing Miss Lily's seizure.

They met at the second swinging door—the one that led directly into the dining-room.

Way! Lily shouted.

Or thought she had.

Chitter—Chitter . . .

Lamb of God.

The flaming wings that would enfold her were descending now.

Out went her arms. With one hand, she struck the open glass door of the crystal cabinet—smashing it and causing a dangerous rush of dark brown blood—while with her other, she struck the side of Agnes's face.

Down went the jug of scalding water—and Agnes with it beyond the door. Lily followed—stumbling over the maid on the floor and into her mother's arms, just as Ede was rising, horrified and turning in her direction.

Blood from Lily's wounded wrist and arm flew off in all directions—over the guests at the nearest table and onto their hair and faces and clothing. All this while, Lily was strangling down in the depths of her throat—*chattering-chittering*—with her head thrown back and her arms flung out and . . .

"STOP!"

Frederick.

He was standing at the far end of the furthest table, pointing at Ede and Lily locked in the frantic embrace of the mortally wounded and the miracle worker.

"Stop that! Stop that! *Now!*"

Every guest was frozen in place.

Lily gave the last of her cries—the one that always preceded the first convulsion. The whirlwind carried her up to the ceiling—so it seemed—and flung her down towards the floor with her mam. All the guests were now rising—one of them screaming—and Frederick went on raging. *Stop! Stop! Stop!*

Charlotte, standing in Bateson's shadow, gave up the cake-knife. Its handle—mother-of-pearl—clicked as she laid it down on Bateson's silver tray.

Well, she thought. *Perhaps some other time.*

16. Frederick was adamant. Lily would *go home* to Munsterfield.

Why?

Because I say so.

Yes. But why?

She is a liability.

Not to me, she isn't.

But she is to us.

Why?

Are you entirely stupid? Are you entirely obtuse? Are you entirely without sympathy?

Sympathy?

OUR REPUTATIONS!

That had been how the subject was raised—at the top of its voice.

And then:

Lily cannot harm our reputations. Only we can harm them.

The appearance of an idiot daughter . . . The presence of an idiot daughter . . . the fact of an idiot daughter . . .

She is not an idiot. Not an idiot.

She behaves like one.

A seizure is not behaviour—it's possession—being possessed.

I will not have it in my presence.

I'm sorry. If that is the case, then I will take her up to Munsterfield.

You will do no such thing. Your place is by my side. Especially now. Especially now, when all this damage has been done.

What damage? She broke some glass—she injured her arm— cut her wrist—terribly. She might have died. But she did no other damage. None.

She has set us back months. That's the damage I mean. The social consequences. God knows, some of those people may never come back to this house. I can't have that—and I can't risk it happening again. We will send *her to Munsterfield.*

Who with?

Browning.

Browning must be with Lyon. I will take her.

No you will not! No you will not *. . .*

Ede was devastated. Beaten.

Then she thought of Lizzie.

17. It was arranged that Bateson would stay with Lisgard, Senior, for one week so that Lizzie could take Lily up to Munsterfield on the train. This would *kill two birds with one stone*—as Ede put it—allowing Lily some favoured company while she settled in and affording Lizzie a much needed holiday from his duties at the Crawford Street house.

Because there was no way to tell Lily why she was being sent away, Ede's ploy had been to say that James and Eliza missed her. "And it's such a bad time here—with all the mud and slush. Up there, you'll have lots of snow to play in—and the barns—sleigh rides and Freda's lovely food. I envy you."

"Why don't you come, then?"

"Because, dear. I'm needed here."

Lily was silent.

Ede said: "you can sleep in our old room. You'll love that."

"With Lizzie?"

"No. That's not appropriate."

"Why not?"

Ede was packing Lily's steamer trunk, folding undergarments and waists into its drawers. She was glad her back was to the child. She had forgotten that, at Lily's age, her own curiosity about the burgeoning world of boys had been intense—and intensely frustrated. She had been a well of ignorance then—ignorance no one offered to dispel. Now it was Lily's turn at the well, and Ede would have to play the adult villain, the reticent interlocutor with the fudged answers—whose determined vagueness could so easily be seen through. *There's something they don't want me to know*, she had decided—rightly. Now, she wondered if Lily could be steered away from the same decision.

"Lizzie is nineteen years old," Ede said—still with her back to Lily, rolling stockings into pairs, lining them up in black and white rows. "Nineteen is too old to sleep with children."

"Why?"

She would ask, wouldn't she.

"Because."

"But *why*?"

Ede sighed.

"Because, when you are nineteen, you desire privacy."

"Why?"

"Because."

There was the slightest pause.

Lily said: "what if I asked him and he said *yes*?"

"He would not say yes."

"Why?"

"I've told you why."

Another pause. Silence fell between them.

Ede heard Lily walk away and sit on the bed.

"Is it because of my illness?"

Ede saw an opportunity for bringing the subject to a close—and seized it.

"Yes," she said. "It is because of your illness."

Damn.

Lily said nothing. The conversation was over.

After a minute, Ede said: "you want me to pack your white cotton dress with the blue sash . . . ?"

Turning, she found that Lily was gone.

Oh, well, Ede thought. *She won't forgive me for this. And then she will. When she finally understands, she might even laugh about it. I did, when Mother told me I was not allowed to sleep in the drive shed with Ephraim. I was ten years old—and, just like Lily, I said* why? *And Mother said:* because.

Of course, because *is not good enough. But it's all you have when you want to save the innocent. And the dreamer.*

Buster went with them on the train and had to ride in the baggage car. When Lizzie was told this, he said: *it doesn't matter. We'll go and sit there with him.* Which they did—all the way to McCaskill's Mills.

18. James and Eliza gave them a royal welcome. It seemed the world had regained all its poignancy and for one whole week, the house was filled with laughter.

Everyone fell in love with Lizzie. He was the *darlin' of every heart and the joy of every occasion.* Freda never stopped feeding him—Eliza never stopped coddling him and one night, James burst into tears.

"What on earth," said Eliza, "is this about?"

"It's as if we'd got our own Jamie back," said James. "It's as if all the boys we'd ever dreamed had returned to us . . . whole and alive."

Eliza wiped his eyes and kissed him on the cheek. "I know," she said. "I know." For her, it was not just Jamie and the Rosary Boys—it was Liam, too, come home in a state of happiness he'd never known.

As for Malahide, he stared and stared, because no one had ever been so alive as Lizzie was. No one had ever been so whole—and so content to be who he was—and this gave Malahide hope. If you can be reconciled to the flesh you are given and the days unfolding with their unique demands of you, then you can have a life as full as anyone's—no matter where or who you are. These, Mal suddenly realized, were the gifts to be reaped, if you said: *I am me—none other. I am this—nothing more. I am here—nowhere else—and here I'll bide. Forever.*

Lizzie had never been on a farm and he revelled in all its unique activities. One of the greatest pleasures was jumping in the hay.

"When we were kids," said Mal, "we used to see who dared to climb the highest over the loft and jump down into the stacks."

"How'd you get up there?" said Lizzie.

"Hand over hand. There's pegs there—you see them?"

Lizzie squinted.

"Yes."

"Then there's the built-in ladders, running up between the posts. My grandad put them there sixty-three years ago—same year my father was born."

"Wow!"

"So . . . when you get up high as you dare to, you walk out along the beams—choose a spot below you and . . . *one—two—three*—you leap!"

"You want to, Lily?"

Lily had been hanging back with Buster, watching and listening.

"Mam never let me do it," she said.

They were standing, staring up towards the sloping roofs where a flock of sparrows was chirping and flitting in and out of the light. Lily had stood there often enough in the past, but Ede had caught her clambering once and called her down. *Too dangerous,* she had said. *Not allowed.*

"Why don't you watch me, then?" said Lizzie. "I'll jump off, and if you like the look of it, you can climb up and try it, too. Remember how we danced in the factory?"

"Yes."

"Well, this is going to be just like that. Except, instead of dancing, we'll go flying!"

"Don't forget she's wearing that bandage," said Mal. "We don't want to start things bleeding again."

Lizzie was already climbing. He had taken off his winter coat and was wearing a bulky sweater and scarf. He was also wearing his hat.

"You oughta take your gloves off," said Mal. "Sometimes they slide off the rungs—and when you're on the pegs, same thing. It's 'cause they're wool . . ."

Lizzie removed his gloves and threw them down. Buster got one, but Lily retrieved it. There were holes in some of the finger ends. If only she knew how, she could fix them for Lizzie. Maybe later, she would ask Eliza.

"Don't go too high," said Mal. "Specially if you haven't ever done this before. Take a practice jump from where you are."

Lizzie was now about thirty feet above them, having shifted from the pegs onto another ladder.

"One beam higher," he said.

"Okay—but take it easy."

Mal moved back a few steps so he could get a better view. Lily and Buster did likewise. Down below them, there were cattle lowing in the stalls and some pigs were having one of their comfortable conversations about the delights of mash and slops. The sparrows had settled along the highest beams and were silent. All their tiny eyes were focused on the climber. What could he be up to, this groundling with his long, pale claws and his russet mane and his cloud-making breath and his face like an owl-face . . . Dangerous.

"Don't go any higher."

"No."

Lizzie left the ladder and went out onto the beam.

"Blondin!" he called down. "Here I am, high above Niagara Falls!"

He began to walk as on a tightrope—arms spread wide—each step laid before the other—one and one and one. And one.

He was at the centre.

Stop.

"How should I land?" he said to Mal.

"On your bum."

"Legs out?"

"Legs out—but not too stiff. Keep everything loose . . ."

Lizzie dropped his arms to his sides. "Hallo, sparrows," he said.

Buster, looking up, gave a bark and a slow, contemplative wag.

"Here I come!" said Lizzie.

And leapt.

Lily raised her injured arm and Mal stepped in beside her.

Lizzie fell forever. *Down. Down. Down.*

"I'm flying!" he cried. "I love it!"

Oh.

Flailing arms and jerking legs—plummeting—down—and all the sparrows rising up above him—down—and the sea of air around him parting, rushing past him—down—swimming down . . . down.

Down.

Oh.

Dust filled the air where Lizzie had landed—but he could not be seen. He had disappeared.

Buster gave another slow wag with his tail and sat—his head on one side—watching.

Where was he?

Mal said: "*Lizzie . . . ?*"

Silence.

Then they heard him.

He came to the edge of the loft on his knees. His face was white with dust—his mouth was open—his eyes were Lily's illustrated eyes—her smudges—and he was looking at her. *Come on,* he said, *it's time you learned to fly . . .*

They were there so long that Freda had to come and fetch them in to lunch. Mal had left them *flying* and gone off to finish his chores—so when Freda arrived, the only one of them she could see was Buster.

"*Liebchens?*" she called. "*Wo seit Ihr?*"

Buster was staring upwards.

Freda followed his gaze.

Lieber Gott . . .

Lily was standing on the highest beam of all. Lizzie was beside her. They were holding hands—and counting.

" . . . one . . ."

Nein!

" . . . two . . ."

Nein!

" . . . three . . ."

Aufhören!

They did not jump.

They fell.

Lizzie leaned forward.

Lily closed her eyes.

At first, they fell flat out, face down.

Lily's long, winding bandage had come undone and was streaming upward behind them.

Ach, nein . . . meine Liebchen . . .

Oh, how beautiful they were. Angels—mid-air—with winged sleeves and blowing hair.

"Now!" Lizzie shouted.

Slowly, they righted themselves, falling feet-first—leaning back, reclining—Lily now wide-eyed—Lizzie now singing . . .

One long, rising note—and the trailing, tailing bandage the last thing to fall—like a flag, an insignia, a badge. An emblem.

The dust rose, caught in the winter sunstreams angling through the spaces between the boards—dust filled with sparrow down—dust filled with sparrows leaping up to reclaim their homeland—dust that was shouting—everyone shouting—birds, woman, dust, dog, children, cattle, pigs and the dinner-gong.

All, they shouted, had been flying.

This was joy.

19. They had journeyed to Munsterfield on the 5th of January—a Monday. On the 7th and 8th, they jumped in the hay. On the 9th, it snowed. On the 10th, which was Saturday, they crossed the road and went into the field to see where Lily had been born.

"Ephraim? You in here?"

This was Eliza in the drive shed.

Ephraim came from the stalls with a curry-comb in his hand. He smelled of liniment and horse hair.

"Can I do aught?" he asked.

"Those snowshoes the boys use, time to time," said Eliza. "Do you know where they might be?"

"I'll see. Boys might've taken 'em—gone off for strays. Snowdrifts, you know—blown in the fields yonder . . ." He gave a chuck over his shoulder with the curry-comb. All this while, he was moving away from her, into where the carriage and the wagon were propped off their wheels, awaiting spring. In the wintertime, the sleigh was kept outside with the sledge, underneath tarpaulins. This, in case a snowfall should encumber the doors. In emergencies, there was no time to shovel.

"What you want them for, then?" Ephraim wondered.

"I want them for the children. They're going to cross the road into Lily's field and I thought if they wore the shoes it would be easier for them."

"Not if I've still got strays," said Ephraim. "We'll know soon enough. If the shoes is wet, they been used—and boys is in the barn. If the shoes is dry, you can't have 'em."

"I know. I understand," said Eliza. "The strays come first. Of course they do."

"Here they be," said Ephraim.

"Wet—or dry?"

"Wet as a rainstorm."

"Thank you, Ephraim."

Eliza accepted the snowshoes, which Ephraim had lifted down from their place on the wall.

"Those kids know how to tie themselves in?"

"If they don't, I'll show them. I wish I had time to go with them. Oh! Do you remember? The fun we used to have snow-shoeing all those winters ago?"

Ephraim gave his version of a smile—the corners of his lips extending—mouth closed, teeth clamped.

"You was good at shoein'" he said. "Mister James, too. All them races we made . . ."

"Well. I'll take them in, now. Thank you, Ephraim."

Eliza started for the door.

"Mind they bring 'em back to that wall," Ephraim called after her. "I won't have nothing out of place in here."

Eliza waved without turning.

"They'll bring them. I promise."

Lizzie stood at the foot of the stile and bound the ties to Lily's boots. Eliza had shown him how to manage this, though his fingers were cold and—having already attached his own shoes—he could barely make a knot.

"You want them loose enough so you can raise your heel," Eliza had told him. "But secure enough not to lose a shoe halfway through a stride! And remember—it's like being a duck. Good wide steps, toeing in. Don't toe out, or you'll step on your own tails . . ."

"There," Lizzie said. "Done."

Lily got down. What a curious feeling it was, not to sink into the snow.

Buster hated the stile. It was much too steep for him and Lizzie had to lift two rails from the fence in order to let the dog across. The drifts were not quite high enough for him to negotiate the pass with a simple leap. It was treacherous snow, layered over other falls that had partially frozen. When these gave way, Buster would flounder, looking like a child who was learning to swim.

Eliza, wrapped in shawls and wearing gloves, watched them from the front porch. How wonderful it was to look out into that field and see children there again. Running, laughing, falling down. And Buster, thinking it was all a game, rushing to lick their faces, preventing them from rising.

She knew that Lizzie was not a *child*. But it seemed appropriate to call him one—to think of him as one. Lily was so *old*—and he was so *young*. She was so serious—he was so gay. Lily made him sombre—Lizzie made her laugh.

Sombre?

Yes.

Eliza had watched him the night before in the lamp and firelight. All of them sitting there together—James and Malahide—Lizzie and Lily. Willa was away—pursuing another man. *That would end in disaster. The poor muddlehead . . . twenty-four years old and doesn't know better than to throw herself down in their path instead of being still and letting them come to her. Oh, well . . .*

But, Lizzie.

Look at him out there now—with our darling girl . . . The boy-man—caught in that moment when childhood ends and the adult world comes rushing through the door. Eliza had watched that moment in all her sons—Jamie, Liam and Malahide—each of them putting on manly airs, hanging back in the company of children . . . lowering their voices in the presence of grown-ups—shrieking soprano in the playground . . . standing awkward in their adult suits, scratching where children scratch . . .

Lizzie was some way *troubled.* Not, Eliza was certain, just because of his father. Something else was feeding on him. What?

The future? His lack of freedom? And the consequences of never being with others of his kind and age. What he needed, she decided, was a roaring crowd of boys—summer cotillions, where he could dance with a dozen pretty girls—and an education that would lift him into the company of men.

The dear, wondrous boy. The best friend Lily's ever had, outside this family. And I dare say she must be the best he's had, what with that daft old man on his deathbed and all his brothers treating him like an exile . . .

Eliza raised her hand to shade her eyes. The snow was blinding white and the sun had just come out from behind the morning's clouds.

If only he could stay here with us, she thought. *It would do him the world of good. And Lily, too.*

Still. He was here now. And she—*the darling girl*—was in seventh heaven.

Eliza turned away and went into the house. Lunch must be ready for their return.

Buster kept standing on Lizzie's snowshoes, preventing him from moving. Lily threw snowballs, and the dog would go bounding, floundering off with a howl of delight.

"He loves it here as much as I do," said Lizzie. "He's going to hate that baggage car on Monday!"

"Why do you have to go?"

"Because . . ."

"Oh, please don't say *because*. Mam's always saying that. I hate it."

Lizzie grinned sheepishly. "I have to go because my father needs me," he said. "Otherwise, I'd stay here forever."

"Would you?" said Lily. "So would I . . ."

Lizzie took her hand.

"You were going to show me where you were born," he said.

They were standing now at the top of the hill, where it fell away into Lily's corner.

"There," she said—and pointed.

"Looks awful cold to me," said Lizzie.

Lily stared at the fence where it made a corner with the tree line. All the trees were barren now, their blossoms down with the leaves beneath the snow. There was a bird's nest there, high in the branches, held in place almost as if a hand were holding it.

Lizzie started down with a wide, free-wheeling gait. So long as Buster didn't interfere, he figured he'd mastered it. Flying *and* snowshoeing, all in one week . . .

Near the hollow where the birth had been completed—the place into which Ede had crawled in order to cut the cord—there were monuments in the snow. Three of them—tall, conical markers, as if to say: *an event of some importance once happened here.*

"What are they?" Lizzie asked.

"Ants," said Lily. "Anthills."

"Why don't they freeze to death?"

"Because they're way down underneath. And asleep. Or sort of."

"Asleep—or sort of?"

"Yes. You know—like hibernation. Only not completely. Sometimes they move."

"How do you know all this?"

"I read about it."

"Oh."

"Don't you do that—read about things?"

Lizzie was silent.

Then he said: "sometimes. A little." He looked at her and she wondered why he wasn't smiling. "Just a little. Sometimes."

Then he looked away.

Lily crouched down near one of the anthills, close as her snow-shoes would let her. She reached out and brushed a bit of snow—a very little bit—away from its base.

"Come here," she said.

Lizzie hunkered down across from her, with the anthill rising up between them.

"They're like the pyramids," he said. "Like the tombs of Egypt's kings . . . I saw a picture once. There'd been a sandstorm—sand over everything, and the pyramids sitting there just like this."

"Take off your glove," said Lily. "Put your hand right here."

Lizzie removed his glove—which still had holes in it—and placed his fingers where Lily had brushed away the snow.

"It's warm," he said, astounded. "Warm!"

"There's thousands of them in there. Sleeping."

Lizzie stared. He had never seen such a thing. And warm. Warm. Alive.

"Sometimes I wish that we could hibernate," said Lily. "Be here—and not be here . . ."

Lizzie watched her.

". . . know things—and not know things."

"Like what?" He was almost whispering—afraid of disturbing her. She was in some kind of reverie.

We'd better go back, he thought. *I don't want it coming on her here . . .*

"Not know what?" he said.

"That you're going to leave . . . and that we'll never fly again . . ."

They were silent.

Buster watched them.

Lily put on her gloves and let a blizzard fall from her fingers until it had covered the place where their hands had rested to feel the warmth of the sleeping ants.

"It's time to go," she said. Rising, she left the hollow and started up the hill. She did not look back.

Beyond her, a wheel of shouting birds flew into the sun.

Lizzie followed. Lily got there first—and Buster, last.

Sunday, it snowed again. Ephraim drove them to church with James and Eliza in the sleigh. They sang hymns, they prayed— with special prayers for *the starving millions of Russia,* where a famine was in progress. They listened to a sermon, which exhorted them to *think upon the great plagues of Egypt, lest, like the Pharaohs of ancient times, they fail to take heed of God's warnings* . . . and they were told to *go in peace.*

All the way home, Eliza fumed. She was incensed that the minister should have implied that *all those starving millions of*

Russians were being punished because *they hadn't paid attention to the word of God!* "That's what the Protestants used to say of us in Ireland," she said, "when the famine struck us down. We died because we were *Roman heathen Catholics*! I ask you . . . as if God punished babies just because they were Irish!" Eliza was so enraged, she fell back into the street-shouts heard in her Dublin childhood. "Them in their English piety!" she hissed. "Westminsterites! Painting us as Pharaoh's children! Their heads belong with Cromwell's on the Bridge!"

To which James replied—dead calm: "you should remember where you sat ten minutes past. I believe that would be in the Anglican Church of St James, which was filled to the brim—if I remember correctly—with *Westminsterites* . . ."

Lily heard all this against the wind. She was watching Lizzie, sitting opposite.

What if I asked him and he said yes?

He would not say yes.

Why?

I've told you why.

Is it because of my illness?

The wind blew.

Yes.

Snow fell.

It is because of your illness.

The sleigh moved off beyond the town. Its bells were singing.

That afternoon, they made angels in the snow.

Lizzie said it was to prove they could *go on flying.*

On Monday, Ephraim drove them all to the station, where Lily watched as Lizzie lifted Buster into the baggage car and climbed in after him.

They did not say goodbye.

20. Lily remained at Munsterfield the whole of January and February. One week before she was to be returned to Selby Street, Ede came up to join her. Lyon and Browning also came. This was the best part of their reunion. Lily even pulled her brother through the snow on a toboggan. Lyon was ecstatic and waved his arms *like a fish*. Lily refused to grant him the status of a bird. This would have given him wings—and flight. Nonetheless, they had an enjoyable time together. Ede, looking out, was delighted.

Browning, too, made a breakthrough in Lily's awareness of her. She taught Lily how to knit—and this way, became her accomplice in *the secret of Lizzie's gloves*.

On the 2nd of March, everyone—even Malahide—went to the Queen's Hotel for a farewell dinner.

Ede stood out in the lobby and told Eliza she would join them in a minute.

"You all right, dear?"

"Yes. Yes. I just want to look around."

Once Eliza had followed the others into the dining-room, Ede went over to the easel she had noticed when they first came in.

Bobby Turner—PIANO WIZARD!

Underneath this headline, it was announced that Mister Turner would be at the Queen's Hotel the following week to demonstrate *THE WONDERS OF THE WYATT!*

Well.

She turned and gazed at the lobby. To her left, she could hear the click of billiard balls in the poolroom beyond an open door.

That was where Malahide had stood, while Ede was dragged away by Willa to see The Piano Man.

Harvest moon of 1889.

Next June, Lily would be thirteen.

Ede closed her eyes.

It all smelled the same—and the sounds were all the same. The poolroom—the dining-room—the showroom . . . potted ferns with dusty leaves—the smell of ink and ledgers—wood and wax and shoe leather. Perfume. Talcum powder. Eva . . .

Little Eva.

She was just a child that night. Eight years old—and now a star, with her *Night of Song*. All of it—all of it—Tom—Lily—Eva—all of it began here.

Ede opened her eyes.

Yes. It was all the same.

And not.

Time had done some damage—and made some improvements.

Mister Willard had done very well by the Queen's Hotel. So well, he'd taken down the musty *portières* and set new damask in their place; taken out the gas and put in electrical lights—even electrical chandeliers. He had also established telephone service at the desk, where *reservations for your ongoing journey can be made with these other fine hotels: the Prince of Wales, the Royale and the Duke of Wellington,* all in Mister Willard's empire.

The Piano Wizard had replaced The Piano Man—and the Wyatt the Williams—but the easel was the same. And its place in the lobby. And her place beside it.

Time.

Time and money. Time and change. Time and . . .

What, she wondered.

Time and me.

21. They arrived at Selby Street late in the afternoon of March 3rd. Bateson was at the door to take their bags. Charlotte, Emily and Agnes stood in the hallway bobbing and smiling—positively gurgling with pleasure. Bateson had taken the liberty of filling the rooms with flowers and even Browning found some paperwhites on her bureau.

Ede said: "where is Mister Frederick?"

Charlotte said: "a message came for you, madam. Mister Frederick is sorry, but he will not be home for dinner."

"Did he give a reason?"

"No, madam. Nothing."

Ede thought: *of course, what can I be thinking? He's never believed in justifying anything he does.* Out loud, she said: "well, that's a disappointment for the children. They were so looking forward to seeing him."

Liar.

That was Lily—already halfway up the stairs.

22. Later—after they had eaten—Lily, Lyon and Browning retired. Journeys were tiring. Everyone was cranky. Ede sat alone with her coffee in the drawing-room. She had also dined alone. Bateson's flowers were radiant by lamp and candlelight. Ede had dressed as though guests were expected— wearing a dinner gown of layered silks, her dinner rings and the sapphire brooch. The children and Browning, as they did most evenings, ate in the sunroom at six o'clock. Ede sat down to the soup at eight, and rose from the *crème caramel* at nine.

Under normal circumstances, it would not have taken her an hour to dine alone—but she had wanted to be at table when Frederick arrived. It would give her a vantage point that was fixed. He did not, however, comply and she went to the drawing-room without him. She was not so foolish as to speculate about his excuses. To begin with, they would not be *excuses* but mere explanations. If he said: *I have been to the moon*, Ede was expected to take this information at face value.

If Frederick was having an affair . . .

If Frederick was having an affair, Ede could not begin to imagine who the woman might be. He wasn't the kind for flash and dash. Whoever she was—if indeed she existed at all—she was more than likely the wife or the widow of one of his associates. If the wife of such a person, then she would be estranged from her husband. Frederick would never dare to tamper with a woman whose husband might be useful to him. This way, Ede decided the woman must be a widow. A widow whose children were grown and therefore, an older woman.

Older than me, that is. And Frederick. Yes. He'd like that. He wouldn't have to court her with the energy a younger woman would require. Nor the expensive proofs of gratitude a twenty-year-old would need to pay her conscience. Older women—lonely women only want one thing: a man they won't have to bury, but who will bury them . . .

Ede gave a start, almost as if she had suddenly wakened from sleep. *Who am I thinking of?* she wondered. *Is it really us?*

23. Lily was holding a piece of amber up to the lamp in order to see the feather caught inside.

Her door was closed. There had been no signal, as yet, of Frederick's return. Browning had heard her prayers. The amber had been her gift.

"I was going to give it to you on your birthday," she said, "but I thought *it's always nice to have something new to come home to,* when you've been away so long."

"Where did you get it?"

"My father gave it to me. He loved such things and had a wide collection."

Browning had then explained how the feather might have got there—caught in the amber *anywhere up to a thousand years ago.*

"Time is wonderful," she said, "passing on its gifts this way . . ."

Off in the world beyond the windows, the Charles Street clock tower told the world it was ten and Lily could hear the traffic up on Bloor Street—trams and wagons, cabs and even motor cars. Though it was cool and damp outside, her windows were open because she wanted to smell the trees and see the stars.

But before she turned off the lamp, she wanted one last view of Browning's gift.

It had to be a redwing's feather, black with an orange crest—pale in the amber, with a faded quill.

"Dead one thousand years," she said to it, "yet I can see you . . ."

Holding it in her hand, she turned out the lamp and went across to the windows. "Isn't that true," she said to the stars. "If I can see you, then you can't be dead."

Everyone—even those she trusted most—had told her the stars were dead up there, no longer able to give off any light. *The light takes millions of years to reach where you can see it, that's all.*

This had been Lizzie. But, no—in spite of the princely source, Lily did not believe it. *If you were right up beside them,* he had said, *they would be like lumps of coal when the coal is all burned out and dead.*

Cinders. That was the word for that. The same as lie beneath the grates when morning comes.

Cinders can still be seen, she insisted. *It's just, they don't give light any more . . .*

Out in the hall, there were footsteps.

Lily froze where she was, leaning along the window-sill with her toes not touching the floor.

"I won't allow you to do this, Frederick," she heard.

It was her mam.

"I will not allow you to do this!"

"It is done," said Frederick. "There. You can see for yourself."

A door was opened.

Where?

"I won't allow it!"

"It isn't a question of whether or not you'll allow it, Edith. The thing is done."

A door slammed.

Which door? Where?

Lily thought of all the doors along the hall, and all the doors when you turned the corner and went the other way along the passage.

Bang!

"You can slam it closed as often as you like," Frederick said. "It isn't going to change a thing."

Lily went across the floor and stood as near as she dared to the light that spread from the crack beneath her door.

Nearby, she could hear a knob being turned and hinges giving a metallic sigh.

"We will go up, now," said Frederick, "and you can see for yourself how comfortable it will be for her."

"No."

"*Yes, Edith. Yes.*"

Lily knew the portent of that tone of voice. It was the law. She knew that her mam would acquiesce.

There was a creaking sound—unmistakably the sound of someone walking up a stairway. Except—the only stairs at Selby Street that creaked were the ones that led into the darkened cellar. Where could these other stairs be?

Now, to her amazement, Lily heard someone walking above her. *There's an attic here, too—the same as at Munsterfield . . .*

Ede's voice—muffled—nonetheless could be heard above her.

"Oh, God," Lily heard. "No—you mustn't do this. It will kill her."

"Don't be ridiculous," said Frederick—equally muffled, as if he were speaking through gauze. "Gain control of yourself. It isn't as if she has to *live* up here. It's nothing but a holding room."

"*A holding room? A holding room! Damn you!*"

Now, there were hurrying footsteps directly over Lily's head. "There aren't any windows," said Ede.

"That's right."

"How will she breathe? She'll suffocate."

"No, she won't. I've taken all that into account. There are ventilators there in the eaves."

"Oh—god—Fred—I cannot bear it. *Please.*"

This was said as words might be said in a dream or nightmare—spoken without a trace of inflection. Just the words, in a hollow space.

Ede, and then Frederick, crossed the ceiling and came down the still mysterious stairs and—after the briefest pause—a door was shut and a key was turned.

"Go to bed," said Frederick.

"Yes," said Ede. Broken.

More steps. Another door.

Silence.

Lily went to the floor and crawled beneath her bed. Browning found her there in the morning—wearing only her nightdress in the cold air and with her eyes wide open and the amber stone in her hand.

24. On the night of April 16th, 1903, there was to be a celebration of Harry Wyatt's thirty-ninth birthday. He remained the most industrious, but still the quietest of the brothers. His presence would hardly be felt were it not for the skill with which he plotted the course of his various advertising campaigns—some of which had brilliance in them. But even so, he did all his work behind a closed door and emerged only when the work was completed—ready for the sales staff to deal with. He continued, of course, to consult with Frederick—but Frederick, watching the numbers climb, was less and less inclined to interfere. Whatever Harry knew about salesmanship, he knew it well and was inevitably right.

The word *sweet* is not very often applied to men unless it has a derogatory edge to it. But in Harry Wyatt's case, it was undeniably his salient quality. His gentle manners were all the more pleasant because there was not a trace of obsequiousness in his character. Neither was there any self-deprecation. He was simply content to be alive and do what he did. It gave him all the happiness he expected. That, and the occasional outburst of song, and the heady pleasure of custom-made shoes.

In 1902, Harry had quietly married an unassuming woman whose name was Maude Gregory. They were a perfect match. She dressed in unassuming shades of grey, wore unassuming hats and had unassuming expectations. When she laid her unassuming hand in its unassuming glove on Harry's arm, it disappeared into the greyness of his own unassuming overcoat. They stood together always on the edge of public events, faintly smiling, sometimes pressed so close together that when they moved, they moved like ballroom dancers, perfect step by perfect step—always in time with one another.

Their voices were never raised and Maude rarely spoke above a whisper. When the telephone rang in the Selby Street closet and Ede went to answer it, if there seemed to be no one there at the other end when she said *hello*, her next words were always: *how are you, Maude?*

What Ede liked most about Maude was her air of innocence. Like the innocence of children, it tugged at one's sense of regret even as it made one smile with genuine delight. And like a child, Maude had a quality that made the most hard-hearted stranger want to lead her safely through the traffic of life to the other side.

Though it rained on the evening of Harry's birthday, it was a gentle rain, and almost warm. The air, thus dampened, was filled with the year's first hint of green. Earlier—in the sunroom, where Browning had sat while the children ate their supper—the rain had tapped against the windows like a stranger wanting in.

All the guests arrived beneath umbrellas and, watching them come up the walk below her window, Lily knew she had lost her only opportunity to see what people might be wearing—and, indeed, who most of the people might be. Aside from the swagger that was obvious in the carriage of Uncle Franklin's umbrella—and the diminished height of the single umbrella beneath which Harry and Maude glided up the walk in lock-step, it was impossible to know who was who. Was that tall man walking by himself Uncle Liam?

She had no way of knowing. Her place on the landing was vacant and would remain so. At any moment, Frederick would appear to escort her to the attic. Her only ray of hope lay in the fact that—at least on this occasion—she would not be entirely alone. Lizzie had promised to bring his dessert and to sit with her while he ate. Buster would spend that time with her, too.

Otherwise, Lily was to be *monitored* in her exile by Browning. While Browning detested the whole idea of Lily's being hidden away up there whenever company came, she was nonetheless determined to play the role she was assigned. She knew too well from past experience that if her protest went beyond her first formal statement, Frederick would let her go. This, after all her good work with Lyon and her growing love for Lily, would be intolerable. *Better to weather the storm in the harbour than sink the ship by risking it at sea.* A precept. One of the dozens by which Browning made her calendar of beneficial disciplines.

Lily heard the Charles Street clock tower begin to strike the hour of seven.

Time.

She took her last breaths of air before she closed her window and turned to face the door. She wore her long blue skirt, a middy blouse and, in her hair, the wide blue bow that Browning had taught her to tie with her eyes closed. On her feet, she wore a favoured pair of carpet slippers. She had removed the offensive itchy black stockings and wore instead a pair of white knee socks. Her hands were empty.

As it had to, because Frederick was on the other side, the door opened just as the clock was giving its final stroke.

"Are you ready, Lily?"

"Yessir."

"Then come with me."

"Yessir."

Frederick—looking splendid in evening dress—waited for Lily to pass him in the doorway and then he moved before her down the hall.

At the top of the stairs, Lily paused while Frederick was inserting the key in the attic lock. She could see her old vantage point on the landing below, but nothing else. Sounds of family merriment were almost foreign to her now. She had shut their meaning away.

"Lily."

"Yessir."

She turned and followed him into the dark. All the way up, there wasn't any light except the least of what could penetrate the stairwell from the hallway. The stairs themselves were so very steep that Lily had to place her hands on the steps to guide herself.

Finally, Frederick stood at the top and switched on a lamp. It hung from the ceiling—a single bulb in a green glass shade at the end of a wire.

Lily stepped to the floor. At Ede's insistence, there was a carpet. There were also, Lily could see, a table, a chair and a wicker settee. On the table, there were books. And flowers.

Frederick handed her a walking stick.

"If you need to use the toilet," he said, "there is a pot in the corner. Also, there is lemonade in a pitcher on the shelf just there—and a cup. This stick is only to be used if you feel your illness coming on. Do you understand?" He was smiling, speaking in the tones a steward would use when introducing a passenger to her stateroom. "I have marked the appropriate place for you to bang it—just over here on this one bit of board above Miss Browning's room. Do you see? I've had it painted bright yellow. When Miss Browning hears you, she will come at once and be with you. Is all this clear?"

"Yessir."

"And you do understand why it must be done?"

"Yessir."

"It must be done in order to protect you from the sort of embarrassment created in December, when your illness overcame you in front of all those guests."

"Yessir."

"We love you," he said. "I trust you really know that."

He turned now, to leave her.

"Lizzie will come with his dessert. There are lovely books to read. And when the guests have left, Miss Browning will come and take you back to your room. Your mam and I will be there to say good-night—and we'll tell you all about the party. All right?"

"Yessir."

"Kiss me, then."

Lily hung back.

Frederick, unruffled, spoke to her evenly. He was smiling, genuinely pleasant. "Remember," he said, "that we always meet and part with a kiss in this family."

"Yessir."

"Come along, then."

Lily went over the carpet to the stairs. Frederick was standing down two steps, his face almost level with her own.

"Good-night, then," he said. "Till later."

"Good-night."

Lily kissed him on the forehead.

He was gone.

She heard the door click, and the key being turned.

She took a deep breath and let it out completely before she went to the sofa. Having inspected the flowers—a potted primrose—she sat down behind the table.

Then, she took out her matches.

Four

1903—1907

Beautiful dreamer,
Wake unto me . . .

Stephen Foster

1. I have a picture in my mind of Lily holding a box of matches. It is part of my private collection—a series of Lily-portraits that have no external counterpart. There are no photographs of what I see, and yet what I see is images—all of my mother—in which she never moves. Time is not in them.

As I see her, Lily is caught in the way that objects are caught and exhibited in museums. The time is always now, yet now holds everything that ever was.

I can summon these private images at will, though getting rid of them is not so easy. Like dreams, they leave a residue of apprehension.

Lily with matchbox. She is seated at a table. She is alone but I am watching. The matchbox is in her left hand. In her right hand there is a lighted match. She is staring at it, fixed and static. Only the flame is in motion. It wavers between us. Lily cannot see me. In her mind, she is alone.

I watch her eyes and I wonder what they see. In all my life with her, I never thought of her as being *crazy*. Never as being *psychotic*. Never as a *madwoman*. But in this picture she is all these things, and I am her only witness. When I testify in my mind, I say so.

It is not her eyes themselves that tell me this, but their gaze with its fixed concentration. In the picture, the flame between us is reflected in her pupils—her pupils dilated, no blue visible, only black—and in the black, fires. Little fires. Dancing. Hundreds of them.

Someone is in there, she would say to me. *Every time I light a match, I can see them . . .*

This is what I hear.

The matchbox is oblong, held on its side. I can see where the match has been struck—an amber smudge on the sandpaper.

I hear this, too: a short, rasping sound and the explosive, sucking noise of the flame gulping air.

There is also the smell of sulphur, endlessly burning—because in this picture the match is never extinguished.

This is Lily as she was when no one saw her. Not even me. But I am able to conjure it—and I do, in my own defence.

When my wife left me, she told me she thought I was mad. Of course, it was only an expression of her anger—only a reflection of her confusion. What else could I be but *mad* if I refused to give her children.

"Why the hell did we marry?" she would yell at me. "I didn't marry you so I could spend half my life with a douche bag!"

Once, we had laughed about this. She had come home in triumph one day with something mysterious—a box done up in the proverbial *plain brown wrapper*—and when she showed it to me, we both had hysterics. It was called EVERY WOMAN'S MARVEL WHIRLING SPRAY! Surely, we thought, there could not be anything funnier in all the world. In its tasteful advertisement it was disguised as a product for feminine hygiene—but, in fact, it was a *sperm flusher*.

Alexandra's volatility was one of the attributes that had drawn me to her—her passionate relationship with life, with being alive. In the days when we were both involved with the band, it had seemed we could survive on love and music—music and love. One and then the other. Food was of little importance. We smoked away our appetite and drank away our cares. Of course, we did eat—and, of course, we slept and did all the normal things that keep a person alive, but looking back at it from here, I remember only the taste of toasted ham sandwiches, lunch-counter fried eggs and Chinese dinners eaten after midnight by the light of paper lanterns.

We slept on buses and in the back seats of other people's cars. We dressed out of suitcases, did our laundry in hotel bath-tubs and often had to make do with sponge baths taken in public washrooms. I must have shaved in every train and Greyhound station in Southern Ontario during our tours of 1935 and '36.

There were fifteen of us on the road together: twelve musicians, a manager and a pair of roustabouts whose job was to set us up and take us down wherever we might be playing. Mostly, we played hotels—but sometimes we played the lake boats or resorts. The best date of all was the Palais Royale at Sunnyside in Toronto. We were called *Baker's Dozen*, after our leader, Ernest Baker—but privately we called ourselves *Alexandra's Ragtime Band* because we were all in love with her—and so was the audience.

Alex had an almost hoarse, smoky voice that was sexy and beguiling. She had only two dresses to sing in. She called them *gowns* because she said that gave them *class*. Everything desirable back in those desperate years was *classy*. One of the gowns was red—and the other was black. She wore them well on her lanky frame, rounding her shoulders to emphasize the cleavage. She called herself a *babe*, but that was just bravado. She didn't think of herself that way. Not at all. She had a lot of self-respect—and rightly so. She'd been orphaned at sixteen, fell in love with singing and said: *to hell with being adopted* and hired herself out as a maid. In the early thirties, she began auditioning for dozens of dance bands and orchestras. They seemed to be springing up everywhere—almost like an exotic disease. In 1935, she landed the job with Ernie Baker and three months later, I was hired as pianist.

I'm not too sure it was love at first sight. Maybe second. It certainly didn't take long. She sat down beside me on the piano bench one afternoon when I was warming up and she said: *you*

*have the nicest thumbs of any man I've ever seen—and what's
that you're playing . . . ?*

My thumbs are not terrific, but she had my attention. I was
playing a song called *I Can't Get Started.* Perhaps it was prophetic.

In January of 1936, King George V died and all hell broke
loose with Edward VIII and Mrs Simpson. There were wars in
Spain and Ethiopia, Hitler marched on the Rhineland and the
Great Depression entered its seventh year. This was the time of
our love affair and, on April 26th, 1937, we were married. That
very same day, bombs fell on Guernica. The world—in every
way—would never be the same.

The following autumn, Baker's Dozen was disbanded. We were
out of work—just like everybody else. Alex didn't mind. *We can
start a family*, she said. *No, we can't* was my answer.

I started tuning pianos then and Alex got some pick-up jobs
with visiting orchestras. She sang for a month with Romanelli's
orchestra at the King Edward Hotel. Full circle.

Almost.

No *full* circle until we had a child.

I won't go on about it. It became a nightmare. We loved each
other—but we were utterly opposed.

At first, when we had sex, Alex used a diaphragm.

"They're not easy to come by," she said. "You have to walk the
doctor around the block three times before he'll believe you really
need it!"

She was wonderful, when you think about it. She kept trying to
laugh it off—her desire for children. She kept trying to make a
joke of it.

At first.

At first, when she discarded the diaphragm because *the pressure is unbearable during sex*, I believed her. And I began to wear
a sheath. And this was accepted.

At first.

At first, when Alex began to speak against my using it, her argument was that it got in the way of spontaneity. "You always have to
stop just when I'm desperate to have you in me . . ." Or: "you look

so silly trying to put the damn thing on, I get the giggles and then I start to laugh . . ." Sexual inventiveness was not my forté—but I had to silence that laughter. This way, but briefly, I discovered other modes of intercourse that Alex at least pretended were acceptable.

At first.

At first, when she started to hide my sheaths—or destroy them—saying: "you forgot to buy more . . ." I began the practice of withdrawal just before climax. Mine. And she would say: *you never told me you were Catholic.* This was her joke.

At first.

I was so desperately afraid of a pregnancy, I didn't know what to do—but my arguments against it were losing their edge—especially given Alexandra's basic desire to have a child.

My own desperation, at one point, drove me to attend a birth-control clinic. This was highly controversial. To begin with, it was illegal—thought of in the same light as abortion. The clinic I had chosen was at St Anne's Anglican Church. This was controversial in itself. The programme had been started by a group of women whose main concern was *the burden of multiple pregnancies borne by the poor . . .*

Well, I was poor. We were poor. So I went.

They offered sheaths and diaphragms, but I explained that my wife had problems with these. They then put forward something called a *pessary.* This was, in fact, a suppository to be inserted in the vagina, where it melted and acted as a spermicide . . . Luckily, it also acted as an enticing lubricant and this is what I told Alex, betraying nothing of its killer aspects. Unfortunately, the pessary acted mostly as an irritant. It was made up of cocoa butter, tannic acid and alum powder—and the alum was my undoing.

"*It burns!*" Alex shouted at me one night. "It burns—you bastard!" She had never called me that before. She had never raised her voice in quite that way. But, of course, by now she was in despair.

This was the beginning of the war that finally drove me from her bed and broke us.

Not that I blame her. I don't. The truth is, I mourn her passing from my life. I love her. But my consolation is that being parted from her, I know that Alexandra will never have to bear the sorrow—or the burden—of giving birth to another Lily.

No more Kilworth babies. None.

None, at any rate, that I would bring into the world.

Lily would not have approved of this. I know that. Her impetus, like Alexandra's, was *life at any price*. But there is a price I will not pay: the price of more deaths by fire.

2. On the night of Harry Wyatt's birthday party in April of 1903, the matches in Lily's hand had again been stolen from the work-bag Agnes carried when she was cleaning grates and laying new fires. On the cover of the box, there was an etching of the Parliament Buildings in Ottawa. *Eddy's Safety Matches.* The image Lily received when she read the label was of an old, old man called Eddy, cutting matchsticks with a paring knife, sitting in his cellar and dipping them in sulphur. By candlelight.

Downstairs, there was music. Franklin was playing the piano. One of the guests had brought a banjo and Lily pressed her ear to the floor to hear it.

> *I come from Alabama*
> *With a banjo on my knee . . .*

Lily was mystified. She had always thought the song was about a man with a *bandage* on his knee.

It was one of the songs that Davey and Richard used to sing at Munsterfield when they came back in with the harvest on the hay wain. That and *Polly Woddle Doodle . . .*

Standing up, she took a turn around the attic, ducking low when the roof angle demanded it. If there were mice, they were silent. Hiding.

The corners were completely dark—like caves. She wondered why she had been given only a single lamp.

Frederick.

But why?

When she got to the shelf with the lemonade, she removed the lace cover from the pitcher, poured a cupful and drank it. Downstairs, they were singing *Drink To Me Only With Thine Eyes*—and she thought: *they will never go in to dinner—and Lizzie will never come—and I will be here forever.*

She looked at the pot with its porcelain lid and its neat little box of toilet tissue standing by. *Pot. Po'.*

Eliza said: *po'.*

Mam said: *pot.*

Maybe po' was a grandmother word.

Lily wandered back to the sofa. The books on the table were her favourites. *Mam must have done that . . .*

Wild Animals I Have Known, by Ernest Thompson Seton.

A Young Person's Idylls of the King, by Alfred, Lord Tennyson.

The Boy Who Loved Insects, by J. Henri Fabre.

All of these, gifts from mam.

And *The Wizard of Oz*, by L. Frank Baum—a gift from Browning.

Lily spread them out on the tabletop.

Their covers shone in the lamplight. Lobo the Wolf . . . King Arthur and Lancelot with Guinevere riding a horse . . . flowers and bees and dragonflies . . . and Dorothy, with Toto the dog, Scarecrow, Lion and Tin Man standing on the Yellow Brick Road.

Dorothy suffered from whirlwinds, too.

Lily sat down in the chair and folded her hands.

This is the way they sit in schools: back straight—head up—eyes front—do not fiddle . . .

She had seen a picture of this in one of Ede's magazines. *Children must be seen and not heard . . .*

Heard, but not seen . . .

That was Lily. But only heard if she got into trouble. Only if she knew she was going to have a spell. Otherwise, not heard—not seen.

I'm frightened.
No, you're not.
Yes, I am.
No, you're not.
Lily waited.
No, she thought. *I'm not.*
She was angry.
Anger is not fear.
Anger is hatred.
"I hate him!"
She said that aloud.
The mice stirred.

Lily gripped the wicker arms of the chair and leaned back against the cushion. The cushion—and something else.

There was something behind the cushion.

She stood up and pulled the cushion forward.

There was a package sitting there—something tall and thin, done up in pretty paper. Blue. With ribbons. When Lily picked it up, she found there was a second package behind it—smaller— this time done up in green.

Inside the first, she found a sketch-pad with an envelope containing a note.

> *This is for you, my darling. Hope you have fun with it.*
> *Love, Mam. XOX*

Lily undid the second package.

Pencils. Coloured pencils.

She kissed the pad and rattled the pencils in their box.

"Presents for everyone . . ." she said—again aloud.

Laying Ede's gifts on the table beside the books, Lily reached up inside her middy and pulled out a package of her own. Soft— pliant. Red.

Inside, there was a card she had made herself, drawn on construction paper.

FOR LIZZIE
TO KEEP YOU WARM
FROM LILY

No hugs and kisses—no *with love*. She had not dared.

Under Browning's tutelage, she had started knitting the gloves at Munsterfield and finished them at Selby Street. They were blue—her favourite colour—and Browning had done the finishing work, the careful sewing, and the tiny knotting inside the finger-ends. They were beautiful. Soft and rich and warm. Lily laid them on the table.

What will I draw?

Mister Eddy making matches.

She sat down on the top step under the lamp and began.

Downstairs, the singing had ended. They must have gone in to dinner. Another of Charlotte's triumphs—and Uncle Harry's favourite: roast beef and Yorkshire pudding. The smell of it was tantalizing. Except . . .

Except.

Lily closed her eyes.

In her mind, a cow was being slaughtered—hanging from a hook, head down . . .

Lily had seen this once, by mistake. She had blundered into Mister Dobson's slaughterhouse, having heard the cattle bawling in his yard. She had gone down the road without permission and run up Mister Dobson's drive when she heard the screaming. Something must be wrong . . .

And it was.

Lily had dodged the Dobson dogs and, racing to escape them, drawn by the clatter of chains and the dreadful scrabbling of the beast as it was being hoisted, she pushed the door wide and . . .

There.

Oh.

Stop . . .

Mister Dobson, already holding the knife, his apron a mass of blood and gore, turned on Lily and . . . shouted . . .

What . . . ?
What . . . ?
What had he shouted?
OUT! OUT!
OUT!

He had pushed her, then, back through the door to the wailing dogs and Lily, fleeing, had not stopped running until she was under mam's bed in the dark.

And now . . .

Lily ran down to the door.

It was locked. Of course.

Open!

She turned the handle.

Stop!

Nothing.

There was not a sound.

No one came.

Browning must be in the bathroom, bathing Lyon. All the others were in the dining-room or the kitchen.

Lily walked back up the stairs.

She was out of breath and did not know why.

Oh, stop, please.

The picture in her mind would not go away—and the cow in its terror went on screaming.

STOP!

Lily almost fell across the table, spilling books and paper, pencils and primrose.

She knelt on the floor.

The wind rose.

From far away, it began to pull at the edge of the picture in her mind. The cow was struggling in a growing darkness, its cries being drowned in Lily's storm . . .

Someone must be made to come.

Stick.

Where was it?

Gone.

She crawled across the floor in search of it.
Stick?
Gone.
The wind increased—still distant—but louder.
Lily sat back on her heels.
Someone must be made to come.
She reached into her pocket and drew out Mister Eddy's matches.
Help.
Lily leaned back and picked up *The Boy Who Loved Insects*. By the time it was in her lap, it had fallen open and now, Lily saw a parade of ants where it crossed down the side of one page and up the side of the next . . .

The whole book was like that—every page was decorated with ants or bees or butterflies . . .

Lily had been about to tear out the frontispiece, but she relented . . .
Don't burn books . . .
She stood up, reeling, dropping the Fabre onto the sofa. There, at the edge of the table, was her new sketch-pad.
Burn this.
She tore two pages from its middle and scrunched them into a ball. Then she went over to the pot and removed its lid.
Fire! Fire! Fire!
The wind was almost on her. She could feel it in her hair.
Hurry.
Hurry. Help . . .
She threw the ball of paper into the pot and set the pot near the top of the stairs.
Hurry! Help! Fire!
She struck a match.
Be quick.
The paper began to burn.
Lily stared.
The tight, round ball uncurled—expanded.
Its flaming was orange—red—yellow . . .
Lily heard voices.

Don't.
They were saying *don't.*
The wind was abating. Its darkness and its roaring ebbed.
Out.
Lily picked up the lid.
Now.
She put it back on the pot.
Smoke.
Lily waved the smoke away with her hands. It began to dissipate.
She smelled her fingers.
Fire and smoke.
"Lily?"
She was rocking to and fro—kneeling—rocking—humming.
Oh . . .
She might have been at Delphi—the priestess sitting in her pan
above the fire.
Oh . . .
She waited.
Nothing happened. Nothing.
"Lily?"
A key was being turned.
Lily sat frozen.
The door opened.
Buster came bounding up the stairs.
Lizzie followed.
"I smell smoke."
"It's all right."
"Yes—but why? Why do I smell smoke?"
"The chimneys," Lily said. "There must have been a down-
draught . . ."
"Why are you kneeling on the floor?"
"I didn't feel well."
"A spell?"
"I don't know. Almost."
Lizzie walked past her. She could see that he carried a plate in
each hand. Spoon handles stuck out over the rims.

"Are you all right, now?"

"Yes. I think so."

Lizzie went over to the table and set the dessert plates down. He picked up the primrose and pencils and placed them at one end.

Lily, having risen, carried the pot back to its corner. Its handle was still warm.

Lizzie saw the matchbox lying on the floor where Lily had been kneeling. He almost mentioned it, but picked it up instead and put it in his pocket.

Most children play with fire, he was thinking. *I did once. Let it go.*

"I've brought some dessert," he said. "Chocolate ice cream and some angel food cake."

Her back was to him.

"There's a present for you . . . somewhere," she said.

Lizzie picked it up.

"You mean this?"

"Yes."

She half turned now, and could see the red parcel in his hands.

"I made them myself," she said—still not really looking at him. "Thank you."

Lizzie undid the ribbons, careful to untie all the knots.

"I hope they fit," said Lily.

Lizzie let the red paper fall and lifted the gloves into the light. "They're beautiful," he said—not daring to put them on for fear they were too big or too small.

"Aren't you going to try them?"

"Of course. But the ice cream is melting. I'll put them on later."

"No. Do it now."

Lizzie closed his eyes and turned his back to her. He pulled on one of the gloves.

He sighed. "Yes," he said. "It's perfect."

And it was.

Lily smiled.

"You can eat in them, if you like."

Which he did. A silver spoon and blue gloves.

They sat on the sofa, side by side, while Buster watched them from the floor.

Lily said nothing.

She had found her way back to the instant when the match had been struck. How it flared. And the rising wind. And the wavering flames. And the first instruction: *don't*. And the second *don't* . . . And the cow, with its abattoir scream—and the silence all at once when she had capped the pot.

The whirlwind had not claimed her. The wings had not enfolded her. Why?

Was it because she had struck the match—or because she had smothered the fire?

"Buster wants to lick the plates," said Lizzie. "You think we should let him?"

Lily nodded.

She was incapable of speech.

Lizzie accepted this. It was not the first long silence they had shared. He put down the plates—to Buster's delight—and then he held his hands up under the lamp. "Can you see them? Look!" he said. "I think I'll wear them forever."

3· April 19th fell on a Tuesday. This was in 1904, almost a year to the day after Lily had struck the match in the Selby Street attic. She had spent many party evenings there, plotting and rejecting other fires. She had also read her books and drawn her version of Egypt under sand and the ant world under snow. She had also played two hundred and seventy games of solitaire, marking them down in the sketch-pad, counting them over with her fingers. Browning had had to rescue her only twice, which everyone but Lily thought was splendid. She had hoped to be rescued far more often—even though rescue meant seizures.

On April 19th, the family ate together—even Lyon, who was

seated in his high chair where Browning could reach him. Because there were no guests, Lily was also at table.

Charlotte's offering was chicken in a cream sauce and a cauliflower *brought all the way from Georgia in a cold car.* Peas were also served—and there were mushrooms in the creamed chicken.

They had begun their dinner at eight. Frederick was greatly excited because the new Wyatt Player Piano had just won a prize in Atlantic City, where a convention of the North American Piano Merchants Society had been held.

"This means we can add another gold medallion to our letterhead," he told them. There were already four of these—quite impressive—two of them from Expositions in Europe and the other two from Montreal and Chicago. The most recent medallion would also mean a good deal more money, but Frederick refrained from saying so. He believed that finance was not a suitable subject at table. *It makes the stomach churn.*

Lily rarely took part in dinner conversations. She was shy about putting forward her interests, knowing from past experience that few—except possibly Browning—were interested in ants or ancient Egypt. When she had first launched the subject of mummified cats, Frederick had turned pale. *Not at dinner, dear,* Ede had said. *It is not appropriate.*

There it was again—the universal dictum: *it is not appropriate.* Lizzie, finance, feathers, butterfly wings, ants—and now mummified cats. *Taboo.*

She had been reading a book about ancient civilizations in which the chapters on Egypt had been the most intriguing. The mummified remains of Ramses II had been discovered *just over twenty years ago, when mam was only three years older than I am now* and when his body had been unwrapped, it had smelled *like dried fish . . . !*

Not appropriate.

Beyond the drone of adult conversation, Lily heard church bells ringing. *Was it Sunday? No. It was Tuesday.*

She sat there, poised above her creamed chicken, lifting a piece of cauliflower on her fork—pretending she was *Isis, protector of children* about to swallow a part of Frederick's brain, without which he would be helpless. *The brain looks just like that,* she had told Charlotte that afternoon in the kitchen, watching her tear the leaves from the cauliflower. *Just exactly, precisely like that. I have a picture of it upstairs. Do you want to see it?*

No.

Not appropriate.

Just as the cauliflower went into Lily's mouth and she was giving it the first revengeful bite—Agnes came at a rush from the pantry. There was now a new, much closer clamour of bells.

The Lamb of God was about to faint. Her eyes were bulging and she was gulping air as if she might be dying of air-thirst.

"Ma . . . ma . . ." she spluttered. "Ma . . . madam!"

"What is it, Agnes? Good heavens," said Ede. "Are you ill?"

"No, madam. No. No. But . . ."

Bells.

"Say it, girl," said Frederick. "Spit it out."

Agnes swallowed and turned towards the front hall, waving her arms in a frantic imitation of semaphore.

"The city, madam! The city, sir! The city!"

"What?"

"THE CITY IS ON FIRE!"

Having said this, Agnes sat down all at once in the middle of the floor. Everyone stared at her—even Lyon—in absolute silence.

And in the silence, the tide of bell-sound rose beyond the windows.

Frederick stood up and went past Agnes into the hall.

Ede said: "you stay put," to the others, and followed him.

Frederick went through the vestibule, out through the front door onto the verandah.

Ede took his arm.

It was true.

The city was on fire.

To the south, the sky was ablaze with flaming cloud shapes and roiling smoke.

Every tower bell, every church bell in the world was now ringing, and the fire bells could be heard on Sherbourne Street. The fire itself made a distant but distinctive sound—a tunnelled and hollow roaring. In the trees along Selby Street, the wind—from the north-west—was making a soughing noise that reminded Ede of the winter winds at Munsterfield.

"What on earth can have happened?" she said.

"I don't know—but I'll find out," said Frederick. "The factory is down there and—heaven knows—it's a tinder-box, with all that wood . . ."

Ede said: "telephone. Can't we telephone the police?"

"Every single citizen of Toronto will be trying to do that," he said. "No. I'll go round the corner to the fire hall. Someone must be there still. They'll know."

He went back into the house to collect his hat and coat, passing Ede moments later with the coat half on.

"Don't let the children be afraid," he said. "There's no point being afraid until we know the details."

Then he was gone—down the walk and through the gate—not running—Frederick never ran—but hurrying faster than Ede had ever seen him move.

All along the street, others had come out onto their porches and sidewalks—facing south, muttering *fire* and *ruin*. Mrs Carmichael, next on the east side of Ede and Frederick, was standing on her lawn with her usual cluster of guests. They were all in evening dress, white damask napkins hanging down from their fingers. *Oh!* they said. *Ah!* they said. *My!*

Ede, still watching the southern sky, heard Mrs Carmichael saying: "come along, now!" to her guests. "The duck is getting cold. Our dinner will be ruined!"

And the voice of the doyenne was heard through the land . . .

Smiling in spite of herself, Ede took her neighbour's advice and went back up the walk and into the house.

"Where is Papa?" said Lyon.

"Papa has gone to bring us the news. In the meantime, we shall have his dinner put in the oven."

She rang the bell.

It was Emily who responded.

"Where is Agnes, Em?"

"Excuse me, madam—but she's upstairs, packing."

"Packing?"

"Yes, madam."

"Why, in heaven's name?"

"So as when we leave, madam, all her things will be ready."

"Leave?"

"Yes'm. She says total fire is coming and nothing's worse, she says, than total fire."

"I see. Well . . ." Ede sat back. "I want you to take Mister Wyatt's dinner out to the kitchen and have Charlotte keep it warm for him. No one is leaving until we have eaten."

"Thank you, madam."

Emily collected Frederick's plate. When she got to the swinging door, she turned her back to it and said: "excuse me, madam—but can I pack, too?"

"No," said Ede. "I shall want you to serve the sweet and bring the coffee to the drawing-room. By that time, I'm quite sure the fire will be under control."

"Yes'm." Emily was gone.

The door swung to and fro.

Lily said: "I wonder who started it."

When Frederick returned, he said the fire had started south of King Street and the wind was spreading it further south and east. The factory was not endangered. But a great many blocks had already been destroyed and the fire was still raging.

"Of course," he said, "I'd feel much easier if I had a proper look at things. So I'm going to ask Bateson to hitch one of the horses to the buggy. I'll leave him here with you and drive to the factory myself. I'll have to make a pretty wide berth to avoid the fire—so I may be some time."

Ede insisted that he finish his chicken and cauliflower while Bateson was harnessing the horse—and they all sat there watching him as if their lives depended on the number of forkfuls Frederick ate.

When Bateson came to say the buggy was at the curb, Ede said: "don't be tempted, Fred. Stay away from the fire."

"I will," he said—and kissed her goodbye.

After Frederick had gone, Lily started up the stairs. From the landing, she heard Bateson talking with Ede.

"Mister Wyatt says I should have the carriage ready . . . just in case."

"Oh, dear."

"It is best to be prepared, madam. It can't do any harm."

"No, of course not. Thank you, Bateson."

Lily saw Bateson making for the kitchen, while Ede remained stock-still in the hall.

It is best to be prepared, madam. It can't do any harm.

Were they going to burn to death?

Lily turned and completed her climb.

Twenty minutes later, she was sitting on her bed with a suitcase beside her. Its lid was open. Lily had not yet finished her packing.

Inside the suitcase, she had placed some books, her favourite cardigan, her jars of stones and butterfly wings, the photographs of James and Eliza in their silver frames, her drawing of Lizzie and the feather in amber. She was trying to decide what else to take . . .

Down the hall, she could hear Lyon crying and cranky. He'd been up too late and now he wanted Browning to take him to see the fire.

Lily got up and closed her door.

She turned out the lamp and walked across to the window.

The sky beyond the roofs across the street was the colour she saw when she looked into the furnace down in the cellar. The colour of fire in a forge, of fire that has gone beyond mere blazing all the way to holocaust.

She raised her left hand and laid its fingers against her lips.

She closed her eyes.

Don't speak.

Say nothing.

When she opened her eyes, she turned away from the window and crossed back over to the bed.

She turned on the lamp.

There was the suitcase. Waiting.

Lily knelt down and slipped her hand underneath her pillows.

Yes.

She withdrew her hand and deposited what she had found on top of the items already packed. Then she reached up and closed the lid.

Ready and complete.

She dragged the suitcase over the edge and pushed it beneath the bed.

When Ede came in and found her kneeling there, she sat on the opposite side of the comforter and said: "you don't need to be afraid. All you have to pray for is the others—in the fire."

I know.

"Good-night, my darling."

"Good-night, mam."

Ede went back into the hall and closed Lily's door.

Lily remained on her knees.

She counted over the contents of the suitcase: *books, cardigan, stones, wings, photographs, Lizzie, amber feather . . .*

And matches.

Beyond the windows, the fire burned all night long—and all night long, she watched it until dawn. There was no way of knowing if the sun came up. The city lay darkened under a pall of smoke for three more days.

4. This is what Lily said about the people in the fire:

I haven't heard the words, Charlie. It may be they speak a language I haven't got. Or had one time, and have forgotten. Sometimes I think it may not be words at all, but only sound— like singing. Songs. Someone singing the tunes of songs way off in something like a cave. What I see is a place at the farthest end of a fiery tunnel and, in it, the shapes of people—though I cannot see their faces. Mostly, they're too far off for me to catch more than shadows—and the sounds they make. Animal noises, sometimes. Not like a roaring—but the way that animals cry in the night—or whisper: where can she be? *when they've lost their mam—or speak triumphant when they've made a kill. That's what I mean— their songs. Their songs, Charlie. Sung from a long way off.*

At first, when I was still a child, I watched her only from a hiding place. Wherever we were, I would find out where the fireplace was, or the kitchen stove she had chosen for her attempt at communication. Then I would find—or create—a hiding place nearby, into which I could easily slip unnoticed when she was under the spell. This way, I could be reassured she was not going to burn down the house or set herself on fire.

I was never Lily's keeper. I was only ever her child—and, on occasion, her guardian and, on occasion, her victim and, on occasion, her accomplice. But I was never her keeper. The *Keeper* in Lily's life was fire. Her jail was her illness, and its key was a box of matches. These let her in and out. Without them, she had no access to either direction. I once heard her yelling: OPEN THE GATE! OPEN THE GOD-DAMN GATE! I WANT TO COME THROUGH! By the time I reached her, she was standing in a darkened closet, setting the clothes on fire.

This was not the first time Lily had done such a thing. The first time was in August of 1906, the summer Lily turned sixteen and Lyon, her brother, was five.

5 • There was a heatwave. The city seemed a wide, calm sea, over which the only universal sound was the shimmering song of the cicada. On Selby Street, this sound was broken from time to time by the restless creaking of Mrs Carmichael's

hammock—next door, in the shade of a chestnut tree—and by the slow and unoiled grind of wheels as the ice wagon made its way along the boulevard, stopping every twenty yards or so to let the iceman off. At the Wyatt house, Lyon ran out to meet him on the walk and Lily, attempting a poise that is denied to most sixteen-year-olds, almost succeeded in portraying indifference when she received the traditional piece of ice that was offered to all the children along the iceman's route.

Lily wrapped this treasure in a handkerchief in order to maintain control of it. Lyon's slid through his fingers, falling to the walk and smashing into a hundred pieces, each of which began at once to melt. The iceman, already having set the Wyatts' block of ice in place, was moving on to the Carmichaels' house.

Lyon roared: "I want more!"

"Be quiet," said Lily.

"I want more!"

"There is no more. He's gone."

"Gimme yours!"

"Don't be ridiculous, Lyon. Of course I won't give you mine." Lily, having said this, took a triumphant side-lick at the frozen tongue protruding from her handkerchief. "We have a pact, remember? Nothing is shared that has already been in the other's mouth . . ."

Lick—lick—lick.

Lyon grew red in the face and reached for the ice. Lily held it aloft and said: "you wouldn't give me a piece of your cake when Buster ate mine the other day. So there. This is my treat, and I'm having it."

Lily retired to the side porch then, where—behind the cup-and-saucer vine—she enjoyed the shade and finished her ice.

The cicadas suddenly were stilled. A majestic silence ensued in which Lyon, thwarted, went around to the kitchen yard, where he sat on the small green bench that Charlotte used when she was shelling peas or snapping beans. If Lily had seen him sitting there, she would have known he was up to something. His expression would have told her this. It was fixed and glassy-eyed and murderous. Even Mrs Carmichael, dozing in the next door garden, must have felt his violent emanations. Her hammock beneath the chestnut tree had stopped its swaying. She was trying to conjure up the word *premonition*.

Lily, on her porch, opened her book and looked at its pictures. She had been reading about The War Between the Ants. The text was mesmerizing—almost the text of a novel for the young. Lily had read the account of the Ant War many times and almost had it off by heart.

The book had been given to her as a birthday present the year after Lyon was born. This was *The Boy Who Loved Insects* and its author was Jean Henri Fabre, the great French naturalist. The stories it contained—the lives of bees, wasps and ants; beetles, moths and butterflies—had been translated into English and edited especially for children. J. Henri Fabre's portrait served as its frontispiece. Lily often looked at him with awe that amounted to reverence. Mam had said he was still alive, though now very old—eighty-three, by Lily's painful calculation.

Fabre had the look of God. He was squinty-eyed, as though he had looked too long at the sun—and he wore a long, white beard. He was shown in the photograph wearing a wide-brimmed hat which, like his coat, was black. Lily for the longest time mistook the name *Jean* for the woman's name it would have been in English. She therefore thought that Fabre must be like Lizzie— men so special they had been given women's names.

The War Between the Ants was waged between the reds and the blacks. Fabre called the red ants *Amazons*, but had assigned no name to the blacks. Consequently, Lily called them *Egyptians* and named their city in the backyard *Thebes* after the royal city shown in *Ancient Civilizations*.

In the war that Fabre described, the Amazons were slave-hunting ants who were quite incapable of taking care of themselves or their children. They could not even find their own food and must therefore have slaves to do their foraging for them. Also to mind their houses and defend them from their enemies.

No one wants to be a slave, of course, so how could the black ants be forced to do these things without rebelling? The answer, according to Fabre, was simple: when they were babies, they had been stolen—carried off to the red ants' nest *in the nymph or swaddling-clothes stage, still wrapped in their cocoons.* In time, the black ants grew up in the Amazons' nest to become both *willing and industrious servants . . .* Slaves.

When Lily first read about these ant-exploiters, she could not help wondering if she and Lyon, Frederick and Ede were also Amazons. After all, they, too, seemed incapable of *finding their own food* or of *taking care of themselves.* There were only four of them, and yet five others had to do all the shopping, cook the meals, clean the house, answer the doorbell, drive the car, make the garden grow and teach Lyon how to brush his teeth. Surely this was slavery.

The thought of all that was being done for her and the sense of incompetence she had as a result of it was an embarrassment to Lily. In daydreams, just as she plotted the burning down of houses and the elevation of Agnes to sainthood, she began to free the slaves as well. Charlotte put a decisive end to this.

One day, Lily had heard the cook threatening Ede: *I shall hand in my notice if madam continues to insist on overseeing everything I create.* (Ede had intruded once too often into the baking of a chocolate soufflé, and the thing had fallen in the process.) *I shall have my own way with a creation,* Charlotte said grimly, *or I shall take my leave!*

The little Lily knew of slavery contained at least the certainty that slaves do not hand in their notice and take their leave. She returned her attentions, thereafter, to the ants.

In the kitchen garden, Lyon had risen and gone in search of mischief. It was not too long in the finding. A rake would help. A trowel would help. He would need a watering can and perhaps the hose. And a hatchet. That would help, too.

In The War Between the Ants, events occurred that Lily had seen herself: the raiding parties Fabre described—the Amazons marching to the Egyptians' camp in a column *five or six yards long.* Of course, she had already seen the ant highway, but that was different. A column—she had looked it up in the dictionary—had a beginning and an end; the ant highway had neither. It might have spanned the earth, for all that she could tell. But the columns marched off the way that soldiers do, each ant following the other in perfect order, laying down a trail that could be followed on their return.

When they arrived at the Egyptians' nest, the red ants pushed the black ones aside and walked straight down the tunnels to where the nurseries were. The Egyptians—who were larger—attempted to fight the Amazons off. Time to time, they succeeded in doing this. But there were more red ants than black, and they overwhelmed the others. Lily would dream about this—that she herself was the next to be invaded. Waking, she would strip her bed to make sure the Amazons weren't there.

In the Ant War, this was when the babies were kidnapped. *The Amazons race back home,* she read in Fabre, *each with her prize, a swaddled baby dangling from her jaws.*

The violence of this was quite alarming, but Lily accepted it as being the way of ants. When Frederick locked her in the attic, that was the way of men.

There were, all told, three large nests of ants on the Selby Street property and another in Mrs Carmichael's garden that fed the ant tree with its highway to the sky. Lily was not allowed to enter Mrs Carmichael's garden—no child was—and she had no way of verifying this latter nest's existence. Still, it must be there. The other three, however, were very well known to her. She knelt on the ground beside them and watched them every day.

The nest where the Amazons lived with their slaves was in the grass beside the cold frames. When she had found it there, Lily had negotiated with Bateson regarding its survival. In the early spring, when he set out the bulbs in their pots and trays of seedlings in the cold frames, the ants were not active, she informed him, and could do his plants no harm. She told him this as if it was news he had never heard before and Bateson, for Lily's sake, allowed as how her great fund of knowledge had brought him up to date with nature. This nest Lily called *Amazonia*.

There was a second nest of reds beside the brickwork that lined the drive where it curved round the house towards the stable yard. The ants who inhabited this particular encampment were the smallest of all the ants on Selby Street. They were, in fact, so very small that, unless there was a congregation of them, you might not know they were there. Their bodies were pale—almost pink—and in certain lights, they were translucent. Lily had named their tribe *Lilliputians*—a pun she extended by calling their city—not the expected *Lilliput*, but *Lily-land*, for herself.

The third and largest nest was over against the stable wall. This, where the black Egyptians lived, was *Thebes*. And this was the civilization of ants that had captured Lily's heart—just as Thebes itself, and its inhabitants, had captured her heart when *Ancient Civilizations* had revealed its wonders to her.

6. At four that afternoon, the bells started ringing in the fire hall on Sherbourne Street. Normally, this would have been the signal for every door on Selby Street to open and for all the people to pour forth onto their lawns—sending out small boys and gardeners to run and inquire: *is the city on fire again?* But this day, the heat and the humidity were overpowering and no one bothered even to think of running. *Later, someone will tell us what happened. Later, in the cool of the evening when anyone with any sense will be strolling beneath the trees. Till then, to stir is madness . . . The city be damned.*

Lily, still on the side porch with Fabre, closed her eyes when she heard the bells, and counted to twenty. This she could do if she concentrated with all her might. In doing so, she warded off the demon vision of flames.

When it came to the neighbourhood congregation of bells, the fire-house bells were unique. A person could not, by any means, mistake them for the school or the church or the knife-grinder's bell. The fire bells had a deliberate urgency—irritating and spiteful: *Wake up! Wake up! Wherever you are!* Lyon adored them, but this afternoon he was content to stay where he was in the yard. He already had the garden hose in his hand and that would put out any fire.

Lyon had been extremely busy in the last half-hour and when Browning received him later that afternoon for his bath, she found him covered from head to foot in mud and grass stains. His clothing would require a whole day of soaking to get it clean and his shoes would have to be stuffed with tissue paper and set to dry away from the sun. They were sopping wet and they squelched—deliciously, from Lyon's point of view—with every step he took. But the discovery of his filthy state did not come yet. First, there came the discovery of what he had been doing.

Over time, Lily had given Lyon guided tours of all the anthills. *Amazonia, Lily-land* and *Thebes* were described as they might have been described in a Baedeker. Histories were provided. Dates. The leading figures were given names—ant heroes and heroines—ant kings and queens. Pharaohs. Gods. There were warrior ants, landowner ants, ants of the aristocracy, peasant ants and slaves.

Lyon had only been mildly impressed with all this news. He had no imagination when it came to thinking of lives and experiences not his own. He had not yet discovered the world of books, but only the world of the park and the zoo and the world, especially, of Bateson's tool-shed and stable. The horses in the stable—there were two—were carriage horses and rather placid. All they seemed to do was munch their hay and stomp their hooves. They rarely spoke. They gleamed like polished leather under Bateson's grooming, and they frightened Lyon half to death. Their names were Rowan Oak and Butevant—gifts from James Kilworth to his daughter and son-in-law.

But the stable itself was a haven for Lyon, who loved to lie in the loft with the hay and the straw piled up around him, and to push open the door of the tiny room where Bateson lived with Toby his dog. This was behind the tack-room. Only Bateson was meant to have access to his quarters, but the partly opened door was irresistible—and Lyon spent a great deal of time in the tack-room trying to figure out how to inspect Bateson's room without going through the door. He would do this whenever Bateson had taken Frederick downtown in the Daimler—or was driving the phaeton when Ede went out to pay her calls.

A trio of anthills meant nothing to a boy with so much else to explore. But that had only been true until today and the moment when Lily refused to share her ice. Now, the anthills were objects of passionate interest—the targets of Lyon's revenge.

With the hatchet, he cleaved the city of Thebes in half—and then again, in quarters. With the rake he scattered the citizens of Lily-land, and with the trowel, he pierced the heart of Amazonia—digging down through its crowded nurseries in which the cocoons of both the reds and blacks were being attended to. He threw them, spoonful by spoonful, into the air. He then brought forth the watering can and inserted its nozzle deep into Amazonia and poured. The can was so heavy, and Lyon so small, he had to use both hands to lift it.

Once all the water had been applied and the appropriate chaos had been created, Lyon rose from his squat and threw the watering can away to one side. It almost landed on one of the cold frames. Instead, it hit the grass and lay there, gently sighing. For a moment, Lyon squinted down at what he had done and then he went back to Lily-land.

The rake was still lying there on the gravel. The tiny pink ants were in panic. Hundreds of them were milling about on the bricks that lined the drive. These bricks, in the dreadful heat of the afternoon, were like the coals of a kiln—almost glowing—sizzling hot. Lyon began to rake along the gravel—*scritch—scratch—scritch—scratch*—burying Lilliputians in pebbles and sand, then—stooping and laying the rake aside—he scooped them off the bricks and crushed them with stones.

All this was satisfying work.

But Thebes was his greatest revenge. He knew that Lily loved it best and had named its kings for the pharaohs of ancient Egypt. He knew that, in her bedroom, she had rolled-up coloured maps which she had drawn herself, depicting Thebes and all its underground passages. Lily's concept of the Egyptian anthill was based on the tunnels running through the pyramids, as shown in *Ancient Civilizations.* Lyon also knew that Lily prayed to the Ant God, kneeling in front of Thebes beside the stable. He had seen her doing this, and heard her humming what sounded like a hymn. An anthem. Now, there would be no Thebes. Already cut into quarters with the hatchet—it was Lyon's intention to obliterate what had been exposed by hosing it—*whooshing it* over the lawn in a biblical flood. This way, Lily would never find its inhabitants again—and Bateson would surely kill whatever ants were left alive with the lawnmower.

7. That night, Lily suffered three convulsions—one, so it seemed, in behalf of each of her cities. She was not to sleep for three more nights, and on the fourth day—a Sunday of terrible silence—she went to the site of Thebes and gathered its king into a matchbox she had covered in foil that had the look of gold.

This was Ramses II, whom Lily kept with her all the rest of her life. Inside his coffin, he was displayed in a strange sarcophagus. Lily had made it for him with the help of Charlotte, rolling it out on the kitchen table. In the garden, she had found some resin oozing from a pine tree. This, she knew from reading Fabre, was the basis of amber. Charlotte had spread an oilcloth over the table and Lily had formed the sarcophagus using tweezers and a pointed knife. Now, the mummified king of all the ants—Ramses II—lay in this translucent wafer.

As for Lyon, Lily regarded him as marked for death. When Monday came, the bells that rang at the Sherbourne Street fire hall were barely needed to bring the whole of Selby Street to the foot of the Wyatts' drive.

Up in the house, Lily had retired to Lyon's closet and, using the matches retrieved from the coffin of the King of Egypt, she had methodically set fire to every piece of clothing Lyon owned. The fact is, she had to be restrained from burning the clothes he wore. It was after this that Frederick decided Lily must be sent away. Permanently.

8. While a suitable school was being chosen—one that would accept a child who suffered convulsions—Lily made the first of her escapes.

This was not, as they came to be, an escape from her demons, but only from Frederick and the house on Selby Street. Having already packed her suitcase, she simply left.

Because it was summer she wore her lightest coat—raw linen— and the hat with the widest brim. In her pockets, she carried the King of Egypt in his sarcophagus, a handkerchief, a box of matches and a ten-dollar bill. The money had been stolen from the change purse in which Ede kept her winnings from the card games played with Frederick in the drawing-room on Wednesday nights. She was so adept at casino, she had already salted away more than a hundred dollars. Lily fervently hoped her mam would not miss it, but would think she had miscalculated. On the face of the ten-dollar bill there was a picture of King Edward, who looked like Queen Victoria with a beard.

The best place to hide, Lily had decided, was in a crowd. She thought of all the crowded places she had been and settled on the electric trolley. This would give her both anonymity and distance. After that, a train. Any train—to anywhere.

Knowing that the trolley conductor refused to accept bills as payment for fare, Lily also collected a handful of nickels from

Lyon's toy bank and put them in her glove. She had once been evicted from the trolley along with Lyon and Browning when Browning had told the conductor all she had was a dollar bill.

Money was not something Lily was used to handling and she had no idea how far ten dollars would carry her once she was on the train. The journey itself could not be conjured. She had never gone anywhere alone.

She left the house after supper on a hot, sultry night when the streets were filled with languid strollers, boys on bicycles and slow-moving buggies whose horses walked at a leisurely pace. Escaping the house was problematical, but Lily decided the best way to leave was to walk out boldly as if she was only going to the garden. For this reason, she carried the suitcase and her hat on the off-side as she passed the drawing-room where Ede and Frederick sat drinking coffee. They were deep in conversation and did not see her pass.

Lily stood on the porch and breathed in the night air. Crickets were singing in the grass and all of Bateson's roses were in bloom. The smell of them was warm and damp and beguiling. Poignant. Through the open windows on the second floor, Lily could hear Browning singing to Annie, the new baby, and, in the drawing-room, Ede was laughing at something Frederick had just said. Lily closed her eyes.

Don't go.

But she did.

She went down the walk and lifted the latch on the gate. Bateson had given up locking it because *Miss Lily had given up her yearning to go beyond it into the street* . . . Now, she was there.

Closing the gate, she turned towards the lights of Sherbourne Street and began at once to move in that direction.

As she walked, she put on the hat and pinned it in place. She was wearing patent leather shoes and they made a pleasant noise on the pavement. *Clickety-click*—like dancing shoes.

Mrs Carmichael was giving another party and all her doors and windows stood open beyond the screened-in porches. Someone was playing the piano. Lily recognized the tune: *Beautiful Dreamer*. It followed her all the way to the corner.

She had decided that she would go to the train station before she made up her mind about the next stage of her journey. She was calm, having succeeded in making her escape from the house—but there was a rolling sensation deep in her stomach—a sensation that reminded her of the hose uncoiling as Bateson crossed the lawn to water his flowerbeds. Something inside her was being undone and she did not know how to name it.

At the trolley stop, she waited with two men and two women who were in their twenties. They did not seem to be married couples but what Browning called *spooners*—lovers, who were so engrossed in one another they took no notice of Lily at all.

Getting onto the trolley car, she chose a seat at the back, from which she could see all the other passengers and watch the buildings passing by on either side. She sat with her feet together and her hands folded in her lap. She had emptied her gloves of the nickels, and wore them undone so that her fingers would not be too hot. The window beside her was open and the breeze created by the car's night passage was welcome. It lifted the strands of damp hair that had lain against her temples and cheeks and blew them up towards the brim of her hat. The air now smelled of tar and horse manure, cabbage soup and cigar smoke. It was exhilarating and mysterious and the spinning aureoles of light from the street lamps and houses had the look of the Midway lights that Lily had seen last year at the Canadian National Exhibition.

"Hello, there," said a voice.

Lily had been staring out the window. A man was standing beside her, smiling down from what appeared to be a great height.

"You all alone back here, then?" he said.

Lily nodded and looked away.

The man was well over six feet tall and he wore an ill-fitting jacket and a bowler hat that could not have belonged to him, they were both so small. His teeth were black for some reason and he needed to shave. Lily was relieved when he took the seat opposite rather than sitting down beside her. In order to prevent this, she lifted the suitcase into the empty space.

She heard the man opening his window and also heard him curse because he had bumped his elbow. Then he fell silent and she ignored him.

The trolley stopped to take on new passengers and let people off. Lily heard the man say: *Dundas Street.* She wished he would leave.

When the car started moving again, it gave a couple of wild lurches, as though there might have been stones on the tracks and then it righted itself and moved along smoothly beneath the chestnut branches.

Lily was thinking: *maybe ten dollars would get me all the way to McCaskill's Mills and I could go and live with James and Eliza . . .*

All the other passengers—including the four young spooners—were far away at the front of the car. The smells coming through the windows now were of market vegetables and fruit and hosed-down sidewalks and the exhaust from motor cars. Lily closed her eyes and drank them in.

"Hey!" she heard.

It was the man. His voice was hoarse and wet-sounding. Odd.

"Hey," he said again. "Girlie . . ."

Lily opened her eyes and turned her head in his direction.

"You like that?" he said.

His trousers were open and he was grinning—black. At his groin, his hand flashed back and forth with something in it that Lily, at first, could not identify.

"You like it?" the man repeated, his hand moving faster.

"What are you doing?" said Lily. It still made no sense. Was he beating time to music? Why was he all undone that way?

The man was sliding down in his seat now—twisting sideways—his hand moving faster and faster—his face contorted and his breathing rapid and choked. He started humming—a low, long note—only one—a single, burgeoning noise that, all at once, Lily recognized.

He was having a seizure.

Surely that's what it was.

She slid across her seat and tried to stand up with the suitcase.

The trolley car gave another lurch and Lily swung out into the aisle, both hands grasping the corners of the seat in front of her.

The man's head was now thrown back in a posture Lily recognized all too well and he was beating at himself as if he meant to do himself harm.

"It's all right," Lily said. "I'll go get help . . ."

She started forward, but was thrown back again by another lurch. The trolley car was passing under an avenue of lights. Just as she was recovering her balance, the man gave a terrible shout.

Lily ran forward.

"Someone's in trouble back there," she cried. "There's something wrong with him . . ."

Half an hour later, Lily stood on the sidewalk in front of the gate on Selby Street. Next door, Mrs Carmichael's party was still in progress and in the Wyatt house, Lily could hear Browning calling out: "Ly—on! Ly—on! Come, dear boy—it's going-to-bed-time . . ."

Lily lifted the latch and went through the gateway. Beyond the screens, she could see that Ede and Frederick had started their game of casino. They hadn't even known she was gone.

Lily took off her hat, set down the suitcase and sat on the verandah steps.

So much for escaping. The world of streets and trolley cars, which in time would become her permanent escape route, had offered her the promise of freedom only to bring her face to face with the fact that, in the streets, she would be pursued by demons other than her own.

For weeks, she would be haunted by the ghost of the black-toothed rider, with his head thrown back and his body arching. And his fingers tearing at himself as if to be rid of his clothes and his flesh. And she wondered if that was what she looked like when the whirlwind rose and threw her up to the ceiling and smothered her with its wings. And the humming noise he had made . . . She knew that, too—with its rising urgency and its strangling grip on her throat.

I must hide, she thought, *where no one can find me. And I will never tell what I have seen, because they will recognize it, too. All of them—everyone who has ever seen me fall . . .*

She stood up then and went inside and climbed the stairs. She emptied her pockets and went down the hall, where she put the ten-dollar bill into her mother's change purse and closed the drawer.

At the top of the stairs, she eyed the door to the attic. Maybe the black-toothed rider had an attic, too, from which he had escaped. Maybe his pockets were full of matches . . .

She closed her eyes and pulled the house around her. Here, for a moment, she was safe. She need not consider escaping any longer. Not now. Not yet . . . The house was creaking. Straining. She could feel it doing this and she knew what it meant. In a while—in a month—it would expel her. She would be gone and the house, without her, would sigh. It knew that she had wanted to set it on fire. It knew that if she stayed it would perish.

Houses do that, Lily told me. *They tell you when it's time to leave.*

9. The school that was chosen was forty-eight miles away, in a field north of Newmarket—almost all the way to Lake Simcoe. The dormitories and classrooms were housed in a large stone building that once had been a convent. It was called St Mary-Margaret and it prided itself on its mastery of difficult students.

St Mary-Margaret could be reached on the radial car that ran between Toronto and Sutton, but on the first occasion—when Lily was admitted there—Frederick allowed Ede to take her in the Daimler. Bateson wore his uniform and they all looked very grand.

They were met on the front steps by the Head Mistress, whose name was Richter. Miss Richter had been born in Germany but raised in England, where her father had been a minor secretary in the Foreign Office.

"The British Foreign Office?" Ede had asked.

"Most certainly not," Miss Richter had shot back. "Heavens, no! My father was in the employ of his Imperial Majesty, the Kaiser. I must tell you, Mrs Wyatt, that he did so very well in the Foreign Service, they kept him on at the embassy in London for fifteen years. I had all my own schooling there in England . . ." Miss Richter had let the sentence drift off into the mists of significant possibilities. "Outside of Berlin, the British school system is the best in the whole world where discipline is concerned," she had said. "And I trust that you will be pleased to hear that I employ that system at St Mary-Margaret. We rule with an iron hand . . ." she had smiled, ". . . in a velvet glove."

Inwardly, Ede had winced. But she was resigned to the fact that strictures were required if Lily was to be controlled. Her seizures had been explained and accepted, her medicines had been provided—the bromides and the muscle relaxants and the chloroform with which Browning had been forced, from time to time, to quiet her. The matron at St Mary-Margaret, Sister Donleavy, had been introduced and instructed in the singular aspects of Lily's condition. And the classrooms and dormitories had been inspected.

This was to be Lily's first long separation among strangers and Ede had willed herself not to show her true emotion. Her principal problem was her fear—her terror—that Lily might perish out of her sight.

They performed a lingering goodbye, which was taken walking in the garden. Little was said. Assurances were given—*not to worry—all will be well.* Ede told Lily that *for the first time ever, you are going to have friends outside the family.* Lily told Ede that for the first time ever, she was going to be alone.

But neither of them cried and neither of them trembled. Ede kissed Lily three times and took her leave. Lily shook hands with Bateson and went up to stand on the steps with Miss Richter as the Daimler was driven away.

When the car had disappeared down the drive, Miss Richter gave Lily's shoulder a pat and said: "well then, let's get started!"

This way, Frederick rid the Selby Street house of its demon. Or so he believed. So far as Lily was concerned, she was finally rid of him. He was gone now—even from memory.

10. In the autumn of 1907, Lisgard Wyatt, Senior, died. He was seventy-five years old, but he might as well have been Methuselah, for all his tragedies and ills.

It had been his dream to fill the world with beautiful furniture—with flamed-birch tallboys and Windsor chairs with saddle-seats and lyric backs, with clocks of satinwood and pianos housed in bird's-eye maple . . . And tables with twice-turned legs.

In 1848, at the age of sixteen, Lisgard was apprenticed to the legendary cabinet-maker, Antony Northey. When Northey offered him a partnership four years later, he took it. Twenty years old and already considered a master craftsman, Lisgard Wyatt began to make a name for himself. But this had been in Kingston, where Northey had his shops, and Lisgard wanted more.

In 1856, he made his way to Toronto and opened his own emporium. There were six employees and standing orders from three great houses—chairs, tables, sideboards—mantels, porticos, newel posts. It was time to marry—time to begin his dynasty.

The rest, we know.

Driven by sorrow, he faltered—and, faltering, he accepted fewer and fewer commissions, offering instead to act as the agent for imported cabinetry. Some might have made a success of such an enterprise, but Lisgard's fortune had been in his hands, not his head; in his eyes, not his mouth—and by the time his second wife had died, he was selling secondhand furniture.

He never carved again—never planed or turned or shaped. That was behind him. His wits dulled. He crawled inside himself and howled with rage at his dying wives and his world of orphans. His eldest sons, in their own attempts to survive, turned their backs on him and moved into the importation of pianos. For twelve of

Lizzie's twenty-four years, the old man held him locked in the embrace of filial loyalty. Now, the embrace had been loosed.

This meant that Lizzie was left alone with Buster in the Crawford Street house and his first reaction was one of panic. For all the years of dreaming freedom, he was suddenly confronted with the real thing and did not know what to do with it. "It gives me headaches," he said.

He stayed at Crawford Street for almost the whole of October, clearing the house from top to bottom. He moved his bedroom onto the second floor and gave the study back its proper furniture. Ede sent a hired char down to help him, along with Bateson, and every floor was scrubbed and every pane of glass that wasn't broken was polished and all the broken ones replaced. The old man's bed was removed from the kitchen and a wicker bed for Buster installed in its place. Curtains were hung, store-bought at Eaton's, and Ede sent carpets that had been languishing in the stable loft and a set of proper dishes and three new lamps. *Dispel the darkness*—that was her motto in this exercise—and seeing the results when all was finished, she could not believe her eyes. Here was a house that would have been worthy of Tom—and its present occupant deserved it no less.

On the 23rd of October, she packed Lizzie off to Munsterfield with Buster. "All this aloneness is bad for you. What you need is a good bumpy ride on the wagon with Malahide and a feast of Freda's cooking! Buster will love it. Real live rabbits to chase!" Then she told him the best news of all.

Lily would be there.

In the throes of one of her seizures at school, she had broken her wrist and Miss Richter had allowed her a two-week holiday. "Just in time for the pumpkins and the bonfires."

11. It was a joyous, rapturous reunion—with Buster crowding between them and the Kilworth dogs going mad with leaping. Everyone laughed and everyone cried and everyone drank a glass of whiskey. Ballyporeen.

James was glad to have another lad in the house. With only Malahide, he had felt hemmed in by women.

"Don't be ridiculous, James," Eliza said. "You've been hemmed in by women all your life."

"Still," said James, "it's nice to hear another male voice."

"All you have to do is go out to the barn for that."

Lily sat at table and stared. Lizzie was more beautiful than ever. Beautiful and free. Beautiful and free . . . and sad.

Why was he sad?

His father had died.

I wouldn't be sad if Frederick died.

Frederick is not your father.

"Will you sing for us, Lizzie?" she asked.

"Yes. But not tonight. I have a headache—and the journey's made me tired. I'll sing for you tomorrow." Saying this, he smiled and winked at Lily. "It's a good thing you broke your wrist," he said. "You're a dreadful piano player—the whole world's worst! This way, Eliza can play for me—and she has the fingers of an angel."

Eliza beamed.

Ede had insisted on having a Wyatt shipped to Eliza. James had given way with graceful resignation. It would do no harm to have music, now. The romantic years—when music had been danger-ous—were over. His children were dispersed—all but Malahide—and music could bring them no harm.

"Can I get you something for the headache, Lizzie?"

"Thank you. No. I'm trying to talk myself out of them. I've had quite a few since Father died. I'm sure it's just the tension. So I try to talk them down. And a good sleep will help."

Lily said: "how do you talk them down?"

"I tell them stories."

"Which? What stories?"

Lizzie gave a faint smile. "Bedtime stories," he said.

All at once he stood up.

"If you don't mind, I'll head up now and turn in."

"Of course we don't mind," said Eliza.

"I mind," said Lily.

"You shush," said Eliza. And then to Lizzie: "if there's anything you need, just call down and Mal will bring it up. I still wish you'd let me give you something . . ."

"No. No. Thank you. I have to deal with them my own way. Good-night, all."

"Good-night."

Lizzie went out into the hall and, until they could hear him on the stairs, no one spoke.

"He really doesn't look well," said Eliza, as soon as Lizzie was halfway up. "Pale and dank-looking. I should have felt him for fever. Did anyone else see how his hand was shaking?"

"I did," said Malahide. "But I don't know him as well as you do—so I thought he was maybe the shaky type. Nervous."

"No. Not at all."

"He was always pale, Eliza," said James. "Even as a boy, when he should have been robust, he had the colour of sheets."

"He's an artist," said Lily. "And artists are always pale."

"Oh, indeed now. Is that so?" said James.

Everyone laughed, even Lily, at how pompous she had sounded. Then, all at once, she stood up and ran out into the hall. At the foot of the stairs, she called out: "Lizzie."

He had not gone into his room yet and came and stood in the lamplight looking down at her.

"Yes?" he said.

"You have to promise me," Lily said.

"Promise you what, Lil?"

"Promise me that you'll sing. All day!"

Lizzie laughed. "All right," he said. "I promise. Cross my heart and hope to die."

He turned then, and was gone.

* * *

When Mal went out to the barn that night, he noted the harvest moon in the frigid sky.

"You're late this year," he said.

Lily, in the front room, looked over across the road at the field spread out in the golden light. The moon itself was behind the house, but every twig on every tree stood out—and every bar of the split-rail fence—and every blade of grass.

She knelt, and stared at all of this, and then said: *thank you, moon, from Lizzie. And from me.*

It was eighteen years since Tom and Ede had found her there.

12. In the morning, Lizzie did not appear at the breakfast table.

"Let him sleep," said Eliza. "It will do him a world of good."

"No one ever says that when I want to sleep in at school," said Lily. "We're always dragged out of bed at six."

"Mal gets up at five," James reminded her. "Build it into your system—you'll soon get used to it."

"What time do your classes start?" Eliza wanted to know.

"Nine. But before that we have to run around the quad eight times, bathe, eat breakfast and go to chapel."

"What is the quad?" Mal asked. He was eating his second breakfast.

"The quadrangle."

"What's that?"

"If you'd gone to school, Mally, you'd know," said James.

"Leave him alone, James." This was Eliza. Then she turned to Malahide. "A lot of schools have them. It's an oblong bit of lawn with a path running round the outside."

"Ours isn't oblong," said Lily. "It's a circle."

"Then it's not a quadrangle," said James. "No wonder nobody

knows anything any more. Calling circles quadrangles! It's those kind of people who must've built all those tumbled houses that came down in the Frisco quake last year. *Oh, yes! We'll just support these walls with a bunch of ROUND QUADRANGLES!* Idiots!"

"James . . ."

"*Idiots,*" James repeated. Then he looked at Lily and said: "now, I suppose it must be those same blasted Yankees who've come up here to *teach!*"

"*James.*"

James sat back, red-faced and apoplectic. "Idiots," he muttered.

After a moment of silence, Lily said: "most of the houses in San Francisco were burned. They hardly any of them fell."

"You're quite right, dear," said Eliza—smoothing the cloth at her end of the table. "That city burned for three whole days."

"Toronto only burned for one," said Lily. "And that was bad enough."

"Qua-*drangles* . . ." said James, barely audible.

Buster padded into the room.

Lily said: "good-morning, Buster. You want to go outside?"

She stood up and started towards the kitchen and the back door. Buster did not follow her. He sat down and stared at Eliza.

Lily said: "if Buster's down, then Lizzie must be awake."

Eliza stood up. "I think that Freda should take him his breakfast on a tray. A little pampering won't do any harm. He spent all those years looking after his father." Passing Lily, she went into the kitchen.

"Can't I take the tray?"

"No, dear. Not with your wrist."

Buster barked.

"What is it?"

He barked again.

"Good old Buster," said Lily. "He's so happy to be here . . ."

Twenty minutes later, Freda, having carried the breakfast tray upstairs, came back down and said: "Mister James?"

"Yes, Freda?"

"Could we have words in your office, please?"

Without waiting for an answer, Freda turned and went back along the hall towards the study.

James, still with his napkin, followed her. "Must be something wrong with that new water closet," he said. "Freda's such a lady, she doesn't want to say *toilet* in front of another woman."

Buster got up and followed him.

While they waited, Eliza and Lily poured themselves more coffee. Malahide had already returned to the barns, where he and the men were building new holding pens for the calves.

In a moment, James came to the door. He was strangely subdued. "Eliza?"

Eliza turned.

"Would you come with me, please?"

Eliza got up and started towards him.

Lily also stood up.

James said, but kindly: "stay put, Lily. We'll be back in a minute."

Lily sat down.

James and Eliza disappeared into the hallway. Buster was nowhere in sight.

Lily wondered what might be wrong—and why Freda had not returned from the study. Maybe Buster had done something bad—eaten a pair of shoes or something.

She stood up and went to the door. The others had gone upstairs and now only James was returning. But instead of making for the dining-room, he went inside the study. Lily heard the telephone being lifted and cranked. Then she heard James's voice—but not what he was saying.

Freda would be with him. Eliza was still—apparently—upstairs.

Lily moved further into the hallway in order to hear what James was saying, but he was speaking too quietly for her to make out the words. Then she heard him hang up. He came and stood in the doorway.

"Lily?"

"Yes, sir?"

"Come to the study, child."

Lily approached and passed him—silent. Something dreadful

must have happened. Freda was seated in one of the chairs, with a blank expression on her face. When she looked up at Lily, her eyes were filled with fear.

James went over to his desk. He still had his napkin in his hand. "Now, Lily . . ." he said.

Lily sat down. She watched him but did not utter. She slipped her good hand inside the sling and pressed her broken wrist in hard against her ribs. The plaster cast was like an iron bar.

". . . we don't know what it is, but something has happened to Lizzie . . ." James told her.

Freda had found him. He was unable to speak and evidently frightened, sitting sideways in his bed, with his knees drawn up and his back against the wall. His head was down and his arms were wrapped around his shins. When Freda told him she had brought his breakfast, Lizzie looked up at her with such an expression, she was stopped in her tracks.

"*Was fehlt Dir, Liebchen?*"

She set the tray on the bureau and hurried to him, asking him: "What is wrong? Tell me." But he only stared at her. Weeping.

Freda crouched before him, looking into his face. The expression there was unnerving—terrifying. It was the same expression she had seen on a dying soldier's face during the French bombardment of her city. That boy, too, had not spoken. His chest and throat had been torn by a fragment of shell. She'd had to watch him die.

"Oh, Mister Lizzie . . . Tell me. Tell what it is."

Lizzie pointed at his mouth, his fingers hard against his lips. He kept on jabbing with them while he rocked back and forth.

"I will bring you someone," Freda said, rising.

At the door she turned and spoke again. "Wait for us," she said. "Wait for us."

Then she brought James.

Doctor Melbourne arrived in his buggy half an hour later. By this time, Freda had also brought Mal and Ephraim from the barn. Ephraim walked the buggy into the yard and let the horse drink from the trough. Doctor Melbourne hurried into the house, where James greeted him, leading him to the stairs.

By now, they were old and good friends. Besides getting James through his stroke, Robert Melbourne had been present at the births of Malahide and Willa—and the death of young James, almost twenty years ago. That had been the last of the deaths at Munsterfield. Melbourne, too, had been the first physician consulted when Lily started having seizures.

In Lizzie's room, Eliza—who had stayed with him—moved away from the bed, speaking quietly. "Thank you, Robert, for coming. We're sorry to call you out so early. He cannot . . . he seems not to be able to speak. He's very frightened . . ."

"With no need to be," the doctor said, turning to Lizzie with a reassuring smile. "Now, let's see what we can find."

The examination took almost an hour. Lizzie was asked to raise his arms and legs and lift his shoulders, turn his head, stand up and walk. Or to try.

The latter was difficult, but not impossible.

Melbourne asked Lizzie to sit down in a chair near the window. He examined his ears, his eyes and his throat. He took Lizzie's temperature and counted off his pulse rate. He squeezed his knees and elbows and wrists and ankles. He listened to his heart. He listened to his lungs.

Then he stood back and looked very hard at Lizzie, thinking.

"Turn your back, Eliza."

She did.

Doctor Melbourne then had Lizzie remove his pyjamas.

"James. Close the window."

He did.

Doctor Melbourne accepted Lizzie's pyjama top and put his hand out for the trousers.

Lizzie undid the strings and the trousers fell. Then he bent over to remove them . . .

Suddenly, he raised both hands to his head . . .

And fell . . .

He dropped to his knees, after which he curled down into a ball, still holding his head, and beginning to rock back and forth, the same as he had done when Freda found him.

James at once stepped forward, thinking to lift Lizzie up. But Melbourne put out his hand to prevent him.

For a moment, the two men were silent, watching the young man down on the floor at their feet. Melbourne was turning Lizzie's pyjama jacket in his hands—turning it round and round—while he thought about it.

Then he thrust the jacket at James. "It's wet," he said. "Wet and sticky. That's mucus. Drool."

"Yes," said James. "I can feel it. What does it mean?"

Doctor Melbourne put a finger to his lips, informing James that Lizzie must not yet hear what he might say. Instead of answering James, Doctor Melbourne said, almost pleasantly: "I had been going to give him a rectal examination . . . see what the glands were up to down in the groin, et cetera. Standard. And the back . . . the liver, the kidneys . . . but I think I'll spare him all that. Let's see if we can get him back on his feet and into another pair of pyjamas."

Without being asked, Eliza left and returned seconds later with a pair of pyjamas taken from Malahide's bureau.

"I can dress him," she said. "You go and talk." She waved them away and turned back to Lizzie. "Don't be embarrassed, dear," she said. "Remember I'm a married woman with three sons."

Three sons.

Jamie.

Going down the stairs, Melbourne said: "I'm afraid this is serious, Jim."

James led him into the parlour, where he uncapped the first decanter that came to hand. Who cared which of the whiskeys it was. The point was—it would be whiskey.

"There," he said, and gave Melbourne his glass. "Well? How serious?"

"Very." The doctor swirled the drink and looked at it. "The mucus—his having fallen—the obvious agony he experienced—and the loss of words . . ."

James waited.

"I think what we have here," said Melbourne, "is a tumour."

"Where?"

"The brain, I'm afraid. It all adds up . . ." He finished his drink.

"Oh, the poor lad. Dear God. A tumour."

"Yes—and we'll have to get it out. Otherwise, I'm afraid . . ."

"He will die?"

"Yes." Melbourne swallowed the whole of his drink.

"An operation. When, do you think? How soon?"

"Right away. As soon as possible."

"Can you do it?" James asked.

Melbourne gave a wry laugh. "Not a hope in hell. He'll need a proper surgeon—and a good one."

"We could take him back to Toronto. There must be someone there."

"No. He's not going anywhere, Jim. Not in this condition."

"What do we do, then?"

"We bring the surgeon to him."

"Here?"

"Here. I will assist him. That I can do. And I can have Miss Bransby come out . . . Tell me where your telephone is."

Melbourne had a particular neurosurgeon in mind—a doctor whose practice was at St Michael's Hospital in Toronto. This was Omar Warren, who had studied in England with the famous Victor Horsley. Horsley's daring experiments and his expertise in neurosurgery were legendary. He was respected worldwide. Students flocked to him. Horsley had made his name in the 1890s by localizing the centres of the brain which control the movements of the body's muscles; as well—and most importantly—the area controlling speech. None of this had been lost on Omar Warren. He was a brilliant student, and had received Horsley's personal endorsement.

What was best about Doctor Warren—second-best, after his surgical skills—was his willingness to perform operations beyond the city limits—his eagerness to bring his skills into communities that other surgeons wouldn't dream of visiting. *I want to solve problems that others won't touch,* he had said. *I want to discover what's out there as far as I can reach.*

Now, he was being asked to reach as far away as Munsterfield—seventy miles and more.

When Melbourne returned to the parlour, having made his call, James could already tell that Doctor Warren would come.

"Come, yes," said Melbourne. "But it's going to cost a pretty penny."

"Damn the cost. Bring him."

"Well—I hope you're ready for this, Jim. In order to get here this evening—and that's the soonest we can expect him—he's going to have to engage a special train. And that costs money. Real money."

"Fine. I don't care. Fine."

"He's going to bring his own nurse with him—but I'll have Bransby standing by. An operation like this will want all the hands we can muster."

"And you will assist him?"

"Yes. I'll be there to administer the anaesthetic. That's all I'm qualified for, in cases like this."

"Thank God you were here, Bobby. Thank God for that—and your knowing of this Warren fellow, too."

"We'll see. There's no one who's perfect, Jim. But we've got the best there is."

13. The kitchen was to be the site of Lizzie's operation. Freda, with the help of the two younger hands—Davey and Richard—had scrubbed the floor and the chairs and the tables. The largest table would serve as the bed on which Lizzie would lie.

Doctor Melbourne had summoned Miss Bransby, who had now arrived. She was a small, grey woman—a deliberate woman, moving at a deliberate pace, watching with sharply focused eyes every move that everyone made. She was also terse. Her voice had an edge to it that told you to jump whenever she said *move*. Everyone in the community knew her, and though wary of her, most were fond of her. Like Melbourne, Bransby had witnessed their medical problems through the years—and her gossip was plentiful, but never mean. She was the perfect colleague for Robert Melbourne, whose charm was his greatest asset. Also his greatest liability. On the one hand, it opened every door; on the other, it tarried overlong, once admitted. Some—though not James, not Eliza—thought of it as *tiring* charm. Bransby, however, cut through situations with the speed of lightning. Melbourne called her *The Scalpel*.

Sheets were hung on the kitchen walls, and more stood by on one of the smaller tables, waiting to be used when called for. Under Miss Bransby's instruction, some of these were torn and scissored into various lengths and various widths, and rolled into bandages. Pails were brought. *There will be blood—and much of it,* Miss Bransby warned them.

"*Pails* of it?" Malahide wondered.

"No," said Miss Bransby. "Pails of sops."

Water was boiled and kept at the simmer in order to sterilize Doctor Warren's instruments.

Meanwhile, James and Robert Melbourne had informed Lizzie of what was to be done and why—a gentle telling. He was only vaguely aware of what they said, being dopey with the weight of his condition. Miss Bransby then arrived with combs and scissors and razors, followed by Ephraim, who carried towels, a pail of hot water and a basin. Lizzie's head must be shaved and swabbed with green soap, after which it would be bathed with the same solution of bichloride of mercury the others would use on their hands.

Lizzie was helped into the straight-backed chair by the window and the shearing began.

At this point, Lily came and stood in the open doorway, watching silently. Buster lay at her feet and slowly thumped his tail. The present activities, with their attendant smells and sounds, were a comfort to him. They had been a daily part of his life while Lisgard lived—the careful sponge baths which Lizzie had administered, the fussing with the hair, the scent of soaps and lathers—these were all familiar. He felt entirely at home.

Lily was in a kind of trance. She was not allowed to take part in any of the present activities—Doctor Melbourne using the excuse of her broken wrist. But he—as everyone—was too aware of the state Lizzie's trauma might produce in Lily, and a seizure must be avoided, lest its onslaught disturb the progress of the operation.

Eliza had already enjoined them all in prayers for Lizzie's survival and the success of the operation. This had been done in the Sunday parlour, where a crucifix—in spite of James's instructions—was in evidence. Only Lily did not kneel down. She refused to admit that there was so much danger it must be prayed away. Prayer was an admission of jeopardy she was not willing to accept. Nonetheless, she stood there and listened while the others prayed.

Once the prayers had been said, Eliza went into James's office and placed a telephone call. While she waited, the telephone operator said to her: "I never had so much long distance in one day before. You folks all right out there?"

"Yes," said Eliza. "Get off the line."

It was Ede who answered. Eliza told her what was happening and asked her to tell Lizzie's brothers. "We aren't going to lose him," she said. "I promise you that. We aren't going to lose him." Then she said: "I want you to go to St Michael's Cathedral. Please. Light him a candle. Light one for all of us." And then: "goodbye."

14. • It was eight-thirty before Doctor Warren's arrival was heralded by the barking of dogs and the clatter of the democrat coming up the drive. Omar Warren came from the wagon almost at a run, as if the sudden stop had impelled him

forward. He was a small, round man with an intense expression which gave the impression of someone who could barely see. "You're Melbourne," he said to Robert. "We've met." And went on into the house.

His surgical bag was in one hand and a leather travelling case for bottles of acid and ether in the other. His coat was undone, his Homburg tipped away to the back of his head and his galoshes flapped as he walked. James caught up with him and introduced himself, telling Doctor Warren that everything had been prepared as requested.

A tall, middle-aged woman with military bearing now arrived in the hallway. She was dressed in a severely tailored dark blue overcoat and a round felt hat. Her hands, also, were laden with bags and parcels.

"This is Miss Trunk," said Omar Warren, already divesting himself of his outdoor clothing, letting it fall to the floor as he did this—Freda hurrying forward to retrieve it.

A tornado might as well have arrived.

Ephraim had gone out to help Davey unload the surgical equipment and now they started to bring it through the door. The first thing Doctor Warren wanted was a *confab* with Doctor Melbourne, after which he would examine the patient. While they went upstairs, Miss Bransby came and took Miss Trunk away, leading her with all her packages down the hall towards the kitchen. Davey and Ephraim carried assorted paraphernalia after them—and suddenly, the front hall was empty, the front door still standing open.

Lily came out of the parlour, then, with Buster padding after her. She wore an overcoat around her shoulders and a woollen hat pulled down over her ears. She stood for a moment looking up the stairs, recalling the sight of Lizzie standing there in the lamplight only last night. She could hear Richard speaking to the horse and the dogs as he walked the democrat along the drive to the shed. She could also hear the crackling of the fire behind her in the parlour and the distant activity back in the kitchen, with its undercurrent of confidential voices.

"Come on, Buster," she said. "You and I will go out and watch the moon."

One hour later, the operation commenced.

15. Davey had carried Lizzie downstairs piggyback fashion, with Lizzie's arms hanging down, swinging lightly from side to side. He was still in a stupor, almost comatose but not. As he was carried beneath the hall lamps, his bald head gleamed with a yellowish tinge from the antiseptic solutions used to wash it. He still wore Malahide's blue pyjamas and Eliza had pulled thick woollen socks up over his feet and ankles.

In the kitchen, he was placed face down on the wide plank table which now had a thick straw mattress on it, taken from one of the beds at Doctor Warren's instruction.

"Make him as comfortable as possible," he said to the nurses. "He'll be in that position for some time. Asleep or not, he'll know it."

The top of Lizzie's pyjamas was then removed and his hands, palms outward, were drawn in against his thighs. A support for his upper body was manoeuvred into place, his shoulders lying in padded metallic crutches and his face pressed lightly into a padded form not unlike a horseshoe, which left his nose and mouth free to breathe. A sheet was then drawn up to his shoulder-blades.

Next to be wheeled into position was a pressure pump, which Doctor Melbourne would control with a lever, using the pressure to urge the ether through a rubber tube and a glass stopper—onto a sieve-like mask covered with gauze. This could be held beneath Lizzie's nose and mouth as the anaesthetic was required. Eliza had been enlisted to hold the mask. Malahide was asked to do this, but he declined. For all his experience in animal husbandry, with its attendant gore, he could not abide the thought of what would be done to Lizzie's skull and he removed himself not only from the kitchen, but from the whole house, fearing that if he stayed, he might hear the sound of cutting.

A quantity of carbolic acid had been added to one of the pots of boiling water and the comforting stench of it filled the lower floor. Doctor Warren's surgical instruments were duly sterilized and then displayed on metal trays. Other trays held collections of small, sausage-shaped rolls of cotton soaked in a saline solution. Miss Trunk had referred to the cotton rolls as *pledgets*.

Doctor Warren spoke to those assembled in the kitchen. "I want everyone present to make use of the bichloride solution, and I want every one of you to wear rubber gloves."

Both doctors and both nurses had already taken these precautions and now Eliza, James, Freda and Davey stepped to the basin and washed their hands in the solution.

"I've never worn rubber gloves," said Eliza as she pulled them on. "What a curious sensation."

Doctor Warren gave her a brief smile and turned to Davey. "You can light that thing now."

That thing was a headlamp taken from a motor car. It functioned by means of acetylene gas and gave a bright white light that no mere oil lamp could begin to provide.

"I discovered how useful that thing is on another of my out-of-town emergencies. I had gone there, you see, in my automobile and, once on the premises, found to my dismay that the household had run out of kerosene—if you can imagine such a thing. So I had the chauffeur bring in the headlamps and lo and behold, they gave such a wondrous quantity of light—especially in the concentrated area of the surgery—that I've used them ever since whenever I go on one of these jaunts."

Then he spoke again to Davey. "I hope you're a good stout lad. You're going to have to hold that thing for some time. Bring it here, now. Let us begin . . ."

Eliza crouched on the floor beneath Lizzie's face. He looked unearthly—marbleized with stillness. His eyes were slightly open, but he was utterly asleep. Two applications of ether had already been given. It bothered Eliza that Lizzie seemed so far away as she watched him—as if somehow he had distanced himself from what was happening to him. His being voiceless made this impression of distance all the more troubling. She felt that in a sense he was being violated, since he could not protest and had no way of understanding the possible consequence of what was being done. He could die, up there above her, even as she watched—and she wondered if this had occurred to him. *The poor dear boy has barely had a life at all,* she thought. *And all his brothers hardly know him. Ede and Lily—me and James—we've been his family. It will be our loss . . . But he isn't going to die. He is not going to die. That's why we're doing this . . .*

She was kneeling in a sort of tent of sheets in which Robert Melbourne joined her from time to time in order to monitor Lizzie's response to the ether. It was in this eerie shade that Eliza spent the next two hours.

After the second stage of anaesthesia, Doctor Warren made the first cut. Having swabbed the lower half of Lizzie's scalp from ear to ear, he made what he described as *a cuticular scratch, barely deep enough to draw blood . . .* This way, he designed the pattern of the incisions which would follow.

All the while he worked, Doctor Warren talked—very much as though he were speaking to a group of students, instructing them as a guide would instruct his charges. "Mas . . . toid to Mas . . . toid . . ." he said, speaking in time to the cuts he was making. "Up above the oc . . . cip . . . i . . . tal pro . . . tu . . . ber . . . *ance* . . . just like the arc of a bridge . . ."

The sound of these cuts was the sound of silk being torn. Eliza closed her eyes.

James could now see a mass of blood surging forward until the nurses applied fresh swabs, each swab discarded in the pails on either side of the table.

Doctor Warren used the sleeve of his gown to wipe his forehead. "Fingers—*fingers*, Miss Trunk," he said. "Use your fingers on the pressure points—you know that."

"Yes, Doctor," said Miss Trunk, applying her fingers near the cuts in the flowing vessels. "I'm sorry, but the flow is fairly hardy."

"Come to the clamps, now, Miss Bransby. Thank you. Thank you. Thank you . . ."

Doctor Warren himself started applying the clamps to the rolled-up edges of his cuts. When he was finished with this, the long, scissorlike implements hung down from Lizzie's skull like grotesque ringlets. The bleeding had been stemmed for the moment.

Omar Warren stepped forward and hovered over what he called *the field of operation.*

"Give me more light just here, young man . . . thank you . . ."

James watched the surgeon leaning forward, poised above Lizzie's head. *What tiny hands he has,* he thought. *Almost a child's hands . . .*

Half an hour later, Doctor Warren had finished scraping the soft tissues from the bone. Now he waited while Miss Trunk and Miss Bransby dealt once again with an episode of minor bleeding. The moment had come for him to perform the *craniectomy*—by means of which the necessary amount of bone material is removed in order to reach the brain.

This part of the operation was performed with a sequence of implements and instruments that resembled a child's carpentry set. Tiny cylindrical saws called trephines were used to make holes in the bone—saw-toothed, flat-handled knives were applied—chisels were driven forward with silver hammers . . . James could not believe his eyes.

Poor Davey had the worst of it—trying to steady the lamp he had now been shifting from hand to hand for an interminable length of time. James could see that he was flagging.

He crossed behind the foot of the table and said to Davey: "because I've only got one good arm, I won't be able to hold that thing for very long . . . but at least I can give you a moment's rest."

"Oh, yes—and thank you," said Davey. "I'm fair gone. Even five minutes with my arms down would do it."

"Bring the thing closer," said Doctor Warren, without looking up.

"Yes, sir," said James, automatically back in his father's sway. *We all become children when we must obey.*

Davey went and sat in a chair, with his arms at his sides.

"I'd sell my soul for a cigarette," he said.

"Well, you won't smoke it here," said Doctor Warren. "Any more than you'd smoke it in an ammunition dump."

"Yes, sir."

"Hold the thing closer, Mister Kilworth."

"Yes, sir."

Under the table and the tent, Eliza wondered why the poor old lamp was always called *the thing. I don't think Doctor Warren has called it by its true name once.*

Minds were wandering—into the past—into speculation of what might be a happier occupation than this—into long meditations on the subjects of food and sleep—into the distance beyond the windows, with its moon and stars and its cold wind rising.

Freda took away the sop pails and emptied them into the stove, where they flared up and dazzled her. Returning the pails to their places, she said to Eliza—whose feet stuck out from the tent of sheets: "you want a pillow?"

"No thank you, Freda. I'm afraid my legs have already gone to sleep."

Robert Melbourne went around the table to take Lizzie's pulse.

"How's he doing?" said Warren.

"Badly, I'm afraid."

"Somebody put another sheet over him. Two. We don't want shock . . ."

Freda spread the sheets, thinking yet again of her dead soldier. Lizzie lay so still. So distant.

At fifteen minutes past eleven, the tumour was exposed.

For the briefest moment, Omar Warren hung above his discovery in dismay. He recognized at once the implacable enemy of an entangled growth. The tumour, encircled as it was with nerves, could not possibly be removed without harming these to such an extent that any amount of paralysis might result.

On the other hand, given the soft, non-fibrous texture of the diseased tissue, if it were to be sectioned and removed piecemeal, parts of it would be certain to elude him, and a stalk from which further growth could occur was almost guaranteed to be left behind.

Worse still—wherever an arterial branch lay hidden within the tumour, one wrong cut could start a flow of blood that might not be stoppable.

Well. Either way, the young man was going to be imperilled.

What was his name?

Robert Melbourne was watching Omar Warren, his view of him angled over the surgeon's right shoulder as Warren leaned forward into the light. In the other man's stance, Melbourne recognized at once the fatal possibilities of this moment, having himself been suspended in similar fashion, face to face with a sinister diagnosis.

"Omar . . . ?"

Warren straightened.

"Yes," he said. "We have the problem I feared."

He called for spoons and told Miss Bransby to come forward with a mass of cotton pledgets. "Make sure they're still damp," he said. "I expect a cavity of some size and we'll want to pack it."

"Yes, Doctor."

Doctor Warren stepped back. He closed his eyes. Here was the moment he had been trained to deal with without emotion. Emotion leads to panic. Panic leads to fumbling. Fumbling leads to death. Precepts. Absolutes. He opened his eyes and gazed at his cohorts. *Remarkable people—all of them—remarkable.*

And who is that?

There was a face at the window. A ghostly face—sad and beautiful. Lily. Doctor Warren nodded, thinking: *quite remarkable. Yes.* Lily turned away. Moonlight streamed where she had been.

Now, begin . . .

"Give me a kidney pan," he said to Miss Trunk, who was already offering a variety of spoons in one hand. She passed him the kidney-shaped metal pan into which he would drop the pieces of tumour as he scooped them from Lizzie's brain.

Go—in. The words were not spoken aloud. Warren's monologue with the world at large had come to an end. He was now alone with the enemy.

He made a single cut and laid aside his scalpel, accepting in its place a spoon of medium size from Miss Trunk. With this, he began to scoop out portions of the tumour in a fashion not unlike the spooning of thick ice cream.

As he worked, every eye was on him. Even Eliza, in her tent, looked upwards—and Davey, who by now had returned to *the thing* even in spite of his aching arms, held the lamp further forward and strained to see what was being done.

Doctor Warren asked for a smaller spoon, and called for Miss Bransby to swab the area around the cavity he was creating. "Are the pledgets standing ready . . . ?"

"Yes, Doctor."

Otherwise, the only sounds in the room were of careful breathing and the soft, wet noise of the spooning. And of the clock, its pendulum swinging like a heartbeat.

Suddenly, Omar Warren spoke again.

"My eyes, Miss Trunk."

Sweat had trickled into them.

Miss Trunk dabbed at his forehead and cheeks with one of the torn sheet bandages.

He turned back and asked for the smallest of the spoons. "I must go further in," he said.

He motioned Davey forward until the lamp shone straight into the cavity.

Down.

He dipped.

More.

And more.

And more.

The kidney pan was almost full of matter.

More.

And then . . .

A jet of blood shot up onto Omar Warren's breast and over his arms.

Miss Bransby instantly stepped forward.

Omar Warren put the spoon aside into Miss Trunk's hand, reached for the pledgets and, using his fingers, began to press them into the bleeding cavity.

He must pack it entirely. Quickly. Quickly. It was his only hope to stop the haemorrhaging.

Don't, he said. *Don't*.

But to no avail.

In that moment, Lizzie died.

16.

Outside in the garden, Lily was seated on the swing. Buster was lying to one side. The swing was hung from an oak tree. Lily had collected acorns here when she was six.

She was staring up through the leafless branches—making her way through the stars. She knew it must be terribly late, but there hadn't been a sound from the house. Mal and Richard were sitting on the side verandah drinking home-made beer and smoking cigarettes. Lily could see their cigarette ends moving through the air like falling stars. The two men spoke in such low tones she was only aware of their voices, not their words. A light wind was rising.

Far away, a dog was barking at some barnyard intruder. A ferret or a raccoon. A fox, perhaps. Lily tried to count the distance—to calculate whose farm it might be and therefore which dog. She had one time known every dog along this road. And every horse. And every cat. But not the people. She had been shy of the people. When Ede stopped to talk to anyone, Lily had moved around behind her, out of sight.

A light appeared on the porch. Someone had come from inside. It was Davey.

Lily looked over at the three men, now revealed in the spill of lamplight. Malahide stood up. Richard leaned forward and stared at his feet.

What is it?

There was a silence all at once.

Malahide turned and stepped down off the porch.

But he didn't come all the way across the lawn. He stopped in the windy shadows instead. Lily heard voices blowing through the branches above her.

Then, at last, Malahide spoke.

"Lily?"

Lily's fingers tightened on the swing rope.

"Lily?"

"What?"

Malahide took one step forward.

"You'd best come in, now," he said.

No.

Half an hour later, Lily went over the dead, dry grass to the house with Buster walking behind her. She opened the door and went inside.

In the yard, the swing went on swaying to and fro—making an endless circle of its path. It was morning before it stopped.

17. In the wicker suitcase there are three mementos of Lizzie. One, you already know: the drawing Lily made of Lizzie dancing. Another is an envelope which contains some cuttings of his hair. It is evident my mother must have gone to his bedroom following his death, and collected a handful of what had been taken that morning in the shearing. This is made clear by the words she had written on the face of the envelope:

> *Beautiful dreamer, wake*
> *unto me.*
> *Lizzie Wyatt*
> *Wednesday, October 30th*
> *1907*

That is all it says, but when I encountered this remembrance first, it was still in the state in which my mother had left it last, the flap of the envelope being tucked, not sealed. And inside, lying with Lizzie's hair, was a cut of her own hair—greying with middle age. Thirty-two years, by then, had passed since his death. And it does not go unnoticed: he died on the date of my birthday.

The third memento of Lizzie is a photograph. At first, I could make no sense of it.

What it shows is a group of workmen, seated and standing in sunlight—gathered together for some anniversary, perhaps. It is one of those formal pictures that were taken in that time, showing the employees of the Wyatt Piano Factory in groupings that were tied to their various skills. *MEN OF THE VARNISH AND RUBBING DECK. MEN OF THE ACTION-FINISHING DEPARTMENT . . . MEN OF THE ORGAN DEPARTMENT . . . THE PLANING MILL,* et cetera.

In this particular photograph, we are shown the *MEN OF THE SHAPING DEPARTMENT*—part of the factory devoted exclusively to grand pianos, whose curvaceous sides and lids required the skills of artisans. There are thirty figures in this picture, not all of whom worked at the Wyatt Piano Factory. Knowing that such photographs were to be taken, the men often brought their children in for the occasion, realizing it would be their only opportunity to show them to the world and record their childhood faces for posterity.

There are three such children in this picture. Three—and two others. Lizzie and Lily.

They are seated in the second row—which is why, at first, I missed them. Benches have been provided, set on the concrete steps leading up to the doors which open into the shaping department. The other three children are seen with their individual fathers—the men in their aprons and overalls, the children in their Sunday best.

Lizzie and Lily are grinning. Clearly, there is mischief afoot. They should not, of course, be there—but there they are. Perhaps it was Lizzie's idea. I tend to think so. There is a hint of triumph in the tilted corners of his lips. He is the only Wyatt not involved in the piano business, yet he would have us think he was involved. Accredited. Acknowledged. After all, he sang. Pianos were his natural allies.

Lily is grinning, too—but hers is a triumph of another kind. She is with her prince. They are side by side. The camera says so. The world will know.

She appears to be ten or eleven—which means that Lizzie is seventeen or eighteen. He was twenty-four when he died. And it is true, as both Ede and Lily told me, he had an unearthly beauty, most of which was got from his vivid presence. No one is more alive than Lizzie seems in this photograph.

I am looking at it now.

Gone, yes. But not.

There they are. Together and alive.

And seated between them, wearing what I can only assume was a red bandanna around his neck, is Buster, the dog. He, too, has the look of triumph.

Smile.

Yes.

Smile forever.

Five

1908—1910

*I was a posthumous
child. My father's
eyes had closed upon
the light of this
world six months, when
mine opened on it.
There is something
strange to me, even
now, in the reflection
that he never saw
me . . .*

David Copperfield
Charles Dickens

1. When laying out the pictures of her life and mine, Lily had the fingers of a card sharp. I have watched her shuffle time away as if it had no place in her personal chronology. The sequence of events which most of us compute in years, Lily compiled according to her moods. She was the mistress of her own seasons. Even her journals had no dates. It was only by identifying the incentive prompting an entry that a reader might guess which year was being described.

Ede, my grandmother, was scrupulous with dates and every photograph or note was marked precisely: *Friday, July 18th, 1908—Munsterfield* or *Charlie's Graduation Day, Brighton, Wednesday, June 17th, 1924*—under which she had written: *Lily's 34th birthday* in brackets. Lily herself did no such thing. She could rarely tell you how old she was, and if someone insisted on having this information—the matron at a clinic, for instance—Mother would have to hide her hands behind her back and count on her fingers.

Now, as I look at the photographs in which—so, my mother told me—my father might appear, I am only certain that the year must be 1909 or 1910. I do know when I was born. The proof is in my certificate of birth, issued in Cambridge, England, on October 30, 1910. My mother's name is given as Lily T. Kilworth, but next to the designation of *Father*, all it says is: *unknown.*

The *T* in mother's name was never explained. Ede had certainly not assigned it to her. I like to think it stood for *Thomas*, though Lily never gave in to being a Wyatt. Nor did she speak much of Tom, The Piano Man. Most of what I know of him, I got from Ede. But Lily's identification of her father was not as vague as her identification of mine. *He was a man, that's all*, she would say. And: *his blood is in you, that I know.*

I have often pondered the twinning of these two absent fathers and I suppose it is inevitable that psychiatry lay the blame for the second squarely at the door of the first. *Like mother—like daughter.* But I disagree with this reading. As Lily's son, I can vouch for the fact that she harboured no resentment of Tom. Though she never said so, she must have felt, as I did, the absence of a father one could reach out and touch, if only in memory.

I know that in my dreams—and waking, too—I long to have some sense of his presence. If he had held me, even once, I could—and I would remember it. If he had laid his hand and spread his fingers on my head, as I have seen so many fathers do with their young, I could hold that, too, in memory. I would know it then for certain. *Who are you?* he might have said. *Where are you going . . . ?* But there was no such moment, so there is no such memory. It was the same for Lily. Tom, The Piano Man died without ever seeing her. He had no notion of her existence.

2. Lily's life, that had been for so long devoid of strangers, was filled with them by the time she left St Mary-Margaret. Her teachers, her sister students, their families and the boys they entertained from time to time had made a crowd around her of candidates for friendship.

After Lizzie's death, Lily still had two more years of education to complete. She excelled in all things creative, but was sorely pressed to keep pace with her classmates whenever mathematics raised its ugly head. She was simply incapable of comprehension once figures entered the picture. Had it not been for an observant teacher by the name of Kenny, who had an imaginative response to her students, Lily would have failed. But Miss Kenny had watched Lily freeze in the presence of numbers and she understood that more was at work in the girl than mere laziness or stupidity.

Having offered Lily private tutoring on the subject, and having persevered in this project for one complete semester, Miss Kenny came to the conclusion that Lily would never master the concept of numbers or the uses of them. Knowing this, she freed her of them. Lily was not any longer required to endure the burden of mathematics—and was given, instead, her personal choice of an extra class in English. It was in this class that she fell in love with poetry—not to say Miss Kenny, on whom she bestowed a kind of loving reverence that sometimes left her speechless in Miss Kenny's presence.

It was around this time that Lily commenced her journals—or rather, her notebooks. This is made clear by the fact that certain names cropped up in her pages—Miss Kenny among them—that were to play an important role in Lily's immediate future. Immediate—and more, in some cases. Phoebe Russell was one of these. Eleanor Ormond was another.

In the notebooks I am compelled to assign to her final year at school, Lily delighted in anecdotal material—some of it demonstrating another side of the teaching staff. This, for instance:

Rose at 6:00. Ran the quad with Eleanor—she in boy's pyjamas (!) me in my slippers—both forbidden. Laughed till we were sick when Pansy—panting and sweating behind us—kept saying over and over: but those are BOY'S PYJAMAS! and those are BEDROOM SLIPPERS! As though we didn't know it. School as per usual. Lovely exam on Greek Mythology ruined by fact I'd forgotten to bring the necessary blotting paper. This drew the following sarcastic remark from Miss Hyslop: is no one buying pianos? Is the firm shaky? Can't your father afford a bit of blotting paper?

*Of course, she thinks she knows all about it. I could kill her. Then
she deducted fifteen points from my mark*—minus 15 for lack of
blotting paper! *When I showed this to Eleanor, she said it meant I
should have had ninety*—but all *I got was seventy-something.*

It was Eleanor Ormond who taught Lily how to ride on the
underside of the milk wagon. This was in aid of making their
escape from St Mary-Margaret—something Eleanor felt duty-
bound to do. Given the school's declared policy of *bringing problem children to heel,* there was every good reason why Eleanor
Ormond should have been sent there. She was determined that
rules were made to be broken and that boys were made to be
explored. The combination of these two attitudes had finally
defeated her parents and off she had been packed to *good old
S.M.M., prison extraordinaire for extraordinary chaps!* Eleanor
referred to anyone she liked as being *a good chap*—or as *chappy.*
Lily was *chap number one.*

Eleanor also taught her *protégé-in-the-art-of-escaping* how to
lasso a chimney with a rope. *You never know when you're going to
have to climb the walls to get back into S.M.M. after midnight,* she
had said. They did this more than once, and the device proved to be
so useful, it became a part of Lily's ultimate repertoire as an escape
artist. In time, she passed the technique on to me—though I've had
little use for it of late. The rope, however, became a standard part of
our equipment—and always had its place in the wicker suitcase.

Because Phoebe Russell, like Eleanor Ormond, played a continuing role in Lily's life after St Mary-Margaret, the following portrait will give some notion both of why she was an *extraordinary
chap* and why she had been sent to *good old S.M.M.*

Phoebe Russell's father was in the British diplomatic corps and
had been sent to the High Commission in Ottawa when Edward
VII had become king. As befitted the late Victorian image of
sobriety and rectitude—Sir Arthur Russell was more than a stick-
in-the-mud; he was a *barge pole!* This from his daughter, Phoebe,
who was delighted at the news she would come of age in the
palmy days of the *Roué-Rex* now occupying the throne.

Once, when asked what she wanted to be when she grew up, Phoebe Russell had answered: *the King's mistress.* She kept a photograph of Alice Keppel on her dresser at school. It was framed, and gave the impression of having familial connections. The truth was, the picture had been scissored from a magazine and mounted on a bit of cardboard. Mrs Keppel was known for her beauty and grace. She was also known for her hats. The given photograph portrayed all three of these attributes—while ignoring the silent fourth, the one that overrode all other aspects of her fame. She was *H.M.'s m—tr—s!*

Driven to a rebellious stance on the subject of this photograph, Phoebe had once blurted out that, not only was Mrs Keppel her *favourite aunt* (they were not related, even remotely) but that she had taught the present king his *lessons.*

She was nearly expelled when it was discovered that she had used "that word" to describe Mrs Keppel's duties. "We are *all* mistresses here on the staff of this school, Miss Russell," the Head had said to her—before she was caned on the bottom. "And I will not have the dignity of such a word maligned by its association with that notorious woman on your bureau."

"Yes, Miss Richter."

There was a pause before the Head Mistress spoke again—and when she did so, she did not quite manage the indifference she had hoped for.

"Is it true," she asked—with a sideways glance at the window, "that Mrs Keppel is your aunt?"

"No, Miss."

"Ah." The Head seemed disappointed and gave a sigh.

"The truth is, Miss Richter, she's my mother," said Phoebe—who gave this sort of performance with some brilliance. She was staring at the floor and just beginning to manage an overflow of tears.

"Your *mother!*" said Miss Richter, almost driven to her feet. "Your *mother???*"

"Yes, Miss. That's why I keep her picture there. Please don't make me take it down."

"Good heavens . . ." The image of Sir Barge Pole Russell

together with Mrs Keppel had clearly risen in Miss Richter's mind.

"May I use my handkerchief, please, Miss?"

"Of course you may. You poor child . . ."

Phoebe dabbed at her eyes and gave a genteel imitation of nose-blowing.

"I suppose I ought to tell you the whole truth," she said.

"You mean there's *more?*" The Head was now on her feet and moving towards a tray of decanters.

"Yes, Miss," said Phoebe. "There's just the one other thing."

Miss Richter turned her back on the child and filled a glass with necessary sherry.

"Well," she said. "What is it?"

The glass was in her hand.

"The King is my father," said Phoebe.

The glass was on the floor.

3. Early in the summer of 1909, Lily set sail for England on board the SS *Franconia*. The only good picture I can make of this is the kind one might see at the movies.

Lily in new clothes and new hats, with new friends and a new life!

Lily on the gangplank!

Lily at the rail!

Lily waving goodbye to a tearful Ede and a smiling Frederick!

Lily blowing kisses to Browning—Browning tweeded, with Lyon in her arms—an eight-year-old boy with a Union Jack on a stick!

Lily looking downward, all the rest—a mass—looking upwards and a thousand handkerchiefs waving!

Every voice shouting—every voice silenced—all but one—the ship's horn blasting: ONE—TWO—THREE!

The crowded shore begins to fade into a multitude of static photographs pasted into diaries. Only the great ship moves on the swell of the sea, black and white and red and outward bound . . .
Everyone's breath is held.
The cheering stops.
Goodbye.

Lily wrote: *it was the land's departure—not the ship's.*

4. She was on her way to Cambridge University, where she would study English Literature in a course especially designed for Empire Students. This had been Eliza's graduation gift when Lily matriculated from St Mary-Margaret. She knew that Ede could not ask Frederick for the necessary funds, his having already sent Lily to boarding school, with all its multiple expenses—and all her medicines and doctors' fees. When Lily spoke of her desire to take the Cambridge course, Ede at first said *no*. Besides the financial burden, there were other considerations: separation at such a great distance—the question of a guardian— a world made up entirely of strangers.

Eliza was not the only saviour. Other factors played into Lily's hand—and I like to think, mine. If Lily had not gone to England, I would not exist.

The first glimmer of hope was raised by the fact that Eleanor Ormond had been accepted as an Empire Student and, while her personal character was *somewhat wild*, her parents' credentials were impeccable. Even Miss Richter approved of them.

Next, there was the offer of Eliza's funding—and finally, Frederick's decision to send his brother Franklin to London, where he would act as British and European agent for the Wyatt Piano Company.

It was then that Ede gave up her opposition and said that Lily could go.

All that remained was gaining acceptance as an Empire Student—and this, with Miss Kenny's assistance and a good many hours of extra study, Lily managed to achieve. It was even conceded that she had *a certain brilliance* where literature was concerned.

That my mother was *an intellectual* had long been evident— but *brilliant?* Ede was at a loss. She kept the letter to herself and its description of Lily's talent was not transmitted. I heard of it only after my mother's first incarceration at the Lunatic Asylum on Queen Street in Toronto.

She indulged in too many dreams, Ede said. *Her brilliance was a curse.* She claimed to have known this all along—but I doubt it. I think Ede's fears for Lily blinded her to some of Lily's wonders.

5 • In choosing Franklin to represent Wyatt interests in London and on the Continent, Frederick was at last conceding the value of his brother's flamboyance. Franklin's passion for theatre and music had produced a largeness of gesture and a manner of personal presentation that was not appreciated in Toronto, where people *simply do not behave like that.* Capes and trilbys, silver-headed walking sticks and hair that curled below the collar might well be the accepted badges of visiting artists with international reputations, but in residence—*in situ—here!*— they were intolerable signs of decadence.

But Franklin paid no attention to his critics. They could do him no real harm—and they even came to his parties, so long as he could promise them Paderewski, Julia Southern or the cast of *The Mikado.* Which he often did.

It was said of Franklin: *he wore his hair long and kept his grudges short.* There was no resentment in him. Life was a gift of wonders to be shared. He was the only Wyatt who freely opened his doors to me and Lily, giving us—over time—both shelter and a joyous welcome.

He worshipped literature, theatre and song—and his gifts were his sense of adventure and invention. *Try this!* he would say. *See what happens when you dare?* Always smiling. Always *jolly*—a word that might have been coined in his behalf.

In 1905 he met and was immediately captivated by Caroline Doge of Paris, Ontario. He was forty-two years old and might never have married if Caroline had not been there in all her wondrous beauty. He had thought, until then, that women were a feast—and the banquet would never end.

Caroline—later called Carrie—was a true southern belle. Her father, Godfrey Doge, had left South Carolina in the eighties, moving his family—and his iron foundry—north in the wake of Reconstruction. Doge had been an abolitionist before the Civil War, and was thought of as a traitor. When the Yankees had arrived, he was seen as their ally. But in time, their contracts dried up and *no true Southerner* would do business with him. This way, he came to Canada.

It was during the search for a foundry outside of Toronto that Franklin had come upon Doge's enterprise in Paris. He was looking for someone who would take on an innovative new design for cast-iron piano frames—and Doge invited him to dinner. There she was—Caroline—one of three daughters—waiting for him as if on order. Franklin had never seen a woman in all his life whose beauty was her equal. Like Eva Willard, she and her sisters always dressed in white—but there the similarity ended. Caroline seemed to be bathed in a quality of light that was all her own. She was irresistible—a magnet of desirability—honeyed with latent passion, trembling with possibilities.

Caroline, for her part, took one look at Franklin Wyatt in his flowing overcoat and the mane of lion's hair beneath his trilby—and fell instantly, emphatically and irrevocably in love.

So it was that on Tuesday, June 22nd, 1909, *Miss Lily Kilworth, Miss Eleanor Ormond and their schoolfriend, the Honourable Phoebe Russell, were embarked from New York City on board the S.S.* Franconia *under the guardianship of Mister and Mrs Franklin P. Wyatt of Toronto, Ontario, Canada. Destination: Southampton.*

In less than a year—there can be no question—one of this party introduced my mother to my father. My problem remains. Since each provides a likely candidate, I cannot tell which one it was.

6. On the ship, they made joyous companions. Dormitory life had been the one aspect of boarding school that offered any prospect of entertainment, and it was this same element of ship life that provided the most pleasure. Sharing a stateroom, the three girls were able to indulge themselves in what Eleanor dubbed *hedonistic déjà vu*—without the prospect of being caught by the likes of Miss Hyslop or Miss Bonnycastle, known as the *Dragon Sisters of S.M.M.*

Miss Hyslop had been given to scathing remarks of a personal nature that could be wounding in the extreme. A lashing from her tongue was looked on as equal to a lashing from Miss Bonnycastle's strap. Caning—the ultimate disgrace—had been left to Miss Richter.

Now, being free of these restraints, Eleanor, Phoebe and Lily gave way to every impulse that had previously been constrained, if not completely thwarted. They sat up all night, talking. They smoked cigarettes. They told rude jokes and performed crude imitations of what it was like to be a boy. Eleanor gave portrayals of seven different men standing at a urinal that had both Phoebe and Lily literally screaming with laughter.

They wore each other's clothes; they went into luncheon wearing no underwear *(very daring)* and to dinner without corselets *(outrageous)*. They made each other up as *courtesans* and practised *seducing older men*—some as old as thirty-five. Eleanor even went so far as to flirt with a well-known concert violinist who happened to be on board.

Of course, their notion of *courtesans* was got entirely from books, with a side glance at Mrs Keppel. Never having knowingly seen a woman of the world in the flesh, their performances were far too grand on the one hand, and gauche on the other. Besides which, they were shy at heart and would have preferred to flirt as themselves with some of the boy passengers—who were so busy pretending to be twenty-one.

The worst that happened was that Eleanor was pursued, one evening, by a somewhat inebriated schoolmaster, who was no doubt taking the same unfettered holiday as the schoolgirl he had followed to her stateroom.

"Phew!" said Eleanor, locking the door. "This one really wants me to do it!"

When the schoolmaster's knocking persisted, Phoebe climbed onto a chair and poured a pitcher of water over him through the transom. "Be off with you!" she said, in a perfect imitation of Miss Richter. "Be off with you! Begone! Scat!"

It was not all games. They could be equally sedate and *proper.* Each had new gowns for evening wear, and the deportment of *ladies* had become second nature, given the emphasis placed on the social graces at St Mary-Margaret. In Franklin and Caroline's company, they were perfect young women who might have been on their way to Buckingham Palace. It was, of course, every parent's ambition to have their daughters presented at Court and, in time, this would happen to Phoebe and to Eleanor. Not to Lily. She had no desire to wear white. And if, as she understood, one was also required to wear ostrich plumes, she would rather spare the ostrich than sport his feathers.

On the second-to-last night at sea, there was to be a masquerade. Franklin and Caroline had come prepared, and he played Faust to her Marguerite—he in doublet, tights and cape; she in a deathly pallor and yards of angel-white chiffon. Lily's only fear was that they might be going to sing. They did not. But they did win second prize for their costumes. Caroline's train was six feet long, and the sight of her waltzing in Franklin's arms, with the train looped over her arm, was the most romantic thing that Lily had ever seen.

Japanese kimonos were currently all the rage as *modern attire for the boudoir*, and Lily, Eleanor and Phoebe had each been treated to one at Worth's on Fifth Avenue, in New York. They were gifts from Eleanor's father (*a negligée,* she told Lily, *instead of the usual negligence . . .*). Consequently, they decided to take advantage of these gifts and went to the masquerade as *Yum-Yum, Peep-bo* and *Pitti-Sing.*

> *Three little maids from school are we,*
> *Pert as a schoolgirl well can be,*
> *Filled to the brim with girlish glee,*
> *Three little maids from school!*

In their stateroom, they stood before the full-length mirror and sang the song at the tops of their voices.

> Eleanor: *Everything is a source of fun!*
> Phoebe: *Nobody's safe, for we care for none!*
> Lily: *Life is a joke that's just begun!*
> All: *Three little maids from school!*

They won first prize. Collectively.

Later that night, Lily disappeared.

7. "When did you last see her?" This was Franklin.
   "We were dancing," said Phoebe.
"Who was she with?"
"I don't know. He was wearing a mask."
They all were.
"Oh, dear," said Caroline—drawling her way to panic. "What was his costume about?"
"His body . . ." Eleanor muttered.
Luckily, neither Caroline nor Franklin heard her.
Phoebe said: "he was some kind of soldier."
"What kind?"

"Oh, heavens—I don't know."

"What colour was he?"

"White . . ." (Eleanor. Another mutter.)

"Red, I suppose—with lots of gold and silver."

"A British soldier?"

"Lord help me—I don't know."

They were standing on the esplanade, overlooking the ball-room. A third or more of the dancers had departed, either for bed or for the bars. It was a beautiful night—calm and moonlit. Eleanor had been eyeing a *Buccaneer*, who appeared to be eyeing her. She was dying to step away.

"Perhaps we should split up and look for her separately," she suggested.

"Yes," said Franklin. "Excellent."

"Oh, I do hope she has not succumbed to one of her . . ."

"Convulsions," said Eleanor. Aloud.

". . . *maux de tête*," Caroline finished. Never having been present during one of Lily's seizures, she still thought of her niece as suffering violent headaches.

When they parted, Eleanor lifted her mask and batted her roughly drawn Japanese eyes. It was she—and the Buccaneer—who found Lily.

"Who did you say she is?" he asked.

"My friend," said Eleanor.

"I thought she was your sister."

"No. She's my friend."

They were standing on some iron steps above the boiler room. They were not, of course, supposed to be there, but a junior Petty Officer had taken pity on them and shown them the way. Eleanor had seduced him with the suggestion that her friend had a *dangerous relationship with fire that might bring harm to the ship*. She did not elaborate.

Lily was seated on an open-work landing, with her hair undone. The expression on her face was one that Eleanor recognized at once. Lily was *lost*.

"Let me do this," she said to the Petty Officer. "She may not know where she is, but she will know who I am . . ."

"Yes, Miss."

The Buccaneer sat down on the steps to wait. He was *big and blond and sweet*, as Eleanor later described him, *somewhere between an ox and early man . . .*

She went past Lily and sat on the steps looking up at her. The workings of the great ship roared around her, but Lily seemed to be oblivious to everything except some inner music, to which she swayed.

"Lil?"

There was no response.

Eleanor took her hand. It was shockingly cold.

"Dear chappy, listen to me," she said—not quite shouting. "We're lost here, and I've just found someone who can lead us back outside. Is that all right?"

Silence. And swaying.

Eleanor was alarmed. She had seen Lily in this state before, though not so severely. Being *lost* could happen two ways. Either it followed a scizure, preceding sleep—or it took the place of the seizure—usurping it, but leaving Lily temporarily helpless.

"Tell me your name," said Eleanor.

"Can't."

Good. At least she was speaking.

"Come along. Be a good chap. I'm going to stand up now, and I want you to do the same. Can you hear me?"

"Yes."

Eleanor rose. The steps were narrow. Dangerous. Still holding Lily's hand, she went and stood beside her.

"Now?"

Lily said nothing, but got to her feet. Her kimono was partially undone. Eleanor closed it and retied the sash. Lily's mask was looped around her wrist, and she wasn't wearing her shoes. Dancing slippers. Silver—with glass buttons.

"You follow me. All right?"

Lily stared. Her eyes were emptied—doubly odd in their

Japanese make-up—as if another person entirely had come to live in her body.

The Buccaneer rose as they approached him, and stood aside.

"Good-night," said Eleanor.

"Yeah—good-night," he said. "I hope she's okay."

"She'll be fine," said Eleanor, still climbing sideways, holding Lily's hand. "Thank you."

It was the Petty Officer who found Lily's shoes. They had been hidden by the metal door when they opened it. He carried them all the way back to the stateroom, while Lily trailed obediently in Eleanor's footsteps, moving as though she were both a child—and blind.

"Good-night, Miss,"

Eleanor accepted the shoes and opened the door.

"Yes. Good-night. And thank you."

Once inside, she sat Lily down on the nearest bed.

"Poor old chappy," she said. "You went off and left me again."

Lily slept all night long under a blanket, wearing her kimono. She did not wake up until 9:00 A.M.

"You here again?" Eleanor said, looking down at her.

"Yes," said Lily. "I'm here."

Eleanor smiled. "Good chap," she said. "Do try not to leave me like that. I miss you."

The next day they entered The Solent and, standing at the rail, they watched as the Needles passed and the giant port of Southampton approached beneath its clouds of gulls and smoke. *England was moving*, Lily would write. *She was coming out to meet us.*

And—somewhere inland—my father waited.

8. Lily would lay the photographs out on tabletops— sometimes by lamplight, other times by daylight. While I watched, she spread the pictures like a game of solitaire.

"These," she would say, "are the fields between Granchester and Cambridge, in England—where you were born. There is a river there—and cows . . ."

She need not have told me about the river and the cows. I could see them in the photographs. But who might the people be on the river-bank? Lily, of course, I could always name. Sometimes—it was curious—she would seem not to recognize herself. I would see her finger pause above her own face before it went down. *Me*, she would say on these occasions. *Me*—but tentatively—almost with a question mark.

The others beside her were young as she was young—with smiles and laughter, gestures that gave the appearance of being amusing, though you cannot tell why. The laughter and the smiles were only in the moment when the shutter clicked.

A hand of solitaire. At the top of each row there would be the *dominant card*—THE FIELDS BETWEEN CAMBRIDGE AND GRANCHESTER. SS FRANCONIA. MUNSTERFIELD. Under these master images—Lily would set out the matching photographs like hearts and clubs, spades and diamonds. The faces in the dominant photo would then be shown in other locales and other lights. Young men and young women—never in equal numbers—Empire Students—laughing, singing or pretending to be serious.

When she laid out the SS *AQUITANIA*, she would say: *this is the ship that brought us home. He won't be there, but you are.* And there I was—aged four—in Lily's arms, or seated between her knees as she sat in a deck-chair, shading her eyes with one hand, holding onto my sleeve with the other. I have no memory of the ship itself, though I have a sense of the sea from that time— the great, wide rolling of it and the colour of it. Green, with spumes of white.

There were also pictures of *RICHMOND PARK* in London, *where the grass is greener than any other green in the whole wide world!* And there stands Lily in white. She so rarely wore white, it was odd to see her as the very image of a young Edwardian— big-hatted, wearing a tight-waisted dress and carrying a parasol.

"Why were you wearing white?" I asked. "You never wear it any more and I thought you hated it."

"I did, once," she said. "And I do now. But I wore it then because of Caroline. She always looked so splendid, decked out in all her white clothes. Don't you remember?"

"What were we doing in Richmond?" I asked her.

"That's where we lived when we weren't in Cambridge. We lived there with Uncle Frank and Aunt Carrie. You remember that, Charlie. Heavens!"

"Yes. But I didn't know it was called Richmond. I only knew it was a big house."

"Such a lovely house, too . . ."

Which it had been. A Georgian home with tall fine windows and bright rooms. Caroline doted on flowers and the house was filled with them. Uncle Frank had made sure they found a place with gardens—and that's what I remember most—the pleasure of sunlit gardens and a nanny who read me *The Tale of Peter Rabbit*.

"Was I born yet, in that picture?"

Lily traced her own elongated figure in its layers of white cotton. "No," she said. "This was when we first arrived, and we used to go out walking in Richmond Park. Very elegant, it was . . ."

"Do you think Frank and Carrie knew who my father was?"

"It's possible. They might, in fact, have introduced me to him . . ." She played another card, laying down a photograph in which she stood in a garden with a wall around it. My garden. The one I remembered. On the wall, there were vines with blooming flowers, probably wisteria. This photograph had been taken in springtime or early summer. Lily wore a dark, slim skirt and a jumper—possibly black, more likely blue—worn over a blouse of some pale shade. Her hands were plunged into the pockets of the jumper and the jumper itself hung down to her hips.

Franklin is standing in the background, smiling broadly. His hands, too, are in his pockets. Caroline apparently took the picture. Lily, it seems, is refusing to smile, though there is something playful about her expression—a deliberate, cheek-biting scowl.

Beside her, though advanced towards the camera one or two steps, there is a grinning young man in his shirtsleeves.

Father number one.

"He would not have been in his shirtsleeves unless he was a friend of the family," Lily told me. "Caroline was very strict about that sort of thing. A stranger never removed his jacket in the presence of a lady."

"What was his name?"

"I don't know."

I knew she was going to say this. It was what she always said. I was used to it—but I always had to pretend that I didn't care.

"Do you remember anything at all about him?" I asked.

"He smelled nice."

Lily smiled. She was being deliberately provocative. She was also playing for time while she tried to reassemble the smiling young man in his entirety. She even picked up the picture and held it to her nose, possibly imagining she might be able to catch a trace of him there. I never knew whether she was joking when she did this. It seemed too earnest for a joke.

"Why was he smiling? Uncle Frank was smiling, too," I said. "But you look as if you're trying not to smile."

"I can't remember. I wish I could," she said. "It's such a lovely smile . . ." She ran her finger over his lips.

His expression had some mischief in it—a broader sense of playfulness than was evident in Lily's scowl.

"Of course," Lily said, "if Caroline took the photograph, the young man might have been flirting with her. Not in any serious sense, you know, but the way young men pay homage to older women whose beauty has not yet faded . . ."

"Can you hear his voice?" I asked. "In your mind?"

She concentrated.

Then she said: "well—he was English. That's for sure. He was always saying *goodness me!* and *crikey!* I don't think Canadians say that. Or Americans . . ."

Now we had a nationality. English.

"Was he a student with you at Cambridge?"

"Absolutely not. For one thing, he's not in any of these other pictures." She reached out and drew the river-bank sequence towards her, leafing through them, picking them up for a closer look. "I think he might have been an actor. Or a writer, perhaps. But he was not a student."

"Uncle Frank was potty about the theatre," I said. "Could the young man have been a singer . . . ?"

Lily, who had been sitting down, suddenly stood up.

"Don't speak," she said.

I sat back in my chair.

Lily lighted a cigarette. She said these helped her to concentrate. *Mes petits feux*, she called them. *My little fires* . . . She would watch the smoke curl up through the air as though it might be a written language. As though it might be going to tell her something.

I was six or seven when we started having these conversations in earnest. It would have been 1916 or 1917 and mother was in her *affected* period. She had developed a taste for long, cotton coat-dresses with multiple buttons all down the front. The shapelessness of these garments accentuated her height and thinness. She would wear the collars open and turned up, exposing her neck. Very often, she bound her hair in dark chiffon scarves, whose tails hung down her back like Chinese queues.

She had also decided in this period that anything worth naming should be named in French. Thus, her *petits feux* had their complement in *feux moyens*—the fires lit in grates—and *grands feux*—the fires lit in stoves and furnaces. What she would have called a burning house in French was presumably left in limbo until she saw one. Or created one.

On the occasion when Lily was trying to recall the name of the man in the garden, she got halfway through her cigarette before she spoke again. The she looked at me and said: "you've never seen Eva Willard, have you?"

"No. Who's she?"

"A singer. *Little Eva Willard* . . ." Here Lily smiled and struck a pose. "*Little Eva Willard and her Night of Song!* Ha!" Then she struck another, more exaggerated pose. "She's a vaudeville artiste—pretending to be a concert star. Always wears white. Yards of it. Bleached white—and dyed yellow hair."

"What's she got to do with my father?" I asked.

"Nothing," she said. Too fast. And then: "everything."

She looked at the photograph again.

Nothing—and everything.

"Singing," she said at last. "Singing. And stages . . . But I don't know. I'm not certain. It's just . . . Little Eva came into my mind and there must be some connection . . ." She was squinting now through the smoke, to wherever it was this memory took place. At first, the words were just words, but slowly she began to sing them, as I sat delighted.

> *Beautiful soup, so rich and green,*
> *Waiting in a hot tureen!*
> *Who for such dainties would not stoop?*
> *Soup of the evening, beautiful soup!*
> *Soup of the evening, beautiful soup!*
> *Soo-oop of the e-e-evening,*
> *Beautiful, beautiful soup!*

Silly as it was—mad as it was—there was something in Lily's rendition of this nonsense that moved me. Perhaps if I had been older I would have laughed—as we are meant to laugh—at the Mock Turtle's song from *Alice in Wonderland*. But I was only six or seven and I was alone with Lily's rendition of it. She sang it as a lullaby—a touchstone for my father's possible identity.

Now, if I was patient, the answer might come.

Lily said: "he was an actor, I think. Maybe he was going to play the Mock Turtle—or sing the song at a theatre party. I don't remember. I haven't the slightest idea. But his name was . . ."

Her eyes closed.

". . . oh, damn."

Then more silence.

And then she said: "he was sweet. He was . . ." She opened her eyes and looked at his picture. "He smelled nice." She laughed.

"He smelled of mint. I don't know why. I can't imagine why anyone would smell of mint—but he did."

"Perhaps he ate mint candies."

"No. Not that. I mean—his body smelled of mint. His hands.
His arms. The back of his neck. His hair smelled of mint. That
was him."

She sniffed at the photograph again—and tapped it with her
finger. If she could only make him talk . . .

"Did you ever ask Uncle Frank what his name was?"

"Frank wouldn't know a thing like that. He never knows anyone's name . . . Unless, of course, they're a star."

"What about Aunt Carrie—wouldn't she know?"

"Why would she know? She's not even in the picture."

"Shouldn't we ask?" I said.

"No," said Lily. "We never talk about your father, or who
your father might have been. She believes such conversations are
indiscreet."

"What's that? *Indiscreet.*"

"Private," said Lily. "Not to be discussed. She doesn't want to
know who your father was."

"Why?"

"It would embarrass her."

Oh.

9. On another occasion, when we were at Munsterfield, I
took the garden photograph and went and stood on a
chair in front of the mirror above the sink in the bathroom.

"*Beautiful soup,*" I sang, "*so rich and green, waiting in a hot
tureen . . .*"

I looked at the smiling, laughing young man—and at myself.
Was that his smile on my face? It could have been.

What colour were his eyes?

His hair was funny.

So was mine.

I reached up and touched it. Right at the crown, there was a bit that would not lie down. And there it was in the photograph—it would not lie down on his head, either.

The next thing I did was smell my wrists.

Mint?

No. Not a trace. Just the faintest whiff of plain yellow soap with the overlay of a dusty afternoon spent in the hayloft.

An actor—or a singer. The impulse to perform had never been in me. Still, it could be lying dormant, waiting only for my father's return to announce itself.

"*Soup of the evening,*" he would whisper, slipping around the door in his dancing shoes, smiling his charming smile. "*Beautiful soup! Soup of the evening, beautiful soup . . . !*"

Then—with a flourish of canes and hats—we would finish the song together:

> *Soo-oop of the e-e-evening,*
> *Beautiful, beautiful soup!*

I produced these final words as a caterwaul, just as great-grandmother Eliza—not my father—stepped round the door. Not in her dancing shoes, either. She was angry. Noise was her enemy.

"What *are* you doing, Charlie?" she asked.

"Singing," I told her.

"Well, stop it," she said. "You'll wake the dead!"

Little did she know that had been my intention.

When she had gone, I climbed down off the chair and went back into the room that once had been great-uncle Liam's. This was where I slept now, whenever we were at the farm and it still bore the imprint of his old precision. In the armoire where once his clothes had hung, each of the wooden hangers had a neat round paper disk slipped over its hook. And on each of these disks, written in Liam's Italianate hand, the hanger's burden was described. *Black Melton Suit, Grey Tweed Jacket, White Linen Suit, Morning Coat . . .*

Now, these hangers only had to bear the burden of a small boy's clothes: a dark blue suit with short trousers—a winter overcoat—a pair of grey flannel shorts—a wool jacket. They didn't tell you much about who I was—the way Liam's every crease and cuff proclaimed his singular person. *Lawyer—scholar—gentleman.* Or so he would have the world believe. He was betrayed, of course, in time by the person he really was. Perhaps Uncle Liam had been just as surprised as everyone else when that person declared himself. Perhaps he had not even known that person was there.

That person.

I had *a person* hiding in me, too. My father. And I knew I would be just as surprised as Uncle Liam must have been when his demon came to claim him, if my father suddenly announced himself and said: *I am here!* No matter who he was, he would still be a stranger coming for me out of the dark. Even my mother would not know him.

I sat on the bed with the photograph of Lily, Frank and the unnamed man in my hand.

Are you my father—with your square-toed shoes and your socks just visible where you lift your trouser legs—because you're about to dance? And your neat round collar and your thin dark tie and your gleaming shirt, like a leading-man's costume, shining in the sunlight. Smiling. Laughing. Unnamed. With a shock of hair standing up on your crown. And nothing more than this to tell me who you were . . . ?

> *Beautiful soup, so rich and green,*
> *Waiting in a hot tureen!*

I lay back flat on the coverlet and held the photograph so my "father" could look down at me.

Perhaps, even now, he was somewhere singing his song. Though I doubted it.

1916 or 1917. I don't remember—but it was during the war that had carried off all those young men. The chance of this smiling dandy still being alive was very slim. *There he was—dressed up in his youth—just waiting for the bugle to call.*

That was how Lily put it. Though, I must admit that was not precisely what she said. What she really said was: *there they were—all dressed up in their god-damn youth—waiting for the god-damn bugle call!*

She was looking at her fellow students when she said this. Not at the smiling young man.

"Youth is their uniform, Charlie. Soon as they catch you wearing it, off you go to be shot. Don't grow up, my darling. Be a child forever."

10. Looking at the Cambridge photographs, she said: "I suppose at that age, you fall in love with practically everyone you meet. I did. I was barely nineteen years old—and there I was without a chaperone, meeting young men by the dozen. That was considered very daring—and very wrong! Going off anywhere without the usual older woman or couple to enforce the proprieties. But we did it all the time at Cambridge. Sometimes, we even swam in the nude."

When she told me this, I thought *the Nude* was the name of the river. *Naked,* I knew, but not *nude*.

Though Lily often went back to Cambridge in other seasons—including the season of my birth—she was only ever there to study in the summertime. She studied English Literature—or, as she would say to me: liter-a-*ture*, as if it was one of her French words. She came away from the lectures deeply in love with Elizabeth Barrett Browning. Her copy of Mrs Browning's poems was in the wicker suitcase, scribbled with rapturous notes in Lily's peculiar hand, with its boxed, squared letters—as though she had copied them from a child's set of blocks.

In the winter, she had lived in London, at Richmond with Franklin and Caroline. This was a time when it seemed that distance from home was curing her brain of its short circuits and her spirit of its troubling visions and images. Her demons, so it appeared, had finally been routed.

We know now this wasn't so. But she was not aware of it then—and in that brief, blinding time of sunny days by the *River Nude,* Lily came to believe that happiness had not been denied her after all.

This, from her notebooks:

There were rowboats and punts and canoes and everyone had picnic baskets. Stone bottles of ginger beer and something called stout, *cucumbers, hard-boiled eggs, potted shrimp, jellied tongue in glass jars, cut loaves of buttered bread done up in butcher's brown paper, sweet tomatoes warmed in the sun—watercress gathered from the river's edge and thimbleberries dipped in cream . . .*

. . . someone had brought a Victrola and we wound it up in the grass. Everyone sang By the Light of the Silvery Moon *and* I Wonder Who's Kissing Her Now. *There must have been twenty of us there in some farmer's field by the river and the cows came and listened to us singing . . .*

El is in love again! Must be the twelfth time this month. She came and got me by the hand and whispered in my ear: There is a willow grows aslant a brook, that shows his hoar leaves in the glassy stream . . . There, with fantastic charms, do naked swimmers come, both youths and maids. Come on! *She dragged me from my partner, whom I rather liked, and ran with me through the meadow off to the river's edge where a clump of willows grew on a rise above the water. Down below, I could see white bodies flashing in the sunlight and clothing strewn on the ground and hanging from the trees . . .*

. . . I thought: I daren't—*but El was already moving down towards them, half sliding, half falling—breathless and eager. I followed her, ashamed and afraid of turning back—equally afraid of joining her. El was undoing her waist and kicking off her shoes.* Come along, *she said.* Hurry, there's a good chap.

It wasn't as if we didn't know each other—all of us, one way or another. It wasn't as if we weren't emancipated . . .

Once we were nude, we went hand in hand to the water's edge. Standing in the reeds was another of El's blond giants. Her current beau. He looked at us candidly and I was proud of what he saw—proud of me and proud of El . . .

Ladies, he said.

We nodded.

Then we stepped down into the Cam and waded through the shallows to the current's edge . . .

What if I hadn't gone with her? I would have missed the wonder of the moving stream, with my hair flowing wide and the water like a satin glove around me . . .

Why are we so afraid of one another in our skins? We are only men and women—we are only human beings—creatures, only—nothing more. And beautiful . . .

In the meadow, dressed again and drying our hair, I watched some dragonflies dancing in the air, beating their wings in time to the record on the Victrola. Someone was singing It's a Long Way to Tipperary, *and we all began to sing it and El and I got up and danced. We danced with each other—we danced with El's blond giant. We danced with the dragonflies. Somebody said:* are you happy, Lil? *And I said:* yes! *I shouted it.*

11. I have already mentioned Lily's capacity for strangers—the habit she had of putting our lives in the hands of what she called *desperados*. She took this word, I think, from a book she had read, or the dialogue cards in movies.

Of course, her definition of a desperado was different than the given. To Lily, a desperado was not a man with a gun who went around robbing banks—but a man or a woman who was lost—someone who would only find themselves in you. *Surely it is right and proper, Charlie,* she said, *that a person should help another person find his way home. It doesn't matter if you don't know who they are; it only matters that you get them there.*

"That's our job, Charlie," she said. "To get other people to the one safe place."

It was not until after Lily's death that I came anywhere near beginning to understand this. Her own *safe place*, which had seemed to be fire, was in fact other people. Other beings.

This way, we come to my second "father."

I find myself endlessly searching the figures of the young men in Lily's pictures. I have looked at them through magnifying glasses in every kind of light my eyes will bear. I would tear out their faces and set them under a microscope if I thought it would reveal some element that would confirm my parentage. But they are only *clowns* in most of the photographs, striking heroic poses, playing at being Horatio at the Bridge or Cortez on a peak in Darien. Their charming foolishness makes them seem too young for fatherhood, though clearly they were not. It was for them—for these young men that Lily mourned when she spoke of *boys dressed up in their god-damn youth and waiting for the god-damn bugle call.*

Dead? Yes. More than likely every one of them gone before he reached his mid-twenties. In Lily's photographs, they would have been eighteen and nineteen years old. There are even one or two who look as if they have not yet begun to shave.

One afternoon, we laid all the Cambridge photographs side by side in the light from a sunny window. It was wintertime. I was nine, perhaps. I might have been ten.

"There," said Lily.

There.

There was no mistaking the tone. Something had been triggered—a key had been turned—her finger had selected one of the young men.

"Red," she said.

"Red?"

"Red."

"Was it his nickname?"

"No."

Had I misunderstood her?

"Fred?" I said.

"No, no. Not Fred. Red."

I looked at Lily. Perhaps his hair had been red. My hair was red. But so was Lily's. Not carrot-red, but auburn. Wyatt-red, as one of the uncles called it.

"Did he have red hair?" I asked.

"Who?"

"The man in the picture."

"No . . ."

But maybe.

That was the reading she had given: *no—but maybe.*

He was standing with two others. This was in Cambridge itself. I don't know all the colleges by name, but clearly this was one of them. Its iron gates were the backdrop against which the three young men were seen. Two of them were wearing gowns—but the designated figure wore a blazer, a boater and white ducks. There was a cigarette in his mouth. His legs were splayed and his hands were in his pockets. He wore such a wayward expression, I thought he was a natural desperado. He also seemed to be slightly older than the others. Two or three years, no more.

I wanted this man to be my father. I looked for him in the other pictures. I wouldn't necessarily choose him now, perhaps, but I chose him then, when I was nine or ten, because he stood the way I wanted to stand. Tough—but easy. The expression on his face seemed to say: *the point of life is fun*—fun and winning and having your way. And nothing else.

I almost missed him in the rest of the Cambridge pictures because he is there in only one other—the one in which Phoebe Russell also appears. He is standing slightly behind her—just enough to obscure one half of his face. Anyone else would miss him entirely because Phoebe Russell is the centre of attention, mocking him by standing with her feet wide apart, her hands in her pockets and a cigarette dangling from her lips.

All the others—including Lily—in this second photograph are roaring with laughter at Phoebe's performance—and laughter closes the eyes. The only eyes—but Phoebe's—that are open belong to the wayward young man, whose one-eyed stare at the camera has lost all its mirth and is devoid of its former recklessness.

I wish I had not found him in this picture. I wish I had seen him only in the other. I had wanted the other to be my father, but I could not accept this hard-eyed version. He was lost in there—lost and somehow broken, and thus a candidate for Lily's brotherhood of desperados. It did not occur to me until later in my life that the pictures of this young man need not have been taken in the same year. Lily, after all, was at Cambridge two summers running, 1909 and 1910.

I asked her if she knew which photograph had been taken first. There was still a chance that his story had been reversed in my original reading of it: the dead man first, and then revival.

But, no—she could not tell. Nonetheless, his was the only image that had provoked agitation. Along with a name.

For it was a name: *Red.*

I came upon it quite by accident in a copy of the *Illustrated London News* that Caroline Wyatt had salted away in her collection of English memorabilia. Yet again, he was shown in a photograph—and, yet again, in a moment of triumph. He had been a long-distance runner, and was seen, in the magazine, breaking the wire at the Stockholm Olympic Games of 1912, at which he set a world record.

He got his name—which mother had misunderstood—from the fact that he wore a red bandanna tied around his head as a sweatband when he ran. There it was in the photograph.

The caption under this picture in the *Illustrated London News* was typically brief and respectful. All it said was: *Famous Athlete Murder Victim.* And beneath that, squared in a box: *The Honourable Charles "Red" Russell has been found dead at his parents' Cheltenham home. Sir Arthur and Lady Russell have issued a joint statement forgoing comment. An investigation is underway.*

And that was all.

The Honourable Charles "Red" Russell had been Phoebe's brother. Mother never knew of his death. Not, at any rate, of its manner. He had been stabbed repeatedly in the groin. I made a brief archival investigation. Phoebe had done it. He bled to death.

That is all I know of father number two.

12. *Father number three.*

1910. The summer Lily was twenty. She is shown with others sitting on blankets that have been spread beneath some trees *by the side of an English road . . . A tablecloth has also been spread. A picnic is in progress . . .*

This is one of the images with which I began my mother's story.

. . . Someone has hung his jacket from the headlamp of a motor car. A low stone wall cuts through the frame beyond the picnickers . . .

Here are Lily and Eleanor Ormond enjoying an outing, kindness of Eleanor's visiting parents. They had come to England in order to act as chaperones on Eleanor's first continental tour. All looks well, but much is not. Nothing is what it seems. Eleanor, like my mother, thought of herself as emancipated. Her sojourn in England had been the result of *absolute freedom*. But, like my mother, she had discovered there were relatives and family friends at almost every turning. Watching. Someone's protective eye was always on them. Franklin's. Caroline's. Others'. In Eleanor's case, the eye was also profoundly inquisitive. A meddling eye—recording. And reporting.

At the age of twenty-one, Eleanor Ormond was to become the seventh richest heiress in North America. Always wealthy, she had not however been destined for these millions until nine months before her parents' arrival in England. An uncle had died, and in his dying moments, his designating finger had fallen on Eleanor's name. Not her father's name—not her mother's—not her brother's—but Eleanor's alone.

There had been a brief threat from a distant cousin, who wanted to contest the will. Money was offered and—as expected—was accepted. The lawyers proceeded to put the inheritance in trust, and Eleanor's parents—Mister and Mrs Douglas Ormond III— were named as trustees.

Around this time, Eleanor had begun to note the presence of a thin, squinny-eyed man with steel-rimmed glasses who seemed to turn up everywhere she went. He was, of course, a private security agent hired by Eleanor's parents to protect her. His name was Angus Rutherford and he was six and a half feet tall.

Lily was then in residence at Richmond with Franklin and Caroline. During the onset of winter in 1909, she had suffered five seizures in a single week, and there was some concern that her illness had returned with force. A doctor was consulted. All the responsible things were done. Bromides offered. Chloroform provided. Clinics visited. Lily was not much able to take advantage of the freedom she had won.

The climate was also at war with her spirit, pulling in storms from the North Sea one week and the Irish Sea the next. The sun did not shine for one whole month. London went into its traditional hiding place—a yellow fog.

It was then that Eleanor went to visit my mother, bringing flowers as though to an invalid. Lily, having resigned herself to Caroline's fluttering ministrations, had taken to lying down in the afternoons on a sofa in the drawing-room. She did this wearing both the expression and the clothes of a valetudinarian character in a melodrama. Camille, perhaps—or Little Nell. She gave an impression of illness rooted in too much reading of Christina Rossetti and Mrs Browning. Tea would be brought by the housemaid, and Lily would *languish* on the sofa before the dampened fire, weeping over *Grief* and other sad poems. This—that was self-willed—only added to the sense of sea-drift in her days. *Not well,* she would write enigmatically in her notebooks. *Not well. Not well.* She was obviously not referring to her seizures.

She had even developed a dainty cough, and would hold a handkerchief to her lips as though expecting blood to stain it. When the blood did not appear, the handkerchief would be crumpled and fisted in the hopes that its mere presence in her hand would tell the visiting world that she was dying.

That Lily was playing a game with her identity was made clear in a conversation I had with Caroline during one of Lily's *incarcerations*. This would have been when I was twelve or thirteen and capable of understanding more—though, sometimes, of visualizing less. With school came a necessary withdrawal from the invented worlds I had co-habited with my mother. Education demands less of our imagination and more of our obedience. The world I lived in then had boundaries—some of which I welcomed. I learned, for instance, there was no more need to *run until the demons could not find us*. A wall kept Lily in—and the demons with her.

I was in that state of denial during which Lily called me *Peter*. And when Caroline told me her tale, I was dubious.

She said: "there was a time when your mother absolutely believed Elizabeth Barrett Browning was in possession of her being. She said she was receiving instructions from the poet on a daily basis—and that I and your Uncle Franklin were to cater to her needs accordingly. It was most bizarre . . ." Caroline played with the folds of her skirt, laying one on top of the other—creating pleats where none had existed. I thought: *she is turning the pages of her story.*

"She took up her place every morning in the drawing-room, surrounding herself with pencils and paper and pens. Books by the dozen piled on the floor. She folded herself in layers and layers of wool and flannel. I had to give up my Paisley shawl, my carriage quilt and my linen throw just to keep her warm. While I froze, of course. It was that kind of winter—damp and frigid. And on top of it, this obsession of Lily's. *When is Mister Browning coming?* she would ask. *I expected him an hour ago . . .* Questions like that can send a shiver down your back. The audacity of her imagination! And her expecting everyone to play a part in it!"

The folding of the skirt was complete. Caroline shook it out and smoothed it with her palms before she began again.

"Don't misunderstand me, Charlie," she said. "I love your mother with every breath I take—but her *episodes*—her make-believe could be the limit. One day, I found her in the bathroom, naked. She was standing in the bathtub, naked as the day she was born. And you want to know what she was doing? She was daubing her skin with extract of walnuts!"

"Why?"

Caroline stood up.

"My question precisely. *Why,* I said, *are you daubing yourself with extract of walnuts?*"

Lily's answer?

"Mister Browning calls me his *little Portuguese,* because there is an olive hue to my skin."

Caroline had been flummoxed by this.

The *olive hue* was decidedly brown.

And there was more.

One morning, Lily had taken up her place on the drawing-room sofa before the rest of the household was up. Not even the maids had risen, and the grate was cold.

When Caroline was informed of this, she went downstairs in her peignoir and found Lily there, and all the lamps turned on. It was 7:00 A.M.

"You have been here all night?"

"Yes," said Lily. "Working. Writing."

"I see. And we are going to pay for all this midnight lamplight?"

"Don't be cross with me, Aunt Carrie. I was working on my masterpiece."

"I am more than cross with you," said Caroline. "I am exasperated and at my wit's end! Sitting up all hours! Painting yourself brown! Turning our lives inside out! How can you!"

"Oh, dear . . ."

"Don't say *oh, dear* like that. Like a bad child. *You are driving me crazy!*"

Lily looked at the dead grate.

There was a silence.

Caroline adjusted her stance and her tone of voice. She was conciliatory. "Sitting up all night—and you so sick—so ill . . . It isn't right. It is not right. I suppose now we'll have to have the doctor . . ."

"No," said Lily. "No. I don't want the doctor." She then held out her hand with a sheaf of papers in it—pages and pages—covered with words.

"What is that?"

"That is my masterpiece," said Lily. "My love poems to Mister Browning. I call it *Sonnets from the Portuguese* . . . Every one of them from me to him. The story of our love . . ."

Caroline sat down.

"But Mister Browning is dead," she said. "Don't you understand that, my dear? Mister Browning is dead."

"No, he's not," said Lily. "I've written him these poems."

Caroline said nothing.

She stood up and left the room.

When she returned, she carried a bottle of Lily's chloroform and a white linen handkerchief.

Sometimes, when Lily was possessed, this was the only remedy. On waking, whoever had been in her would be gone.

As Lily slept, Caroline gathered the sheets of paper and squared them into a bundle. When she was finished, she looked down and saw the words: *How do I love thee? Let me count the ways* . . . Written in Lily's hand.

"All night," Caroline said to me. "All night, copying every word."

I thought about it.

I had seen such things. The Ant God being worshipped. The intellectual, turning her world into an exercise in French. The star-gazer, lost at the window. The fire-watcher, crouching near the flames. I had run with her from demons. Watched her *playing with matches* . . . But I had never met Elizabeth Barrett Browning. And I was dubious. There was always Lily's mischief to contend with. Her avoidance of reality by pretending she wasn't there.

And yet—the *Browning Game* had another aspect to it. It prepared her for her encounter with my third father.

"Hallo," said Eleanor, one day. "I've brought you these."

They were oriental lilies—richly scented—pink and white and maroon.

"Thank you," said Lily Barrett Browning, giving a consumptive sigh.

Eleanor ignored this. Instead, she said: "why are you that peculiar colour?"

Lily said: "it's part of my condition."

"You mean—as in jaundice?"

"No," said Lily. "Not as in jaundice." And then: "why are you here?"

"I'm in trouble," said Eleanor.

The maid who had brought in a tea tray, went to put the flowers in a vase. Caroline was in the dining-room arranging the placement of guests for that evening's dinner party.

Lily gave a cough. "What sort of trouble?"

"The sort of trouble a chap could help me solve, if she was willing."

"Me, you mean? How?"

"You'd have to give up dying," said Eleanor. "I suspect what I'm proposing is rather strenuous."

"Give up dying?" The plaintive tone was not well played. Eleanor knew her friend too well.

"Yes," she said. "Surely you must be bored with it by now."

Lily said nothing at first. She turned away and set the crumpled handkerchief out of sight behind a pillow. She then gave her attention to the book in her hand. "The trouble with dying," she said, "is how tiring it is." Eleanor wanted to laugh, but waited. Lily said: "I suppose there are some things a chap just can't pretend to be."

"Yes," said Eleanor. "Like a corpse."

Lily laughed. At last.

That was better.

Eleanor opened her leather bag and removed a flask. She poured an ounce of brandy into each of their cups. "On the other hand," she said, "there are some things you can pretend to be with great success."

"Such as?"

"Such as a person's best friend."

"I don't understand."

"I want you to pretend to be me."

The maid came back at that moment, with the lilies in a Waterford vase, and placed them near a window. When she had departed, Lily said: "why should I be you?"

Eleanor explained about the man in the steel-rimmed glasses. Of course, she did not intend to put her friend in jeopardy. "I need a ruse," she said. "I need a chance to get away from him. Just for an hour."

Lily smiled. "Is he handsome?" she asked.

"I told you. He's six and a half feet tall."

"I don't mean him," said Lily. "I mean the man of the hour."

Eleanor roared. "Lily's back," she said. "Thank God—and welcome!" She leaned down and kissed Lily's forehead. "Yes," she said. "The man of the hour is more than handsome. He is godlike. Glorious. *Divine!*"

"Blond?"

"Have they ever been anything else?" Eleanor took Lily's hand. "Well?"

Lily set Mrs Browning aside. "Yes," she said. "I would love to be you. For a change."

13. I had never met Eleanor Ormond, and had thought I should never find her. I had looked for her name in telephone books and registries, but there was not a word. Calls to those I thought might have been relatives turned out to be blanks. Then, one day three weeks after Lily's death, my telephone rang. It was Eleanor Ormond. Married now for the

second time—and, for the first time divorced, she was using her first husband's name. I knew nothing of this man, but learned he had died in the War.

"This is Eleanor Hess," she said. "I was so relieved to find you listed in the book. I have only just heard of your mother's death and wondered if I might invite you to come for drinks at the King Edward Hotel. I was at school with Lily and I adored her. Please say you'll come. I'm only in town for three days."

I said *yes, of course* and when I'd hung up, I looked down and saw a faded picture of Eleanor, Phoebe and Lily leaning on the rail of the SS *Franconia*, summer of 1909. It was as if the photograph had spoken.

The King Edward Hotel in the 1930s, even though there had been some architectural modifications, was still the bastion of everything its name implied. The two-storey lobby was still a palm court with marble floors and pillars—the mezzanine still had its host of entertainment rooms, each in a different style, and the clientele still represented international wealth and the local *beau monde*. The aura—as it had when I first encountered it in 1916—still provided an atmosphere of almost sensual safety—of well-being and comfort—a genteel mix of gaiety and sobriety.

To be there, waiting for Eleanor to arrive, was to be in Lily's company.

She had brought me here for my early encounters with Ede. Lily being Lily, these *secret rendezvous* were staged in the open arenas of public restaurants and hotel lobbies. This was where Ede would pass us money and Lily would pass her lies about our lives. That was how we survived in the days before Eliza had set up the trust fund that would support us for so long afterwards. Mother called these earlier times *our palmy days*, because of the potted palms in the lobby of the King Edward Hotel.

Later, in 1917 and 1918, when I was seven and eight—Lily had brought me here in her quest for *viable strangers*. Because of the War, it was a time of many strangers—most of them in uniform, all of them lost. It was also the time of *thé dansant*—afternoon dances to which the young were especially attracted because of the ragtime music and the atmosphere of determined hilarity. I still remember the jagged rhythms of those afternoons and the laughter—each provoked by desperation.

Lily loved to dance. But she had no escort. None—that is—of her own age. That was why I was there. She took me along as her *beau*. Sometimes, she would dance with strangers. More often, her feet would start moving and her fingers tapping and she would look at me and say: *Charlie . . . ?*

Out we would go to the dance floor. Partners.

I, of course, was barely breast-high. I was also a good deal lighter than Lily. Dancing, I could be lifted off my feet and spun above the floor—a small toy child—dizzy and breathless and frightened that she would let go of me. She never did, but sometimes I think I came quite close to flying through the air like Peter Pan, without any visible means of support.

It was odd, sitting there that afternoon, waiting for Eleanor Ormond. Surely I was thinking back to a Lily not unlike the Lily she must have known—*the chappy with the dancing shoes*—Lily *Dress-up*—her escapade companion. And mine, also.

Thés dansants were the invention of Irene and Vernon Castle, ballroom dancers who had a club in New York called The Castle House. Tea dances were its greatest attraction. The fact was, Vernon and Irene Castle revolutionized everything they touched—dancing styles, women's shoes, men's clothing, music. Irene Castle was the first American star to "bob" her hair. All hell broke loose. Vernon Castle held his partner closer than any other man had done. They were nearly run out of town. Furthermore, they didn't *fox trot*—they *walked*.

Mother adored it.

One spring afternoon when Lily was in search of strangers, she brought me to the King Edward Hotel and marched me through the lobby straight to the elevators. I will never forget that day. Never. Even as we rose, she was dancing. We could hear the music and I swear the band was playing just for Lily. When the doors at last were opened and we got off, there was a horde of others—talking, laughing, milling. Lily strode through them, heading for the ball-room—with me in hand.

Just as we arrived, the band struck up *The Charleston Rag*—one of Lily's favourites. She danced all the way to the table, with the maître d' as drum major. This was *Lily's parade . . .*

I sat down.

"Oh no you don't!" she said. "Take off your coat."

She was already taking off her own—looping it over the back of her chair—setting down her bag—getting out her cigarettes.

I took off my coat and was laying it aside when the band exploded into *The Castle Walk*.

Lily grabbed my hand. I didn't stand a chance. There—in front of two hundred people—she strutted me onto the floor.

You have to realize—when Lily danced back then, she *was* Vernon Castle. I was Irene. Backwards—backwards—always backwards. *The Castle Walk* is backwards all the way for women. Not a vertebra out of line, ramrod straight, with shoulders squared, staring into space—no eye contact with Lily-Vernon—and the steps so small, so quick—no heels, all toes—a danced precision drill—perfect for soldiers—perfect for Vernon—perfect for Lily—hell for Irene—and hell for me.

But—oh—I loved it!

So did Lily.

So did everyone.

Other dancers left the floor.

A circle was formed.

We *walked.*

The band played on and on and on.

We *walked.*

Backwards—backwards—backwards—round and round— Lily laughing—me holding on for dear life . . .

And the music racing ahead of us, pulling us faster and faster—everyone applauding—everyone clapping in time to *The Castle Walk*—all their faces turning to watch us—*Lily-Vernon* and *Charlie-Irene—King and Queen of the King Eddy Ballroom—Spring of 1917.*

Make no mistake of it—Lily knew happiness—Lily knew joy. We both knew heaven.

All those years ago.

I might not have known Eleanor if I had passed her in the street. She had put on weight, though not so much that it altered her essential features. What had changed was her sense of self. The vivacity was gone—the mirth which had animated her presence in the pictures I had seen. She was more profoundly changed than even Mother had been. Her expression was sad—resigned. She had lost, I think, her eagerness to evade whatever restrictions had chased her through those early years—and had given in to their persistence. She was someone's captive, it seemed—or the captive of a circumstance she could not resist.

In spite of the added pounds, she was still a handsome woman— square-faced, with a generous mouth and large dark eyes—so dark, in fact, that I could not tell their colour. They must, I suppose, have been brown.

"So, you're Charlie Kilworth," she said.

We sat in an elegant bar looking out at the lobby. Our drinks had been ordered. Eleanor had lighted a cigarette. Its smell reminded me of Lily. They had probably started smoking together at school.

Eleanor was staying at the hotel, but perhaps had been off at an engagement. She wore a hat and her topcoat rested on a third chair. The hat had the appearance of a flowerpot that had been crumpled. That was its colour, too—red clay—and a long green feather sat up on one side. Variations of these two shades were played out in a linen suit and a blouse with a bib that made her look like an attorney in a technicolour court. Her lipstick gave that impression, too—as though it had been applied to be visible for miles.

Waiting for the drinks to come—they were highballs—we filled in the blanks of what we needed to know of one another. This was when she told me she was reverting to her first husband's name. "I won't even bother to tell you the other one's name," she said. "He was—he is a perfect bastard. That is all you need to know."

There were no children from either marriage. "I didn't want to be a mother," she said. "And now, it's too late."

"Would you have children if you could?"

She eyed me sideways and smiled. "Why?" she said. "Do you want to be adopted?"

I laughed.

"No," I said. "I'm perfectly happy just the way I am."

The drinks came.

We toasted Lily and then sat back.

"Did you ever actually meet your father?" she said.

My heart stopped.

She must have known who he was or she would not have worded the question that way.

"No," I said. And then: "did you?"

She considered her answer carefully.

"I'm not sure," she said finally. The tone of this was impossible to read. Although there was tension in it, I could not tell whether it had to do with who the man might have been—or perhaps with her uncertainty as to whether or not she ought to tell me what she knew.

"What did Lily tell you?" she asked.

I explained that the authorship of my life seemed to have been misplaced. Clearly, it had to be someone with whom my mother had relations late in January of 1910—possibly in early February at the outside. I reminded Eleanor Hess that I had been born on the 30th of October in that year.

She said: "I know. I was there."

She lighted another cigarette.

"Has she ever told you—did she ever tell you the story about her impersonation of me?"

"Yes. But I could make nothing of it. There was a blank in the middle of it, the way there was in so many of my mother's stories."

"And then—I forget the rest . . ."

Eleanor gave a perfect impression of Lily's voice and manner when she said this. It had been one of mother's trademark statements.

"That's right," I said. Then I said: "when did you last see her?"

"After you were born." Eleanor rolled the ash from her cigarette. "I saw her two or three times, then. But after that, I was carted off to Paris by my parents and I didn't see her again until just before the War."

"She brought me home to Canada in September of 1914," I told her. "I think, in fact, the War had already started, hadn't it."

"Yes."

The terseness of this answer was in league with one or two other things she had said and I had to wonder what it was about. But I could not ask—I would have to wait for it to reveal itself. If she allowed it to.

"You said you had seen my mother just before the War."

"Yes. Summer of 1914. You were three years old—plus whatever. I remember your being brought into the room. You had a nanny, then, and when she brought you in you were laughing, and you put out your arms the minute you saw your mother and I swear you flew straight out of the nanny's arms into hers! I can see that moment as if . . ."

I waited.

". . . as if it had never ended. As if we could all turn back to that room this instant and be there. Lily was so proud of you. She took you round to every person in the room and said: *this is my boy, Charlie. This is my boy, Charlie.* My husband was with me— Karl—and he insisted on holding you. This worried me, because I thought: *oh, dear. Children are so often frightened of uniforms.* Karl was a soldier, you see, and he was wearing a lot of insignia. He looked very grand, of course, but I thought he might intimidate you. Not at all! We practically had to tear you from his arms when it came time for your nanny to carry you off to bed."

Again, she fell silent, as if she were still inside the scene she had just described. Then she said: "shall we have another drink?"

Yes.

I signalled and the waiter came and departed.

"Right from the moment we knew she was pregnant she hadn't the slightest idea who it might have been," said Eleanor.

"You make it sound as though she had any number of men to choose from." I said this lightly. Smiling.

Eleanor waved the idea away. "There were choices, yes. But not any number of them." She looked at me with an amused expression. "Does it bother you to talk about your mother this way? Anyone listening to us might imagine we were talking about a loose woman."

"Yes. But I know she wasn't. I lived with her all those years. She was lost, that's all. She thought she was being pursued—but that was her only sense of danger. She ran straight into the arms of strangers. She would have trusted Genghis Khan."

Eleanor laughed. "You're right," she said. "But—oh—she was such tremendous fun to be with. You could get completely carried away—and then, before you knew it, she would be running out into the middle of traffic or leaning out of a window seventeen storeys above the street. Or lighting one of those damned fires of hers. She ought to have been killed long, long before she was . . ."

Her lips closed.

Finally, she said: "I'm sorry. That was tactless."

"Please don't worry."

We sat in silence a moment and then I said: "you started to tell me something about the time she pretended to be you."

"Yes."

Eleanor thought her way back to the moment before she spoke again.

"There was this man with steel-rimmed glasses."

"Yes," I said. "I know about him. He was a detective."

"No," said Eleanor. "Not a detective. A Security Agent. All he had to do was keep an eye on me."

"Because of your money . . ."

"Yes." She smiled. "Because all that money was attached to me—and my parents didn't want me to go wandering off. If I went, the loot went with me. It wasn't my honour my parents were worried about. Not my person—just my purse." Another smile. "My problem was—and I'm sure Lily must have told you this—I was in my *promiscuous* stage. I fell in and out of love about once a week . . ." She caught me smiling and laughed. "It wasn't serious, you know. It was more like a game. I didn't really fall in love until I met my first husband. *That* was serious."

"Was he blond?" I grinned.

She laughed again. "Aha! She *did* tell you! Yes. He was blond. *Mein Blondes Baby* . . ."

She grew pensive. "That's a song Miss Dietrich sings. *Mein Blondes Baby*—Karl . . ."

I watched her.

He was dead, of course. Gone.

He died again just then. I could see it in Eleanor's expression. She had conjured him—and now she had to let him go.

She returned to the present, rolling the ash from the end of her cigarette. Now, her expression was sardonic.

"I stole him from your mother," she said.

"Oh? How is that? She never mentioned him to me."

"No. She wouldn't."

"Why?"

"Because she didn't know she knew him."

There.

I knew what Eleanor was saying. Karl Hess had been another anonymous player in one of Lily's episodes.

"What happened?"

Eleanor said: "we had devised a plan in which Lily would dress up as me. She would wear my overcoat—my scarf—my gloves—my hat. It was wintertime, and the clothes back then were fulsome. Lots of collar to turn up—lots of material in which to hide. She even wore a pair of my shoes—a very handsome pair of boots . . . Well. The idea was that she would draw—or try to draw Mister Steel Rims off my tail. If he really thought it was me, he would follow her."

"And . . ."

"And I would be able to skip out the back door to a waiting cab."

"And . . ."

"And meet with the man of the hour at the Dorchester."

The waiter had brought our second drinks. Beyond the bar, the lobby was filling up. The sound of a distant orchestra was mingled with a throng of voices.

"What happened?"

"He followed her. I stood in the window behind the gauze curtains and watched them. Lily had my walk down cold. I couldn't help laughing. I cheered. Like a fool . . ."

"Why like a fool? It was a success."

"Yes. And no."

"No?"

"I was living in The Boltons—off the Old Brompton Road . . ."

"I don't know London. I don't remember it."

"It's immaterial. The houses are charming. There's a gardens. Mister Steel Rims—whose name was Rutherford—Angus Rutherford—used to use the gardens as his sentry post. I'd had a key made and gave it to him. Only residents can use the gardens, so he'd open the gate and sit in there and watch. It was from there he'd gone to follow Lily. My problem was, I didn't know where she'd gone. Off down the Old Brompton Road, no doubt—but there were miles of that and she might be anywhere."

"Hadn't you decided on a place where the chase would end?"

"No." Eleanor waved it away. "That's how stupid I was. We'd been so excited about her dressing up—and she was so much better than she'd been, I assumed common sense would tell her to walk around the block—come back into the house and that would be the end of it. Steel Rims Rutherford would think I was safely back in my nest."

"Good Lord."

"Indeed. When I realized she'd gone on walking—I was alarmed. I waited as long as I dared—and, finally, I went to the back and told the cab driver not to wait. When I went into the front room again and looked out the window—there was Steel Rims. But no Lily. Not a trace. She was gone."

"When was this? Wintertime, you said."

"Yes. It was wintertime."

"But when—exactly."

"Oh heavens! I don't know. November. December. Wintertime."

"Not January? February?"

I could see that Eleanor understood what I was saying. She sat back and looked at me.

"No," she said. "I really don't think so. There was a touch of Christmas in the air. That I do remember."

She could see that I was crestfallen.

"Do you want me to finish the story?"

"Yes."

"I was desperate," said Eleanor. "We'd just been through Mrs Browning—and here was another . . . disappearance."

"What did you do?"

Eleanor smiled. "You won't believe this," she said, "but I went outside into the gardens and walked right up to Mister Steel Rims. His mouth fell open, of course. We very rarely spoke—I hardly acknowledged his presence. I said to him: *Mister Rutherford—please—I believe you just followed me while I was taking one of my walks* . . . He looked at me blankly—said nothing—just stared. Then I said: *can you tell me where I went?* And he said: *no, Miss. No. I never saw you. It was cold out here,* he said, *and I went to the pub for a toddy . . .*"

She was gone. Lily.

And the next thing that happened was that someone found Eleanor's overcoat and hat in Kensington Gardens. The police brought them back to her because her name and address were on the labels sewn inside.

14. It was now quite late in the afternoon and drawing on to evening. The financial district in which the King Edward Hotel was located closed its offices at 5:00 P.M. and a throng of men in summer suits invaded the lobby. The circles of leather chairs expanded. The distant orchestra gave up all pretence of having an audience and was quiet. Otherwise, we could hear the sound of early diners arriving in the lobby with their children. We watched them passing over the carpet—the parents like shepherds, the children like sheep.

There were also a number of men in uniform. Another war was in the offing. This, too, was reminiscent of other times.

We had ordered our third and final drink and were partway through it when Eleanor asked me if I would take my dinner with her there in the hotel.

There was no one, Alexandra being gone, to whom I was responsible, so I agreed to dine with her on the condition that I might be her host. To this, she acquiesced. I was relieved. I am too old-fashioned—even now—to be the guest of a woman in a paying situation. Even if, like Eleanor, she was the tenth richest woman in North America. Tenth, no longer seventh, because since Eleanor had first inherited her millions in 1909, a woman named Barbara Hutton, another named Doris Duke and a third named Peggy Guggenheim had all arrived on the scene.

In the dining-room, we sat with fewer others crowded round us. I was comfortable, now, in her company. There was a wistful eagerness in her desire to remember as many details as she could, because she felt she owed their retrieval to Lily. And, I think, to me. There was still a sense of something being withheld, however—of something left unsaid—but I could also tell that she was debating the exposure of this information even as she spoke of other things.

Here is what I have retained of her story.

Three days passed. The first evening, Eleanor had the presence of mind to telephone Franklin and Caroline Wyatt in Richmond. She told them Lily had decided to stay a few days in The Boltons at number 28 the Gardens—*because we've been having such a good time.* She also told Caroline, with whom she had a second conversation the next morning, that Lily was in the best of health and the best of spirits.

"Yes, but what will she wear?" Caroline wanted to know. "She didn't even take her night attire." Caroline, as ever, chose appearances and the proprieties as her first concern. "I hope you aren't going to be taking her into other people's houses wearing those dowdy clothes," she said. "It was just a simple house-dress, if I recall."

"Well, no," Eleanor lied. She had dealt with Caroline before. "It was white—very pretty and most becoming. You know the one—with the heavenly sleeves and the dear little collar." Eleanor was describing a dress of her own.

"Oh, yes. Yes, of course. The heavenly sleeves and the dear little collar." Caroline's voice drifted off into Southern vagueness. *The heavenly sleeves—the dear little collar* . . .

"Besides which, Lily's been using some of my clothes, Mrs Wyatt. She loves dressing up. We really have been having a most entertaining time."

Caroline was mollified. Eleanor Ormond had such very good taste in clothing, and there would be nothing, therefore, in Lily's appearance that could cause the family embarrassment.

Messages of love and tender concern were exchanged and at last the ordeal of the obligatory report was over.

On the second day, Steel Rims Rutherford returned to the scene. He rang the bell at Number 28 and expressed his concern at having seen the police at the door, when the coat and hat were returned. Eleanor explained that the clothing had been *stolen some time ago and was being restored to its rightful owner.* The culprit, she said, was at present in a cell.

At four o'clock on that afternoon—the telephone rang.

It was someone German—a man whose accent was almost a complete impediment. But, at last, enough was made clear for Eleanor to know that she was to go to number 44 Tedworth Square where—the German informed her—*we have reason to belief there is someone you have lost.*

Eleanor, eschewing all caution, threw on her hat and coat and boots, took up her handbag and umbrella and ran past Steel Rims Rutherford at such a great speed that she was gone to the Old Brompton Road before he fully realized it was her. This made twice. The first time, he had gone for a toddy.

15 • Tedworth Square was in Chelsea, not a great way off from the Thames River and connected to the Embankment by Tite Street, where Oscar Wilde had been living when he was arrested. Whistler and Carlyle had lived nearby and the district had once been the haunt of Henry James. Eleanor knew of its reputation from her fellow students at Cambridge. *Chelsea is art—art, Chelsea*, one of them had said. *That is all ye know of London and all ye need to know!*

Eleanor arrived in a taxi. Number 44 was at the top of the square with a view of the gardens, which were gateless. This meant that anyone could use them and, in the summertime, men came up from the River and slept there under the bushes. The trees, being leafless, had little charm, but otherwise it was a pretty place, though ordinary. Unlike most of the squares in London, its houses were constructed of red brick—now faded.

Eleanor suddenly realized, as she heard the taxi drive away behind her, that she was walking into a situation of which she knew nothing. Nothing but the fact that a man with very little English awaited her beyond the door and that with him, she prayed, would be Lily.

But a man did not answer her ring. A woman in her forties did, clothed in a yellow Japanese kimono. Her hair, which was honey-blonde, was piled on top of her head and held in place with a lacquered comb.

"You are Miss Ormond," this woman said in a surprisingly cultured and friendly voice. "I am Elizabeth Frejus. Do come in."

"Thank you."

Eleanor entered a vestibule which gave into a narrow hallway at the end of which she could see a staircase rising to a landing. On the right, before the stairs, there was a sitting-room that apparently had been commandeered as a bedroom. Passing by its open door, Eleanor could see very little else but an enormous mahogany bed in which an old woman was ensconced against some pillows.

"The rent, Miss Frejus!" this woman said. The voice of a harridan was immediately recognizable.

"Yes, Miss Quigley," said Elizabeth Frejus, continuing to lead Eleanor towards the stairs. Turning beyond the door, she smiled and said in a low voice: "the rent isn't due till tomorrow, but she loves to terrorize her tenants . . ."

"Who's that person with you, Miss Frejus?" the voice from the bed called out.

"Another visitor for Robert, Miss Quigley. We're rather hoping she'll buy something. That should make you happy." More smiling and a wink from Elizabeth Frejus. She and Eleanor were now partway up to the first landing. "If she buys just one," Elizabeth called back, "that could mean half a year's rent, Miss Quigley. Wouldn't that be lovely."

"Yes. Well . . ."

The bedridden voice of the landlady faded.

"She'll go back to her gin, now—and be asleep in half an hour. Thank goodness. I'm sorry you had to be subjected to that."

"It doesn't matter," said Eleanor. "Who is Robert?"

"We're going up to see him now. He's a painter. Robert Shorecross. I'm his mistress."

Eleanor muttered: "oh."

"I suppose you're not used to being handed information like that, but there's not much point avoiding it. Everyone knows we're not married. Sooner or later, you'd find out, anyway."

They were now on their way to the top of the house.

"It's a long climb," said Elizabeth Frejus, "but there's a lovely huge skylight up here and an irresistible view of the city. Do you know many artists, Miss Ormond?"

"No. None that are professionals, at any rate."

As they went from the third to the final floor, Eleanor counted the last of the open doorways that could be seen along the various corridors. Twelve rooms in all.

"We're all artists here," Elizabeth told her. "Artists, or writers. And one musician. Karl. He plays the flute and is German."

"German?"

"Yes."

"Is he the man who telephoned?"

"Yes," said Elizabeth. She turned and gave Eleanor a knowing smile. "He has made your friend very happy," she said.

"Her name is Lily," said Eleanor. What did *very happy* mean?

"Good. At last," said Elizabeth Frejus. "A breakthrough in the mystery. Her name is Lily."

"Yes. She didn't tell you?"

"That's right. Didn't tell us—because she couldn't. Shall we go up? She will be there, now. Robert is painting her portrait."

Eleanor hung back.

"Just one question before we go," she said. "How, if she couldn't tell you who she is, did this German fellow know he should telephone me?"

"Your name is on the labels in her boots."

"Of course. I see."

All at once, Eleanor was glad of her mother's insistence that every piece of her clothing be marked. First the coat and hat—then Lily.

"How did she get here? The last time I saw her, she was up in The Boltons."

"She and Karl were both in Kensington Gardens watching a band rehearse. Karl plays the flute. He was interested. So was your friend. But when he went to leave, she followed him. She had no coat, no hat. He didn't appreciate being followed but he could see she was ill. At last, he gave in and brought her here."

"She said nothing?"

"Nothing. She was—and is—mute. In the end, we found your name in the boots."

"And so I was telephoned."

"The assumption was that your husband would answer. Your husband—or one of your parents."

"But this German fellow—this flautist, or whatever they call themselves—why on earth was he chosen to speak to me? I could barely understand a word he said."

"Yes. But you see, your friend is in love with him. He feels responsible."

"She is *in love* with him?"

"Yes, Miss Ormond. Passionately. I hope you will forgive my saying this so boldly, but—your friend, Miss Lily, refused to leave Karl's bed both yesterday and this morning. We had to go in and rescue him."

"Rescue him?"

"Yes." Elizabeth was smiling again. "Figuratively speaking, of course. She would not let go of him and he—being a gentleman— was afraid of using force for fear of harming her. She's very strong, you know."

Eleanor did, indeed, know Lily's strength. It had been her ally during their escapades at school.

"Please do come up," said a man who could not be seen, but whose voice was coming from the studio above them. "I'm dying to meet the real Eleanor Ormond."

16.

Robert Shorecross, the man who had spoken, was standing with his back to Eleanor and Elizabeth Frejus as they came to the top of the steps and entered the studio. He was tall and wore an old shirt as a smock on top of another, somewhat better shirt. The figure on his canvas could not be seen because he stood in front of it—and the canvas itself, on its easel, obscured the sitter.

"The light is almost entirely gone from the sky, and I really do hate to paint by lamplight," he said. "And so . . ." he turned around. "I will stop."

He had a long, almost comic face—dark-eyed and amused. His hair was shoulder-length and when he was painting, he pulled it back and tied it with a rag. He looked like a gypsy.

"I have to clean my brushes," he said, "so I won't shake hands. But a gent never does shake hands with a lady. Is that still true? I'm completely out of date with all that rigamarole. Forgive me. You've met Liz Frejus, I see. And here . . . well . . . here is your friend."

He gestured at the canvas.

There she sat. Lily in a green chair, wearing a white dress dotted with blue flowers and her hair let down as though she was a girl again.

The expression in the painted eyes was one that Eleanor had seen. They were bright—and feverish. And the corners of her mouth had the look of someone who smiles because there is a secret only she has access to. Her hands both lay palm upward, one arm resting on the chair and the other slightly raised and extended—as though the hand were expecting something to be placed in it. In her lap, a spray of flowers had been loosed, as though they had escaped from a vase.

Having deliberately taken the time to read the portrait, Eleanor was now more or less prepared for what she would find as she rounded the easel and approached the sitter's chair.

The chair was empty—the flowers had been thrown to one side. Lily was standing with her back to Eleanor, plaiting her hair into a single braid. As she did this, she was humming. The light around her was partly cast from two brass lamps that hung from the ceiling, and partly from the northern sky beyond the vast and multipaned window. The sun was on the verge of setting and snow was falling on the roofs of London—vivid and translucent—the colour of a blood orange.

"Hallo, Lily," said Eleanor, barely raising her voice.

The figure turned and, for a moment, its features were so still that Eleanor was startled. The hands, with their fingers tangled in hair, were marble-white and looked almost like the paws of an animal. The head, already leaning into the pull of the braiding, was bent even further as the eyes looked up and sideways at the apparent stranger who had spoken. There was not a glimmer of recognition.

So far as Eleanor was concerned, it was not Lily Kilworth. It was another person wearing Lily's body.

17· Steps were heard as someone came upstairs in boots all the way from the ground floor.

It was the German, bringing with him a cloud of wintry cold and the smell of snow.

Eleanor watched him as he came up past her—seemingly bald because his hair had been cut so short. He was wearing a great-coat and carried a cap. Seeing Eleanor, he threw the cap against his body, holding it there with his left arm. With his right arm, he saluted her. He also clicked his heels.

Elizabeth Frejus said: "this is Cadet Hess, Miss Ormond. Karl Hess—from Munich."

"Born Munich," Karl corrected her. "Lie-ving one year in London now. Students exchange."

Eleanor watched him closely while he talked, noting every step he took and every move he made—removing his greatcoat and then his jacket—taking up a glass and bottle—drinking—almost laughing—turning to Lily—toasting her, but refusing to cross the threshold into her half of the room. This was the man with whom Lily had been so passionately bedded that another man and a woman had had to come and remove her.

This is the end of what Eleanor told me:

She had said the man's name was *Hess*, and I said: "your name is Hess."

"That's right."

"It was him you married, then? Karl, the flautist?"

"Yes." She laughed. "Of course, I had no inkling when I saw him first that I was even remotely attracted to him."

"What happened?"

Eleanor gave a sigh. We had reached the stage in our meal between the dessert and the coffee.

"It was all quite true," she told me. "The part about your mother's passion for Karl. He told me so himself. Though the passion was not reciprocated, he admitted there had been intercourse. She would not let go of him. She clung to him, he said, as one would cling when drowning. She had to be torn from his arms. It was, he told me, terrifying. His way of explaining her behaviour was: *panic*, not passion. Those were his very words: *she was panic-stricken.* He was not even sure that she knew it was sex."

I had no reply to this.

Before I left her, I showed her the photographs that had seemed to show the most likely candidates in the search for my father. Eleanor had known them all—and, of course, had been married to one of them.

The laughing young man whose song had been *Soup of the Evening* had not, in fact, been an actor, but a music hall entertainer whose name had been Humphrey Carroll. His real name, Eleanor told me, had been Carroll Humphries. *But he'd hated that and switched it round.* He was talented, she said—*but rash.* In the War, he was killed while crossing No Man's Land. *Stark naked, Charlie. In the dead of winter, singing . . .*

"*Soup of the Evening?*" I asked.

"No," she said. "Singing *Auld Lang Syne.*"

As for Charles "Red" Russell: "the less said the better. By the time that was over, I had a lot of sympathy for poor old Phoebe. Still, they were a pair, and in their crazy way I think they somehow cancelled one another out. They could never—either of them—ever in a million years have made another human being happy."

And then—there was Karl.

"Since you're so sure this happened in November or December—is there any chance she saw him again? I mean . . ."

"You mean in January? I'm afraid I can't help you, Charlie. I know that he went back to Germany briefly. In the spring, he returned and started courting me."

"And the others?"

"In January?" Eleanor thought about it. "She could have seen any of them any time. I suppose."

We sat in silence as we looked at them—three men in three photographs. I considered their names. *Carroll. Charles. Karl.* Each the name of someone who might have a son called *Charlie.*

Six
1914—1918

What's the use of worrying?
It never was worthwhile.
So pack up your troubles
In your old kit bag,
And smile, smile, smile . . .

Pack Up Your Troubles
Felix and George Henry Powell

1. I was brought out of England in September of 1914. The War had started, but to date there had been nothing more startling than huge recruitment rallies in which thousands of men filled the streets, eager to don the uniform.

Our reception at Selby Street in 1914 was spectacular, to say the least. Lily had given no warning of our arrival, and the news of my existence having been so ill-received at my birth was no better received in my presence. We were immediately banished to a hotel.

The first hotel we lived in was the Newtonberry Arms on Jarvis Street, which placed us more or less around the corner from Ede and Frederick. It was at this time that Lily paraded in front of the Selby Street house, pushing me in a pram I no longer needed—a picket line of two with a placard that read: *WYATT PIANO COMPANY UNFAIR TO UNWED MOTHERS!*

The whole street turned out to see us with our placard and Mrs Carmichael, next door, sent a boy to see if she ought to prepare for a militant demonstration. Should she lock her doors and shutter her windows? The police were called.

Mrs Carmichael was placated. Mother was gently reprimanded. In the end, she set the placard aside and contented herself with telling her news to Bateson, who came to the fence to say how glad he was to see her—and to meet me.

When this was done, he said: "there's one piece of news you may not know, Miss Lily. Sad news—but not. Old Buster—Mister Lizzie's dog—came here to be mine after Toby died. Buster was greatly old, Miss—you knew that already. Well, he had two more years with me here. Good years—nosing through the garden— sleeping in Toby's old bed. That's where I found him one morning. Died like a dream in's sleep . . ."

"Dear old dog."

"Yes, Miss. And a great one. Same as Toby. I put them both back there by the cold frames."

"Thank you, Bateson."

And that was all. Toby and Buster dead. Lying, restorative, where the Ant King died all those years ago. Lily said: *bless all dogs for being*. And we left.

Lily never had qualms about making her statements to the world. She was prepared to kill in defence of the animal kingdom and of children. And of the mentally bereft. Her emotional reactions disintegrated when the red flag went up. And yet, in spite of the fires she lit and the fists she raised, there had been no deaths and no harm given—beyond the shock of being confronted by a madwoman.

This word must itself now be confronted. *Madwoman*.

When I was first presented to the family on Selby Street, I was unaware of the kind of blackmail that can be used when people are afraid—as Frederick was—of what they perceive to be madness in others. But the consequences of this fear entered my life at that time. And the blackmail, of course, was Frederick's ability to have Lily put away: committed. Neither Ede nor Eliza could protect her from this. It was a man's world then, in which only a man could have his legal way with such a decision.

His emissary in our lives was Ede. She would arrive—apologetic—with his edicts—his conditions concerning our relations with the rest of the family. We could not go to them. Not at Selby Street. If we wished to see them, or they to see us, a secret rendezvous must be arranged. Thus, our meetings with Ede at the King Edward Hotel. There were other meetings, as well, at the Newtonberry Arms. These were the only times I ever heard my mother make war against Ede—and Ede against her. Other arguments between them never achieved the fireworks I remember from when I was four or five years old.

When the shouting between them began, it was always at a distance from where I played in sunlit rooms or had been put to rest beyond closed doors. This is the way it is with children. Violence that is incomprehensible because it is emanating from people you love and trust always seems to be coming from another part of the forest. *Why are they yelling? What does it mean?* By the time they walk into your presence, their anger is restrained, though none the less alarming. Its voice is coasting now on an undercurrent of rage, but tempered with the thought: *don't frighten the child.* As if the child were not already terrified.

While Lily stood aside, the very image of dampened fire, Ede would bend down and kiss me goodbye, still rigid with fury.

2 • The hotels we lived in were often little more than glorified boarding-houses. In the present world, they no longer exist. What you had was a suite of rooms and the use of a parlour and a drawing-room on the main floor, if you should wish to entertain large numbers.

The dining-room provided separate tables, upon which you could build up your own array of condiments. Lily was very fond, for instance, of a blue glass cruet which we carried with us everywhere. It had a silver setting and its handle depicted a partridge at rest. The bottles—there were four of them—contained sugar, oil, vinegar and mustard. The sugar bottle had seven wide holes and I remember my fascination with the streams of sugar falling onto my morning porridge. I thought of them as waterfalls and alpine avalanches. Sometimes, my pourings got completely out of control and mother would catch me with half the shaker emptied. The mustard jar had a lid with a hole—for a long, curved spoon, and the handle of the spoon was a silver partridge feather.

Maids brought the food. There was rarely a choice. These dining-rooms were not like restaurants. You took what you were given, but it was always excellent food, beautifully prepared and served. You dined off the best of china—Spode and Wedgewood—and the settings were always of silver, never of plate. Another thing we had was our own silver napkin rings. These, too, were like resting birds and the underside of one said *Charlie* and the other, *Lily*. Charlie was my name. I was never called *Charles*.

The family saw to it that neither Lily nor I ever had to worry about having money—only about its management. Lily had a realistic sense of frugality and money was never wasted—though Frederick would have said so. He would not have approved, for instance, of the first-class accommodation Lily provided for us. Our hotels were expensive, but their ambience was a tonic and their addresses provided us with instant recognition as *persons of consequence*.

"We may not believe in the class system," my mother often said. "But we do believe in *class*!"

This sense of class was not reflected only in our accommoda-tions. It could also be seen in every piece of clothing we wore and the few indispensable objects which made up our domestic posses-sions: a rosewood chair—a Japanese vanity with inlays of brass and ivory—a tilt-top circular table, again of rosewood, on which—every time we moved—mother would reset her collection of silver-framed photographs and the silver birds she had begun to collect in England. The blackbird feather and Ramses II did not sit here. These were holy objects, the equivalent of Lily's icons. Embedded in their amber tombs, they were always displayed on Lily's dressing table with her silver mirror and brushes, the trio of stoppered per-fume bottles and the photographs of James and Eliza Kilworth.

Among our possessions there was also and ever the wicker suit-case—packed and ready for our escape. *Escaping* was never explained to me. I suppose it did not have to be. We had been *on the run* since the moment I was born, and it was simply a state of being that I accepted.

When I was four years old, I experienced the first *escape* I can remember in detail.

It was night-time. I was sound asleep. This was at the Newtonberry Arms. It was dead of winter—there was a snow-fall in progress beyond the windows. Lily was standing beside my bed. She was fully dressed and wore a hat. She had a way of waking me I have never heard anyone else describe. She would place two fingers on the pressure point behind my ear and speak my name.

Charlie.

Instantly, I was alert.

"Get up. We're leaving."

"Why?"

I sat on the edge of the bed. Lily went across the room and turned on a light.

"I can't explain. There isn't time. Hurry."

She spread a large red bandanna over the lampshade to dim the bulb. This cast a fiery glow over everything, including Lily's shadow where it moved across the ceiling.

"Get dressed. Be quick. And put on your overcoat."

"Yes, Mother."

I pulled my clothes on over my pyjamas. I was shivering.

Lily was putting a few extra things into the already packed wicker suitcase. A sweater of mine—a shirtwaist of hers. My pair and her pair of bedroom slippers. A candle.

"Where are we going?" I asked.

"I don't know. Away."

That was all.

She carried the suitcase over to the door of the bedroom and looked out into the little hall that led to the drawing-room.

"Turn the light out. Bring the red handkerchief."

I did this and joined her.

"We will leave here," she said, "as quietly as possible. We will cross the drawing-room to the vestibule. We will go out into the main hall and walk down the stairs to the lobby. If the night clerk is there, we will say nothing. In the street, we will run . . ."

"But where, Mama? Where?"

"Just run. Stay with me."

We moved then through a darkness lighted only by the street lamps shining through one set of windows. Drawing-room. Vestibule. Main hall. Stairs.

In the lobby, the night clerk sat asleep in his chair. He did not waken.

At the front door, mother flicked the latch over and pulled.

A blast of cold wind entered and passed us.

Out on the verandah, the snow began to pelt us. We went down the steps and along the walk.

Mother took my hand and said: "now—run!"

And we ran. I was frightened and confused. I kept thinking: *someone must want to catch us. Someone must want to push us into the closet and turn the key . . .*

We ran up Jarvis Street all the way to Bloor, with the contents of the suitcase bumping and banging. Across the road, we could see the night-lights of St Margaret's College for Girls. Above us, the giant elms were shaking in the wind—a north wind against which we had been running all this while. I looked back down the avenue to see if there was anyone there. No one. The street lamps were barely visible in the blowing snow. Mother was still holding onto my hand.

"We will cross over here," she said.

We hurried to the other side of Jarvis where St Paul's Cathedral loomed, waited barely a moment and then went over Bloor Street and began to run again, westward.

I could hardly breathe. Mother was running at her own pace, forgetting mine. It was almost impossible for me. If she had not been holding onto my hand, I would have fallen. We turned then and began to run on the road itself until we came to a laneway that dropped into the darkened ravine.

For a four-year-old, running downhill is no easier than running on the flats.

I kept trying to say: *oh, please—please stop!* But I could get nothing out. What was wrong with her? Why were we doing this?

At the bottom—by some miracle—mother slowed her pace and finally stood—irresolute—in the lee of some trees. She stared off into the dark—this way and that way—as if there must be someone there. The wind had faded, and at last we were standing still. But I was burning in every muscle and my lungs were cramped and bursting.

Because the snow provided some light, we could see the fences standing along Ravine Drive. They were like arrows, pointing the way to limbo, beyond the curtain of falling snow.

"We can walk now," Mother said. "Come along."

I wanted to say: *I can't*, but I knew it was useless.

I was wearing only shoes and socks—no galoshes. I wore long black stockings, pulled up over my pyjama legs—a shirt—a sleeveless sweater and a jacket, plus my overcoat. Also, gloves and a cap. No scarf. I was already cold and now, I was wet. At least my feet and ankles were.

Mother let go of my hand. I was free to adopt my own pace, and fell somewhat behind her.

We walked this way through the dark for about ten minutes.

"Here is someplace," said Mother.

Above us, the iron trestles of the Sherbourne Street bridge rose out of sight. Way, way off, its street lamps glittered like fallen stars.

"We will go up here."

I was afraid she meant we were to clamber up the bridge. Instead, we turned to our right and began to zig-zag under it, climbing over the hillside until we had almost achieved street level.

"This will be fine," Mother said. "Just fine."

"Where are we?"

"Never mind. We're safe."

I doubted it. "Are we going to stay here all night?"

"Yes."

"Why?"

Mother ignored this question. It had not, she decided, been asked.

Instead, she busied herself creating a haven for us, hard up against the underside of the bridge where it met the embankment. There was no snow here, but only a mass of autumn leaves and old blown newspapers.

"Perfect."

She gathered and piled the leaves until there were enough to bury us. I don't think I thought it then, but in retrospect, when I conjure this picture, I can only think her concentration in that moment was manic. I would not have understood the word, but if someone had explained it to me, I would have said: *Mother . . .* She moved on that hillside beneath the bridge like an animal preparing to hibernate. Her focus was absolute. She was alone.

I waited.

"Now," she said. "We will lie down here and be perfectly warm and perfectly comfortable. Nature provides," she added. "Nature takes care of us."

She opened the suitcase and took out my sweater. "You can use this as your pillow."

She did the same with her shirtwaist.

When I had lain down—fully dressed, overcoat and all, still wearing my cap and gloves—Mother shook out the blanket kept in the suitcase and covered me in my nest of leaves.

She took off my wet shoes and stockings, fitted my slippers onto my feet and tucked the blanket end around them. "There," she said.

Lying down beside me, she pulled her half of the blanket over her shoulders and, facing away from me, said: "good-night, Charlie. Sleep well . . ."

Sleep well.

I did not sleep at all. I didn't dare close my eyes. I kept thinking: *my mother is crazy. I am living with a mad person. What is going to happen next?* Or the child equivalent of such thoughts. I had always accepted her, until that night, as being the way most mothers were—imperious, but trustworthy. Odd—but lovingly so. I had never felt imperilled by her madness. Now I was.

I waited for her to fall asleep, thinking perhaps that I would run away from her. Escape. But she didn't sleep. So I stayed.

We lay that way until dawn.

When we had risen, Mother took me up onto Sherbourne Street, where we ate our breakfast in the Sherbourne Hotel. Nothing more was said. I only know that something—someone— had been survived.

In time, of course, I began to see the patterns in her behaviour. I understood, for instance, that an excess of fire-watching signalled an episode of panic—and, therefore, another escape. On the other hand, an excess of pensiveness—the long hours spent sitting in her chair while staring into space—tended to bring on bursts of high-powered energy. These always ended with us dancing—playing physical games—or dressing up as movie actors and laughing ourselves sick.

Lily's favourite role for me was Charlie Chaplin.

"After all," she said, "he stole your name, so you have a right to steal his face . . ."

I had a black paper moustache attached with paste, and a bamboo walking stick and a miniature hat Lily found in a Woolworth's store. I wore my pyjama pants with braces, dropping them down so I could "trip" on the cuffs. Lily taught me Charlie's walk, and how to clean my fingernails with the bamboo stick, which I also used as a toothpick.

Her own disguises ranged from a wide-eyed Lillian Gish to a kohl-eyed harem girl. As the first, Lily tried to see how many times she could bat her lashes in half a minute. As the second, she danced with veils—the veils being bath towels and my pyjama tops.

The movies had entered our lives as the result of escape episodes.

Sometimes, when we were running away, Lily would hire a horse-drawn cab, but—having no destination—all we did was drive in aimless circles. Other times, we went to the farthest edge of the city and spent the night in a travellers' hotel. We never slept under a bridge again. But if our escape was being made by day, we went downtown and took up residence—suitcase and all—in a movie house. This way, Lily achieved the double safety of darkness and romance. *Anyone's life but mine,* she would write.

The dark of movie houses could also be dangerous. With their flickering lights, they kept Lily poised on the verge of seizures. And yet, this seemed to be a source of energy. It roused her, but it didn't pull her all the way over the edge. Looking back from here, it occurs to me that Lily flirted this way with her seizures—the way some people flirt with disaster—walking on tightropes, riding wild horses. There is, for such people, exhilaration in jeopardy, stimulation in peril. From Lily's point of view, the movies were the next best thing to flames. There were phantoms up there on the shimmering screen, just as there were in her fires. And their voices, too, could be heard only in the mind.

When I see the memory of Lily now in that eerie light, the pallor of her face and the bright expectation in her eyes force me to realize she was already fleeing from her demons. Even then, before they had been identified.

The movies became her drug—her *good, safe place*—her world within the world, where no one could reach her—no one could harm her. She believed, I am certain, that even if Frederick himself had come to sit down beside her, she need only rise and walk away through the streets that appeared on the screen. *Goodbye,* she would say, and close a door held open for her by Douglas Fairbanks or Wallace Reid.

Someone did come to sit down beside us—but not in the movie house. It was Liam, and he came to the Newtonberry Arms.

Lily and I had been to see *The Count of Monte Cristo* with James O'Neill and I had been going about in a velvet drape. That was meant to be my *noble cape.* It wasn't very noble, I'm afraid. All it did was wind itself around my legs and trip me. As Liam came through the door, I fell.

"What are you doing here?" said Lily.

"What is that child doing down on the floor? Is it Charlie?"

"Yes. That is Charlie."

Lily totally ignored my predicament.

"What are you doing here?" she said again.

Liam took off his hat and set it aside. I had never seen him before. As I looked up at him, he seemed enormously tall and distant.

"I wanted to see your son," he said. "My nephew."

He reached down his hand and hauled me—noble cape and all—to my feet.

"How do you do?" he said.

I shook his hand. Or tried to. He ended up with a fistful of velvet.

He did not remove his coat. I know now he was concerned that Lily should not see his suit. I suspect it was more or less threadbare.

Lily offered him tea. She did not keep liquor on the premises. Not then. The tea would have to be got from the kitchen. A maid would bring it. *No*, said Liam. *No tea.*

I divested myself of the drape and we all sat down. His shoes were muddy.

Lily told him an amusing story about seeing Frederick in the street and accosting him. *Don't you want to meet your "grandson"?* No, he said. *I have no grandson.* Lily described how she pushed me forward. *Such an appealing child. Wouldn't you like to kiss him?* she asked. *I don't kiss children!* said Frederick.

Lily gave a raucous shout of triumph. *Then I kissed him!* she roared. *On the lips! Right there in the street!*

Every word of this was a lie. None of it had happened. I looked at Liam to see if he believed her.

"You're almost as good a storyteller as I am," he said. "But not quite."

Lily did not appreciate this. She had meant to entertain him. Instead of laughing, he rebuked her for it.

He got up then and went to the table where his hat was waiting. He stood there for a moment with his back to us.

"Lil," he said—not turning.

"No," she said. "We're broke."

Money.

She went with him to the door. I did not. I stood in the sitting-room, watching.

Lily put her hand on his shoulder.

"Thank you for coming to see Charlie. No one else has. But mam, of course . . ."

Liam put on his hat.

Lily opened the door.

Liam walked through.

"Goodbye," I said.

He did not look back.

The door closed.

"Well," said Lily. "I guess that's that."

"He seemed quite nice," I said. And meant it.

"He is," said Lily. "Very nice. For a dead man."

3. I have said that we lived in hotels and this was true. But we were also given some respite through visits to Munsterfield. There, Eliza, approaching seventy, made us welcome. James had died of his heart in 1912, the last of Eliza's Rosary Deaths. Every night, she prayed for his immortal soul beneath the crucifix in the parlour. Lily showed me his office—largely the same as when she had seen it last in 1909. Even the abacus was still in its place.

Malahide was a man in whom I found a good companion. He was almost forty now—still and ever unmarried—still and ever totally uninterested in any form of settling down. The house, the barns, the fences all had his attention. But not the land. Not the fields. Not the life of it. Uncle Mal could sit beneath the sky and never look at it. *Hot*, he would say. But the sun . . . ? He'd never seen it.

He was fair enough to look at and pleasant enough to be with. *Any number of women would have had him*. I believe that's how such things were couched back then. He was short and strong and brown from the sun and his hair had a honey tint to it. He always wore a bandanna around his neck and kept another in his pocket for mopping his brow. They were red—with white polka dots. I have one still. He showed me how to tie it round my neck and pull the knot to the back so the bulk of the bandanna made a three-cornered bib above the throat. It was his trademark.

Davey and Richard had gone away to the War, but Ephraim was there, greatly old and retired. He *pottered* in the drive shed, polishing harnesses—grooming the horses. He still drove the democrat from time to time. But mostly, he sat in the kitchen and dozed. Thinking back to the three of them—these men my mother had known, but I had not experienced—I understood at last what it meant to *hire oneself out*. Ephraim, Davey and Richard had only had the barns as homes. No wonder the horses fared so well in their time. The horses were their brothers—separated at birth.

The only help that Malahide had now was from boys too young for the War and a man who, wounded, had been returned to Canada. His name was Michael O'Hare. There was shrapnel in him still, and he told me *one day, it will make its own way out of my body and fall down onto the floor* . . . I waited breathlessly for this to happen. *When, when, when will it fall?* I said. *I want to see it.* Michael said: *Maybe next Thursday* and everyone laughed—but me. I was bitterly disappointed.

Freda Hoffstaeder now was seventy. Minna, her daughter, had married happily and moved away. She had found another who, like herself, was deaf and Freda was proud of the fact that her one-time *idiot daughter* was seen to be a respectable wife and mother raising children of her own.

Freda was still the dominant force in the kitchen. She had suffered some insults from two of the shopkeepers in town who disapproved of her German name. But she had hurled their insults back at them, shouting: *I Canadian! I Canadian!* They had been silenced when Eliza threatened to cut off her patronage. *And,* she had said, *I also want your apologies to Mrs Hoffstaeder.* She got them. In writing.

I loved it there, on the farm. Lily would spread a blanket and sit with me in the field where she was born. It became our special place—our haven and our sanctuary. We would take out books and stoppered bottles of water and lemonade and she would read to me in the shade of the buckthorn trees and the honeysuckle, now gone wild, that had witnessed her birth. The fence to which Ede had clung through the hours of labour was now our occasional backrest and the birds whose songs made up our spring and summer serenade must surely have been the fifth or sixth generation of birds whose antecedents had called out Lily's name. Or so Ede told us. The bobolinks, the meadow larks, the killdeer and the veery in his woods beyond the river had all cried *Lily Kilworth!* on that morning in 1890. So, it seemed, did their descendants.

The cicadas sang and the grasshoppers ground out their tunes and bees the size of my childish thumbs hung from the clover heads nearby. I sat in a state of endless wonder. And Lily introduced me to the ants.

In the field one afternoon in the summer of 1916, we looked at an anthill there and Lily explained the process by which the ants identified themselves to one another. I was five, and in a month or two would be six. The War still raged. That was the summer of slaughter on the Somme. Still—we were safe in our field, and the world was a world of ants—not of men.

"We are not alone here, Charlie," Lily said to me. "It's their world, too. But we have taken—we are taking it from them—breaking it over their heads . . ." We crouched beside the anthill. "Look how delicate they are, Charlie—delicate and fine. Look how their bodies shine and what perfect precision there is in everything they do."

She let one large black ant climb onto the palm of her hand and showed it to me. "You must never kill an ant," she said. "You must never step on one or pick one up and pinch it. If you pick one up, you must look at him and let him go. These are the wonders of the world, Charlie—all these creatures here . . ." She laid her hand on the earth—and the ant walked away. "These are the people of Ramses II," she said. I already knew about him, having seen him in his amber coffin.

One of the books Lily read from in the field—and sometimes, too, in the evening on the lamplit porch that faced the field—was the book of insect stories by J. Henri Fabre that Ede had given her years before. I doubt that she read to me then the words that follow here, but I know she read them to me sometime because—looking at them now in order to copy them out—it is Lily's voice I hear most clearly. Fabre is addressing his fellow scientists in anger:

You kill and rip up the insect. I study it alive. You turn it into an object of horror and pity. I cause it to be loved. You labour in a torture-chamber and dissecting-room. I make my observations under the blue sky . . . You pry into death. I pry into life . . .

Lily called this *the spirit of Fabre*. It is also, I think, *the spirit of Lily Kilworth*. For me, it was a way of learning—the field my schoolroom and Lily my teacher.

"Now, watch and see what they do here, Charlie. Watch and see what they do . . ."

She pulled the grass aside just enough so that I could look down onto one of their tracks and the ants going to and fro.

"They're kissing," I said.

Lily laughed. "It certainly seems so, doesn't it."

Time and time again, an ant coming back along the trail towards the hill would meet another ant who was going in the opposite direction—and they would stop to exchange what looked like kisses. They also seemed, at times, to be embracing—their feelers waving frantically.

Lily explained.

"Each one puts a tiny bit of food from its own mouth into the mouth of the other . . ." she said.

"Ugh!"

"*Ugh* maybe to you, Charlie—but not to them. For the ants, it's how they tell each other who they are—not just a way of saying *hello*—but of saying *this is me*. That's what's going on all over this field, right now. All the ants in creation are walking up to each other and saying: *this is me—who are you?*"

Lily had been kneeling—I had been hunkering. Now we sat back and watched the anthill.

"Because they keep exchanging food," Lily said, "every ant who lives in there will taste the same when they greet every other. And every ant who comes along that path will also taste the same. And if they don't—well, it's best not to think about it."

"Why?"

"Because, when an ant doesn't taste right, that means he's a stranger. And strangers don't fare well in the world of ants any more than they do in the world of people." She reminded me of Freda's experience in the town.

"What happens, then, if it doesn't taste right?"

"It's driven off," she said.

This imagery had not yet entered my lexicon.

"Driven off in a motor car, you mean?" I was looking down at the ant path, wondering if such a thing as an ant car existed.

Lily lay back on the blanket and laughed. She laughed until I thought she was going to be ill.

"Oh, Charlie," she gasped. "Oh, Charlie—Charlie! I shall never mind being a stranger again, so long as I'm driven off in a big Rolls-Royce!"

4. On an afternoon in April of 1918, when we were still living at the Newtonberry Arms, Lily dressed me in a sailor suit that was deliberately one size too large. *Economy*, she said. *Economy*, buttoning my equally oversized raincoat and pulling a beret onto my head. Her own clothing then was the usual blue—but whatever had flowed now hung in close to her body. I remember long, slim dresses with long, slim coats and woven hats like helmets made of dyed blue straw. Each of these hats had a peak that leaned out over her eyes. I think she wanted to look somehow like a soldier. Like one who was at war. Thus

attired, and with her umbrella, she led me out of the hotel and walked me up to Bloor Street, where she bought me ice cream and chocolate cake and said: *let's go to the movies.*

There were theatres then in Toronto named for the royal dukes: *The Prince of Wales, The Duke of Kent, The Duke of York* and *The Duke of Gloucester.* As theatres, these were all quite small. More than likely, the buildings had originally served in some other capacity—as shoe stores or cafés. The auditoriums were not yet raked as they came to be in the glory days of movie palaces. Consequently the audience sat in rows of wooden seats that were so uncomfortable they might have been designed for penitents in a monastery.

Lily always tried for seats at the end of a row. If the need should arise for an escape, she wanted every chance to make a quick exit. Her seizures were increasingly rare—as I remember—though of course my experience of them was uniquely my own. It was only later, when grown, that I learned of their appalling frequency in her younger years. Maturity, her doctors told her, often brings some relief to those who suffer such *disabilities.* Mother hated this word. *I am* not *disabled,* she would say. *I am merely hampered.*

On that April afternoon in 1918, the theatre Mother chose was The Duke of York, on Yonge Street north of Bloor. It was showing a Chaplin film called *Shoulder Arms* and a film with Theda Bara called *Salome.* It was from this, I think, that Lily got her dance with the veils. I remember Theda Bara's flamboyance and I remember the head of John the Baptist on a tray. It was wonderfully dramatic—and several people cried out in horror. In the Chaplin film, he played an enlisted doughboy who couldn't master his rifle—or, as usual, his trousers. They kept falling down—as did everything else around him. I thought this was riotously funny. Lily did not laugh. She had been sobered by *Salome,* and by the newsreels, the latter showing the dreadful realities that Chaplin spoofed. I was too young to believe that what I was seeing in the newsreel had not been staged—like everything else we saw at the movies.

The music at The Duke of York was played by a woman who always wore a silver grey hat. This hat was not unlike a fedora—smaller, but having the fedora's brim and crown. It was worn straight on—no characteristic angle—and it gave the woman the same authority a tam-o'-shanter gives a Scot. Once seen, never forgotten.

She appeared to be in her late thirties and she always wore, besides the hat, the same pale coat—pearl grey—and a pair of gloves. I never understood the gloves. Perhaps they kept her fingers warm. Whenever she prepared to play the national anthem, with which each programme began, she would remove the gloves with elaborate ceremony—finger by finger by finger. Also removed at this moment was a quantity of rings and two or three jangling silver bracelets which she laid on the piano one by one, as if to display her wealth.

She was small, this woman, with a round, corseted figure and a back held in place with whalebone stays. She stood and sat like the statue of a revered national hero—masculine and noble. Exercising a born conductor's authority, she would enter before the lights went down, remove the gloves and rings while staring around the auditorium—make a gesture much as to say: *please rise*—and as we did, she would commence *God Save the King*, which she had mastered in a standing position.

Just before *Salome* was about to begin, a young man with water-plastered hair stepped forward—obviously out of breath—bowed to the silent audience and raised a bow to a violin. The next thing we knew, he had played the first six notes of the national anthem . . .

"I've already done that," said the woman in the fedora. "Sit down."

"Yes, ma'am," the violinist said and, drawing a wooden chair from behind the piano, he sat in it, facing the screen. The pianist hit middle A with her finger and the violinist responded in perfect pitch. Behind us, we heard the projector stammer into action and *Salome* began to flicker to life on the screen. The violin began to sing.

What we heard cannot be described any other way. It was music rising, so it seemed, from a human throat.

The young man might have been humming a contralto tune for all we could tell. I was mesmerized and mystified. I barely saw the beginning of the film at all. I could not take my eyes from the young man's figure.

At seven and a half, a person's attention wanders if the activities up on the screen are remorselessly adult. Whatever Theda Bara's interest in John the Baptist involved, it did not involve me. Not at first, at any rate. There were endless languishings on balconies and stairways, along the railings of which Theda Bara laid her bare arms while making eyes at a variety of young men in very little clothing. She carried a rose in her mouth in at least one scene and I can remember wondering why its thorns didn't puncture her lips and drag her out of what seemed to be an endless lethargy. Her heavy-lidded eyes were always half-closed, suggesting sleep. This, no doubt, was her famous *vamping*—but it was entirely lost on me.

What did hold my attention was the music. The lady in the hat sat up so straight before the piano, she was like a mechanical man I had seen in one of the arcades where Lily went to buy her cigarettes. The mechanical man was turbaned and he wore a "diamond" pinned to his tie. If you put a penny into the slot beneath his glass booth, he would tell your fortune. His torso never moved—only his head and arms were animated. He waved his mechanical hands above a deck of cards laid out before him, while his head moved up and down and sideways, as though he were studying your future. A bell would ring, all at once, and down your printed fortune would fall, through a little chute. Suddenly as his mechanical deliberations had begun—they ended. *Ding!*

Now, in the shaded light that shone upon her at The Duke of York, the lady in the hat was performing her music just as if someone had inserted a penny and thrown her into gear. Her arms reached out towards the keyboard and her hands moved up and down—up and down—up and down, with no sense of tempo and no sense of volume. And yet, she never lost her place and she never missed a cue. She even provided pauses, in which she drank from a porcelain cup that rested without a saucer at the soprano end of the keyboard.

As for the violinist, he was not yet twenty, but older than sixteen, I surmised. He wore a white shirt and a green bow-tie and he rested the violin beneath his chin on a red square of cloth that matched his wide, elastic suspenders. In contrast to the piano player, his shoulders and his back were extensions of his instrument—lifting and falling, leaning into the music the way a swimmer leans through the water towards his destination.

Tangos, fandangos, pavannes and sarabands were played that afternoon—fantasies, rhapsodies and marches. Also, towards the end—in keeping with the fate Miss Bara had foisted on John the Baptist—the violin sang an extended *liebestod* that caused much sobbing.

When the lights came up after *Shoulder Arms* and it was time for us to go, I noticed that Lily seemed to be disoriented. Instead of heading up the aisle towards the rear of the theatre, and thus, its lobby—she began to walk towards the wall to the right of us, where I could see there was no exit. In the meantime, the two musicians had also risen and, switching off their lamps, they were preparing to go backstage until the next performance. The woman in the hat was making a show of putting on her rings and bracelets.

The wall towards which my mother was heading was hung from top to bottom with heavily draped brocade. I cannot tell why this should have been, but perhaps the cloth was standing in for wallpaper. Desperately trying to find an opening through which to exit, Lily became entangled in this curtain and very quickly began to panic.

She was, of course, enduring the vision of flames that preceded her seizures. The whirlwind must have been rising. Under the impression the curtain was on fire, she had moved towards it either to stifle the flames or to save the people who were trapped inside. I had seen all this before and I knew more or less what to do.

Above all, she must not be surrounded by hordes of inquisitive people. That was rule number one. I began to pull at her skirts and sleeves to see if I could turn her away from the wall before the seizure struck her down. But she would not turn around. In fact, she struck at me and knocked me to the floor.

No sooner had I fallen than the violinist was there.

"May I help you?" he said. "Is there something I can do?" His violin case was in his hand.

"Yes," I said. "My mother is sick. Any minute she's going to start yelling."

"I see," the man said. "Okay. Let's get her out of here."

By now, I was on my feet and he thrust the violin in my face. "Carry this," he said, "and follow me."

Lily was making her strangled noises. Her head had started its backward plunge to the floor. I was terrified.

The violinist caught her and, not being very large himself, he almost dropped her. Finally, he draped her over his shoulder and staggered with her towards the steps that led backstage.

Playing doorman—failing entirely to acknowledge my presence—the woman in the fedora stepped in behind the young man and caught Lily's head in her hand. "What is it this time?" she said to him. "Another pregnant ladyfriend?"

"No, Mother," the violinist said, very nearly out of breath. "This woman is a perfect stranger."

We were walking now along a semi-darkened corridor with a cement floor and many closed doors.

"She doesn't look like a stranger to me," said the woman in the hat. "Hanging across your back like that, she looks downright familiar."

"No, Mother—no. Would you please let me in?"

The woman in the hat went ahead of him and opened the door to a small red room filled with mirrors. The light switch was on the wall in the hall and as she leaned out to turn it on, I could see the man beyond her laying Mother down on a narrow cot. Lily's body was arching now. The convulsions had begun.

About to shut the door, the woman in the hat all at once caught sight of me.

"Who the hell are you?" she asked.

"Charlie Kilworth," I said. "I belong with her." I nodded at Lily, who was now in the throes of a violent seizure.

"You know what to do about this?" the woman asked. She seemed amazingly calm.

"Yes," I said, and crossed the room.

"Don't you drop that violin," she said.

"No, ma'am."

"There's a life in that violin," she insisted. "Hand it over here."

I did so and went to kneel on the floor beside Lily.

The man said: "does it last for long?"

"No," I told him. "And when it's over, she'll want a blanket."

The woman in the fedora was filling her porcelain cup from a bottle. She seemed almost divorced from the rest of the scene. Before she drank, she removed the hat and sat down. I heard a long, long sigh.

"Well," she finally said, "you never know what the cat's going to drag in next . . ."

No, I guess not.

We settled down and waited for it to be over.

This way, we had our first encounter with Neddy Harris and his mother, Ada. They would be a part of our lives until their own were over.

5. Neddy Harris was seventeen when we met. Seventeen, about to be eighteen. One of his many "ladyfriends," as Ada called them, had already handed him the infamous white feather. He wore it stuck into the brim of his peaked tweed cap for all the world to see. It was not that he didn't care—only that he knew his own intentions regarding the War. The minute he was eighteen, Neddy Harris would be *gone for a soldier*, as one of the songs then had it.

Ada made fervent daily prayers in his behalf, kneeling wherever the spirit moved her, to beg the gods to spare her son and let the War be ended before his moment came. She would do this in the most unlikely places—never in churches or the privacy of her own rooms. I saw her fall to her knees in Child's Restaurant, in public parks and even on streetcars. She would enjoin her fellow diners, strollers or riders to kneel alongside her, making a chain with linked hands while she led them all in prayer. *Who but a cretin could fail to do so?* This was Ada's blackmail. Down they all went.

Ada's voice had a quaver in it and her words took on the rhythms and the notes of songs. *Oh all ye gods of mercy and forgiveness,* she would pray, *lend us your ears and grant us your attentions. Look upon Edward, my son, and tell us how it should be that one so blessed and talented should be fed into the cannon's mouth and blasted to Kingdom come!*

Neddy would ride out these storms of piety without apparent embarrassment, but when they were over and all had risen to consume their soup, walk their dogs or continue on to their destinations, he would lean far back in his place and say to Ada: "you'll have to rework that bit about being fed into the cannon's mouth, Mother. It sounds too much like a circus act . . ."

On the occasion of our first meeting, it became quite clear that Neddy Harris was already intrigued with Lily. He stroked her wrists and stared and stared as she lay there beneath her blanket. The blanket had been got from the manager's office where it was kept, along with a phial of smelling salts. Ladies overcome with fainting spells often had need of such things during the movies shown at The Duke of York. During *Birth of a Nation*, nurses had been hired. Signs were posted: *NURSE IN ATTENDANCE!* This of course brought people thronging through the doors.

When the time came for Neddy to rejoin Ada for the next showing of *Salome*, Neddy Harris stood up and leaned in over Mother and kissed her on the mouth. I was astounded, never having seen such a kiss performed in real life. Kisses on the lips had thus far been reserved, in my experience of them, for actors on the screen—or for ants on greeting one another.

"You stay here," he said to me, as if I was Tom Mix with a gun. "And make sure she doesn't leave."

I stared at him blankly. No one but Lily had ever spoken to me that way before. Not even Malahide or Eliza at Munsterfield. Worse than this, when he took up his violin and left the room, he locked the door behind him.

"Where are we now?" Mother said, as she began to awaken from her sleep.

"In a room somewhere behind the screen," I told her. *Locked in*, I almost added—but knew better. A locked door was anathema. If someone else was in charge of the key, it threw her into immediate panic.

"What are we doing here?" She was trying to sit up.

"You were ill," I said. "They've let you lie down here until you're better."

"Is there anything to drink?"

There was a sink, but the taps only gave off a rusty dribble and started banging. Nothing more was forthcoming. I shut them off.

"There's something in a bottle," I said—and brought it to her.

She propped herself up on one elbow and took Ada's bottle in her other hand.

"Gin," she said.

I had thought it looked like water.

"See if you can open it," she said. "I'm too fuzzy at the moment . . ."

She leaned back against the single pillow, which had no cover—only ticking—and I pried the cork loose as best I could. When Lily drank, she made a face and then smiled. "Good," she said—and fell, at once, into another sleep.

I retrieved the bottle and took a mouthful—quite unprepared for its fiery effect in my throat. It was dreadful tasting—but after a moment, when it began to work its magic on my nerves, I thought: *yes—that was good*—and drank some more.

Later that night, the night clerk of the Newtonberry Arms Hotel was awakened from his slumber behind the front desk to find two tipsy women, a drunken child and a youth whose tweed cap sported a small white feather—two-stepping one by one through the lobby.

"Don't say a word," the young man said to the astounded watcher as he led his charges dancing towards the stairs. "We don't want to wake the manager."

*   *   *

In the morning, we made our final Newtonberry escape.

Lily, recovered by dawn, gathered the rosewood chair and table, her Japanese vanity and the inlaid box with its cargo of perfume bottles, silver birds, hairbrush, mirror, framed photographs and the blue glass cruet and lowered them out of the window to the yard below. Six leather travelling bags of clothing followed. She then descended the rope herself, and carried each item through the yard out into the delivery lane beyond the high board fence. *St Mary-Margaret forever!* she had said to me, climbing over the sill. Shades of Eleanor Ormond.

When Lily was back inside the room, she checked to make sure that everything we owned had been removed. Satisfied, she dressed me once again in my sailor suit, raincoat and beret and said to me: "we will now walk down the stairs and leave by the front door. I won't have anyone saying we absconded in the night . . ."

On the bureau she left an envelope containing one month's rent—a tip for the maid—and a note that said: *GOING AND WILL NOT RETURN. SINCERELY, L.T. KILWORTH.*

Taking up the wicker suitcase, into which she had repacked the lasso, she took my hand and led me to the door.

Now, at last, she leaned down and kissed me. Smiling, she held her finger to her lips.

"Don't say a word," she told me. "We don't want to wake the manager."

Our life at the Newtonberry Arms was ended—and our life at number 84 St George Street was about to begin.

6. St George Street runs north and south between Dupont and College in what has long been known as the Annex. It is a district near the University of Toronto with large Victorian

houses that were meant to have been the flagships of the upper-middle class. But in late-nineteenth- and early-twentieth-century Toronto, the classes kept outdoing one another—even outdoing themselves—and a good many large-sized houses were built and abandoned within a year or two by families on the upward spiral.

Number 84 St George was one such house. It had been given a manorial name by its original owner—a man in hardware. He called it *Ecclefechin*. This was in honour of the town in Scotland from which he had emigrated. But no one could pronounce the word, and the house became simply *Number 84*—an address that, in time, took on its own manorial ring.

Rambling, spacious, with suites of rooms inhabited by wealthy widows and professors emeriti, it offered two separate dining-rooms—one with potted palms—three withdrawing-rooms and two parlours. It was also possessed of wide green lawns and gardens that were tended by wounded veterans of the War still raging. Their injuries were mostly to the spirit and thus invisible. They had, we learned over time, been variously buried alive, gassed, half-drowned in mud or deafened by shell fire.

A palpable silence enveloped these men as they worked. They were attired in green canvas aprons and dark green trousers which gave the appearance of a uniform. At their head, a man of sixty-odd years—once a gardener at Kew—led them through their duties the way he might have instructed children—raking, digging, pulling weeds and cutting deadheads. Six of these young men had been hired to care for the grounds at Number 84—which gives an idea of its size. It gives no idea, however, of the haunted presence of those men, who often—as I witnessed—stood frozen on the grass and wept.

Mother was clever at playing the lady. To begin with, she clothed herself—and me—with flawless taste. That she favoured dark colours gave the impression of a genteel tragedy hovering in her background. Perhaps a dead hero had been her husband—perhaps my father had worn the Victoria Cross. Who could tell? And who would ask?

The question was rarely put.

A person's grief and mourning—especially during that time of war—were private matters and to be respected without hesitation. Mother had a way with sighs that said all this, though not a word was ever spoken concerning her "bereavement." I had been taught how to bite my lip so that a tear could appear in my eye if the word *father* was ever mentioned out of hand. The phrase: *and who was your father, my brave little man?* had a triple response that we could produce in seconds: *my bitten lip, my tear, Lily's sigh.* The answer was never given.

Meanwhile, Lily's quest for who my father might have been continued. I have vivid memories of her laying out *solitaire* hands of photographs at Number 84, just as she had at the Newtonberry Arms. This way, we took up residence amongst the aging widows of other wars and the dons of another age in April of 1918. It was to be my home through a time of wonder—and disaster.

7. Lily's private joy at Number 84—and my private fear—lay in the fact that our suite of rooms had a fireplace. We had our own bath and WC, our own sitting-room and a bedroom each for Lily and me. The fireplace was in the sitting-room which meant, at least, that I had more access to it than I might have, had it been in Lily's bedroom.

Our windows overlooked the long side of the garden and the window from my bedroom overlooked the terraced lawns at the rear of the house. Through a door that opened off the sitting-room, there was a small, shaded balcony with a balustrade and an awning. The awning had blue stripes on a green field. Lily's colours. Flying for all to see.

In April, 1918, the War—which now we know would be over in November of that year—gave no appearance of ever coming to an end. For all the wonders inherent in the burgeoning world of

May, the feeling in the air was one of universal despair. The leaves that were now about to burst upon the trees might just as well have been shells about to burst upon our landscape. When the birds returned, they were greeted with silent lawns over which a muted population walked in apprehension. No one had understood there could be so much death.

The casualty lists in the papers that once had been a cause for private mourning were now so long that whole communities were stricken. The story was told of an entire class of boys from one Toronto school being wiped out together during the Battle of Lys fiasco. Day by day, week by week, the lists proliferated. The dreaded yellow cablegrams that arrived to tell of a death or wound were now so numerous, some were delayed and did not arrive before a parent found a son's name in a public notice.

A large group of black-clad women—the mothers, sisters, aunts and grandmothers of these dead boys—paraded down Bay Street and stood in silent protest before City Hall. They carried the flags of the province, the country, of Britain and of France and they trailed them through the dust, finally spreading and standing on them in mute anguish. That evening, in the twilight, the women faded away, leaving their emblems of despair behind them. In the dark, a group of city clerks came through the doors and down the steps with canvas bags and brooms. By midnight, the flags were gone and the sidewalks swept of every trace of grief. Not a word was said. Not even *amen*.

In her bedroom, Lily brooded by candlelight. She took up making entries again in the notebooks she had abandoned after my birth in 1910. Though I had no notion what she was writing until the notebooks surfaced in the wicker suitcase now before me, I am absolutely convinced the decline they describe was triggered by the presence of the fireplace at Number 84. She kept these pages locked in the inlaid box whose key she wore with her other keys on a chain around her neck.

Now, in my eighth year of life, keys were still forbidden to me. Lily's fear apparently prompted the belief that I might prove to be her warder—and lock her in, if I possessed a key. That I might turn the key against her and bring *the authorities* to steal her freedom.

These fears were not universal from day to day, but only in her darkest moments—when the silence fell and she took up her pen.

He was here again, she wrote on the twelfth of May, 1918. *Charlie was bedded and the doors between us closed. I said: I don't understand how you found me, though I knew that of course he could find me no matter where I was. He is probably watching now as I write these words. If so, then I tell him once more:* I CANNOT COME WITH YOU YET. THERE IS MORE THAT MUST BE DONE.

He had the same burnt-over look, his clothes all hanging down in shreds. His hair had been cut away in patches. Of what remained, the strands were tangled—some of them weeping over his forehead, the fringes singed—and his scalp a mass of scars . . .

He never speaks. He never speaks.

I don't know where to hide.

He never stands behind me, always where I can see—must see—his dreadful wounds and feel the heat of his presence.

Sometimes he is on fire—but I have no way of putting out the flames . . .

I know, I know who this man is.

I know, I know—but I dare not speak his name.

Once named, he will know I know him and then he will know that I cannot resist.

Last night, I went into the sitting-room and wrote his name on the back of a card that was on the mantelpiece. I will not write it here, where he can see it. I dare not.

I held the card to my forehead. He hadn't followed me. He couldn't see this.

Go, I said. And I set his name on fire.

When I returned to this room, he was gone.

These Gothic visitations might have been written by Mary Shelley or Horace Walpole.

Again in the night—at 3:00 A.M., *with a burning book in his hand* . . . is how another of Lily's entries begins.

And: *he has tried to wrench the keys on their chain from around my neck. I cannot bear his presence any longer. There are burns where his fingers held me* . . .

And: *Charlie has come to the door, and only his knocking drove my tormentor away* . . .

Knocking is hardly the word. On more than one occasion I went to the door and pounded on it. In her dreaming—or her nightmares or her seizures—Lily would cry out and babble words that, as always, had no connection to any language I recognized. Except once. Once, I distinctly heard a name. *John.*

John.

John. Repeated, and then cut off in mid-syllable, as if a hand had suddenly covered her mouth.

But she never let me through, and if she spoke anything coherently, it was only and ever to tell me: *thank you, Charlie. All is well. You may go back to bed now.*

Thank you, Charlie.

All is well.

You may go back to bed now.

I never did. Not ever, when these episodes occurred. I would bring a blanket and pillow and make my "bed" by the door. If fires had been lit, I could always smell the smoke, and then I would pull my day clothes over my pyjamas, just in case we would have—yet again—to escape.

As for the reference to *burns where his fingers held me*, it was true. What seemed to be burn marks had appeared on her neck. My own interpretation is that Lily must have made them herself, pulling at the key chain in panic.

These were spring nights I describe, when Lily wrote in her notebooks. Our windows all stood open and the warm air teemed with peeper song and distant music. Distant, and not so distant. Someone played the piano next door—people sang and records spun. But the music was pensive—some of it noble—all of it sad. One night, not a great while after we had been ensconced at

Number 84, a violin began to sing in the dark beyond the casement. It sang and sang—and I thought, in my bed, I will never hear such songs again. It sang *I Love You Truly* and it sang *Love's Old Sweet Song* and it sang *On the Banks of the Wabash Far Away* . . .

I heard the key being turned between my bedroom and the sitting-room. I heard the door being opened onto the balcony. I heard the words: *but soft, what light through yonder window breaks* . . . ? I heard all this before I slept.

My mother's midnight visitors were not all phantoms, it seems. One of them played the violin and wore a cap with a small white feather in its peak.

8. Once, when I had been asleep long enough to dream, I suddenly woke up and knew that something was happening. Beyond the sitting-room door there were voices. Not the desperate *voices* of Lily's previous encounters. She was laughing. Neddy, I thought, must have told her a joke. I heard her say distinctly: *oh, you are terrible!* in the way that people do with mock offence.

"No," Neddy said—and he was laughing, too. "I'm *wonderful*, Lil—and I can't believe two wonderful people shouldn't get together . . ."

Their voices then became indistinct and I began to drift again to sleep. But before I slept the second time, I watched the light beneath the door—and I swear their shadows were dancing.

In the spring of 1918, Lily closed the doors with Neddy Harris inside more than once. This is not to say that, inside or outside, Neddy succeeded in his quest to seduce my mother—*during the first reel,* as he put it. The impression I have of a longer pursuit cannot be entirely wrong. There were just too many occasions when Neddy came to woo her for me to believe that his wooing was anything but ardent in the absolute sense. If success was already his, he would not have been so persistent. That, at any rate, is my belief.

Very often, there was the same charmed laughter I had heard on the first occasion. Whatever else, they shared a teasing, wistful sense of humour. Lily would say: *why would a nice girl like me go out with a wild boy like you* . . . ? And: *gentlemen never put down their violins in the presence of a lady* . . .

But—in time—she would have him as her lover—of that I'm certain. She had placed him already in a league with Lizzie Wyatt. You couldn't get better billing than that with Lily Kilworth.

9. Through the War years—barring Ede's occasional visits— we didn't see a great deal of the Wyatt family. Once—only once—we were all together under one roof. This was at the Massey Music Hall, on the night of December 14th, 1917—when Lily and I were still at the Newtonberry Arms. The occasion was a War Rally, with a multitude of entertainers and standing-room only in the house. All the surviving Wyatts and all the surviving Kilworths—even Malahide—were there. Two of them were on the stage—my mother's detested sisters.

Annie, that year, was twelve—a shy, tiny child with serious eyes. She never smiled, and she hated what she had been asked to do. But she did it—namely, play *an English rose* in the tableau that marked the First Act Finale. Sister Alice—ever precocious, ever dancing, ever wide-eyed and ever conniving—got to skip across the stage as one of the fairies attending Madame Emma Albani's astonishing Titania—astonishing because the Diva was in her seventies. She had consented to appear only because she was not required to sing, merely to *show herself*. Her Oberon was thirty years her junior, and at that, too old for the Fairy King. All of this was in aid of an orchestral performance of three selections for Mendelssohn's incidental music for *A Midsummer Night's Dream*.

When Madame Albani—smiling a lacquered smile and bound unto death in whalebone—showed herself to the audience, she received a standing ovation—which Alice at once appropriated as her own. Dazzled by the applause, she dropped the Diva's train—and curtseyed. The audience—some of us excluded—were so charmed by this, they laughed and pointed at her, *oohing* and *aahing—isn't she sweet!* Alice beamed. It was to be her first—and last—laugh.

It had been a dreadful year—capped by the devastating Halifax explosion the week before the concert. Sixteen hundred and fifty-four lives had been lost. The destruction was beyond imagining.

In November, the Bolshevik Revolution had begun in Russia, when the battleship *Aurora* fired its guns at Petrograd and rebellious troops had stormed the Winter Palace. The Tsar had already abdicated in March. Russia was gone as our ally. Civilization seemed to be in a state of collapse. When the battle of Passchendaele—begun in July—ended on November 10th, there had been 400,000 British casualties—among them an alarming number of Canadians. The only good news of that whole year—aside from America's declaration of war on Germany—had been the great Canadian victory at Vimy Ridge in May.

There we sat—and stood—four thousand strong in all our splendour—under the scalloped ceilings and fluted arches of the Massey Music Hall, caught in all its shimmering lights—mourning our dead—shouting our approval—singing our anthems and applauding our stars. Mother hated it, but she was mesmerized. *The lights,* she kept saying, *the lights—and all that white . . .*

All that white was us.

Looking up from where we sat at the end of a row in the orchestra, I could see Ede and Frederick, Lyon and Alice (who had given her performance)—sitting in one of the boxes above the stage. Ede wore a blue so pale it could not be seen beneath the beading on her breast and shoulders. In her hair, some egret feathers had been pinned with sapphires. Her long satin gloves had been rolled from her fingers, and tucked with diamond bracelets—and all her rings in a knuckled row sparkled and shone. Lyon—as though he, too, wore a costume—was a handsome *sailor boy*, middied and tied in white and blue—a surprising choice for a lad of sixteen. Alice had retained her fairy wings of Chantilly lace and her ringlets had sparkles in them. White—white—white.

To one side, above them, Franklin and Caroline, Harry and Maude were seated in another box—Maude demure in pale mauve, Caroline sumptuous in flowing organdie—white on white—each of their husbands, as was Frederick, dressed impeccably in white boiled shirts, white ties and cobalt studs and cufflinks. Their coats had silk lapels, adorned with white carnations.

Bright light—and white, Lily wrote. *One might have thought we were there to surrender!* And, indeed, in some way we had. We had buckled under the weight of all that propaganda: yes, we will give our energy—yes, we will give our money—yes, we will give our sons to kill and be killed by the Kaiser's sons! We will sing *God Save the King* and *Land of Hope and Glory* and, when the singing is done, we will give our voices over to *The Burial of the Dead*: The War gave, and the War hath taken away. Blessed be the Name of the War . . .

Bright, bright—and white.

The Kilworth clan were installed in a block of seats to the left of the stage, diagonally opposite the Wyatt boxes. Eliza, as matriarch, was seated in the front row, next to the pillar. The stage was not more than twelve feet away from her. Diagonally opposite were the Wyatt boxes.

Eliza did not wear white. She wore silver. Silvered lace over a dark blue velvet gown. James had been dead, now, five years—but Eliza still kept turning, as though she expected him to be there. Behind her, Willa sat with three of her children. The rest were too young to attend, and had remained at home with their father. Willa was gaining weight again, but whether it was because of gluttony or another pregnancy, a person could not tell. She wore, predictably, a garish yellow gown that made her look like an ill-costumed character in a farce. Malahide—awkward and squirming in his late father's evening clothes—was her escort.

Lily and I were not seated with the clan, Lily having already turned down Ede's invitation to sit in one of the Wyatt boxes. She had also been nervous of sitting with Eliza, lest the subject of my father should be raised. Eliza had made it her business to *press and press and press* the return of his name to Lily's memory and the pressing had become a kind of badgering. Consequently, we had taken aisle seats, from which we could escape at a moment's notice.

I might have been Lyon's negative twin. Lily had dressed me in my oversized navy blue sailor suit—dark as his was light. Lily herself wore a long, slim gown that accentuated her height. It was completely unadorned—and grey, the colour of smoke.

Liam did not show up until a moment before Eva Willard's entrance. He was standing under the balcony, right of the stage, where he could see, but not be seen by the performers. On the other hand, Eliza could see him—and so could we. Just. He wore a somewhat old-fashioned version of evening dress—a tailcoat with square-cut tails and squared lapels. His hair, now thinning, had lost its sheen, and his skin was pale and mottled.

Eva Willard had reached the pinnacle of her career. She was called *The Lily Maid of Song*—which made Mother laugh—and *The Angel Patriot*—the latter because of her war work. She had sung to the troops in France. In England, her *Nights* (and *Days*) *of Song* had been performed with great success in convalescent hospitals for the wounded. The Prince of Wales had attended one of her concerts in uniform. Little Eva Willard had become a very large star.

And everywhere that Eva went, a Wyatt went with her.

On the night of December 14th, 1917, all the Wyatts and all the Kilworths were gathered in her aura.

Her entrance was greeted with ecstatic cries of *Eva! Angel! Lily Maid!* and flowers were thrown—all white—as she made her way to centre stage and the waiting Wyatt grand. Her accompanist was an older man whose name—so the programme informs me—was Ambrose Taylor.

Eva must have been all of thirty-six that night. She reminded me of Mary Pickford—tiny and childlike, painted and dyed. Her long white sleeves had been designed to hide the girth of her arms and her neck was hidden in a dozen layers of buoyant chiffon. The effect of this costume was much the same as the effect of Alice's fairy garb—everything floated—everything shone—everything hid the body beneath its folds. Her hair, again like Mary's, was ringleted and girlish—but, unlike Mary's, it was almost white with yellow dyes. Her cheeks were rouged. Her eyes were the eyes of a child who is constantly "surprised." But her lips were the lips of manly dreams—scarlet and wet and pursed for kissing.

But—Little Eva Willard could sing.

Standing in cathedral lighting, *The Lily Maid of Song, The Angel Patriot*, raised the roof of Massey Hall that night with *Pack Up Your Troubles* and *Tipperary*. She sang *Over There* and *You're in the Army, Now!* for our American cousins as the Stars and Stripes were paraded on stage. She broke our hearts with *Keep the Home Fires Burning* and she lifted them again with *Roses of Picardy* and *The Bells of St Mary's*. At the end, she got us all standing up to sing with her—and we roared *For Me and My Gal* and we shouted *Hail! Hail! The Gang's All Here!* until it seemed the chandeliers would fall.

When she left the stage, there was another cascade of flowers—all white—and a ringing of all her names: *Angel! Angel! Lily Maid! Eva!*—over and over and over again, until at last she had to come back out to break our hearts again with *The Minstrel Boy to the Wars Has Gone.*

It was then that Liam turned away and left.

I remember all this. I remember it well. And so, for whatever reason, did Lily. It was she, after all, who kept the souvenir programme. On its cover, decorated with portraits of the King and Queen, surrounded by golden maple leaves—she had written the words with which I began this memory: *Once—only once—we were all together.*

All that singing—and all that white—so long ago.

10. Because there was a law forbidding theatres to open on Sundays in Toronto, Sundays became our *days of riot and song.*

There were four of us, now. We had become a family—Neddy and Ada, Lily and me. We called ourselves *The Wabash Gang*, because *On the Banks of the Wabash* was Ada's favourite song.

Of course, there could be no riots at Number 84. Not, at any rate, the kind of riots we indulged in. Much gin was consumed—Ada played the piano and Neddy played the fiddle. (*Violins* were also banned on Sundays. This was Neddy's edict.) Lily recited poetry and did the cakewalk. I was variously Charlie Chaplin and Douglas Fairbanks. We all sang songs. It was wonderful—but definitely not Number 84. Consequently, *The Wabash Gang* convened at Number 37 Alcott Street, where Ada lived with Neddy in a boarding-house.

The boarding-house was owned and run by a woman whose early life had been spent in the circus. She had been a *horseback dancer*—a tumbler, who one day fell and was injured in such a way that she was forced into the role of wardrobe mistress. Now, in her sixties, she had retired from *the world of lights*—and was "mother" to a houseful of entertainers. Her name was Nora Gresham—once known as *The Pony Girl.*

She limped, but only slightly, and had put on a good deal of weight. Cigarettes had ruined her breathing—and in the silences between our songs we could hear her wheezing in the dining-room, setting the tables for supper. Mrs Gresham enjoyed our riots and gave us a good deal of leeway—*so long as you don't bring in the neighbours.* We never did, though neighbourhood children would sometimes gather on the sidewalk to listen to our singing.

Lily and I would arrive after lunch in the afternoon and stay until supper had been eaten. There was a piano in the parlour and we rolled back the rug so we could dance. Ada broke loose from her eternal grey and greeted us in yellow, orange or red kimonos—worn over a second kimono of another colour. She continued to play the *grande dame*—organizing our riots as though the whole world were in her charge—*you do this and you do that, and we'll all . . .* but there was fun in her voice and we were all obedient.

Lily would forsake Mrs Browning and give dramatic readings of story poems, with gestures.

> *The wind was a torrent of darkness*
> *among the gusty trees,*
> *The moon was a ghostly galleon*
> *tossed upon cloudy seas.*
> *The road was a ribbon of moonlight*
> *over the purple moor,*
> *And the highwayman came riding—*
> *Riding—riding—*
> *The highwayman came riding, up to the old inn-door.*

When *Bess, the landlord's daughter* started *plaiting a dark red love-knot into her long black hair,* Lily plaited. And when *she loosened her hair i' the casement,* Lily undid the plait and shook her hair out to one side. We all had to *tlot-tlot, tlot-tlot* with the palms of our hands slapping our knees whenever the *horse-hoofs ringing clear* were heard—and we all had to blow and hum like *the wind is in the trees* and we all had to *tap with our whips on the shutters* when they were *locked and barred.* It was very exciting, and very theatrical. We had certainly been to the movies often enough to get the melodrama right.

Lily also read Robert Browning's *Incident of the French Camp*—at the end of which I had been schooled to participate. When *smiling, the boy fell dead*—I did it rather well, falling backwards onto some pillows—with the widest grin I could manage. This inevitably brought applause.

That Mother enjoyed these days of riot and song goes without saying. We all did, and it was then that the bonding of Lily and Neddy was most familiar—and familial. It became an accepted ingredient of all our lives. Because of my days and nights at the movies, I was more comfortable than I might have been with the subject of *romance.* Seeing my mother holding

Neddy's hand—watching them as they danced, I could believe—and did—that they were merely echoing the gestures of Mae Marsh and Richard Barthlemess in *Blossom Time*. I did not, however, fully comprehend the sexual connotations of their friendship.

Yes. Of their friendship.

That was still my word for it.

When I say that a great deal of gin was drunk, I mean that most of it was consumed by Ada Harris. Lily and Neddy drank on the sidelines, so to speak. They would sit together on a tall-backed Victorian sofa with the pale blue glasses Mrs Gresham provided in hand, and nudge each other knowingly as Ada became increasingly sentimental and—finally—tearful.

"Play me my song," she would say at the end of every Sunday afternoon. "Play it for me, Neddy—do . . ."

By this time, she would be incapable of playing it herself.

"All right, Mother," Neddy would say—and when he rose, Ada always took his place beside Lily. Sometimes she would take Lily's hand in her own and give it an emotional squeeze.

Neddy would pick up his fiddle and Mother and I would sing the Wabash song, while Neddy's fiddle sang the obligato.

> *Oh the moon is shining bright*
> > *along the Wabash,*
> *From the fields there comes the*
> > *smell of new-mown hay.*
> *Through the sycamores the candlelights*
> > *are gleaming,*
> *On the banks of the Wabash far away.*

As the song was ending, Ada's tears would flow, and all of us would sit—contented—silent—and, so it seemed—fulfilled.

Nora Gresham had a natural ear for cues. Five minutes after the final *far away*, she would come to the door and tell us that our supper was *spread upon the tables* wanting our company.

In the parade that followed, Neddy led the way and I brought up the rear. Lily walked with Ada—side by side and upright. Just. This way, our days of riot and song inevitably ended. Sighing happily—in one another's company.

11. Early in June of 1918, the garden parties began at Number 84. These were held as a matter of course each year, and the residents would be petitioned by various charities to sponsor them. This way, war amputees and orphans, schools for the blind and deaf, various missionary organizations—and the increasingly forceful, seemingly ubiquitous Women's Christian Temperance Union—each had a chance to invite the wealthy and the powerful to join them on the lawns of Number 84, where *afternoon tea will be served by the ladies* of whichever charity had won the day.

Mostly, the garden parties occurred on Sunday afternoons, which meant—if Lily and I attended—giving up our day of riot and song. But: *Sunday*, one of the resident widows stated bluntly, *puts the fear of God into a rich man's heart—and the hand of God into his pocket.*

A marquee would be raised and many tables and chairs set out by the men in green aprons. Flowers would be displayed in large blue vases. Four silver tea services were deployed on damask cloths laid over boards and trestles. The ladies of that day's charity would take turns pouring tea into china cups.

Lily bought herself a wide straw hat with a floppy brim for these occasions. Her only concession to colour would be the red silk peonies with which she adorned the hat, her jacket or her bag. The rouge on her lips was barely discernible.

On Sunday the 16th of June, there was a round of visitors we had not expected. The occasion was a Strawberry Social given by the

Royal Society for Crippled Children. It was the week of Lily's twenty-eighth birthday. The garden parties would last from three in the afternoon till five. The weather that year was extremely kind. It never rained on Sundays.

Lily had sent me back into the house to collect her cigarettes and matches. She was notorious for smoking openly in public—a thing that women *never did*.

Coming back downstairs, I heard the piano in the parlour being played and, going in, discovered that Ada Harris was sitting there in her grey fedora.

"Whoever you are," she said without turning around, "I hope you haven't come to tell me I shouldn't be playing in here. I cannot resist a Wyatt, and this is one of the sweetest I've ever heard."

I said: "hello, Mrs Harris. Is Neddy with you?"

Ada spun the stool and faced me.

"There's a dear boy," she said. "This is not quite like the Sundays we're used to, is it?"

"No," I said. "But the Wabash Gang is here, isn't it?"

"True, but I do miss the gaiety." She glanced at the windows. "*Society* is so dull, isn't it, Charlie. They never seem to have any real fun."

"No, ma'am."

"You play on this?" she said, indicating the Wyatt.

"Sometimes. One finger only."

"Lovely beast, the Wyatt. Best piano made. Did you know that?"

"Yes," I said—speaking so starkly, my answer must have seemed arrogant.

Ada smiled. "Ohhh!" she said. "You do, do you? Well—well. For one so young, you seem to know a lot."

"My grandfather makes them," I told her.

Of course, she did not believe me. Lily never spoke of her Wyatt connections—and if she had heard me calling Frederick *my grandfather* she would have cursed me. Or worse.

Ada was looking at me quizzically. "You putting on airs?" she said, with a dip of her head as she opened her bag.

"No, ma'am," I said. "It's true. Where's Neddy?"

"Neddy's off somewhere," said Ada, producing her flask and muttering. "Pay no attention."

I watched her drink and thought of the hot acid taste of gin and hoped she wouldn't offer me any. Always polite, I would not have known how to refuse. But Ada was Ada, and every drop in her flask was hers. It was not like The Duke of York—or Mrs Gresham's—where the bottles were everyone's.

"Go on," she said, releasing the flask back into her bag and giving the bag a pat. "Sit down and play me something."

"I only use one finger," I reminded her. "It really isn't worth it."

"Charlie, Charlie. You never play at our house. Play me a tune. I'm asking you."

"All right," I said—and went to the piano. I placed Lily's cigarettes on the ledge where Ada's rings and bracelets should have been and gave the stool a spin. Ada had wound it down too low. "What should I play?" I asked.

"Anything you like," she answered.

My mind had gone completely blank. I could think of nothing—not a note.

"Ask for something," I said. "I don't remember any tunes."

"Ask for something . . . Let me see . . ." This was gin-talk. Befuddlement. Ada was off behind me, perched on the arm of a chair. "What about *For Me and My Gal*?" she said.

"I don't know it," I said. We had sung it at Massey Hall with Eva Willard, but I couldn't remember the tune.

"Not know *For Me and My Gal*? Charlie Kilworth!" Ada was laughing.

"Hum it," I said. I was getting impatient, worried that Lily would be angry if I didn't soon return with her cigarettes.

Ada began to sing.

> *The bells are ringing for me and my gal!*
> *The birds are singing for me and my gal!*

Immediately, I began to play. One finger only, of course. But the tune came back to me quickly.

"That's good," Ada said. "Sing along with me, now . . ."

And she began the song again.

"It's much too high," I said. For, though my voice had years to go before it broke, it was never a soprano voice. Mother had wept when she heard me singing, first. *It's Lizzie's voice,* she had said. *Contralto.*

Now Ada said: "all right. Try this . . ."

She pitched the tune a notch or two down, and I began to play again. I also began to sing. But before I had sung the second line, Ada was on her feet and by my side. She had given up the singing altogether—and seemed, I could not tell why, excited.

I stopped playing.

"What's wrong?" I asked.

"Nothing's wrong. Nothing's wrong," said Ada. "You're *wonderful!*"

That was Neddy's word. The one I'd heard through Lily's door. *Wonderful.*

"Why?" I asked.

"Wait a minute. Wait, wait, wait," Ada said. She got out her flask and had a long, deep swallow. She closed her eyes. I was watching her.

Then she began to sing.

> *It rained all night*
> *The day I left,*
> *The weather, it was dry . . .*

I played.

"Stop!"

I stopped.

There was another pause. Then, she sang again—this time higher than her normal range. She almost didn't make it—but she did.

> *Shine on, shine on harvest moon,*
> *Up in the sky.*

> *I ain't had no lovin' since*
> *January, February, June or July.*

I played.

All with one finger. Every note.

"You're a genius!" Ada said. "You're a genius, Charlie Kilworth!"

Then she stood up and began to dance.

This alarmed me. No one at Number 84 would dream of dancing in the parlour on a Sunday afternoon.

"Why?" I asked her—not quite sure what a genius was.

"You have a gift from God, Charlie. Angels must have landed on your cradle!"

"Why?"

"Perfect pitch!" she shouted at me. "*Perfect pitch!*"

I was totally mystified, but secretly pleased. Whatever it was I had, I was obviously destined for greatness. Theda Bara—Charlie Chaplin—and me.

"Every song I sang for you, Charlie—every single one—I put in a different key. And you didn't falter once. *Not once!*" Ada had stopped her dancing and was beaming at me. "We have to go and tell your mother. Tell your mother—and celebrate. A son with perfect pitch is a sign! A sign, I tell you, Charlie. I ought to know. All Neddy has is talent, but what you have is genius! A musician's dream come true!"

That is how I found my gift—my life to be—my place. Not quite eight years old, and destined to be a piano tuner.

12· The entrance to the garden was made through doors in one of the drawing-rooms that opened onto a raised terrace. As we came to these doors, I heard the sound of a gypsy violinist beneath the trees and I turned to Ada expectantly. *Neddy?*

There was not a trace of recognition in her expression.

"Come along, dear," she said, and gave me a gentle pat on the back. "We must find your mother."

Weeping is the word most often used to describe the rhapsodic longing expressed in gypsy music. On the lawns that Sunday afternoon at Number 84, the *weeping* had moved all the way to *sobbing*. It was a glorious, almost ridiculous, sound. Somehow, because the music was so entirely out of place, most of the guests were confounded by what they were hearing and stood with teacups in hand, faintly, nervously smiling—wondering what might be going to happen next. A dance troupe? A famous singer? Surely *someone* was about to make an entrance.

Ada and I had the advantage of the terraced heights as we looked for Lily. Even so, it was quite impossible. Too many wide-brimmed hats were being worn and some of the women had brought along parasols and raised them.

"You go that way, I'll go this," said Ada, pushing me towards the furthest reaches of the garden. "If you find her, tell her nothing. I want to be the Gabriel in this. *Your son has perfect pitch!*" She hurried off into the crowd.

The gypsy violin was still sobbing. A cluster of women was moving towards it en masse. I avoided them.

At the rear of the garden, there was a high board fence masked by a mass of mock orange and lilac trees. In the corner, under a shingled roof, there was a garden house. It was here that the Master of Kew and his crew kept their rakes and spades and edgers, their garden forks and their baskets of trowels and weeding sticks. I have no idea why I went there to look for Lily. It was there—I suppose that's why.

I could hear the party and the violin in what seemed, beneath the trees, to be a kind of distance. Muffled, almost. Clouded. There was a closer sound of crickets. And of voices.

"Mother?"

I stood in front of the door. The door was closed.

The voices fell silent.

"Mother?"

There was no reply.

I opened the door and peered into the gloom.

"Charlie?"

Yes.

She was there with one of the wounded gardeners. He was naked—and so, in a way, was she. Her dress was undone down the front.

I saw this. And I didn't.

The light was bad. Filtered—spotted.

All I could think was: *they've been—or they're going—to the River Nude.*

Even then, I knew it was a crazy thought. But so was what I saw. It made no sense at all.

Finally, I said: "are you all right?"

Lily was doing up her dress. The man had risen to his knees and was trying to pull on his shirt. He was the thinnest man I've ever seen. He was almost skin and bone.

"You shouldn't be here, Charlie."

I wanted to say: *nor should you.* But I didn't.

"What are you doing?" I said.

Lily didn't even think about it.

"Mister Arbuthnot and I are friends. We were talking."

Naked?

I was silent.

Lily continued: "there are things people talk about that don't concern you, Charlie. And this is one of them."

She got to her feet and stood in front of Mister Arbuthnot. He, too, had risen, and had turned his back. He was pulling on his trousers. I knew him, of course. I had seen him in his green apron out on the lawn and working in the flowerbeds. I liked him, though we rarely spoke. He had large black eyes, and I think he was partially deaf. If you had a conversation, he watched your lips. Now, he said nothing.

Lily's wide-brimmed hat with her red silk peonies on it was lying in a wheelbarrow. She picked it up and smoothed her skirts.

"When Mister Arbuthnot is ready," she said, "we will all leave together."

This is what happened.

He put on his apron and ran his fingers through his hair. We were all, as Eliza would have said, *assembled.*

Mother went first.

She took my hand and waited until I was beside her. Then she reached back and took Mister Arbuthnot's hand.

"Ready?"

Yes. And no. But . . .

"Yes," we said.

The three of us, side by side, rejoined the party.

When we reached the first group of guests, Lily said: "Mister Pierce? Mrs Ballantyne? Miss Shenstone? This is my friend, Mister Arbuthnot . . . And my son. Charlie Kilworth."

The effect of this was interesting. Each of the guests was clearly baffled as to why they were being introduced to a gardener. One who, by the light of day, appeared to be unshaven. *Does one shake hands with such a man?* This was Mister Pierce's dilemma. The ladies, of course, need not even consider it.

Mister Pierce looked askance at Mister Arbuthnot.

"Been in the War, have you?"

"Yes," said Lily. "Mister Arbuthnot is unable to hear you."

"I see. Well." Mister Pierce gave a nod at the young man and said: "keep up the good work." His hands, by now, had made their way to his coat-tails, where they rested, safely locked in their folds.

We walked away.

Mister Arbuthnot pulled at Lily's sleeve.

"Please," he said, speaking very clearly. "I want to go, now."

Lily nodded at him, and smiled. She rounded her lips so he could read them. "Goodbye, Mister Arbuthnot. And thank you."

He bobbed his head and turned to me. "Goodbye, Charlie."

"Goodbye."

He went then, back the way we had come. He did not turn round, and I noted that just as he was passing them, Mister Pierce and his party developed a sudden interest in the tea marquee.

Having seen their reaction, Lily shook her head and spoke

sardonically. "Never bother with your betters, Charlie. It isn't worth the effort."

She then took my hand and we moved off over the lawns in search of Ada.

There the violinist stood, rolling his shoulders, dipping his hips as he played. He wore a loose white shirt and tight black trousers and, on his head, a magenta silk kerchief whose ends hung down his back. He made a half-turn, as I watched, and I saw that his eyes were closed. I also saw that, neatly tucked beneath the kerchief's edge, just beside the violinist's left ear, there was a small white feather.

Neddy. Of course.

Lily was stopped in her tracks.

She was watching him with the same amusement I had expected all the others to exhibit. *What are you doing here? You must be mad!* That kind of look. But Lily was alone in producing this reaction. For the rest, there was a continued sense of nervous apprehension. *Am I really looking at a gypsy violinist . . . ?*

Yes.

And no.

At the movie house, Neddy had a keen sense of drama. But this was melodrama—overstated—overstrutted—overplayed. The violin swept too far to the right—and then too far to the left. It was a performance imported from Budapest. Or, perhaps, Bucharest.

Ada, who I suspect had been into her flask more than once since we parted, came and stood beside us.

"Good, isn't he," she said. "I taught him everything."

Wonderful.

Lily took a step towards Neddy.

I wondered if she was going to tell him about Mister Arbuthnot.

Instead, she gave him a kind of curtsey—almost a dance step— almost a bow.

At this precise moment, a voice spoke beyond my right shoulder.

"Hello, Charlie," it said.

It was Ede.

13. Lyon was with her. Annie and Alice. They looked
remarkably beautiful. If I had been able to take a
photograph of that moment, it would have borne all the
traces of its place and time. *This is what upper-class matrons in their
fifties wore in 1918 . . . their children would be presented thus . . .*

Lyon, who was not quite seventeen, was wearing a new blue
suit whose jacket was belted at the back. To deny that Lyon Wyatt
was handsome would do him a gross injustice. He had the Wyatt
hair and eyes, and the squared-off look of one who is self-confi-
dent. His figure was thick and well-proportioned—broad in the
shoulders, narrow at the hips. His one unfortunate feature was his
mouth. He had Frederick's thin, tight lips. "Oh," he said. "So it's
you."

I nodded. "Yes."

They had not yet approached Lily, though Ede without doubt had
seen her. They hovered—and Ada hovered at my other shoulder.

"Charlie?" Ede said, and gave that little cough that people give
when they want an introduction.

"Yes," I said—and turned to Ada. "This is Mrs Harris."

She stepped forward, grey and substantial—reeking of gin.

"This is Mrs Wyatt," I continued, thinking I must not mention
Frederick's name. "This is my uncle, Lyon, and this is . . ."

Annie and Alice had gone to stand behind Ede.

Ede said: "these are my daughters, Mrs Harris." And she drew
them forth.

I had not much experience of Annie Wyatt and Alice. Annie
had always been retiring, watchful and—I thought—resentful of
my existence. Alice, on the other hand, gave a fair performance of
having no idea who anyone was. The world was one big audience—anonymous. She was always looking somewhere else and
fidgeting with her clothes. At the gate, when they entered—since
Neddy's music still filled the air—I'm sure she came in dancing.

Ede drew her furs about her and stepped away. She gave the
impression she might have been on the street and collided with a
stranger. Ada was quickly ignored.

There was Lily.

In a moment, the distance between mother and daughter had been closed and Ede was saying: "I only wanted to see you because it's your birthday . . ."

"Hello, Mother."

They kissed—not as ants, but as Europeans kiss—one cheek and then the other. This was Lily's doing. Ede would not have been familiar with such a procedure.

"Lyon is with me," she said. "And your sisters. You remember Annie . . . Alice . . ."

Lily gave Ede a look that said: *I wonder what sort of ingrate you think I am,* and held her hand in Alice's direction. Alice curtseyed. Lily knew that Annie would have died of embarrassment if forced to say hello, and she barely looked at her.

I stood aside. It was a meeting I could not fathom. Too many unsaid words were in the air; so much tension was evident, I felt I wanted to run away.

Suddenly, Lily turned from Ede and took a step in Neddy's direction.

Ada put her hand on the top of my head as if to restrain me. For all that I wanted to flee, there was not an ounce of energy in my legs. I stared at Lily's arm as it linked itself with Neddy's. *What was going to happen . . . ?*

The violin was hanging down towards the grass and I saw for the very first time that Neddy Harris was wearing rouge on his lips and cheeks. Also, a golden earring, dangling beneath the feather.

When Mother spoke, I thought the world was going to end.

"This is Edward Harris," she said to Ede. "My fiancé. We will be married as soon as he returns from the War."

Mid-sky, the sun had stopped. The earth no longer turned.

Ede was frozen. Lyon glared. Annie stared and Alice looked away, her interest caught by a passing tray of strawberries and cream.

"How do you do?" said the gypsy violinist.

"Yes," said Ede. But that was all she could produce.

A moment passed. I have no notion what its length might have been—a minute—an hour. When it was over, Ada spoke.

"Charlie tells me your husband makes the Wyatt piano," she said to Ede.

Ede looked sideways, knowing at once by some mysterious code that she was being confronted by a future in-law who would prove to be problematical.

"No," she said. "My husband is a businessman, Mrs Harris. His employees make the pianos. Why do you ask?"

Ada was more than Ede had bargained for.

"Oh," she said. "It's not of any real interest. It was just a way of cutting through the chill."

Ede smiled. We waited.

"Perhaps," Ede said to Neddy, "you would be good enough to remind me of your name . . ."

That way the players met, whose lives so soon would be blown apart in the world beyond the lawn on which they stood.

14.

Neddy's last escapade at Number 84 took place the day before his eighteenth birthday—July 2nd, 1918. It was a Tuesday.

It began at dusk with fireworks.

All at once, the diners in the dining-room were seemingly under siege. Strings of mini-bangers blew off all around the windows. This was like rifle fire. Rockets burst from the lawn like exotic birds flying up into the darkness, letting down streams of golden feathers. Roman candles popped in all the colours of the rainbow. Six large Catherine wheels—yellow, green and white—spun ecstatically, pinned to the trunks of six tall trees. An array of sparklers, spelling out *LILY KILWORTH*, seemingly floated into the garden and stared in through the windows. Somewhere, a band was playing *Keep the Home Fires Burning*. (It was a record.)

All of this ended with a gigantic burst of magnesium flaring out on the terrace, sizzling Lily's name. Everyone rose from the tables—all of them stood in awe, their glasses still in their hands. Only the least imaginative person in the world would not have known what had happened. Neddy Harris had said *goodbye*, and departed.

It was not, however, quite over.

In the morning, when the gardeners arrived and were confronted with the debris of Neddy's fireworks, they were also confronted with a phenomenon which none of them could explain. Every peak in the gabled roof was a seeming fountain of helium balloons. And on the lawns beneath the trees, adorning the wreckage of last night's display, there was a mass of small white feathers.

When I looked out at 7:00 A.M. I had thought I would see a scorched and ruined landscape. Instead, I saw my mother in her bathrobe, moving over the grass with an apple basket, picking— as she might have gathered daisies—a harvest of *memento mori* from the man she loved.

Six green-aproned soldiers—including Mister Arbuthnot— watched her for a moment, mute and mystified. But when Mother stood up from her stooping, she smiled at them and held out her hands. *Will you help me,* she was saying, *win the War?*

15. When Neddy had joined the army and was gone, Mother and Ada became inseparable. I began to be on my own for extended periods. Not for days, of course, but for longer and longer hours while Lily sat in The Duke of York and watched the same movies over and over again. In between showings, she and Ada would go and stand in the alley-way behind the movie house and smoke cigarettes, or they would sit together in the dressing-room where Neddy had first kissed Mother. What they talked about—or did—I will never know.

I could not tell—and cannot, to this day—whether Ada Harris shared her gin with my mother. Maybe—maybe not. Lily may have had her own gin, for all I know. She gave no appearance—ever—of drunkenness, but I could smell it on her sometimes when she came in through the dark to kiss me good-night.

When we were in the sitting-room, I would watch her there while she dozed or while she read and, for the first time ever, I came to realize that I would never fathom the meaning of her silences. She was passing, in that time, beyond the definable walls of her mystery—withdrawing entirely into the castle of her enigma.

16. It had been back in December of 1917—around the time of our visit to Massey Hall—when the *passing* had begun to show its violent side. Unaccountably, there would be sudden outbreaks of temper. They would arise from nowhere; the doors would all at once burst open and Lily would be raging. *I CAN'T! I CAN'T! I CANNOT!* Or: *I WON'T! I WON'T! I WILL NOT!*

She seemed, in these moments, to be addressing someone who was following her—or attempting to follow her. When the doors flew open, she would turn and slam them behind her. Once—only once—when this had been done, she whirled on me and shouted: *DON'T LET HIM IN HERE, CHARLIE! IF YOU DO, I WILL KILL YOU!*

When the first of these outbursts occurred, I telephoned to my grandmother, knowing that something must be done. I was not afraid for myself—I don't know why—but I was terrified for Lily's sake. I knew she would never harm me, even though from time to time she hit me. She would never strike me with the kind of force that injures—and, certainly, she would never kill me. Being hit, I had learned to roll with the punch and by the time I had backed away, Lily had recovered her equilibrium. Enough of it, at any rate, not to hit me again.

Ede had come at once—it was about Christmas, that first time—and had the good sense to have Bateson drive her. Bateson had a calming effect on Lily. She trusted him implicitly and he seemed to understand her anguish. He would turn slightly away with her, taking her arm with his gloved hand, and he would talk to her, both their heads bowed, in words that sounded like a prayer. Or, perhaps, a catechism. I never knew what they were— these words—nor did Ede, but Lily could be heard replying: *yes. Yes. Yes.* And they would turn again and she would look for all the world like one of the green-aproned soldiers out in the yards who never spoke. *We can go, now,* Bateson would say. And all of us would climb into the Daimler.

There were six of these episodes. Six or seven. I suppose it is immaterial, except to say that their frequency was sufficient to warrant serious concern. We would drive to Omar Warren's clinic on most of these occasions—the same Doctor Warren who had failed to save Lizzie. But his clinic was renowned far and wide for its treatment of neurological disorders. He was even claiming he could perform operations in which he could solve the problem of seizures. In time, these came to be called *lobotomies*. We never saw Doctor Warren. That would have been impolitic. The doctor we saw was young and innovative—bringing to his treatment a new-fangled knowledge of psychology as well as his neurological training.

His name was Peterson and I think his first name was Anders. In Europe, before the War, he had studied with Doctor Jung at Zurich. Mother trusted him. She called him *Hamlet* because he was Danish—and teased him about his white-blond hair and albino eyelashes. Our visits to him were treated as opportunities to sail on a wave of medication, the effect of which was much like a wave of morphine. Lily, who had been so tense that a seizure might have been forthcoming, would inevitably start to relax the minute she was brought into Peterson's presence.

Hello, Hamlet, she would say in her sleepwalker's voice.

Hello, Mrs Browning, he would reply. *Welcome to Elsinore.*

And the door would close.

Ede would sit and remove one glove and then the other. She did this with the kind of concentration other people reserve for rearranging the marbles in a puzzle. Each finger of each glove was regarded separately and pulled with the implication that this might not be the move she intended. She would think about it. Analyze it. Reconsider.

During these deliberations, Ede would give the impression she was entirely alone in the waiting-room. I think she had no idea that she was being observed. She was considering her failure, I think, to have saved her daughter from the fate that had brought her to this moment. Blame was the burden of all Ede's concern. She told me so on other occasions. She told me at length, when Lily died. *I didn't* . . . she would say. *I couldn't* . . . she said. *I tried* . . . And, inevitably: *I failed.*

Ede, over time, had acquired a kind of poise that, while it was studied, had been studied so effectively that no one would guess it was not inherent. The woman who once had sworn at Liam in the halls of the Queen's Hotel, Toronto—the girl and the woman who had thrown her head back and laughed out loud at the world around her—now sat stilled and immutable. Her posture would not have changed if you had told her a cobra was lying at her feet. She counted this as a strength. I count it, now, as a tragedy.

In September of 1918, when I asked Ede to take us to Doctor Peterson for a treatment, she came at once with Bateson. This had now become a routine. I, however, was on the verge of no longer being able to cope with it. I resented most of all being thought of as the child of someone "crazy." Everyone—Ede included— wanted to save me from Lily, my mother.

"Charlie," Ede said, when we had taken Lily back to Number 84 and left her resting in her room, "come out and sit with me on the lawn. There's something I need to say."

The gardeners were working in the flowerbeds. Some of them were removing the spent blooms of roses from their stems and others, including Mister Arbuthnot, were digging in the earth. We chose a wrought-iron bench to sit on. It was painted white and sat with a table by its side beneath some maple trees. Ede set her handbag aside and I waited for her to begin the debate with her gloves. Instead, she folded her hands in her lap and looked away at Lily's window.

"Aside from the obvious problems when your mother is suffering one of her episodes, Charlie, are you happy here?"

"Yes. We love it."

"Yes—but you, Charlie. You. Are you sure you can live this life?"

"What life?"

"The one you're living. With someone who needs help. You're awfully young. Now you are almost eight and . . ." She paused and looked at the gardeners. "Most children of eight go off to school every day."

"I don't know any children," I said. "Except Auntie Willa's."

We both knew what that meant. Ede smiled. "Well," she said. "That's just the point. It's time you had more time with people your own age. A person has to have friends, Charlie."

"I have friends, Gran," I told her. "Ada, Neddy, Uncle Mal."

"But they're all adults, Charlie. Annie and Alice are both in school and have lots of friends. Lots of them. Lots." It was as though she did not quite believe this herself. I would not have believed it of Annie. Annie would never leave her corner.

"What I am driving at," said Ede, "is—sooner or later, the sooner the better—we'll have to get you into a school." Inadvertently she looked up at Lily's curtains where they blew out into the breeze. The connection was clear to me, even then. Ede wanted to separate me from my mother. This was not about *school* at all.

"What do you think, Charlie? Tell me."

"I won't go," I said.

"Charlie . . ."

"I won't go anywhere without Mother. I'm the only one who knows how to defend her."

"Defend her?" Ede was astonished. "Defend her?" she repeated. "Who from?"

I bit my lip.

"Charlie—tell me. This is impossible. Are you telling me someone has tried to harm your mother?"

I went on biting my lip—scuffing my toes against the grass.

"Don't do that, Charlie. Think of your shoes. Now tell me . . . What do you mean you have to defend her?"

I was still. I rested my hands on the edge of the bench, leaning on them until they hurt.

"Someone comes in the night," I said. "She talks to him."

Ede waited. Clearly, the image I had given evoked a kind of danger I did not comprehend. I could feel—the way all children can—the decision being made not to tell me something. Finally, Ede said: "you like this Neddy person, don't you."

"Yes."

Was that who she thought had come in the night?

"Would you have him for a father?"

"Yes."

There was another pause. "He's dreadfully young, Charlie," she said. "Much too young for your mother."

"No, he's not," I said. "She loves him."

"Oh, Charlie . . ." Ede looked away. Now, of course, I know exactly what she was thinking, but I didn't know it then. She was remembering Lily's father—Tom, The Piano Man—and setting Neddy, with his violin, beside him—seeing them both as impossibly impractical—impossibly impetuous—and impossible to resist. Even impossibly wonderful, perhaps.

Neddy's word again.

When she leaned around in my direction, I could see that Ede had begun to cry.

"Oh, dear," she said. "Forgive me."

She reached into her bag and retrieved a handkerchief.

"It's all right," I said. "Mother never cries. I think that's unnatural."

Ede blew her nose and looked at me. She laughed.

"You're very wise," she said. "Mister Know-it-all! Very wise—and very knowing . . ."

"For someone my age," I said, giving her sentence its inevitable ending.

Again, Ede laughed. "No, dear," she said. "I wasn't going to say that. Wisdom begins in the cradle."

What about *knowing*, I wanted to ask her. But didn't. What I did say was: "if I'm already wise and knowing, why do I have to go to school?"

More laughter. "Goodness! Heavens!" she said. "What have we spawned?"

Some of the gardeners turned and looked at her.

"Good-afternoon," said Ede to the nearest of them.

The man nodded. His lips moved, but there were no words. I knew him. His name was Alec. He had been buried alive in the Second Battle of Ypres, when a mine went up.

Ede looked away. The expression on Alec's face had sobered her. She pulled at the lapels of her coat and dropped her hands back down to her lap.

"Charlie," she said.

I knew that something bad was coming. I didn't speak. I waited. That was all I could do.

"The moment is going to come when your mother will have to go away for a rest . . ."

"She's not insane," I whispered, knowing instantly what was being said.

Ede went on without pause. "When this happens," she said, "something will have to be done about you."

"She isn't crazy."

"Charlie—oh, my darling. Listen to me. Lily is my baby—don't you understand? *I love her.* And I cannot let her suffer any more. She must have help. She needs . . . she must have . . . it is imperative. We have to save her life."

I said nothing.

Then I said: "she is not crazy. I won't go."

"Charlie," Ede said, "do you think I don't know what Lily is suffering? Do you think I don't know? I've been with her all her life. I know every ounce of what frightens her by heart. But this is different. This is worse. This is the worst she's ever been."

This said, she sat there and watched me—waiting for me to respond.

When I spoke, I could barely hear my own words. I hated

them because in saying them, even in whispering them, I was betraying my mother. I was telling Ede that it was true: that Lily was mad. "The man she talks to at night—when I don't think there's really anyone there . . ." I said, "she says that his name is John."

Nothing had prepared me for Ede's reaction.

Silence. Absolute silence. And then: "Oh dear Jesus!" she almost shouted—and clapped her hand to her mouth.

I stared at her.

Her eyes were Lily's eyes when Lily came through the door in one of her rages.

"Oh dear Jesus God," Ede said again—but now as muted as I had been. "Oh dear Jesus God. How can this be true . . ."

I reached out to take her hand. To comfort her. But she snatched it away.

Then she stood up.

Her voice, all at once, was hard and clipped as the voice of Lyon, her son.

"Has Doctor Peterson been told about this?" she said.

"What?"

"Charlie—I warn you," Ede said. "All her life, I have defended your mother—protected her—kept her back from the edge. *That was my job!*" She was shaking—with anger, I think. "Now you tell me this figure has appeared. This . . . this . . . *John* person . . ." She looked away. She knew, of course, who he was, but she would never say so. For Ede, as for Eliza, John Fagan was a forbidden image. He must not be thought upon.

Now, with more control, she looked down at me and said: "your mother needs a kind of help that none of us can give her. Not you. Not me. Not this *Ada* person. Not this *Neddy* person." She said their names as if they were as dangerous as John's. "We can do nothing. Nothing." She took a deep breath. "Listen to me, Charlie. If you think I am going to let Lily go—if you imagine that I am going to let her go . . ."

"She isn't crazy," I repeated.

"Oh, Charlie! Charlie!" she said—and sat back down on the

bench. "Who cares what it's *called*! Who *cares* what it's called! She's dying of a terror—and someone has to save her."

"I will save her," I said. "I already have. I can do it again."

Ede looked out at me, staring from a cave into which she had crawled with her fear.

"Something must be done," she finally said, exhausted. "Something must be done—and only Doctor Warren can do it . . ."

Doctor Warren. Knives.

I stepped away. Ede had already departed, though she remained on the bench like a mourner by a grave. Slowly, as I watched her, she began to work the fingers of her left glove—thumb first—and then the others, one by one.

From the terrace, I looked back. The gardeners went on turning the earth and cutting deadheads from their stems. Mister Arbuthnot, even if he had been standing right beside us, could not have heard what we had said. He seemed so placid—almost serene—out there, digging. Then, as I was about to walk away I saw that Alec was stepping out from the flowerbeds. He paused a moment and moved in Ede's direction.

When he arrived, he stood before her, leaning forward, both hands hanging down at his sides. Then he took one last step and handed her a rose. Already dead, its petals fell into her lap.

Ede looked down at them. She seemed, almost, to be counting them—turning them over with her fingers. Alec drifted away and I went into the house.

By the time I had reached our rooms and could see the garden from the window, Ede was gone and the petals, having fallen after her, made a path of where she had walked. It was white, and not unlike Neddy's feathers. Not unlike snow. But not at all like the rose it once had been.

17. Ede was soon to suffer one more tragedy and, although it will seem that I am piling tragedies ruthlessly one upon the other as we reach this part of the story, it must be understood that the War and its aftermath were like that. Ten thousand men had died on the Somme in a single day. Multiply ten thousand men by ten thousand families and you can see how the tragedies mounted upwards.

In October, I had my eighth birthday. I felt as if I was now an accredited adult. *Eight*—and small for my age. *Eight*—and serious. *Eight*—and a man of the world. There was little I did not know about the human condition that any child can know, who has been given a loving parent and a place to stand. But I was not just *any* child. I had also been given silence and music—poetry— a unique religion of reverence for life—a profoundly mysterious companion and a sense of being wanted and cared for by someone whose whole concern for me could be defined in a single word: *wonder*. I was also given someone to decipher—someone to protect—someone to ponder. To say that I was *old* at eight is simply to state a truth.

Two days before my birthday, Ede arrived on foot at Number 84. She carried flowers—chrysanthemums from a hothouse. She was wearing white—as Caroline or Eva would have done—from head to toe. White in October is unheard of, unless you mean to appear on the stage. And it was like that—a costume.

She wanted some tea, she said—and might we have it in one of the drawing-rooms—me and Lily and Ede, alone?

This was arranged.

Lily was sombre. Aloof. Her dark blue clothing gave her the look of someone in a religious order.

The tea was brought. Until the tray was set and the maid had retired, there was total silence.

Ede had placed the flowers aside on a table. Their scent was thick with implications of glassed-in gardens—earth that was freshly watered—moss and stones and fountains.

We waited.

When Ede spoke, it was without a trace of pity. She simply told us a story.

"Lyon contracted the Spanish flu two weeks ago," she said. "Because he was strong, he resisted it. We kept him at home. Doctor Cooper believed that was best. The hospitals have special wards for it now. But these, almost everywhere, are full. Apparently the greatest number of victims in the city have been nurses. The paper published a list of them last week. Thirty-five in one day. Thirty-five nurses." She was sitting very straight in her chair. "Doctor Cooper said that Lyon would be better off at home, where Miss Browning and I could take care of him . . ."

Ede poured cup of tea and pushed it across the table in Lily's direction. Lily was standing, and did not come forward to claim it.

Ede said: "Miss Browning died three days ago."

Lily sat down.

Ede said: "she was ill for less than forty-eight hours. We did the best we could—but she went. She was ready, I suspect . . . I had the feeling she wanted to die. At any rate—she's gone."

Ede looked across the room at Lily, seated now in sunshine.

"She told me to say goodbye to you, Lily. As you know, she was very fond of you."

Lily said: "yes." And folded her hands.

Ede poured a cup of tea for me. I took it. While she poured her own, she said: "Frederick, of course, was desperate to save his son. The only son we have . . . The War had not taken him. We were so relieved—so grateful. Lyon will be seventeen until next August, and surely, by then . . ."

The thought was left unspoken. War's end.

"Frederick ordered an iron lung for Lyon. A dreadful, ghastly contraption people came and set up in his bedroom. All day and all night, the thing made its ghastly noise . . . breathing—but inhuman . . . It was breathing for Lyon. Breathing for him—in, out—in, out. Dreadful. I shall hear it to the end of my days . . ."

We sat in silence. Listening.

Ede said: "there was nothing more to be done. The boy was in this thing and barely conscious. Perspiring . . . the heat of the machine—the heat of the disease. I kept going over to dry his face. His hair . . ."

Lily was sitting, now, slightly forward.

Ede said: "poor little Emily . . . poor little Agnes . . . Charlotte. They all took turns with me. But I would not leave him. Nor would Frederick. He sat at the foot of the lung and both his hands . . . his hands . . ." Ede made a double fist of her own and held it up for us to see. "Hours on end," she said, "he squeezed them together, in, out—in, out—in, out. As if he, too, was breathing for Lyon . . ."

She pulled her hands down into her lap and spread her fingers. "Wednesday—Thursday—Friday . . ." she said. "What's today?"

Friday.

"Miss Browning died on Tuesday. The iron lung arrived on Wednesday morning . . . and . . ."

Ede pushed her cup away and stared at it.

"And so . . . *this* morning," she said, "it stopped. Frederick shut it off. At 4:00 A.M. . . . because Lyon was dead. Had died. We did everything that could be done—and he died."

Nobody spoke.

Ede looked down and lifted the skirts of her dress to spread them wider over the chair, smoothing them free of creases.

"I wore this dress especially. I haven't been out of it since Wednesday. I wanted Lyon to see me at my best. And this was the best I had."

That was all.

We sat there while the tea grew cold.

Finally, Ede stood up and collected the flowers, now slightly wilted.

"I had thought I was going to leave these with you," she said to Lily, "but now—I think I will take them home again. You hated Lyon so . . . I'm sure you need no flowers to remind you."

And then: "goodbye," and she was gone.

18. At the eleventh hour on the eleventh day of the eleventh month, the War ended.

A week before Christmas, a cablegram was waiting for us when we returned from a shopping spree. Our arms—in the expectation of Neddy's arrival any minute—were full of presents. When he walked through the door, we would shower him with gifts. It was also Ada's birthday. We meant to surprise her, too.

Lily, with all her packages still in hand, looked at the cablegram where it sat on the hall table. "It will tell us when Neddy's going to arrive," she said. "Open it."

I set down my boxes and drew the cablegram from its envelope. It was yellow.

"Read it," said Lily again.

"I can't," I said.

"READ IT!"

She must have known already. It told us Neddy was dead.

On the eleventh day of the eleventh month at two minutes prior to the eleventh hour, Neddy Harris had been the last Canadian to die in the War. It happened at Mons—where the War had begun.

Merely to say that *these things happen* is to slander irony itself—and its will to strike us down when we are least prepared. It is what it is: the root of barbarism.

Lily laughed.

She laughed as if laughter had just been invented. I was terrified.

She ran out into the street and began to throw our parcels at passing motor cars. She went on laughing—and shouting with every pitch: *Merry Christmas!* she shouted. *Merry Christmas to all! Merry Christmas to every one!*

When the presents had been exhausted, she started throwing snowballs, sticks and handfuls of icy gravel snatched from the drive. She threw her hat. She threw her coat. She threw her purse. She threw her shoes. She took off her beads and threw them, too.

By the time she had started throwing her clothes, the laughter had stopped and had been replaced by wordless chanting—rising from disorientation—signalling an oncoming seizure.

The seizure did not occur. Instead, Lily did something I had never seen her do before.

Four or five people—men and women—had run from their houses to see what the commotion was about. They were concerned, in part, for me. As the tirade of shouts and presents, snowballs and clothing had mounted, I was left stranded on the walk of Number 84, catatonic. One of the neighbours—a woman whose dog I sometimes walked for a nickel—came and stood behind me, folding me into her arms. Her name was Mrs Crawford.

"What is it, Charlie?" she said. Her voice was like a mother cat's.

I explained that Neddy had been killed and Lily had just found out.

"But the War is over."

"Yes. He died the last day."

Mrs Crawford let go of me and gently urged me to step aside.

The other neighbours were attempting, now, to restrain Lily's flailing arms. But all she did was fight them off and shout abuses.

Mrs Crawford reached the boulevard.

"Leave her alone," she said.

"But . . ."

"Leave her alone."

Mrs Crawford did not raise her voice. She spoke with such authority the others fell back.

Lily stood in the snow, looking like a cornered animal. Her head went back and I thought: *the seizure is going to begin . . .*

But all she was doing was inhaling gulps of air.

She put her hands on her hips. Her legs were splayed. Now, the cornered animal was gone and she looked like a triumphant gladiator.

Mrs Crawford waited patiently. She did not even shiver, although the others, who had also left their houses without their coats, were beginning to cringe in the cold and to stamp their feet.

When Lily had recovered her breath, she dropped her arms and stood up straight. She took one piercing look at the sky and closed her eyes.

Mrs Crawford said: "Mrs Kilworth, is there anything I can do?"

"Thank you," said Lily. "No."

This was when she did what I had never seen her do before. She wept.

She put her face in her hands and I could see her shoulders shaking. No one went near her. No one moved. She wept for almost a minute, and then she took her hands away from her face and shook her head, as if to rid herself of the tears.

After that, she took a deep breath and stepped out through the snow towards the walk. As I watched her approach, I moved further off to the side. Lily went past me, on up the shovelled bricks to the porch. She was in her stockinged feet, but she seemed to have no awareness of that.

I thought perhaps she might have spoken to me as she passed; called me to join her before she went inside. But she was already on her way to the rest of her life.

That night, I went into her bedroom to discover Lily was gone. And with her, the wicker suitcase. She had made her last escape— without me. I was now, for the first time ever, entirely alone.

19. In the morning, I pretended my mother was ill— recovering from yesterday's events—and I took up a tray of breakfast from the dining-room. I did not want any adults to interfere in my search for her. I knew too well how eager all the widows were to be of service to their *little man*. I had been patted and pinched and hugged possessively by all of them.

Most of the other residents of Number 84 were aware of the scene that had taken place on the boulevard in the snow the day before. *Grief*, they muttered, *lays a different hand on every shoulder*. In their minds, mother's "husband," of course, was already dead. *Perhaps a brother had died . . .*

I said nothing. I told them nothing.

In the bathroom, I flushed the scrambled eggs down the toilet and poured the coffee down the sink. I had already eaten my own breakfast, thinking it best to put up a show of normalcy. Still, I drank Lily's glass of milk and I ate her toast.

The first place I looked was The Duke of York. But it did not open till noon. Then I went to Alcott Avenue.

When I got to Number 37 and asked for Ada Harris, Mrs Gresham said: "out cold. What do you want with her, Charlie?"

"I'm looking for my mother. Is she here?"

Mrs Gresham said: "no, hon. I'm sorry. And, like I said, Mrs Harris is out cold. Her boy died. She's drunk."

"Could I see her anyway?" I asked. "Maybe she'll know where my mother is."

"All right, then. I'll take you up. But I wouldn't hold out much hope." She was leading me along the narrow hallway towards the narrow staircase. I had never trespassed beyond the lower level. "She's on the third floor. Ada has the front two windows. Her boy—that lovely boy—used to have the back two, before he went in the army and got hisself killed."

Mrs Gresham's breathing was so bad, it took us hours to climb the stairs. But, at last: "here we are, then. I'll knock. You stand back. Sometimes, when she's in this condition, Ada gets rebusive . . ."

She pounded on a door with the number *3-A* on it.

Nothing.

She pounded again.

A voice from downstairs shouted up: "shut that racket!"

"Shut your own racket!" Mrs Gresham shouted back—and winked at me.

Then she pounded again.

"Mrs Harris? Ada? I got someone here for you, dearie," she said.

At last, the door opened.

Ada's face appeared—grey as her usual clothing. Her hair was hanging down in straggles. For the first time, I could see that she was almost bald. The fedora was finally explained.

"Neddy?" she said.

"No, not Neddy, Mrs H. Neddy's dead—you know that." This was Mrs Gresham.

"Oh."

Ada's voice had flattened into a monotone. The smell that came from her room was foul—a mixture of cigarettes and vomit. Gin.

I stepped forward.

"It's me, Mrs Harris. Charlie."

She tried to make me out, but couldn't. Her brain was completely befuddled.

"I'm looking for Lily," I said.

"Lily's not here."

"Do you know where she is, please?"

"No." Ada thought about it. "If I were you," she began. And then: "Sure as fate, she'll turn up at The Duke of York. She's there every afternoon."

I knew that already.

"I need her now," I said.

"Can't help you, Charlie. I don't know where she is. Neddy's dead. That's all I know. Last day of the War. The bastards . . ." Ada looked at me. "Sorry, Charlie. I never use language—not unless they kill my boy. The bastards!"

"Yes, ma'am."

"Go to The Duke of York," she said. "Lily will be there."

Ada began to close the door.

"Bye-bye, Charlie," I heard her say as she turned away. And then, before the latch had clicked: ". . . the thieving bastards!"

Ada was right. Lily was at The Duke of York when I arrived there at noon. At first, I failed to see her, because she was not yet seated in the auditorium. The film was to be a romance called *The Last Rose of Summer*. Constance Talmadge was in it. And Wallace Beery.

Children could not attend the movies alone in 1918, unless it was a Saturday matinee. But I got in because I knew about the alleyway at the back and the door that Ada used. I went and looked in the dressing-room.

There was the wicker suitcase.

I gave a shout. I couldn't help it. I hadn't realized how afraid I'd been that Lily might not ever come back.

I lifted the suitcase onto the make-up table and leaned down to kiss it. Lily's familiar scent was on it.

The cot had been slept on. The blanket was there, unfolded, and the pillow without a cover. All at once, these were beloved objects. Lily had used them. This is where she had spent the night. Her coat hung down from the back of the door.

Still, she did not come, and I could hear the movie beginning. The Duke of York must have hired another pianist. Someone was out there playing away in a fashion that Ada could never manage. The familiar *rumpity-dumpity, bumpity-bump* of her rhythms had been replaced by someone who was in love with waltzes.

I went down the corridor then and pulled aside the curtain. The auditorium was dark, of course, and for a moment there was nothing to see but the beam from the projector. I went up the side aisle, feeling my way along the hangings that had entangled Lily.

Constance Talmadge was on the screen in close-up. If I had been older, I would have fallen in love with her there and then. Her face has haunted me ever since that afternoon for reasons that have more to do with my search for Lily than *The Last Rose of Summer.* Nonetheless, I will never forget her.

I chose a seat at the very back because I wanted a vantage point from which I could see my mother wherever she might appear. But she did not. The film had played for fifteen minutes and there was still no sign of her. All at once, I smelled smoke. At first, I think I may have been the only one to smell it—but gradually others, too, became restless.

"Is something burning?" someone asked.

I don't know why I didn't instantly make the connection. But, I suppose for a myriad of reasons, I did not. Neddy's death—Lily's disappearance—my visit to Ada—Constance Talmadge—all made a contribution. It was not until the flames themselves appeared that I knew they were a signal of Lily's presence.

The screen was on fire.

The hero, whose name I've forgotten, had *gone for a soldier.* It was not Wallace Beery, but a younger man and he was leading his men up out of the trenches and *over the top*. There were bursting shells and flames in the movie itself—but, of course, they were not in colour. The flames we began to see were blue and orange and yellow.

"FIRE!" someone shouted. "FIRE!"

"Fire—fire—fire!"

That was Lily.

The auditorium became a mass of fleeing people. As if they themselves were rising from the trenches, they clambered over the backs of their seats and down into the laps of others who were also struggling to escape. They ran each other down in the aisles—they jumped without looking from the flimsy balcony. They clawed at Lily's draperies. They sank to their knees and pounded the floor with their fists. Everyone was screaming—yelling—cursing.

I alone went running against the current. Perhaps because I was small and light, I could run across the backs of the chairs without tipping them. This way, I made my way to the front and stood on top of the piano. The pianist had been amongst the first to escape. She had run up the steps to the corridor behind the screen and out into the alley.

"Mother!" I shouted. "Lily!"

Of course, there was no reply.

Still, I persisted. *Mother! Lily!*

No.

I scrambled down from the piano. The screen and all the curtains were now a mass of flames, and the fire had spread far out into the auditorium. The smoke was chemical and yellow. Everyone was gasping. I ran over to the steps and lunged past a man who was running the other way.

"Mother! Lily!"

I ran through the smoke until I reached the dressing-room.

There she was.

Lying on the bed.

Her eyes were closed. Her hands were folded. She had removed her shoes.

I thought she was dead.

20. She had wanted to be dead—and in a sense, she was. From that moment forward, I never met the woman again who had been my constant companion since birth. Instead, I was given the remnants of her—the incohesive remains.

She had intended to burn The Duke of York to the ground so that it could be her funeral pyre. And Neddy's.

She had stolen his violin from Ada and it lay beside her on the floor. The wicker suitcase was beneath her feet. Some kind of poison had been ingested—something she had purchased in a hardware store.

In the hospital, she fought the nurses and the doctors who were trying to save her life. She fought them so effectively, somebody had to knock her out. When her stomach had been induced to give up its contents and a shot had been administered to calm her down, she still persisted in her kicking and shouting until, at last, she was captured and restrained and put into a strait-jacket.

That was when I saw her. She was sitting slumped in a wooden chair, with her arms tied down inside the padded garment, giving her the appearance of an amputee. Her hair was wet with perspiration and it hung like a gorgon's nest of snakes. There was not an ounce of life in her face—it was just a plaster cast of desperation, the heavy-lidded eyes half-closed, the mouth drawn down, its lips with blood on them.

I went in alone. An orderly was already with her, seated opposite, so that he could watch her. Ede had come with me, but she waited in the anteroom, unseen. It had been thought I might be good for Lily. *If she sees Charlie,* the reasoning went, *there might be some flicker of recognition that would make her want to live.*

Whoever had thought so was wrong.

"Hello, Mother," I said.

The lowered lids were raised, but the eyes did not turn in my direction.

"Mother?" I repeated. "It's Charlie . . ."

For a moment there was silence. Her feet moved, allowing her to readjust her balance in the chair. At last, she looked at me. Stared at me and saw me.

I wish she hadn't.

Her jaws began to move, and her mouth began to open. She made a great, wide O with it—the way she had when she pretended to be the wind in *The Highwayman*.

There was not a sound.

The orderly sat watching.

Lily spat at me.

Then she lunged forward, chair and all, and bit me on the hand.

When I was pulled away, she started screaming: *kill him! Kill him! He's a traitor!*

That was the last I saw of my mother for the next eight months. She was taken to the Queen Street Lunatic Asylum where she was confined at first in a padded cell. She was then kept under close observation in a ward with others who were considered to be *dangerous individuals*. I never saw her there. Children were *not allowed*.

Of course, we had to give up Number 84. I was sent to live with Franklin and Caroline. Theirs became my home. But not my dwelling place. I was in my ninth year, and old enough to be sent away to school.

21. I will only mention this once. Lily never knew I knew it, and even as I wait to set the words down, I feel her watching me—wondering how I will say this—tell you this.

It is such a bitter thing. And difficult to contemplate. And so I never think of it—not ever.

This:

In the Lunatic Asylum, Lily gave birth to a stillborn child.

Neddy's—for certain.

It was a girl.

And that is all I will say.

Seven

1918—1939

Somewhere the sun is shining,
Somewhere the songbirds sing.
Somewhere, there's no more pining—
There's joy in everything . . .

Beautiful Isle of Somewhere
Pounds and Fearis

1. In my earliest talks with Ede, following Lily's death, all I got from her was recrimination and guilt—an endless stream of regret in which every sentence began with the words *if only . . . If only I hadn't* this, that or the other. *If only Frederick hadn't been so unbending—if only I had been stronger—if only she hadn't gone to England . . .* Et cetera. Et cetera. Finally, I gave up listening.

Caroline wept. It seemed that she was always in tears. Towards the end of her life, her clothes were damp with them. I called her Niobe. But her tears for Lily were nothing but a tributary to the Amazon she wept for Franklin, who had died in 1937. She also wept for *the past, the past, the past.*

Liam's life had somehow been wasted—thrown away because he could not accept Eva's refusal to continue their love story. Malahide would never leave Munsterfield. That was certain. Willa described herself as the *mother of hundreds*, without a moment to spare. I was not, I must admit, sorry when she failed to turn up at Lily's funeral. If she had, we would have been inflicted with her brood, which I think was made up of one dozen children, fathered by an auto mechanic who had finally deserted her for a younger woman with whom he promptly commenced a second brood.

So much for the aunts and uncles. Lily's half-sisters—Annie, born in 1905, and Alice, born in 1907—the year of Lizzie's death—were equally unhelpful in piecing together the history of my family. Annie, always deeply serious, rarely smiled and had become involved with the Pentecostal Church. Lily had frightened her. Worried her. Alarmed her. The manner of Lily's death had overtones of holy retribution. It was safest to stay away from the subject, lest God misinterpret your interest.

Alice Wyatt, as might have been predicted, had gone to Hollywood, California, thinking there might be a place for her on the silver screen. When David O. Selznick was scouring the world for new talent to claim the role of Scarlett O'Hara, Alice had begged Aunt Caroline for lessons in *Southern accents and manners* before she climbed on board the Santa Fe Superchief in Chicago and, like her uncle Liam, melted into the populace at large.

Harry Wyatt was still alive, but had lost his memory. Maude, his wife, spent all her time coaching him in forgotten language and habit. *Here is your coat, dear. C-O-A-T, coat. Put it on. That's right. Now, these are buttons, Harry. Buttons. B-U-T-T-O-N-S.* This had become his life—and hers.

And so the rest of Lily's story—with a single surprising exception—must be told from my own memories. Memories of my school years—and of the years that followed.

The school of choice for Lyon Wyatt had been Upper Canada College. If there had been a social register in Toronto, more than half of its men would have been students there. Staid and proper and wealthy, it perfectly suited Frederick's wishes for his son.

The academy chosen for me was King's College in Brighton, east of Toronto. It was chosen as much for its locale as for any other reason. This put me at a *good safe distance* from Lily and I was to stay there until my education was over.

I liked it well enough. I made a few friends who still turn up in my life from time to time. A few—not many. No names. Why embarrass them? I was neither popular, nor unpopular. I was simply there. Some hopes were raised on the playing fields when it was told that I had *perfect pitch*. But when it was discovered I could not even throw a ball, the boys involved lost interest in me entirely. Music was not a subject many thought of as having boy-importance. My destiny—my future work—awaited me, but there was little use I could make of my talent at school.

The music classes taught us something of theory and how to read notation—how to sing and how to play the triangle. Some of the boys played other instruments—cornets, bugles, trombones. No one played the flute. There was a military band which they encouraged us to join. I was still fiddling with the piano—but you can't take a piano on parade. I progressed to two-handed, fully chorded capabilities over the next ten years and, by the time I left the school in 1928, I had hopes I might find work in a dance band.

As a student of other subjects, I was proficient enough to skip grade five. We didn't call them *grades*; we called them *forms*. The British mode was pretty well adopted throughout the system. The masters wore gowns and the students wore uniforms—grey. Dormitories, up until the time you were twelve—were large. You slept with eleven other boys till then and after that, with three. Prefects—a station I never achieved because I had no ambition for it—slept in rooms of two, and the head prefect slept alone.

We ate in a noisy, boisterous dining-hall where grace was said in Latin and the food was traditionally foul. It was nourishing enough, but absolutely tasteless. We lived on white bread and condiments. We went to Chapel every Sunday and some of us sang in the choir. This I did until my voice broke. My contralto was a relatively rare phenomenon and much use was made of it. I was given solos to sing and took some pleasure in them.

Singing solo created a private place it is impossible to achieve in any other way. You are alone with the music—and every ear, including your own, is bent upon your performance. I always closed my eyes when I sang alone. I kept it as a place where I could sing to Lily.

Our mutual lives—mine and my mother's—took on a pattern over time that was more or less easy to live by. At school, I was an "orphan" for the first few years, until Lily was sufficiently recovered—and medicated—to have some part of her life beyond the Asylum. When that time came, and she made one or two appearances at the school, I was careful to explain to my friends that my mother had *been in a coma* until then, brought about by *the most frightful motor-car accident.*

I talked like an imported English schoolboy. We all did. We got our language from *Chums* and *The Boys' Own Annual,* where *lads* and *fellows* and *chaps* were always involved in *jolly* adventures and had *ripping* fun and suffered *frightfully* from adult interventions in their lives.

I say! we said, when impressed. *Bad show,* we would say, when not. No one ever *exclaimed* when they had *ripping news* to tell. They always *ejaculated.* "I say, have you seen George's sister!" *he ejaculated.* "Ra-ther!" This, of course, left us in stitches, once we were old enough to ejaculate in earnest.

Ede became my surrogate mother. Caroline had few motherly instincts. She and Franklin had no children for the best of reasons. They needed none. He was her child—and she was his. They lived, with great success, the joyous lives of those who never lose touch with their youth. They were in their sixties then, and Franklin had been installed at the Wyatt Piano Factory as its resident *inventor.*

Caroline never gave up her Edwardian mode of dress and she remained a woman of almost ethereal beauty. Her gestures always gave the impression of someone who might have been swimming languidly in a warm lagoon. Her accent, too, retained its Southern edges—or lack of edges. Her sentences, spun out of gossamer, floated on the air and drifted off without endings. She was enchanting—an enchantment. *You again,* she would say whenever I returned for holidays. *I cannot begin to imagine where the time has gone. Were you not here, my darling, just two shakes of a lamb's tail ago . . . ?* Then she would gather my face in her hands and kiss me on the forehead. She smelled of dark flowered perfumes always and her rooms were filled with light.

It made a decent life—secure in ways I had never known. I no longer had anyone's focus on me twenty-four hours a day—yet I was loved and befriended. And there were no locked doors.

2. Lily's first asylum—the one on Queen Street in Toronto— was appalling. The buildings, for all their windows, gave an impression of darkness. Inside, there was always someone screaming.

Ede was faithful to Lily every day of her incarceration. Incarceration is the correct word here, though the staff never used it. After all, Lily, at first, was in a padded cell. But Ede was always standing at the door—willing to walk on through if only they would give her permission to do so.

Permission for visits was very hard to come by at Queen Street. Observation privileges, on the other hand, could be arranged, and Ede took advantage of them over and over again. There were rooms where you could not be seen, but from which you could observe your wards and charges at play—or at work, as the case might be. Also, when sedated. Sometimes seated on the floor.

The time then came when doors were opened and Ede walked through.

"Hello, Mother."

"Hello, Lily."

Ede was careful never to embrace her. Also, never to approach beyond the limits that Lily set. If Lily wanted contact, she would come to you. If not, you sat on opposite sides of the room.

Uniforms were worn by the patients—mostly so that patients could be identified immediately when there was trouble. A melee of nurses, orderlies and rioting madwomen could be problematical if everyone was wearing white. The patients were dressed in green.

"What can I bring you?" Ede would say.

"Nothing."

"A sweater? Are you warm enough?"

"A sweater would be nice. Blue, please."

"Yes."

"I would also like a bottle of perfume."

"Are you allowed to have a bottle of perfume?"

"I don't know, Mother. And I don't care. I want one."

Ede nodded. "I will bring you a bottle of perfume."

"Thank you."

"Anything else?"

"Some ants."

Ede was not sure what her reply should be. She waited.

"It's all right, Mother. You can smile." Lily, herself, was smiling. "You could also bring me some matches, if you were so inclined."

"No. No matches, Lily."

Lily did not speak again for a moment. Then she said: "some ants *would* be nice. Some butterflies. A bird or two. We could plant a tree over there," she said, "if they'd let us dig through the floor . . ."

Ede sat forward and watched her. Lily could never not be beautiful. Even now. They had cut her hair off for fear she would use it to strangle herself. Women had done that—wound their long braids of hair around their necks and hanged themselves. Now—all hair was cut. A matter of course. That and trimmed fingernails.

"Mother?"

"Yes, dear?"

"Where is my Charlie?"

"He's in school."

"Where?"

Ede told her.

"Does he ever mention me?"

"Of course he does."

"Can he come to see me?"

"No." Ede modified the starkness of this by reminding Lily of the rules. "He will come when it's allowed."

"Can I go to see him?"

"I cannot answer that."

"Are there rules at his school forbidding visits by crazy mothers?" Lily was smiling again.

"Possibly," said Ede.

She, too, smiled.

"I want a hat," said Lily, suddenly.

"You have no need of a hat, my darling. Not in here."

"I've been told I can walk outdoors, if I'm good."

"That will be nice."

"Not *nice*, Mother. Not *NICE*, for heaven's sake! It will be *wonderful!*"

Ede said: "yes. I quite agree. It will be wonderful. *When.*"

$3.$ In time, Lily was considered well enough to leave Queen Street. For a while, she would live in a hotel—and then she would need to go into another kind of home for the mentally ill. Her second asylum was for *private patients only*—as if all patients don't want privacy. On the other hand, this particular institution—to which my mother was committed on three separate occasions—was extremely well run and set in the midst of a terraced garden. The buildings were part of an estate in North Rosedale that had been left by its owner especially *for the care of madwomen.* Not mad *persons*—not mad *men*—but mad *women.* The late owner's daughter had been schizophrenic and had committed suicide. The family name was Glenville and the estate had the name of the *Cloisters.*

Something must be said about our finances, I suppose. If I were reading this, I would want to know *where their money came from. All those expenses, with her in asylums and clinics and rest homes—and him all those years at that school.*

It's a good question. The answer, of course, is: *our finances are none of your business.* But that's not good enough when you're telling the story of somebody's life. Real people eat real food and wear real clothes and live in real houses. How did we do it?

Well—we know about the house. That was kindness of Franklin and Caroline. In her brief bursts of freedom, Mother would live in hotels—and I would stay with her there. This had to do with the fact that Lily refused to be scrutinized. *I will not live anywhere where I am being* watched! *However kindly their concern, I will not have Frank and Carrie staring at me noon and night. I've had enough of that in prison . . .*

Prison.

That was her impression of it. Rightly, I suppose, given her particular condition. Given her experience. *Frederick used to lock me
up there in the dark*, she would say to me, pointing at whatever
roof we were under. It was as if the Selby Street attic was always
above her, waiting for her return—waiting for its inhabitant—its
prisoner—its ghost. Its fire-starter.

But Frederick had never locked her in the dark. The dark was
a state of mind she could not escape—and she blamed him for it,
though in her lucid moments I think she knew better. He was not
the monster she had made of him—he was just a visible part of
her nemesis. He was there—she could see him. The rest was hidden, and she would never have blamed him for that. She knew
better. He was not John Fagan, but only Frederick Wyatt—and
there was all the difference in the world.

Eliza's trust fund provided us with most of what we lived on. Ede
would augment it from time to time. In the long run, she told me
so—though Lily never knew it. Lily knew when there was cash in an
envelope slipped between them when Ede was visiting—but not
when there was a cheque in the envelope sent to the Trust Company.

I had to deal with some of it. This only when Mother was living on *the outside*. I dealt with it because figures were a nightmare
to Lily and it fell to me to keep track of her chequing account and,
on occasion, statements regarding the fund.

None of these statements survived. Nor, for that matter, did her
cheque stubs or statements from the bank. Lily always had me
destroy them as soon as I had dealt with them. *Who cares how we
spent the money?* she would say. *As long as everything gets paid, and
there's some left over, that's all that matters.*

One aspect of the fund, however, did survive—namely a meticu-
lous accounting of my school fees. This accounting was in the suitcase—a whole sheaf of pages, suitably dated, on which the payments
were duly noted *with thanks*. Each of these pages bears the crest and
letterhead of King's College. And each one—typewritten—shows the
amount of the fee and the annotation: *received, with thanks, from
E. Anderson.*

Mother had collected all these sheets in a single envelope marked: *Charlie—School.*

I have to assume *E. Anderson* must have been our Trust Officer back in the old days. Whoever he was, he has gone to his grave. The man who replaced him (there is still some money in the fund—though precious little) is just *sincerely yours* and a signature legible as typing can make it: *E.P. Jones.*

If a man won't sign his own name, we have come to a pretty pass. But that is the world we live in, I guess. It's all so impersonal. The next thing we know, our names will be numbers—in which case Lily would have had to spell hers on her fingers, holding her hands behind her back.

4. When Frederick died in 1933, Lily had been allowed a one-day pass to attend his funeral.

In the morning, while his casket was still on view in the Selby Street parlour, Lily took me in to look at him. I was twenty-two when he died, but I had never known him. I had seen him at Massey Hall and sometimes, I had seen him in the street. *There goes Frederick Wyatt.* In Homburg and overcoat, looking neither left nor right, stepping from or ushered into motor cars. But I had never heard his voice and I had never touched his hand.

Standing in his presence, looking down at his grey face, Lily was silent at first. And then she said: *the circle now is broken.*

I looked at her.

She was smiling. Privately. It was not at all a smile of triumph— nothing to do with revenge. She had survived him, that was all. He was gone, and with him, one of the keys that had locked her in.

Goodbye, she said. And that was all.

I had never said: *hello.*

5. • All stories have an ending, but some end out of sight—off stage. To be accounted for, you must be seen. But some of us disappear. As Liam did.

I cannot tell if Liam is still alive as I write these words. If he is, he would be sixty-eight years old. Ede is seventy-three—and she is still here. But something informs me Liam is not. It's just a feeling. Just a fear.

The last time I saw him, it was raining. April, I think—but I don't know when—which year. It was some years after his appearance at the War Rally in 1917. Somewhere in the 1920s.

It was one of the times when Mother was out of the Cloisters, and living in a hotel. We had been to the movies. That's a certainty. Where else could we have been? And we'd come out into the rain and under our umbrellas. I suppose we were walking on Yonge Street. Heading north.

Liam was standing by a traffic signal, watching for the lights to change. We could see him, ten or fifteen yards in front of us. He had no umbrella—only an overcoat—and a rain-soaked hat with its brim turned down. His hands were in his pockets—his shoulders rounded forward—his face quite expressionless, as if the rain had washed all his feelings away.

We failed to reach him before he crossed—and, watching his progress, we could sense he would not have wanted to see us—or be seen. He was not so much drunk—as tranquillized. A dream walker—somnambulist. He simply put one foot before the other—nothing more.

We could see him from the far side—tracking him, but not. Seeing him—but not *watching*.

Ede had told us that from time to time he would turn up at Selby Street. Grey. And emptied. With some great effort, he would have eschewed his drink before these visits. He still had that much pride. That kind of pride that said: *I will not let you see that part of me.*

Quite simply, he was there for money. Sometimes Ede fed him—but got no information from him. Nothing but his needs. He always came when he knew that Frederick would not be there. He could not have borne that witness. And so Ede would hand a bill or two—ten—twenty—thirty dollars from her card winnings—and he would leave.

This had stopped happening some months, I think, before we lost him.

I shall not forget it—that moment before we lost track of him. Nor did Lily. Once, he had been her storyteller—once, so it seemed, he had been her enemy. Not any more. When he went, he was gone. His story ended—or will end—in a Memory Potion dream that might, at least, bring with it happy visions of Eva Willard, dressed all in white, in the time before she said *no*.

6. Frederick's death was greatly mourned by his staff and business associates—less at home. Ede gave a sigh of relief that she likened to the loosening of a corset. Two years later, in 1935, the Wyatt Piano Factory faltered and failed—done in by progress and the Depression. First the Victrola and then the radio had undercut the piano market. When the Depression hit, the business buckled, so to speak, and fell to its knees. Harry Wyatt, who was still keeping total senility at bay, was then in charge. He went down to King Street on a Wednesday morning in January of 1935 and, with tears in his eyes, he assembled and then dismissed the entire body of employees. *You must go now*, he said. *We have done all we can.*

There had been some hope that the Christmas season of 1934 might improve the financial picture. It did not. One hundred and eighty-five men, women and boys—with more than three hundred already gone—lost their jobs in a single moment. They did not, however, lay the blame for this at Harry's door—or at Frederick's. On the contrary, they were full of praise for the fact that so much effort had gone into trying to keep the gates of the factory open. When Harry stood in the cafeteria that day and shook the hand of each employee as he presented the final pay envelopes, he was thanked again and again for trying to pull them through.

As for the Cloisters, however well run it was, Mother's visits there finally came to an end. They were too expensive for Ede to manage, now that she was a widow and the factory was gone. A gentle irony played into her hand at this moment. Having sold the Selby Street house, she moved into our old rooms at Number 84. This was in 1936, and the girls were both independent by then. Annie lived away—Alice was lost in America.

The room that had once been mine was used to house the last of the family's Wyatt pianos. Ede would sit there of an evening, playing *Beautiful Isle of Somewhere*—singing *Love's Old Sweet Song*. In another year, when Franklin died, the piano was moved into the sitting-room and Caroline took up residence where it— and I—had been. This circle has a pleasant symmetry, and I like to think of Ede and Caroline as having lives that will bring some pleasure to their days. Watching them, seated beneath the maple trees on the lawn—where Ede and I once sat—it is gratifying to think that each of them, in a way, is the embodiment of a song.

Two old women sitting arm in arm—one of whom sang a garden in her mind—the other of whom had given birth to her child in the corner of a singing field.

7. If Lily's privileged visits to the Cloisters were ended, so too, finally, were her stays in hotels. She was eventually deemed stabilized enough to take up residence in the Asylum for the Insane at Whitby, Ontario. This, too, was east of Toronto—but not so far east as Brighton, where my school was.

Our reconciliation was now complete. Her fear of my *betrayal* was a thing of the past. When she had called me a traitor, she had imagined I was in league with Ede to harm her. Harm her by making her live, thus preventing her from discovering who was waiting for her in the fire.

Something extraordinary happened the very first day she was ensconced at Whitby. Walking onto the lawns to explore the tables and chairs set out beneath the chestnut trees, Lily saw a familiar figure. Familiar, but not familiar. Something was wrong with the shape of this person's body—but the way the body sat on its chair, and the way it thrust out its chin—now *chins*—was unmistakable.

"Ada?"

Lily had moved around in front of the woman who sat there, forlorn and seemingly emptied of everything but size.

"That's me," the woman said—not looking at first at the questioner.

"I'm Lily Kilworth, Ada. Don't you remember me?"

The eyes shifted—filled with suspicion.

"Lily Kilworth died by fire in The Duke of York," the woman said. Now, without doubt, Lily knew she had found her old friend.

"Do you know how long it is since I last saw you?"

"I don't even know who you are."

"I'm Lily Kilworth, Ada. Just a minute . . ." Lily counted the years on her fingers. "Eighteen years ago, Ada. Eighteen years—and here we are again!"

"How do you do?"

"Don't say how-do-you-do. Stand up and kiss me!"

"No," said Ada. "I never kiss strangers."

Lily could only be amused at this obtuseness. She stood back, smiling.

"Ask me what your son's name was," she said.

"Neddy," said Ada.

"Don't *tell*! *Ask* me. Let me see . . . what colour hat did you used to wear? That's a good question . . ."

"Grey.

"Oh—honestly! This is madness."

"Why not? I'm mad." Ada sounded as if she was afraid someone would deny it.

Lily knelt down in front of her and took her hands and stared into her face. As Ada watched, Lily began to sing.

> *Oh the moon is shining bright along the Wabash,*
> *From the fields there comes the smell of new-mown hay.*
> *Through the sycamores the candlelights are gleaming . . .*

"On the banks of the Wabash, far away," Ada said.
She squinted.
She held on tight with both hands.
"Lily?" she said.
"That's me."
"Oh . . ."
The hands relaxed and Ada sat back.
Then she said: "where's Neddy?"
Lily waited. Standing up, she dusted off her knees before she spoke.
"Neddy couldn't come," she said. And then she said: "but he will."

This way, arm in arm like Ede and Caroline, they lived out what remained of their days.

8. In 1937, the year that Franklin died, I married Alexandra Lamont. I was twenty-seven and we were both in the music business. Alex sang with a band, when we met. I was the pianist. This has all been said. In 1938, she left me. You know why.

Because I had not told Alex the truth about Lily, I did not tell Lily about Alex. It seemed the simplest way to deal with the situation. If I'd told her, she would have insisted on meeting her.

"You married yet, Charlie?" Mother asked one day. It was winter and we were walking on the Whitby lawns in the snow. Lily wore a tam-o'-shanter, then, and a huge blue wrap-around coat with a collar that covered her ears.

"No," I said.

"You going to?"

"I don't know."

"I wish you would . . ."

"Oh, Mother . . ."

"Don't be impatient with me, Charlie. Everybody wants a grandchild . . ."

"I don't."

"Of course not! *Yet.* But you will, one day."

No, I wouldn't.

"Find some girl and fall in love," Lily said—holding tight to my arm. "Find some pretty girl and fall in love with her and have yourself a family."

We walked a moment more and then she stopped.

"Promise me, Charlie."

"What, Mama? What?"

I was cold.

"Promise me there will be at least one child."

She looked at me with a sudden and dreadful anguish which I did not then understand—knowing nothing of her stillborn child.

"You have to," Lily said. "It's a promise I've already made— and she's out there waiting for you."

"Who? Who's waiting?"

"Your daughter, Charlie. Your child."

There—again.

The unborn—waiting.

"I've always said so, Charlie. I've always, always said so. Someone has to make us visible. Someone has to pull us out of the fire . . ."

She was drifting—almost lost again in the old way, as if there had been flames nearby to cue her.

"I tell you, Charlie, I was there waiting in that field. Waiting for Ede and Tom to find me. You don't think two people come together for nothing, do you? They were together because I was waiting to be found . . ."

Then she looked straight into my face and said to me: "you knew it, too, Charlie. All that time you waited for me to find you. What if I hadn't? What if I'd said: *I won't?*"

She turned and, clinging to my arm, she surveyed the fields of snow that stretched away to the confining walls.

"Neddy," she said. "He died, didn't he."

Yes.

"Did they hurt him?"

"It was the War, Mama. Wars hurt—you know that."

"Yes."

A wind had begun to rise. Off in the field there were flurries lifting from the ground, dancing almost. Whirling. Lily watched them.

"Do you think he died by fire?"

I knew he hadn't—but I didn't want to tell how it had really happened. There wasn't a way in the world he might have died in that moment in that place that would have given her any peace.

"I don't know how he died," I said.

Far away—for so it seemed—her voice said: "Merry Christmas to all . . ."

She remembered that much.

That was enough.

"I don't tell Ada," she said out loud. "I don't tell Ada Neddy is dead. I tell her any minute she will see him. Any minute she will see him. Any minute."

"Good, Mama."

"I told your daughter the very same thing," she said.

A chill that was not the wind passed through me.

"I told her: *wait. Wait,* I said. *Charlie will come for you . . .*" She looked at me. "Won't you, Charlie . . ."

Well—god help me: *yes,* I said. Yes. But it was the same old lie.

9. Out of the blue, thinking she was gone from my life, I had a letter from Eleanor Hess. Eleanor Ormond. A letter and a parcel.

The parcel contained her personal copy of Elizabeth Barrett Browning's poems. She told me: *this is the copy I had the first summer your mother and I were at Cambridge together. 1909. I want you to have it.*

I glanced at it briefly and set it aside. It was the same edition as the one I had found in Lily's suitcase.

My dear Charlie,

I had thought I would not do this, but I now understand that I must. There are things you have a right to know, in spite of my own longing to keep them from you. Please bear with me, and please understand. I did not mean to hurt you by withholding this information. I meant to protect myself—and to hoard the one private thing I knew that gave me solace.

I know who your father was.

I turned the page. My eyes hurt. I was afraid. I sat down.

Your father was my husband—Karl.

Karl Hess.

Your name is Hess—if you want it.

I met him first when I went to collect your mother from that house in Tedworth Square. In telling you the story, I deliberately withheld the date, saying I could not remember—saying I thought it might have been in November. It was not. It was late in January of 1910. Nine months before your birth. It is very hard for me to say this, but of course, that is not the point. The point is, you must understand what happened.

You have seen your mother give up her being to that stranger who lived inside her. You have seen her disappear—even though her body remained and even though it went on moving—walking—being. I have seen this, too. And I saw it there at Tedworth Square. She was with Karl. She had followed him. And he had taken her in. They had all taken her in, not knowing who she was.

Something in Karl—or of him—had pulled at your mother's

*other self and I know—or at least I think I know—what it was.
It was his music. It was the flute in his hand—and the way he carried himself—his stature.*

*You look like him, Charlie. You have his back. You have his
head. You have his eyes. You wouldn't know you had his head
unless you cut off all your hair. That was the other thing that
pulled at Lily—that captured her. In the book I have sent you,
there is a poem called* A Musical Instrument. *Read it, and you will
understand. She thought he was the Great God Pan. Of course,
he was no such thing, but in Lily's absence, the other one—the
wild one in her—thought so, and wanted to believe it.*

*She lived in another version of the world, Charlie. You know
that. It wasn't the world we live in, you and I. It was the world
she was born in—a corner of a field, and a river winding by, with
reeds in it. Never forget that, when you want to conjure him. Karl
belonged there too, in his way. With his music—and his generous
heart. It was part of what I loved in him—just as it was part of
what I loved in Lily.*

I gave up reading, then. I was shaken. I was shaking.

This is the rest of what she told me—Eleanor. Of how my
father died, and of how she never lost sight of Lily, though Lily
had long lost sight of her.

My father was a junior officer in the Imperial German Army. This
was in 1912. Nominally, he was classified as a musician, but his
flute was soon enough discarded. He died, as Eleanor said, *on the
wrong side of the Somme* in July of 1916. She had intended to sit
out the War in Berlin. Everyone had thought it would be over—
win or lose—in five or six months. People who said it would take
a year were thought to be crazy.

When Karl was killed, Eleanor purchased her freedom by giving
a quarter of a million dollars to a German society for the protection of war orphans. This allowed her—this, plus friends in high
places—to seek asylum in Sweden. She went to Paris when the War
was over and motored to the Somme. There wasn't a grave for
Karl Hess. There was only the earth which had swallowed him,

together with over a hundred thousand others. She knelt upon the earth and then prostrated herself, remaining on the ground in that position for twenty-four hours.

When she rose, she turned her back on Europe and, for a while, on Karl. She knew that I was his, but she had settled her feelings about that when Karl was still alive. There had been no forgiveness; none was needed. But when he was killed—and she knew that she would never bear his children—she hated him. She hated him the way all people hate their lovers when they die in wars and accidents, because a sudden death is like desertion. She also hated Lily for having his child, and me for being the progeny she had been denied. This hatred stayed with Eleanor Hess for several years—not as virulent hatred—not as a source of energy. She was not compelled to act on it—even to voice it. It was simply there.

In time, she remarried and, perhaps because she was embittered, she married an embittered man—mean-spirited, dishonest and cruel. These are her descriptions. His name—as she said—was of no importance. The marriage ended, so far as Eleanor was concerned, with a supreme act of revenge. She left the man ruined, but justly so. He had made an underhanded play for her money and lost a good deal of it in crookery. She left him penniless and shed him the way a wound will shed a scab.

It was, I knew, in some way significant that Eleanor Ormond reclaimed my father's name in 1939—the very moment when Germany held the world yet again at gun point. It was almost, in its way, an act of atonement. His country had willed his death—and now, as it prepared to kill a new generation of its sons, Eleanor raised Karl Hess up from the dead and returned what he had lost with his life: his beloved wife and, in me, his immortality.

In Eleanor's copy of Mrs Browning's poems, I made two discoveries—one she intended me to make, and the other inadvertent. At least, I suspect so.

Written in the fly-leaf was Eleanor's name:

Eleanor Ormond
Cambridge
July 1909

And under this:

Eleanor Hess

And under this:

Eleanor Anderson

My heart stopped.
E. Anderson.
And now I know. Not only who my father was, but who my benefactor was, who sent me to school.

I will not tell her I know. She did not want me to have this knowledge. That is why, even in her letter, she spoke of her second husband's name as having *no importance*. She had known that if I heard it, I might guess.

And, since my father could not see me provided for, she had provided for me, herself.

The second discovery was this:

Pasted on the inside back cover, written in Lily's hand, was the following:

In the summer of 1910, on a still June morning, he took me up the river to the town. Not a sound. No people. Only the splash of a frog or a turtle sliding from the bank. And the reeds all silent on the shore beneath the shade of the willow trees. And yet, when I listened down, I heard a whispering chorus of insects making a seething noise. We drifted there almost an hour and neither of us spoke. In the town, he went away and I never saw him again. And yet . . .

The sun on the hill forgot to die
And the lilies revived, and the dragonfly
Came back to dream on the river.

If only . . .

Under this, she had written: *see pg. 54.*
    Turning the pages, I found: *A Musical Instrument.*

> *What was he doing, the great god Pan,*
>   *Down in the reeds by the river . . .*

A bell rang.
    I had read the poem in one of Lily's notebooks, copied there in her own hand. When I'd encountered it first my only reaction had been that Lily, being enamoured of Mrs. Browning, had simply written down some favourite verses. But when I searched for it, the poem was nowhere to be found. I began to think I must have been mistaken. Then—all at once—there it was.
    A Musical Instrument.
    The poem began on a left-hand page and was continued on the right. When you spread them open side by side, the pages had the look of a decorated manuscript—especially given Lily's squared-off letters. As in the text of her Fabre storybook, there were illustrations in the margins—beetles and butterflies, water lilies, cat-tail reeds and a red-winged blackbird. Hovering over it all, a dragonfly with veined, translucent wings was superimposed on the poem's first lines.

> *What was he doing, the great god Pan,*
>   *Down in the reeds by the river?*
> *Spreading ruin and scattering ban,*
> *Splashing and paddling with hoofs of a goat,*
> *And breaking the golden lilies afloat*
>   *With the dragon-fly on the river.*

He tore out a reed, the great god Pan,
     From the deep cool bed of the river.
The limpid water turbidly ran,
And the broken lilies a-dying lay,
And the dragon-fly had fled away,
     Ere he brought it out of the river.

'This is the way' laughed the great god Pan
     (Laugh'd while he sat by the river),
'The only way, since the gods began
To make sweet music, they could succeed.'
Then dropping his mouth to a hole in the reed,
     He blew in power by the river.

Sweet, sweet, sweet O Pan!
     Piercing sweet by the river!
Blinding sweet, O great god Pan!
The sun on the hill forgot to die,
And the lilies revived, and the dragon-fly
     Came back to dream on the river.

Now I know the poem by heart. Whether I am the reed or its music, I cannot tell. I only know that I have found my father. What my mother may have called him—how she might have named him in the drowning panic of conception, I can only guess. But he, for me, is now a surety. It is true that he died before I knew him—but not before he knew me. There was, after all, that moment which I must have retained without awareness—when he stood in the living-room at Richmond Park and held me in his arms—with his fingers splayed to the shape of my head. As Eleanor Hess described our parting—I had to be dragged from his embrace.

As Lily once had been.

10. The rest you know. Or have guessed.
It was fire, of course.

There will always be some debate about whether or not she started it. Smoking was allowed in the Asylum. Smoking, but not matches. Not lighters. When a patient wanted a cigarette, she had to go and ask the nurses or the orderlies for a light.

Still, Lily was Lily, and she had her own ways of coming by matches. Ever since Agnes and the matches in her work-basket, Lily had figured out how to steal them.

Twenty inmates perished. Most of them were caught in a stairwell whose door somehow got locked behind them. At the bottom, there was thick wire meshing—and no way through.

Lily was on the floor above—the fourth floor—the top floor. Six were with her, gathered in a circle—seven bodies altogether of which both Mother's and Ada's were identifiable. The rest, perhaps so—but that was not my job.

I think back now to all my life with Lily and I hear a moment—see it—smell it—that happened at Munsterfield when I was five or six years old.

One night—it was summertime—we sat on the floor with our arms along the window-sills in the room we shared at the front of the house and we watched the field across the road in the moonlight.

This was the room that had once been Ede's and had now been set aside for visitors. Lily had requested it because it was the room where she had lain on the truckle-bed as a child, safe in the presence of her mother and the field whose earth had been her cradle.

"When I was your age," she told me that night, "I used to watch the world from this very same window. Sometimes alone—and sometimes with my mother. Nothing changes," she said, "though everything is altered."

She put her hand on the back of my head and smoothed my hair and scratched my neck.

And then she said: *don't speak*—as if I had spoken. But I had not. *Listen,* she said. *The whole world is singing . . .*

And it was.

Frogs and crickets. Nightjars. Owls.

Sing, said Lily, whispering. *Sing. Pass it on.*

"You hear that, Charlie?"

Yes.

"That song—those songs are just the same as what I was telling you about the ants. *This is me,* they say. *This is you. This is us.* All songs pass from one to another—the songs of ten thousand years of nesting together—of being one—of being *us.* And the frogs are saying just the same—except their song is more about place than food. Not this *taste* is me—but this *place* is me—this bit of grass—this lily pad. This taste—this place—this song. These songs . . ."

She looked out into the dark—the two of us kneeling, now—and she urged me forward with her. Beneath our hands, the roof made an angled drop towards the yard—and beyond the yard and its wall was the road—and beyond the road was the field.

Pass it on! Lily whispered to all the singers.

"Say it, Charlie. *Pass it on!*"

We whispered it together—knowing it must not be shouted because a shouting would destroy the song and its harmony.

And so we knelt there—leaning down to the roof—and I could see her profile in the moonlight and smell her hair and the garden below us—the trees, the earth, the wall, all rain-wet from a storm that had passed half an hour before. And I could smell the road and see it gleaming, and I could hear the grass. I swear I could hear it growing, but Lily said: *that's just the worms coming up to the top because it rained.* And they would be singing, too.

We—and the small stream burgeoning out of the storm and the stars above the field and the sky with its endless curving. *Us. Us. Us,* they said. *We're singing. Us.*

This was my mother's teaching.

I received it then—but I had no notion until her death of its potency.

Pass it on, she had said.

Pass it on.

I was five that night—not quite six—and when I almost slept, she lifted me up and showed me to the world—the same as Ede had done with her.

"This is my son, Charlie," she said. I heard her. And I know she said it to the stars.

Just now, I looked at the opening words of this book: *I had seen her just the day before—a day of pale blue skies and summer breezes.*

And . . .

We had stood on the lawns beneath the chestnut trees and she had said: the leaves are talking to me, Charlie.

And . . .

Yes.

And . . .

"The time will come," she said, "when there will have to be a gathering—everyone brought together in one safe place . . ."

And . . .

"This is not a safe place," she said. "In spite of its being an asylum."

And . . .

"People like me, Charlie," she said. "I guess we aren't safe anywhere. Not in this world."

No.

Not in this world. Never.

But surely, in the world she found inside the fire. She had always told me there were people in the fire—who beckoned to her. Called to her. Singing. She had always told me they wanted her to go in. It was written in her journals, again and again: *come in . . .*

Of course, she was afraid of them. Of course, she was afraid. This had been why she had fought off the image of John Fagan for so long. And with such fury. *I can't. I can't. I cannot! I won't. I won't. I will not!* He, too, wanted her to go in. Or so she believed.

In the journals, she had written: *It is all a gathering. A gathering of us—all of us all the way back to the people in the caves— the caves where the first of us were born—made visible . . .*

And elsewhere: *John had wanted to get back to them—but his parents locked the door . . .*

The caves where the first of us were born.

Doctor Peterson had said: *the skull is a cave where the mind is hiding.*

Hiding.

Afraid.

Lily.

There are those who would demand of madness a kind of logic. A kind of logic that, by its very nature, madness cannot provide. *Why did she do that?* people would ask me of Lily.

How could I answer them? *Because she is mad?*

This would not have been Lily's answer. Nor will it be mine.

Lily Kilworth returned to the caves where the first of us were born, and only she will ever know why.

But in those caves, as in the circle of fellow inmates with whom she and Ada died, I like to think there was a singing. I want to believe there were songs.

There is a song we used to sing at King's College—and Lily, I know, had sung it, too, at St Mary-Margaret. She also sang it in the Asylum. I heard her sing it there with all the others out on those lawns beyond the green chairs. It was sung to the tune of *Auld Lang Syne:*

> *We are because we are,*
> *Because we are, because we are!*
> *We're here because we're here!*
> *Because we are here,*
> *Because we're here . . . !*

This is me, Lily.

This is you.

This is us.

This is the story of everything I know. Of who we are and how we've lived. And where we come from.

Circles. See the circles of endless repetition. Tom and Karl. Lizzie and Neddy. Lyon. Ede and Lily. Me . . .

Well.

There's a war coming now. Another circle closing around us. More young men dressed up in their youth. And me? I can hardly say no. There are few enough pianos left to tune, and even though I'm twenty-nine, there must be something I can do. In the army.

Yes, there's that circle, too. The circle in which my father fell. Still.

What would my mother say. *Be a child forever.* Children—the only guaranteed safe good place.

And so.

Pass it on?

I will try.

Coda

In the War, I was wounded. Severely, I must add, though not so badly as to leave me crippled. The word that would best describe my wounds is *disfigured*. Altered—never to be the same.

Consequently, my greatest apprehension afterwards was in being reunited with Alexandra. In 1940, she had come back into my life and we had tried again to make our marriage work. And we did—make it work. After all, we loved each other.

I went overseas in 1942—the darkest and the worst year of the War. And the brightest in my life.

In April, 1943, while I was in England training for the invasion of Sicily—which took place later that summer—I had a letter from Alex telling me that a child had been born. Our child. Her child. Mine.

Thinking of our old wars, she had not dared tell me she was pregnant. Nonetheless, she thought of the pregnancy as her victory. I knew it was mine. It must have happened during my embarkation leave.

I went out and sat on the roof of our barracks the day Alexandra's letter arrived. It was evening. Twilight. The letter was in my hand. I must have read it a hundred times. At last, I put it away in my pocket and stared out over the surrounding hills.

I found her, Lily, I said. *She was waiting, just the way you told me. And I found her. All is well.*

I sat on the roof until the bugle called. Then I went down—and slept.

Now that you know that, I can tell you about my wound—my *disfigurement.*

I stepped on a land-mine—a land-mine waiting for me in a field near Ortona. 1944. Some of my toes went missing, but—worse— I was emasculated. There is no *nice* way to say this.

I was strangely ashamed—as if, somehow, I had emasculated myself—as if my foot had been guided by my will and not by happenstance. I knew it wasn't true—that fate had done it to me, not volition—but I still had a sense of shame. I was no longer whole, though anyone meeting me in the street would not have thought so. How could they tell?

Looking back, it was—of course—impossible not to remember all our skirmishes about conception. Lily's urging that I should *pass it on.* My determination not to. Alex conniving her way around every prophylactic I provided. The yelling. The insults. The hurt of it all. And, dear god, what if I had won? What if *no* had meant *no forever?* Followed by a land-mine.

In the end, I said *yes.*

Yes.

Her name is Emma.

The story ends where it began—in Lily's field.

I took Emma there last week. June 17th. Lily's fifty-sixth birthday.

Em is three, now. Three years, two months. I had to carry her on my shoulders, the grass was so tall. Alex came after—picking flowers.

When I put Em down, I turned back to see Alex coming from the incline into the corner. Just as she reached me, Em gave a tug at my leg.

"Look what I have," she said.

She held out her hand.
It contained a large black ant.
We were not—and we will never be—alone.

About the Author

Timothy Findley is the author of seven acclaimed novels including, most recently, *Headhunter*, which won the City of Toronto Book Award. His previous novels include *Famous Last Words*, *Not Wanted on the Voyage* and *The Wars* which won the Governor General's Award for Fiction. He is also the author of two short story collections, *Dinner Along the Amazon* and *Stones* and a work of non-fiction *Inside Memory: Pages from a Writer's Workbook*. His latest play, *The Stillborn Lover*, was the winner of an Arthur Ellis Award. Timothy Findley lives on a farm in the countryside beyond Toronto.